The Girl is not

By Emma

Published by Emma V. Leech.

Copyright (c) Emma V. Leech 2020

Cover Art: Victoria Cooper

ASIN No.: B08BNJW3VG

ISBN Ebook: 978-2-492133-17-6

ISBN: 978-2-492133-18-3

All rights reserved. Without limiting the rights under copyright reserved above, no part of this publication may be reproduced, stored in or introduced into a retrieval system, or transmitted, in any form, or by any means (electronic, mechanical, photocopying, recording, or otherwise) without the prior written permission of both the copyright owner and the above publisher of this book. This is a work of fiction. Names, characters, places, brands, media, and incidents are either the product of the author's imagination or are used fictitiously. The author acknowledges the trademarked status and trademark owners of various products referenced in this work of fiction, which have been used without permission. The publication/use of these trademarks is not authorised, associated with, or sponsored by the trademark owners. The ebook version and print version are licensed for your personal enjoyment only. The ebook version may not be re-sold or given away to other people. If you would like to share the ebook with another person, please purchase an additional copy for each person you share it with. No identification with actual persons (living or deceased), places, buildings, and products is inferred.

Table of Contents

Chapter One

28th November 1818, Stir it up Sunday.

Too many mouths…

"Tol' you she had one in the basket again."

Livvy noted the smug expression on Mrs Pengelly's face with a frisson of irritation. She might well have guessed before Livvy had. It didn't make the news any more welcome. Another poor mite to add to the chaos and, more to the point, another mouth to feed, and another body to clothe. Please God, let it be a boy. At least then they wouldn't need a season and a dowry, though there was school, and university, and… oh, it was hopeless.

"Do you reckon she even knows where babies come from?"

Livvy sighed and pummelled the bread she was kneading with increasing vigour. "I did try to explain to her, and that there were… methods…."

Gelly snorted. "Bet she took that well, from her unmarried sister-in-law."

Despite everything, Livvy let out a breath of laughter. "She turned an odd puce colour and told me never to speak of such things again."

The laugh that burst from their rotund cook wobbled her plump jowls and made her bosom heave rather alarmingly, but Livvy felt some of the tension leave her shoulders.

"Oh, Gelly, whatever are we to do? She swears blind she only bought trifling little gifts for the children for Christmas, but you know what she is, and Charlie can deny her nothing. If only she would economise, we might manage well enough, but he's no better...."

Livvy blew a lock of hair from her eyes, aware she was whinging and, worse, repeating herself. She had been singing this same hopeless song for at least four years and, no matter how hard she remonstrated, nothing ever changed. Ceci would get herself with child again and spend too much money again, and Charlie would just give his wife an adoring smile and shrug. She can't help it, he'd say, and then he'd scold Livvy for making Ceci feel bad when she'd not been raised to live in poverty. As if Livvy had

Gelly shook her head and turned her attention back to the pie she was making.

"What can you do, pet? 'Tis not your fortune, more's the pity. They'll run through it till it's spent and lament once it's gone, like it were someone else what done it." The cook fixed her shrewd dark eyes on Livvy. "You'd do best to get out, whilst you can."

Livvy paused, her fists sunk into the bread dough still. "I'll not marry that… that odious creature, not for anyone."

"Don't blame ye for it, neither, but you'd have a home that weren't fallin' down 'bout your ears, and bairns of your own."

"And what would happen here, I ask you? Who would see to the children if I did not? They'd be feral within a sennight if I did not make some attempt to take them in hand."

"Reckon," Gelly agreed, nodding.

Livvy harrumphed and divided the dough in two, setting each half aside to rest in a greased bowl. She washed the flour off her hands in cold water from the pump and looked out of the window at a day that was draped in fog like a blanket of wet wool.

"I wonder what time Charlie will get back? I expected him yesterday, but I suppose he got talking to some old friend and forgot the time. *If* he comes back for Christmas, I suppose we ought to count ourselves lucky."

"Nonsense, he'll be back, now Missus is here. A week apart is all he'll stand."

Livvy nodded. That was true enough. Ceci had returned from London a week earlier as she'd been too tired to stay longer, and her brother loved his wife to her bones. She could do no wrong, and no matter how time and too many babies had taken their toll on her lovely features and slender frame, to Charlie she was still the most beautiful woman that had ever lived. Livvy wondered what it felt like to be adored so thoroughly. Livvy suspected she would find such credulous adulation more than a little suffocating. Just as well it was not a problem she would ever have to endure.

Before she could make herself utterly maudlin, the kitchen door burst open with a crash and the children piled in.

"Is it time?" Jane demanded, guileless blue eyes staring at Livvy, bright with expectation.

"Hmmm," Livvy said, reaching into the pocket in her skirts for the heavy gold fob watch that had been her father's. It ought to be Charlie's really, but Papa had left it to her, and Charlie had never complained about it. "Well, you tell me, Jane."

Jane studied the watch, her little face screwed up in concentration. "The big hand is on the six and the little hand is on the eight."

"And so?" Livvy pressed.

"Half-past eight?"

"Clever girl!"

Jane beamed at the praise. "And we've had breakfast and we're all dressed, even George."

Livvy gave the children a nod of approval, astonished to discover that George, who was not quite three years old, was indeed dressed in a rather worn skeleton suit, but it was clothes, and he was wearing them. Quite an accomplishment. Livvy cast a critical eye over the children. Harry, at fourteen, was the eldest: all legs and arms that never seemed to be quite where he expected them. He was gangly and clumsy, like a newborn colt, and very aware of the fact he was becoming a young man. That his shirt cuffs were fraying and his cravat not properly starched were all minor miseries that wore upon him with greater force as the weeks and months passed. However, he was a good-hearted lad, and kind to his siblings. Today he carried Birdie, who was not yet a year old, her chubby arms looped about his neck. The older girls, Susan, Lydia, Rebecca and Jane, were thirteen, eleven, nine, and seven respectively.

"Well then, I should say it was certainly time. Susan fetch the currants and raisins. Lydia, you get the suet and the treacle. I shall fetch the ginger and nutmeg. Rebecca, can you measure out the flour? We shall need a pound."

Rebecca gave a stern nod, adjusted her spectacles, and went to the large flour jar. Jane bounced with impatience, waiting for her task.

"Eight eggs, Jane," Livvy said. "Take the basket, and be careful not to break them this time."

Jane gave a little squeak, grabbed a shawl and the basket, and ran out into the garden towards the hen house, letting in a blast of cold, damp air as she went.

"S'pose I'd best fetch the charms, then," Gelly said with a wink.

Livvy smiled. Despite the constant worrying that made her feel as frayed and worn as poor Harry's cuffs, she enjoyed Christmas and all the preparations. Stir It Up Sunday had been a favourite time ever since she was a little girl and Charlie had needed to help her carefully stir the thick, dark pudding mixture from east to west, like the journey the magi had taken. The carved wooden spoon sat over the kitchen mantel all year, only coming down to be washed and oiled and used to stir the pudding. It felt like magic, or at least it had when Livvy was a child. The tradition was ancient and adding the thirteen ingredients, representing Christ and his disciples, had always seemed like alchemy, especially the charms. Yet it had been a long time since she had believed in magic, or believed in anything except trying to keep stockings darned, the chimney from smoking, and the pantry stocked. Her greatest challenge, however, was getting her brother, Viscount Boscawen, to understand that the worthless investments he'd made would never bring more than the pitiful amount that barely kept all their heads above water. Heads he kept adding to because he couldn't keep his blasted fall buttoned for above five minutes.

Livvy sucked in a deep breath and let it out again in a slow exhalation. She would not spoil this for the children, for they still felt the magic. It was in their eyes, their blue eyes, all varying shades from the most delicate duck egg to the deep indigo of her own. Even Harry, struggling to become the young man he was destined to be, still felt it. She recognised the tremor of anticipation, of hope for a season of goodwill and roaring fires, of yule logs and gifts tied with bows, and mantels decorated with evergreen and prickly holly, stabbing soft fingers and drawing shiny drops of blood like berries. The traditions resonated through her, through the walls of the ancient house, down to the soil, connecting past and present, the long dead and the yet to be born.

With a sigh, she remembered the new life Ccci would bring squalling into the world, whether or not they could afford it, and returned her attention to the Christmas pudding.

By dinner time, the house was full of the perfumed spices of the pudding, lingering like an exotic taunt beside the more prosaic scent of boiled mutton and cabbage. Charlie would complain. If he arrived in time to eat, that was. He hated cabbage, yet it was cheap and grew plentifully in the kitchen garden, so he could dashed well lump it. The scrunch of carriage wheels over gravel announced her brother's return from London at last, and Livvy hurried to the front of the house.

Charlie stepped down from the carriage and gave her his usual bright grin. "Well met, Livvy. How are my little thieves and baggages?"

Livvy snorted and embraced him. "As wicked and dreadful as ever, brother dear."

"Excellent, I'm glad to hear it," Charlie replied and then wrinkled his nose. "Cabbage? Really, Livvy? Is that any kind of meal for a man to return to?"

Livvy folded her arms and returned a stern look, he gave a wistful sigh.

"Ah, well. I shan't complain, as penance for having done something you shall scold me for, I don't doubt."

Livvy's heart plummeted to her worn slippers, and she didn't dare ask. She just waited, with a sick feeling swirling in her guts, to discover what ridiculous thing Charlie had spent their last shilling on.

"Oh, don't look so Friday faced, it's not that bad," he said, impatient as he turned back to the carriage and swung open the door.

As he seemed to indicate she ought to look inside, Livvy took a tentative step closer.

The carriage was worn and musty, like everything belonging to the estate, and the air inside was sour, smelling of sweat and... there was a figure slumped in the corner, breathing heavily.

Livvy took an instinctive step away.

"W-Who?" she demanded.

"Now, Livvy," Charlie said, his voice uncharacteristically firm. "I'll not have you fly into the boughs. I owe him. He saved me more times than I could count at Eton, and after too. He's a good fellow despite... well...."

"Who, Charlie?" Livvy demanded.

"Kingston."

It took a moment before Livvy realised she was standing with her mouth open. She closed it with a snap and tried to gather herself. Harcourt St John, the Earl of Kingston, or, as the scandal sheets had dubbed him, the *King of Sin.*

"You can't be serious," she said.

Her words were faint but trailed a wispy cloud on the frigid evening air, proof she had spoken aloud.

"Deadly serious," Charlie replied, his expression stern. "He's sick, Livvy, and… well, I feared what might happen if I left him alone. He'll stay with us until he's well again, and that's an end to it. No argument, no discussion. I shan't be moved on this, so don't think to try."

Livvy knew he meant it. Mostly, Charlie was the easiest going of men, too easy, but now and then he'd dig his heels in and nothing would budge him. She could see in his eyes that this was one of those times, so she might as well save her breath, but… to have such a man in the house, for *Christmas*. Good heavens.

"What's wrong with him? For if he's sick and the children—"

Charlie gave a curt shake of his head. "He's dipped too deep, that's all. Needs to rusticate for a spell. Fresh air and good food and some time away from—"

"Dissipation and vice?" Livvy suggested, her tart tone giving the words a bitter edge.

"London," Charlie finished, glowering.

Livvy snorted. As far as she could tell it amounted to the same thing.

"Papa!"

There followed several minutes of hugging and excited chatter as the children came out to greet their father, who dispensed the sweetmeats he'd brought with kisses and a fond words.

Livvy urged them to get out of the cold evening air. "Harry, take the children inside and send Spargo out to help with the baggage, please."

"Yes, Livvy," Harry said, as he chivvied the brood back into the house.

Charlie had climbed back into the carriage and was attempting to wake his guest.

"King. King, old man, we're here. Stir yourself, there's a good fellow."

There came a deep groan that seemed to resonate through the walls of the carriage and on into the darkness, and Livvy shivered.

"Miss Penrose?"

Livvy turned to see their butler appear on the front step. He was a big man with a grizzled grey beard and a fierce demeanour, who never said a word if a grunt would suffice.

"Would you help Lord Boscawen with our guest, please, Spargo? You'd best give him Harry's bed for tonight, until we can prepare the blue room for him."

Spargo nodded and headed towards the carriage.

Livvy waited, seething with frustration. Yet another mouth to feed, another load of laundry to see to, and heaven alone knew what kind of influence he would be on the children. Not a good one, that much was evident.

Muttered curses had her turning to see Charlie and Spargo half-carrying the earl from the carriage. Spargo was a strong fellow and her brother was no weakling, but they were struggling beneath his weight. In the dim light cast by the carriage lamps, Livvy got a glimpse of an arrogant profile, of the severe planes of a face that showed no trace of softness. He was barely conscious, a sheen of sweat on his skin, and she caught a furious glitter in his feverish gaze.

"Get off, get off you devils, let me be," he protested, but weakly for such a big man, and Spargo and Charlie wrestled him up the stairs.

She followed them into the house as they hefted him to Harry's bedchamber and all but threw him down on the mattress. He didn't stir, limbs akimbo, one long leg hanging off the side of the bed.

"Dead?" Spargo asked, peering over the bed at him.

"Dead drunk," Livvy said in disgust. She smelled it on him, a pungent mix of liquor and perfume and cigar smoke, of sweat and sickness. With a burst of fury, she turned on her brother. "Well, Charlie, he's your guest, so you deal with him, for I shan't. I wish you joy of him."

With that, she stalked out and made sure to slam the door behind her. She was halfway down the corridor before Charlie caught up with her.

"Livvy, wait."

Though the urge to keep walking and tell him to go to the devil was fierce, she forced herself to stop but didn't turn back.

"Do you remember the time I got sent home from school, beaten black and blue? The worst time." Charlie stood behind her still, his voice grave.

Livvy nodded, she could hardly forget. He'd been in a terrible state. Charlie had been sickly as a child, and had been a scrawny, weak boy until he was almost sixteen: an undeniable temptation for bullies. He'd been a magnet for them, but that second year at Eton had been hard

"I remember."

"That was the last time it happened."

Livvy turned round to face him and saw pleading in her brother's eyes.

"King saved me, Livvy. He beat the boys who made my life a misery and told them they'd get

worse if anyone laid a finger on me again. We…
We were never close friends. I don't think King *has*
close friends, but I owe him. He didn't have to look
after me—he was older, and so popular, and I was
just a snivelling little runt—but he did. He looked
out for me and made them stop. And now I shall
look after him. Please, Livvy. I need your help."

Livvy cursed inwardly. This was her brother all
over. He was so bloody nice you couldn't help but
forgive him for making your life impossible. She let
out a breath of exasperation and stared at the ceiling
for a moment.

"Very well," she said, and stalked back to
Harry's bedroom where they'd left the earl.

Chapter Two

Still the 28th November 1818, Stir It Up Sunday.

Damned devils, blasted boots, goblins, crows, and pigs...

King was dying.

He knew it, and the fact did not much surprise him. What was a little disconcerting was the realisation that he wasn't ready to go. He'd made a bloody mess of everything, but all the same, he wanted to carry on with a desperation that startled him. His body did not seem to be in accord with his mind. King had little to recommend him to the Almighty, though, and was in no hurry to meet him just yet, which might come as a shock to those who knew King best. The Earl of Kingston had been on the road to perdition for as long as anyone, and certainly as long as he himself, could remember. Now that the pearly gates beckoned, King was damned if he was ready to go through. Assuming of course he wasn't due to visit a location with a far

15

warmer clime. It would hardly be an unreasonable supposition.

The problem with living was, it was so much bloody effort. Especially right now. Right now, he was sweating and trembling, and the room was spinning in an alarming fashion. More to the point, he hadn't the faintest idea where this room was? A dim recollection of a friendly face and an interminable carriage ride made some sort of sense, but who? And where? And now some devil was manhandling him!

"Gerroff," he mumbled, vaguely aware of his words slurring beyond recognition.

Christ, he must have been on one hell of a bender.

"Sit him up or we'll never get his coat off."

The voice was feminine, tart as citrus and sharp as a knife. It cut through his tender brain and made explosions go off on the way through. Hands mauled at his person, an indignity he never would have suffered if he'd been in any state to protest. He tried again anyway, mumbling words that were incoherent even to him as the room swayed and pitched. His stomach roiled and burned, and he let out a perfectly audible "Oh God," before he cast up his accounts on a pair of dainty blue slippers.

"Son of a—"

"Livvy!"

Charlie snapped her name, censure glinting in his blue eyes. His disapproval was evident and Livvy knew well enough that he was frustrated by her, but then the feeling was mutual. They were siblings, and they loved each other dearly, but they were as alike as snow and sand.

"He's ruined my slippers," Livvy replied, impressed with the restraint she showed in not simply walking out the door and leaving them to it…except then the blasted earl took their attention by passing out cold.

Charlie sent Spargo to clear get the necessary to clear up the mess whilst they dealt with the earl. By the time they'd wrestled him out of his coat, waistcoat, and boots so splendid the cost of them could have kept the family fed for an entire year, Livvy was breathless.

"Help me with this," Charlie said, cursing as he tugged up the fine linen shirt that was now rumpled and stained with sweat and vomit.

Livvy blinked and then let out a huff of laughter. This was Charlie all over. He would scold her for not being more ladylike and for swearing like a navvy, and then expect her to help him undress one of his friends without batting an eyelid. Sometimes he forgot she was a young, unmarried woman…well, unmarried, anyway. Then he'd remember that her marrying a rich man would solve all their problems and remind her to watch her mouth, make more effort with her hair, and not to ride astride, even if no one was looking. Not that he would sell her to the highest bidder—as if such a thing existed—for he loved her too well for that, but he'd get a wistful look in his eyes that made her stomach roil.

Livvy kicked off her soiled slippers and stepped gingerly around the revolting mess on the polished floorboards. At least he'd missed the rug. Charlie had gotten both of the earl's arms free of the shirt but was struggling to get it over his head. With a bit of careful tugging and shifting, they got it free and then Livvy found herself staring down at a chest of such magnificent proportions she could only blink. Lord, but the man was big. Big and muscular and *hairy*. None of the Boscawen men were built like this fellow. When they all went sea bathing in the summer, Livvy had noted a scattering of golden hair on her brother's chest, but….

A low groan rumbled through the object of her attention and she realised he was trembling hard, almost panting, his breath coming in hard little gasps. His skin was grey, with dark circles beneath his wild, feverish, rolling eyes.

"No, get away, get away…." He swiped an uncoordinated hand out towards some unseen object, and Livvy jumped back out of the way. "Devils, you'll not have me, not yet, not today. N-Not ready to die."

Livvy shot an uncertain glance at her brother, who gave a tight smile.

"When a man has drunk as much and for as long as King… well, when a fellow finally stops, he… he sees things that are not there, as the alcohol leaves his body. He'll be wretched for a good few days, but little by little he'll come about. He's the strongest man I've ever known."

"He's a foul creature, Charlie, can't you see that?" Livvy said, shaking her head at the wreck of a man before them. "You must have read the scandals, seen the print shop caricatures. He's a libertine, a hell-born babe, and this man will be here, among your family, for Christmas."

"Ah, Livvy, where's your sense of charity? Goodwill to all men, remember?"

Livvy snorted and looked her brother in the eyes. "I remember, and I'll remember to tell Harry the same when you admit you can't afford to send him to university, and Susan when she realises there will be no come out for her. Yet we must share our meagre Christmas luxuries with a man who'll just turn around and destroy himself all over again."

Livvy turned on her heel, trying not to let the stricken look in her brother's eye make guilt stab in her heart as if it had been pierced with a blade. When had she become so cruel, so callous? She had never been one to see a fellow creature suffer, never been one to stint on charity. Yet the past years had hardened her, dried her up into the desiccated old spinster she was destined to become.

Only four and twenty, she reminded herself as a panicky sensation rose in her chest. Only four and twenty. Not old, not *so* old, not yet. It didn't matter. She may as well be ninety-four. She was trapped here, beloved auntie to her nieces and nephews, skivvy to her kind-hearted, ridiculous brother and his feckless wife, and there was no escape.

King lurched in and out of consciousness, unable to tell which was which. His dreams were lavish nightmares, scenes of debauchery in a fiery landscape where brimstone singed the colourful gowns of beautiful women. Except they weren't women at all, but devils in disguise, demons waiting to devour the next lustful man who turned his attention their way. There were pitchers filled with wine that turned to thick, bubbling black tar if he tried to drink and burned and burned, searing him from the inside until his lungs blistered and his stomach roasted from within. Occasionally he woke, or thought he did, to a simple bedroom with whitewashed walls and a fire that burned in the hearth. For a little while happiness would fill him up, tears stinging his eyes at the relief of discovering himself still alive, still in the world after his brush with hell. The linen sheets were worn smooth and soft, and smelled faintly of lavender...

but then he'd see it sitting in the corner, a deformed, gnarled devil grinning at him, drawing back thin black lips, wrinkling skin like an alligator to bare rows and rows of dagger-like teeth as it laughed and laughed.

"Please," he begged, shaking his head. "Please, no... no...."

It seemed that Livvy was not quite as cruel as she'd believed herself to be, as the Earl of Kingston suffered through a third day of bone-racking shaking and sweating and whatever it was that terrified him so he wept like a little boy. She stayed with him through it, wiping his brow and murmuring reassuring words, holding his hand when he was so terribly afraid.

He was a handsome devil, she'd give him that. Even with his skin the colour of rancid milk, his dark hair plastered to his face with sweat, and the stench of sickness clinging to him, he was beautiful. It was a dark, harsh kind of beauty, like the Cornish coast that sparkled like a sapphire on a clear day and would wreck an unwary ship with ease if it got too close. Finding safe harbour in those strong arms was an illusion though, and she wondered how many foolish young ladies he'd ruined. Just as well she was past the age where she believed a man could change his character. A good-natured fool would ever be thus, and a rogue would be nothing more. Pretty he might be, but the Earl of Kingston had the morals of a tom cat and, if he was suffering now, it was no more than he deserved.

Still, she was not vindictive, despite her earlier harshness to her brother, so here she sat by the fiend's bedside again, attempting to spoon a little chicken broth down his throat. He coughed and spluttered, but managed a few spoonfuls, though some dribbled down his chin. Livvy reached for the napkin in her lap and dabbed it away, then yelped as a hand as strong as a vice clamped about her wrist. Her gaze flew to his, and she gasped. His eyes were dark, so dark they were almost black and burning with intensity.

"Who are you? Are you another devil?" he growled.

"L-Livvy," she stammered, immediately furious with herself. Why on earth had she given her first name, her *pet* name? She straightened her spine, meeting his gaze and firming her tone. "I am Miss Olivia Penrose. Sister to Lord Boscawen. You're in *our* home, my lord."

For a moment he just stared at her, then he looked so bewildered she almost laughed.

"Y-You're… you're real?" he asked, his voice raspy and cracked.

Livvy nodded, realising this was his first lucid moment since he'd arrived. No wonder he was disorientated. "I am."

"Livvy," he repeated, and passed out.

His grip loosened on her wrist. She tugged herself free and let out a shaky breath. Well, that was what she got for playing the good Samaritan. She ought not be here at all, alone in a room with such a man. Yet their one and only maid would not come near him, Gelly had no time, and Spargo was helping one of the tenants repair yet another hole in the roof. They were paying the tenant with two of their spring lambs. It was a good exchange, though still more than they could afford, yet it had to be done before the entire west wing collapsed. Oh, and Charlie... Charlie was walking with Ceci in the garden because his beloved looked peaked this morning and needed some air. That Charlie had brought Lord Kingston here in a fit of human charity was one thing, but actually dealing with the result of that kindness was something he'd not have given a second thought. Hardly anything new there. *No,* she scolded herself, she would not be bitter and mean-spirited. There was a job that needed doing and she'd done it because no one else would

At least Kingston was sleeping now, and a little more peacefully than before. Livvy reached over and straightened his covers, tucking them in and trying not to notice his powerful chest as she did so. They'd not bothered trying to wrestle him into a nightshirt. On their first attempt he'd given Spargo a black eye, and Livvy had proclaimed that quite enough of an effort to make the man decent. He was clearly beyond saving, and she doubted very much it would be the first time he'd slept in the altogether. A wicked corner of her mind could not help but be pleased about it, though. She was resigned to the fact she would never marry, but she took no pleasure in it. So what if her curious brain was gratified to see what a naked man looked like in the flesh? One that wasn't her brother, anyway, and she'd not seen him since he was a young man, skinny dipping. It wasn't as if she'd have another chance, either. Still, she wasn't so lost to propriety as to peek beneath the bedcovers, and she'd turned her back when her brother and Spargo had removed the man's breeches. He might have no sense of decency, but she did, and she'd not invade a man's privacy in such a way when he was out of his senses. Besides, if even a fraction of the rumours about the man were true, he'd show her himself with very little encouragement. That thought made her cheeks burn, and she hurried from his bedchamber as fast as she could.

King peeled back one wary eyelid. He thought perhaps he was still alive, but wasn't about to put money on it, if they even had such a thing as coin in the hereafter. Then again, if he was dead, he would likely be roasting over some fiery pit and, whilst he certainly felt ghastly enough to be dead, he was cold. Shivering, in fact.

He jolted as the door to his chamber opened, the sound like a bullet to his brain. Except this wasn't his bedchamber. Uncertain of where he was or with whom, he closed his eye again and played dead. Facing anyone right at this moment did not appeal. Hopefully it was just a maid to see to the fire or, better yet, his valet. Come to think of it, where was his bloody valet? The least the devil could do was bring him a drink, for he needed one so badly he was trembling with it... or was that the cold? Both, he decided. This room was like a bloody icebox, and he needed a brandy.

Soft footsteps padded towards the window and King slitted open his eyes again to investigate, and cursed as a figure flung back the curtains. He had a fleeting impression of a female form before the light seared his eyeballs and forced him to look away. The evil fiend who tortured him then compounded their efforts by opening the bloody window.

"S-Shut the d damned window and close the c-curtains," he stammered to whatever witless maid had dared do such an idiotic thing, infuriated by how weak and feeble he sounded.

"Ah, you have deigned to grace us with your presence, at last. Good afternoon, my lord Kingston, and no, I will do no such thing. The room needs airing, it smells like something died in here and, as you've decided not to do the world such a favour, we must have some fresh air."

King opened his eyes again, wide this time, so affronted by the temerity of the young woman who worked in this establishment that he was momentarily lost for words.

"I'll have you dismissed, you impudent wench!"

The outrageous creature just snorted in amusement. "I'd like to see you try."

King blinked, trying his best to focus on the fuzzy image which appeared to have some misshapen hump on its back. On closer inspection, it turned out to be a baby, strapped to the woman by means of a long swathe of fabric. King watched the babe and the woman wearing it suspiciously, assuming at any moment that one or the other of them would grow horns and a tail, and gnash pointy teeth in his direction. However, the hallucination—for it could be nothing else—took a different direction this time, and he watched a sleek black bird fly in the window and settle on the disrespectful female's shoulder.

"Good day to you, Mr Moon," the woman said to the bird. "Gelly has saved some lovely bacon rind for you if you go and tap on the kitchen window."

The crow, for that was what Mr Moon appeared to be, gave an ear-shattering squawk and flew back out the way it had come.

King swallowed. Good God, he'd lost his bloody mind.

Livvy watched her pet crow fly away to the kitchens and turned back to face their unwanted guest. He was staring at her with undisguised horror. He was also shivering so hard his teeth were chattering. No wonder he'd wanted the window closed, she thought with a stab of guilt. Still, she would not let him fester in such a fetid atmosphere. Her grandfather had been a strong believer in the power of fresh air and exercise, and she'd never had cause to doubt his word as he'd been as hale and hearty at seventy as any man twenty years his junior. If only he'd not fallen from his horse, perhaps they'd not be in this terrible mess, but there was no point in lamenting that fact all over again. With a sigh, Livvy went and stirred up the fire, getting a hearty blaze going again. She'd air the room for half an hour, and it would warm up soon enough once the window was closed. In the meantime, she'd put another blanket on his bed.

Once Livvy had pulled the blanket out of the chest where such things were kept, she moved back to the bed, a little alarmed to see King pull his legs up and scramble away from her.

"Stay back," he said, breathless with terror. "You'll not have me."

"I don't want you," Livvy said in disgust. "I can't imagine why you'd suppose I would."

She moved closer and King made a sound of distress, staring at her with wild eyes.

"No!" he said, shaking his head, breathing as though he'd been running for miles. "No, I won't go."

"No one's asking you—" Livvy began and then realised. Oh, Lord. He was still seeing things. No doubt he thought she was some goblin or demon, come to carry him off to the fiery pits. Summoning her most calm and reasonable voice, the one she used on unruly children, she tried again. "Lord Kingston, you've been very unwell, and I know you are all about in your head at present, but I promise you I am no devil come to take you into the darkness. I'm Miss Olivia Penrose, and I just wish to put this blanket on the bed to make you more comfortable."

Kingston stared at her for a long moment. So long she wondered if he had lost his wits entirely.

"L-Livvy?" he asked cautiously.

Livvy sighed. "*Miss Penrose.*"

He hesitated.

"There was… a bird."

Good heavens, she supposed that would seem odd. Especially if one had just left off seeing things that one ought not.

"Oh. Yes, my crow. Mr Moon. He's quite harmless, I assure you."

Kingston looked doubtful.

Livvy turned towards the sound of the door opening and her heart sank as Jane came in, followed by a black piglet. Kingston squeezed his eyes shut.

"It's not there," he muttered. "It's not real. Get a grip, King, for the love of God."

Livvy sighed. "Um, actually, that is real, though it ought not be in the house. Really, Jane, what were you thinking? You know not to bring the piglets inside. They are not pets!"

"Yes, but Barnaby was cold, and—"

"Piglets do not feel the cold like we do, Jane, and I've told you a dozen times, we don't name our dinner. You must not get so attached to them. It only ends in heartbreak."

"Oh, but—"

"No buts. Take him back to the sty at once."

"Yes, Livvy, but Harry said to tell you he's collected a whole basket of rosehips."

Livvy let out a breath of relief. "Excellent. I was worried it would be too late in the year. I completely forgot to check how much syrup was left, and I must replenish the stocks."

"I can help," Jane said eagerly.

"Certainly you can, but take Barna— I mean, take the pig back to where it came from."

Jane scowled but bent to lift the piglet, who had been running about the room, snuffling as it went. She closed the door behind her.

Livvy turned back to the bed.

"You can open your eyes now," she said gently.

Kingston did, though he still looked appalled.

"A pig," he said. "A black pig?"

Livvy nodded. He did not look convinced.

"It was… a *real* pig?"

"You were expecting a hippopotamus?" she demanded and then sighed. "I beg your pardon. No doubt this does seem like a madhouse to you. I can hardly deny it. Yes, my lord. It was a real pig, and a real crow, but anything else unnatural to a bedchamber has certainly resulted from your wicked lifestyle and a feverish imagination. I beg you to forget it. I shall return later with some soup for you. Do try to rest."

Deciding she'd tormented him enough for one afternoon, no matter how thoroughly he deserved it, Livvy covered him with the blanket, closed the window, drew the curtains, and left the earl alone to suffer in silence.

Chapter Three

1st December 1818.

For services to womankind…

"Well, you're still alive then."

King glowered at Miss Penrose as she strode in, bearing a tray of soup and bread and butter. The urge to fling it across the room was tantalising. Lord, what he wouldn't give for a good sirloin and a decent Burgundy. On reflection, he'd just take the Burgundy. He was so desperate for a drink he'd have delivered his soul to the devil for a mere sip. If he'd had the energy, he'd ransack the bloody house, but he was as weak as a kitten and no one but a huge Cornishman by the name of Spargo, or the frosty Miss Penrose, ever came anywhere near him. King was aware he was in a very bad skin and in a foul temper, but Spargo seemed to be some manner of a deaf-mute who communicated via a system of unintelligible grunts, and Miss Penrose had a heart of granite.

"And a good day to you too, my lord. I am quite well, thank you for asking," the wretch continued, as if King had been foolish enough to say such a thing.

He did not wish her a good day at all. He wished her to the bottom of the blasted ocean and well she knew it.

She placed the tray across his lap and King glowered at the bowl of green sludge.

"What the devil is that?"

"Vegetable soup. It's good for you. I suggest you eat it."

"I want meat."

The she-devil folded her arms and stared at him. "You may think you do, but I promise you, your stomach will not tolerate it. Eat the soup, my lord."

"Stop *my lording* me, for the love of God. It's not like you mean it. Call me King. Everyone does."

"As you wish, my lord."

King narrowed his eyes at her, well aware she was baiting him. "You don't like me."

"My, we are perspicacious this morning," the outrageous chit said cheerfully as she bent to stoke the fire.

King admired the view of a very fine backside even as he seethed. Well, he really wasn't dead yet.

"Why? What did I ever do to offend you?" he demanded, discomfited to realise there was any number of ways he might have done so whilst out of his senses. In normal circumstances he'd apologise for the imposition of foisting himself upon them, as it was, he was struggling to keep hold of his sanity let alone his temper. A little voice told him he was being a bad tempered brute and deserved her contempt, but it was drowned out by the angry shouting in his head that demanded he find a drink at once.

Miss Penrose straightened and turned a pair of piercing blue eyes in his direction.

"Let me see," she said thoughtfully. "Firstly, you are another mouth to feed, and you add significantly to the laundry. Secondly, you vomited on one of my only pairs of slippers. And, thirdly, I consider it a service to women everywhere to hold you in contempt."

King snorted. "As I recall, I have given a great service to a good proportion of the female race. Never had any complaints, anyway."

If he'd expected her to blush and stammer and run from the room, he was doomed to disappointment. Miss Penrose was like no gently bred young woman he'd ever encountered, for she simply held his gaze, a considering expression in her eyes. "I'm sure all the women you've ruined would concur, my lord."

"I don't go about ruining innocents," he retorted, stung by the implication. He had become something he hardly recognised of late and there were many things he'd done wrong in his life but never that.

Though there were stories that implied he'd done just that, he knew the truth. More than one foolish girl had set out to trap him into marriage and come a cropper. He wasn't some flat to be tricked into harness with some manipulative creature. If he'd done wrong, he'd own it, but he'd not suffer for some silly woman's attempt to catch an earl for a husband. That was their own lookout.

"I'm certain you are a paragon of virtue," Miss Penrose replied with a smile so false it made him want to gnash his teeth in frustration.

"Hardly that, but I don't see how I can add to the laundry when I have no clothes. Or do you prefer to keep me naked?"

Ah, that brought a pleasing surge of pink rushing to her cheeks. She turned away and busied herself opening the blasted window again to let in an arctic blast of cold air.

"Since you have been incapable of dressing yourself, and you gave poor Spargo a black eye when he attempted to help you, you find yourself as you do. It's no preference of mine, I assure you, and you add the laundry as we had to scrub heaven alone knows what from the clothes you arrived in, and there's the bedlinen now, too, not to mention my *slippers*!"

"Then I must send my regrets to Spargo and I apologise for the blasted slippers, I'll buy you a new pair, but why must you take it as a personal affront? It's not like you wash the clothes yourself."

King watched, curious to note another wave of heat flush her cheeks, and his gaze drifted to her hands. They were red and chapped. She moved, busying herself once more, and keeping her hands out of sight. He frowned.

"Charlie brought me here?" he asked, still a little hazy about where here was and how he'd got come to be here.

He had a vague recollection of Charlie Penrose, Viscount Boscawen, telling him he'd be right as ninepence in no time. Charlie lived somewhere in the wilds of Cornwall, if memory served.

"Yes." She turned to look out of the window she'd just opened, and tugged her shawl closer about her shoulders. "Boscawen feared you were dying. He tells me he owes you for keeping him in one piece at Eton, so, in a fit of compassion, he brought you home to be cared for. Except his charity ended at bringing you home. I have no fond feelings for you, but I must do the Christian thing on his behalf, it seems."

"Why?" King demanded, not understanding that in the least and discomfited to remember it had been her who had stayed with him when he was out of his senses. "You don't owe me anything. Get your servants to tend to me."

The aggravating creature just snorted and shook her head, glaring at him.

"You really do not understand," she muttered, and stalked from the room before he could ask what the devil she meant by that.

With little else to do, King regarded the bowl of green whatever it was with distaste but picked up the spoon. His stomach thought his throat had been cut and was clamouring for sustenance. It wasn't a steak, but it would have to do.

To his relief it tasted a deal better than it looked, and the bread was good and thickly spread with butter. So, one hunger was appeased for the time being, though the desire to find a drink was as fierce as ever. King set the tray aside and threw back the covers. He moved slowly, easing his legs over the side of the bed until his feet touched the floor. The effort left his head spinning. Determined, he tried to get to his feet and almost fell on his face as his legs gave out. Somehow, he clung to the bedhead, forced himself back onto the mattress, and lay there, shaking and sweating. God. Was this what he'd been reduced to? No wonder Miss Penrose held him in such contempt. He closed his eyes for a moment and breathed deep. Clean, cold air from the open window filled his lungs, and he could smell the sea, a salty tang that cut through the stench of sweat and sickness… of *him*. He opened his eyes again, and noted a small looking-glass on the bedside table. He reached for it, and even that trifling task left him breathless, his hand trembling. How pathetic. He'd been a damned Corinthian once upon a time, until drink and despair had pulled him down into the mire. Though he didn't want to, he knew he must, must face what he'd become, and he raised the looking-glass.

An old man looked back at him. Christ, he was only five and thirty, yet the man in the glass appeared to be half dead. Grey skin, bloodshot eyes. He looked utterly haggard, and to think once upon a time he'd fancied himself a handsome fellow. None finer. Blasted peacock. He'd likely ruined himself, and all for what? To spite his father, a man who had never given a snap of his fingers for him anyway. Well, he'd never do the old man's bidding, but he'd been a damn fool to let things go this far. He'd nearly given in, too. If Charlie hadn't found him when he had….

Anyway, killing himself might infuriate the old man and avoid his grand plan, but it would hardly do King any favours, not when his soul was as black as pitch.

This had to stop. Charlie…Charlie, had done him a service, a great one. He'd pulled him out of the dark hole he'd fallen into, and now he had to stay out. He must sober up and get strong again, and…. Well, he'd think about that when he was feeling less like a shipwreck. For now, he would sleep.

❧ ❧ ❧

6th December 1818. St Nicholas Day.

The giving of gifts and thanks and slippers…

"King!"

King did his utmost not to grimace as Charlie's voice shot through his head. He assumed the headache would leave him eventually, but it was bloody persistent. Though he'd almost balked at the indignity of leaning on the silent, morose Spargo to get down the stairs, King thought he really might run mad if he had to spend another day alone in his room. After their words the other morning, Livvy—Miss Penrose—had avoided him. For some reason, this irritated him even more than her presence. If nothing else, being lashed by the sharp side of her tongue had given him something else to think about other than the fact he was crawling out of his skin with the desire for a drink.

Now, however, he was being welcomed into the bosom of the family by Charlie, who came over and shook his hand.

"Good to see you up and about, old man. Thought you'd breathed your last when I found you that night. Gave me quite a turn, I don't mind telling you."

"I owe you a debt of thanks," King replied, meaning it. He knew it was quite likely Charlie had saved his sorry arse. Not Charlie alone, though.

"Well, I owed you first, so we'll call it quits, eh?" Charlie said, with a lazy grin. "Now I'd best introduce you to the horde."

King noted that no mention was made of Livvy's aid to his recovery. Charlie might have bundled him into a carriage and got him here, but Livvy had fed him soup, wiped his fevered brow, and endured who knew what mad ramblings. No matter how much she despised him, she'd cared for him. He knew it had been her who had tended to him more than anyone. He'd gleaned that much from the taciturn Spargo. The only maid was a God-fearing soul and afraid to come near him, and no one else had the time or desire to help. He looked across the room to find that quite startling pair of blue eyes watching him, a look of wry amusement lingering there. King saw from her expression that she'd not expected to receive any credit, but then she'd said as much, hadn't she? Her brother made the show of largesse and received the thanks, and she paid for it.

King nodded and made appropriate comments as he was introduced to Charlie's wife, a faded little blonde woman with a sweet smile and a languid way about her, as if the act of staying awake required great effort. There were so many children King did not even attempt to learn their names, though the baby—Birdie—was one that stuck in his mind. He was uncertain if it was a pet name or her real name. Going on what he'd seen of the household to date, he would not be the least surprised if she'd been christened Big Blue Parrot.

Throughout the introductions, his gaze kept returning to Livvy. She was quite tall for a woman, and well made, with generous curves and slender limbs, and an unruly mass of curly hair that was the colour of dark honey, with lighter blonde threads that caught the sun. She was not beautiful by any means, but there was something arresting about her. It wasn't just her eyes, which were a very dark blue and certainly worth a second glance. Perhaps it was the formidable will of iron lurking beneath her soft exterior that shone through and made a man take notice? It had taken King little time to realise that the few staff in this ramshackle house turned to her for instruction, not the viscount. Once the introductions had been made, Charlie told Spargo to bring some sweetmeats for the children, and the man looked to Livvy before obeying. She gave a discreet nod, and Spargo did as Charlie had asked. King wondered if the viscount knew or cared.

His father had never gone in for the traditions associated with the Christmas season, or any season come to that. It was ironic, given he was so bloody passionate about the traditions that went with the damned title, and the need to marry an appropriate bride, no matter if the girl was...*unsuitable*, to put it mildly. The Penrose family were different. For a start, they seemed to like each other, which was a novelty in King's experience of family life. They were undoubtedly the noisiest collection of individuals he'd ever come across. Even Lady Boscawen could hold her own with an uproarious bellow of laughter, which seemed far too large for her frame or character.

As the tradition of the day was for the giving of gifts, the children were already overexcited, not that anyone but Livvy did anything to temper their high spirits. Indeed, Charlie seemed to add fuel to the fire by playing the fool and chasing them around, until one of the girls fell over, bumped her head, and began to wail, and the smallest boy disrobed in the middle of the room, pronouncing he was "'Ot. Too 'ot."

King sympathised. The noise was making his ears ring, and he was sweating. The unpleasant sensation of his shirt sticking to his back provided an extra irritation. Thankfully, Livvy quieted the girl with a hug and kiss and stern admonishment not to make a fuss as it was only a little bump. She ignored the boy, who was down to his small clothes and socks. King wondered if she would ignore *him* if he tore his own clothes off too. Probably.

Finally, the children settled down when Livvy told them no presents would be exchanged until everyone was behaving themselves. Peace reigned. King could almost have kissed her for that.

As everyone went to fetch their gifts, King shifted on the settee, feeling uneasy for having no gifts to give, and for the knowledge that his hands were shaking. He scanned the room, hoping to see a decanter of brandy and finding nothing. He swallowed, trying to steady his breathing, which was coming faster now as anxiety kicked in. Perhaps Charlie kept a bottle in his study. He'd never been a drinker, King knew that much, but damn it, the man must have a brandy now and again. Hell, he'd drink sherry if he must.

The children ran back in and exchanged their gifts with each other. They were all homemade, with varying degrees of skill: a conker on a piece of string, an embroidered handkerchief, little watercolours, samplers, and poems.

"This is for you, my lord."

King looked up, a little startled to be addressed by the eldest child, a boy on the cusp of manhood. He was thin and gangly, all arms and legs, and had a serious, anxious expression as he held out his gift to King. The boy's eyes were blue, a lighter shade than Livvy's but the same shape, and with the same golden brown lashes.

"Thank you," King said, a little taken aback.

"It's nothing much, but… well, everyone should have a gift at Christmas time."

King unwrapped the brown paper to find a small painting of a horse. It was well done, the creature's head finely wrought, though there was something not quite right about the angle of the legs.

"Oh, it's lovely, Harry, well done," said a decisive voice.

King looked up to discover Livvy had sat beside him and was looking over his shoulder.

"Isn't it lovely, my Lord Kingston?" she asked, a note in her voice that suggested he agree with enthusiasm or face the consequences, likely dying a slow and painful death.

King bristled, a little aggrieved she should think him cruel enough to say anything less, but then she didn't know him at all, and he'd hardly given her any reason to think otherwise. So far, he'd been rude and surly and caused her a great deal of trouble. What a paragon she ought to think him for that. It was a wonder she hadn't thrown him out.

"It is very well done. You have a good eye," he said, trying to arrange his features into something approximating a smile. It was remarkably hard to do, as if he'd forgotten how.

"Thank you," the boy said with a sigh of relief and a look in his eyes that was somewhat daunting.

It appeared perilously close to admiration, though why King could not fathom.

"Here, Livvy, these are for you." Charlie threw a parcel across the room to Livvy and grinned at her. "I think you'll find the timing apt."

King caught the parcel before it hit the ground, as Livvy had made no move to do so. In fact, she'd gone stiff as a board, all but vibrating with tension. King handed her the gift, which she took, though she looked none too pleased about it. How strange. Surely everyone enjoyed being given presents?

"Aren't you going to open it?" he asked, curious.

She stared at the parcel for a long moment, as though someone had handed her a dead mouse. He heard her sigh before she opened the paper, and he noticed her hands did not seem entirely steady. Inside was a beautiful pair of silk dancing slippers. They were a deep green, embroidered with gold thread, and King would have laid money on them pleasing any female of his acquaintance. Not Miss Penrose, however. Her jaw was set and she looked positively murderous.

"I believe it is the custom to say thank you," he murmured, relishing the opportunity to criticise her behaviour for once. It made him feel slightly less of a monster to know she was hardly perfect.

She turned her head and looked him in the eye. "They won't notice if I throw them directly on the fire. It's the buying of them they enjoy."

With that, she stood and stalked out of the room.

King turned, wondering if he ought to make an excuse on her behalf but, sure enough, no one had noticed her leave. Charlie and his lady were all smiles as they passed another gift to one of their children. Too curious to leave well alone, King stood, pausing for a moment until the room stopped spinning, and then followed after Livvy. He found her easily enough, standing by an open door at the back of the house, staring out at the gardens beyond.

"You have a penchant for fresh air that will see you with pneumonia one of these days," he remarked, noticing the slippers and the wrapping paper thrown down on a nearby chair.

"I've never been ill a day in my life," she retorted, though there was none of the usual acid in her tone. She sounded tired, wistful even, as though the idea of being ill and going to bed was one she longed for.

"You do not care for dancing?"

She gave a huff of laughter and gestured to the wilderness beyond the door, which must once have been a pretty garden. "Shall I cavort with the fairies, my lord?"

"I wouldn't bat an eyelid if you did. I've seen enough goblins these past days not to dismiss the idea. I might even join you."

He got a smile for that. A proper one. Well, naturally if he discussed his own shortcomings, she would be pleased, the wretch.

Encouraged, he pressed on. "Surely there are assemblies and the like even in the backend of beyond, like… where the devil are we, anyway?"

"About three miles from Bude, and yes, certainly there are, though they are few and far between."

He knew better than to poke at her with a stick. She always came back fighting, yet the urge to rile her was undeniable, plus the fact that he wanted to know. "Then why not thank your brother graciously for the thoughtful gift? Why were you so furious your hands were trembling?"

"Are you blind?" she demanded, swinging around to face him. "Have you spent so long in a haze of alcohol and debauchery that you see nothing beyond your own nose? Or do you simply not care?"

"Mostly, I don't care," King shot back as irritation got the better of him.

She looked him up and down, an encompassing sweep of those vibrant blue eyes that dismissed him as being good for nothing and made him feel like an awkward youth, a sensation even his father could no longer provoke.

"You astonish me," she replied in disgust. "And whilst I'm about it, I ought to tell you that you'll find no liquor in the house, nor wine in the cellar, so don't bother searching for it. Charlie has never been much of a drinker, and we sold most of the wine years ago. I told him we must remove temptation whilst you remain here. You'll not find so much of a drop of sherry, so don't bother looking. It's all hidden away in a smuggler's hole and, if the Revenue never found it, you certainly won't."

After that lovely bit of information, she turned on her heel.

Furious at her words, and at being dismissed in such a manner, King reached for the shoes.

"Miss Penrose," he called. She set her shoulders but stopped, turning to face him again. "You forgot your gift."

She stared at him for a long moment.

"Why don't you *eat* them?" she snapped inexplicably.

King watched her go, wondering what the devil she'd meant by that.

Chapter Four

7th *December 1818.*

A valet returned, too many apologies, dented pride, and the lure of wickedness.

As if the bloody earl hadn't caused her enough aggravation, it was compounded the next afternoon by the arrival of his blasted valet. To be fair, Mr Walsh seemed a decent sort. It had taken him all this time to track down the earl and follow him, with the man's belongings in tow. He appeared fiercely loyal to his master, which spoke well of his nature, if not his intelligence. At least the man would see to his master's clothes. That was something, but it was another mouth to feed. Livvy spent the rest of the day staring down at the household accounts with a knot in her belly. At least she was too miserable to eat, which meant there was more for the children.

She told herself to stop it. They wouldn't starve. Things were tight, yes, but not desperate. They had a home, a roof over their heads— mostly—and there was enough in the larder to see them through another three months, plus they had the piglets and the lambs, chickens too. The garden was producing reasonably well, and then there was her mad plan to save them all, which would likely do nothing of the sort. All of which was fine and dandy if there were no debts. If Charlie hadn't done something unbelievably stupid. *Stupider.*

He would never let her look at *his* accounts. It was one of the few times he put his foot down as head of the household, except she suspected it wasn't pride that stopped him from allowing her, but fear. For if she knew how bad things were… no. She would not think that of him. Charlie wouldn't do that to her. He loved her. He was foolish beyond measure, but he would not ruin them all beyond saving. He would not ruin *her* with his idiocy. The investments he had made had been ill-advised—what an understatement—but with careful management they could all manage well enough. Livvy put her head in her hands, drew in a deep breath and tried not to remember Christmases past, which had been full of lavish gifts, good food, guests, and parties. Then their parents had died in a boating accident when Charlie was sixteen and she was eight. Though it had been a devastating loss, the presence of their indomitable grandfather had lessened the blow. Gramps had been a huge figure in her childhood, strong as an ox, good-hearted and principled. Everyone had loved and respected him.

Losing him when she was fourteen had hit her far harder than the loss of her parents.

It had hurt Charlie, too, and he had been forced to take over the running of the household long before he was ready. Even Livvy had known he was immature for his years. He'd run away with Ceci and married her the moment he was out of mourning, and Livvy knew Grandpa would not have allowed it. Ceci was sweet but frivolous and silly, and only encouraged Charlie in his own foolishness. She'd been due to marry a duke, and her family had disowned her for eloping with Charlie and withheld her dowry. Everyone knew it was a disastrous move, but Livvy had been too young to make her brother see it, and there was no one else to gainsay him without Grandpa there to talk sense. Charlie had tried to make the household a happy one, but Ceci and Livvy were chalk and cheese, and Charlie had made so many disastrous decisions—things that had made Livvy wild—but she was only his sister and could not keep him from folly. He was the man of the house and foolish or not, he never let her forget it.

Livvy groaned and curled her fingers into her hair, tugging at the roots. Was this to be her life, forever scrimping and saving and worrying over each blasted penny, while Ceci and Charlie were oblivious? Well, she could always marry the odious Mr Skewes. A shudder ran down her spine at the idea. He was a wealthy landowner who lived a little over five miles from Boscawen. It was hardly a secret that he wanted to marry her. He'd been very clear on that matter. Mr Skewes was thirty years old, fit and eligible, and easy enough on the eye. He was polite to his neighbours, did his bit for charity, never drank to excess and never raised his hand in anger, and yet... and yet there was cruelty in his eyes. He had a way of saying things without really saying them that made Livvy uneasy. She knew he had his eye on Boscawen's estate, and suspected he saw his way in via her. She neither liked nor trusted him, and instinct told her that putting herself in his hands would be akin to putting her head in a noose.

No.

No, she'd work her fingers to the bone before she allowed a man like that to own her. Though what would that mean for Susan and Lydia, Rebecca and Jane and poor little Birdie? There would be no dowry for them. How would they ever marry and leave home without a season, or at the very least new frocks for the local assemblies? Tears pricked at her eyes and she scolded herself. *Stop that now, Olivia Penrose. You're getting maudlin for no good reason.*

Things might not be as bad as they seemed, and Susan was only thirteen. They had a good few years yet, and anything might happen in that time. Just because the girls wouldn't have the chance to go to town and marry fine, wealthy gentlemen didn't mean they would not marry good men who could keep them and their families in comfort. They'd just have to lower their sights.

Livvy swallowed down her anxiety and her misery and closed the book of accounts. No amount of worry and staring at the figures would change them, but perhaps some fresh air would clear her head.

❧ ❧ ❧

"You can stop grinning at me, like that. It'll go to me head if you keep on."

King snorted from his position slouched on the bed, watching as Walsh put away the last of his clothes. "Nonsense. You've not a conceited bone in your body, and I was never more pleased to see anyone in my life."

"Aye, well, I might say the same. Truth be tol' I reckoned you was dead for a while there."

There was a despairing note to his valet's words that King heard with a heavy heart. He did not know why Walsh bore with him. The man could easily find a better position, one that actually paid him a decent wage, and with a master who wasn't a pathetic sot. Guilt and disgust rose inside him like bile.

"Sorry," he muttered.

Walsh shook his head. "The drink had a grip on ye. Dragging you down, it were. I've seen it afore, but I never saw anyone turnabout like you have. Boscawen saved your skin, I reckon, my lord."

King frowned. It was an odd sensation, knowing one would be dead in some filthy corner of London if not for an old friend taking pity. He was pitiable too; he knew it and it made him burn with shame. Worse was knowing that, if someone put a bottle of brandy in front of him right now, he didn't know if he could stop himself from drinking it and starting the whole spiral downwards off again. He couldn't even remember when it had become so bad, when escaping boredom and sorrow had become a descent into hell. He looked up as a shadow fell over him to see Walsh watching him with concern. He was getting on in years now, his faithful valet must be sixty at least. Walsh had been with King since he was twelve years old, and had been more a father to him than King had any right to expect. It had been Walsh who'd comforted him as a boy, when he'd been on the receiving end of one of his father's furious rants for crimes he'd never understood. Walsh who'd taught him the value of good manners and decency, though he seemed to have forgotten those lessons of late. Walsh was a good man. God knew he'd have to be not to have given up on King two decades ago.

"Don't do it again, lad, I beg you."

King blinked hard. He'd never asked Walsh to *my lord*, him—indeed, he'd begged him to call him King as everyone else did—but the man was stubborn. Yet, every now and again he'd crack and address him as he might a son, usually when King had done something so dreadful he'd frightened the poor devil half to death.

"I'll try," King replied. "I will, I promise. I'll do my best."

He looked up and saw the fear in Walsh's eyes and guilt bloomed in his heart. No one else had ever given a damn for him. Oh, he'd been indulged by his parents and given every advantage, but it was the title that had mattered to them, not *him*. His parents had never listened to him, never given his hopes any credence, never allowed him the freedom to choose anything for himself. It had been stifling, and he'd rebelled against it as hard as he could, not that it had ever done him a damned bit of good.

"This is the best place for you for a spell. Couldn't get farther from society if you tried, I reckon." Walsh sounded altogether too pleased about that.

King snorted, trying to find some humour in the situation before he wept with shame. "Fine, I'll just die of boredom."

Walsh shook his head. "You'll get your arse out of doors and some fresh air, get strong again. I've never seen you so grey and worn to a thread, and that's the truth. You need feeding up, though I reckon I'd best slip the cook some coin to help out.

Won't do to insult Lord Boscawen, but he can barely feed his own brood, if you ask me."

"What?" King sat up, startled by this information.

Walsh rolled his eyes at him. "Surely you've seen it? The children's clothes are all wash-worn, cuffs and collars turned about more than once, I reckon. This place is falling down around their ears and no repairs in sight. Boscawen's got pockets to let."

"Why don't you eat them, my lord!"

Livvy's sharp words returned to him with unpleasant clarity. That's why she had been so furious, so overset that her hands had trembled as she unwrapped her feckless brother's gift. She knew they couldn't afford such things, but her brother had spent the money anyway.

"Are you blind? Have you spent so long in a haze of alcohol and debauchery that you see nothing beyond your own nose? Or do you simply not care?"

"I didn't. I didn't see it," King admitted.

Walsh shrugged. "Well, you've had your own troubles."

"Do we have any coin left?" King demanded, horrified to realise he had no idea.

Since his father had cut him off, he'd been living off his winnings at cards…winnings which had dwindled with his ability to concentrate as his drinking got heavier.

Walsh shifted, looking a little uneasy. "We do. Not a vast amount, but enough for a few months, if we go careful."

King stared at him, realising Walsh must have taken the money and hidden it so King couldn't piss it all up the wall like he'd done with the rest.

"I hope you took your wages out first," King said gruffly.

God, he was a sorry excuse for a man. His father was a brute and his mother was an icicle, but he was an adult now, not a snivelling boy. So what if his father hated him, so what if the man took a malicious joy in destroying everything King tried to build for himself. He'd been born to privilege, he had education and brain in his head, surely he could have done better. Allowing himself to sink to such depths was pathetic and vile. How had it happened? At what point had he gone from wanting a drink to *needing* one? He knew the difference between right and wrong—though he often ignored the distinction—but he knew the difference between a good decision and a bad one, too. He had no one to blame but himself for this wretched state of affairs, and now he'd landed his miserable carcass on a family who could hardly look after themselves.

What pitiful mess had Boscawen created for them? The man had never had the sense he was born with. It had been no surprise the bullies tormented him so mercilessly. No wonder either that Miss Penrose had been so revolted by King landing in her lap. It was a wonder she hadn't tossed him out on his arse that first night. Likely she'd tried, but her foolish brother had not allowed it. She had certainly inherited the brains and fortitude her sibling was missing.

The unnerving realisation that he owed Miss Penrose an apology was not a pleasant one, and it nagged at him. In normal circumstances he'd just have a drink and indulge his baser nature until such inconvenient pangs of conscience were drowned out. The desire to do so was tantalising but he could not go back to being that man. He'd become a disgusting, pathetic creature, someone he did not recognise and could only hold in contempt. It was little wonder Miss Penrose agreed with him on that. Worse was the awareness that he *needed* to stay here. Walsh was right. He needed to keep clear of society if he was to have any hope of keeping himself sober, of kicking this pernicious addiction that had taken a hold of him. Livvy—*Miss Penrose*—had hidden all the drinks in the house to help him do that.

He supposed he ought to thank her, but he wasn't feeling quite that charitable yet. He gritted his teeth and made himself remember the devils, demons, and goblins that had hounded him through those terrifying hours when he thought he'd died and gone to hell. Livvy had stayed with him and he'd not deserved her kindness. She certainly did not deserve his loathsome presence in her house. She might be prickly and aggravating but he'd merited little else from her. Very well, he'd thank her and mean it too. Damn her eyes.

As much as the woman infuriated him with her waspish nature, she had dragged him out of the darkness, chased away the devils and the goblins, and she was strong enough to keep him from falling back into the pit. He needed to stay here, with her, until he was recovered and could stand on his own two feet again. It was a lowering realisation. He was a pathetic mess of a man and he had earned her disgust, but he would rally. He would stand tall again, and she would see that he was better than that. Why he felt the need to prove himself to her, he had no idea. Well, no, he had a fine idea. No young woman had ever spoken to him with such contempt. In general, they swooned, they simpered, or they flirted. If they didn't, he'd been too drunk to notice before now in any case. Being reviled was a new experience, and one he did not enjoy in the least. No. He would show Miss Penrose who he really was, who he had been once, and then she would sing a different song entirely. He had enough self-awareness of his own pride and stubborn nature to know he would be far less likely to fail with her keen blue gaze trained upon him, waiting for him to put a foot wrong. She would expect him to return to his boozing and debauchery at the first opportunity, and she would be smug with disgust when he did. So he wouldn't. That the idea of failing made him tremble with fear was something he would not think about. He *could not* fail, could not go back to being that… that… No, he would not fall again and if he needed to use Miss Penrose and her disgust of him as a crutch then so be it. He'd show the starched little madam, and then she'd owe *him* an apology. What for, he wasn't entirely certain, but he didn't doubt he'd think of something.

❧ ❧ ❧

Livvy fiddled with the big iron key, her fingers numb from the cold. Finally it turned and she locked the door in the thick stone garden wall that led to the abandoned farm buildings. It wouldn't do for the family to learn about her little experiment. Certainly, she didn't want her brother to know. If he got wind of it, he'd likely think their troubles were over and spend even more money on the strength of a glimmer of hope. It was nothing more than a glimmer, after all. If the winter was a hard one, that spark of hope would snuff out like a candle in a breeze.

"Ah, Livvy, there you are."

Livvy jolted in surprise. No one came out to this part of the property, certainly not on a day when there were thick black clouds overhead threatening a downpour at any moment. That the voice belonged to Lord Kingston only compounded her shock. What the devil did he mean lurking about in the grounds, and calling her *Livvy,* damn him!

"I did not give you leave to use my Christian name, my lord," she said, clutching the cold iron key in her hand. "You may address me as Miss Penrose, or not at all. I prefer the latter, I assure you. Good day to you."

To her annoyance, he only laughed. It was a good sound too, a rumble of amusement that came from deep within him.

"I deserve that. Indeed I only said it to rile you, which was foolish of me when I have come to beg your pardon. You will be unsurprised to hear I have little skill or experience for such an undertaking."

Livvy regarded him with suspicion. The path was narrow so she couldn't walk past him and get away. What in blazes was he playing at?

He snorted and shook his head. "By the look on your face I see I am doing worse than I imagined, so I will try to make this as painless as I can for both of us. I am sorry that you were forced to endure my presence when I was… well, in whatever disgusting state you were forced to deal with. I am profoundly grateful to your brother, and especially to you, Miss Penrose, for all you have done for me. I realise I am a burden to your household you could well do without, but I will do my best to keep that burden to a minimum. I would leave, but—"

"*No.*"

Livvy clamped her mouth shut, furious with herself for having spoken. What he did was none of her affair, but if he left and returned to the same way of living, he'd be dead in six months at best, likely a lot less than that. Looking at him now, big and tall and so imposing, that seemed impossible, even if his skin was still a ghastly shade, his eyes sunken and shadowed, and his coat hanging loose where he'd lost so much weight.

To her surprise the earl did not make some lewd remark about her not wanting him to leave, instead he just returned a rueful smile.

"Indeed. My chances of staying sober seem far greater if I remain here for a while under your hawklike and disapproving gaze. I fear my charming presence will not make up for the lack of drink in the house for your festivities, however."

Livvy shook her head.

"My grandfather disliked drink in any form, for his father was a drunkard, and his brother too. We were given a healthy fear for the perils of overindulgence. Charlie drinks to be sociable in town, but he won't mind missing it to keep you in one piece. He thinks the world of you," she added for the sake of fairness.

He had apologised after all, and quite prettily in his own fashion. It must have stung for a man like him. He was proud, she could see that, though his pride must have taken an almighty dent of late.

"I have no idea why."

There was bitterness in the words that surprised her. For all he was smarting for her having seen him at his worst, she assumed he would take pride in who he was, in the fact he had saved her brother at a time when he'd been unable to save himself.

"Because you protected him," she said, seeing no reason to deny it. Charlie had been weak, weaker than Kingston, and the earl had shielded him. "You didn't have to. He was a younger boy, beneath your notice. You didn't need to step in."

He shook his head, a sharp movement that spoke of impatience with the subject. "Nonsense. Pray do not colour me in saintly shades. I don't doubt I enjoyed smashing his tormentors' heads together as much as they'd enjoyed beating him. I'm little better, only that I prefer not to pick on those who cannot fight back. I just happened to be there. I'm sure anyone else would have done the same."

"No, they wouldn't, and they didn't," Livvy said, folding her arms and wondering why she was labouring the point. "He was being beaten and terrorised almost daily until you stopped it. Plenty of other boys could have stepped in. None did. Only you, and it wasn't only the once, so don't make out like it was."

He huffed out a breath and raked a hand through hair which was thick and dark. "I cannot abide bullies. Sadly, the place was riddled with them. Still is, I don't doubt."

Livvy nodded. "Well, you may stay until after Christmas, providing you behave yourself and don't set a bad example to the children."

She walked towards him, expecting him to step aside and let her pass. He did not.

"What about you?"

Livvy frowned. "I beg your pardon?"

A wicked glint entered his eyes, something dark and amused lurking there. Livvy's heart picked up. He looked exactly like what he was: a bad man, a man so sunk in depravity he'd almost killed himself. The Earl of Kingston still carried the scent of liquor and sickness, still looked like a man who'd ruined himself with drink and dissipation, and yet there was something magnetic in his gaze, something that made her skin prickle with awareness.

"May I set *you* a bad example?" he asked, his tone mild.

"Certainly not," Livvy replied briskly, glaring at him. "Now step aside. I do not have time to waste with this foolish chattering."

He did so, the faintest quirk of his lips mirroring the amusement in his eyes as she hurried past him, but she felt the weight of his gaze follow her all along the path until she was out of sight.

Chapter Five

8th December 1818.

The bitter truth, a betrayal, and a straw to cling to.

With hindsight, Livvy should have seen it coming. She should have known better than to hope they might yet survive her brother's foolishness. Well, now she saw it with such clarity she felt dazed by the glare. Her brother was still talking, still explaining all the reasons marrying Mr Skewes was the best thing for everyone, and her especially.

"He's a good man, anyone can see that, and it's a fine house too. It's hardly a death sentence, Livvy, to be told you'd live in such a splendid place, with money at your disposal for frocks and pretty things, and he doesn't care about the dowry. He'll pay off all our debts and only take the land off our hands in return. It's not like we're making anything from it…."

Her brother rambled on and on, and her fists clenched tight around the iron key. The metal was warm now, and she could not remember having picked it up that morning. She'd been on her way out when her brother had asked to speak to her. The iron had been cold then, the touch of it against her hand making her shiver. Her mother had told her stories of the fae folk when she was a child. They were allergic to iron. Was it iron and lemon juice, or salt? Had that been it? She couldn't remember now. Livvy had made herself forget a lot of things over the years, silly things that were of no use to her now. Like how she'd dreamed of going to town and having a season, of beautiful dresses and meeting a good man, a clever, handsome man who would make her laugh and think her pretty and… and what nonsense. Such things were best forgotten. She stared at the hand clutching the key, saw how chapped and dry the skin was from too much hard work and not enough care.

"No."

Charlie stopped talking and looked at with an air of mild surprise. "Sorry, what?"

"No, Charlie. I will not marry him. Not even to save the family. I'll work my fingers to the bone for you, I'll scrimp and save and skivvy if I must, but I will not give that man the right to me, to own me. No. I shan't."

"What nonsense is this?" Charlie said impatiently. "You act as though I would sell you into slavery!"

"You *are* selling me into slavery," Livvy retorted. "Just because I would live in a fine house and wear dresses that aren't five years out of date would not change the fact that I would belong to a man I despise."

"You don't despise him."

Livvy shot to her feet.

"Don't you tell me what I feel!" she shouted in fury, tears pricking at her eyes.

She had been a fool to trust her brother. He was weak, and his weakness would be her condemnation if she wavered now. Livvy took a deep breath and forced her voice into something resembling a reasonable, calm tone.

"Hear me, and hear me well, Charlie, for I'll not say it again. I will not marry that man to save you from a situation of your own making. I tried to warn you against your friend's ridiculous investment scheme, and you refused to listen, but you'll listen now. I'll leave and not come back before I allow you to betroth me to that man, and if you think to persuade me or cajole me into it, stop now. One more word on the matter and I'll never speak to you again."

Her brother stared at her, his colour high as his own temper flared, but she didn't care. If she didn't beat him over the head with her meaning he'd think she would come around, that she just needed time to think it over. Well, she'd thought it over. She'd sacrificed a great deal for this family—her own future and happiness, for one—she'd not sacrifice what little freedom remained for them.

"You're being hysterical," he said, stalking to the window and glowering at the rain sheeting down beyond the glass.

She stamped down with difficulty on the desire to show him what hysterical looked like, but her reply was quiet and serene, even if she was throwing things at him in her mind. "Do I sound hysterical, Charlie? Good heavens. I'd no idea how sensitive you were. Perhaps you should have a lie down, you'll give yourself a migraine. Now, if you'll excuse me, I have things to do."

Somehow, she left the room without giving into the desire to beat her brother about the head with the nearest object, though her hands trembled so much she could hardly turn the door handle. Outside, she almost barged into Mr Walsh and murmured an apology before she fled, heading for the gardens, for escape, for the path that led down to the sea, though the rain was pelting down still. It soaked her to the bone in no time at all, but Livvy did not stop.

"Well?" King demanded as Walsh returned, looking grim faced.

70

He had often believed the man wasted his talents as a valet. He'd have made an exceptional spy. Walsh could read people with ease, always seemed to be aware of any upset or scandal in a household, and could smell an intrigue from a mile away. It had saved King from a great deal of unpleasantness over the years. When Walsh had brought him his breakfast and told him there was something amiss in the house, King had listened. Not that he gave a hoot for whatever problems Boscawen had brought down upon himself. That was his own affair. He might not want to burden the man further, but he wasn't a blasted priest or a shoulder to cry on, and he had no financial help to give beyond a few extra coins for his keep. Yet, if the place was about to fall apart, they'd want King out and he couldn't have that, not until he was stronger. He'd woken feeling utterly wretched, so tired the very idea getting out of bed was akin to climbing a bloody mountain, and miserable besides. He wasn't a surly fellow by nature, not until recently, but everything seemed so damned black he felt like curling up under the blankets and never coming out again. The only bright spot in the past few days had been the knowledge that he'd unsettled the unflappable Miss Penrose.

"He's trying to marry Miss Penrose to some bloke what lives nearby. A Mr Skewes."

"And she won't have him?" King guessed with a smile. Well, good for her. He could not help but feel a burst of fellow feeling for someone standing strong against being forced into a marriage they did not want.

"Not only won't have him, despises him. Told her brother she'd leave rather than marry Mr Skewes, and would no longer speak to him if he mentioned it ever again."

A bark of laughter left King as he imagined her icy response to Boscawen's interference in her life. He could see her now, looking down her nose at Charlie, regarding him as though he'd crawled out of cheese.

"What's her objection? Is he fat? Old?"

Walsh shook his head. "According to Gelly— that's the cook here—he's a good-looking fellow, few years your junior. Got money, too, and a fine house."

For no earthly reason he could think of, King felt a burst of irritation at that description. Perhaps it had been the 'few years your junior' comment, or that the fellow had money. "Then why won't she have him?"

Walsh rolled his eyes. "Supposing you ask her?"

King returned the expression. "Ah yes, I can imagine the reception I'd receive if I posed such a question to Miss Prissy Penrose. Christ, she'd bite my head off for my impertinence."

"Shouldn't blame her none, either," Walsh said, chuckling.

King sighed and settled back against the pillows.

"Well, anyway, it's only a family squabble, nothing to worry about." He sat forward again, as Walsh's expression was not a restful one. "What?"

"Gelly reckons it's only Miss Penrose what holds this family together, not that Boscawen and his lady recognise it, but your old mate is close to bankruptcy. I reckon young missy has to marry that fellow, or at least one with a few quid, or they'll all be in the basket."

King gave a despairing groan. "And what do you propose I do about it? All I need is a quiet place with no booze and no temptation for a few weeks, while I get myself together. I have no desire to land myself in the middle of a family dispute."

Walsh leaned back against the chest of drawers and folded his arms. "Well, you're 'ere, in the house, so you *are* in the middle, like it or no. May as well meddle a bit if it'll get you the peace and quiet you need. Boscawen is bound to be grateful. I mean, you could have a little chat with her, and maybe you could meet the fellow what wants to marry her too, see what he's like. If he's a nice fellow, p'rhaps you could talk the lady round. Lord knows you can talk 'em out of their petticoats when the mood takes you."

"Flattery will get you nowhere," King grumbled. "I'm hardly in a state to persuade Miss Penrose of anything. Besides which, she quite clearly despises me."

"A challenge for you, then. You always used to like the tricky ones the most."

He narrowed his eyes at Walsh with suspicion, wondering if he was up to something, but the man just returned a blank, innocent expression. King sighed. "God, you're annoying. I can't think why I keep you around."

"Can't think why I stay, neither," Walsh remarked with a grin. "I'll fetch some hot water."

The devil sauntered off with a smug expression.

King closed his eyes and let out a heartfelt curse. "Bloody, buggering hell."

Once he was suitably shaved and attired, King forced his aching limbs down the stairs only to discover Miss Penrose was not in the house. It seemed best to approach her first and get the lie of the land, as he wasn't gallivanting about the countryside looking for Mr Skewes in this weather. He regarded the sombre grey clouds outside with misgiving. It had poured all morning and looked as if it was set to come down again any time now. Well, he'd have a quick stroll around the garden and, if she wasn't there, he'd try again later.

Livvy dragged her sodden skirts back along the path that led to the gardens. She was still holding the key, her fingers curled about it and blue with cold. Not that she was going to visit her little project now. She didn't have the heart for it. Every time she remembered her row with Charlie, her heart ached anew. She had trusted him. He was a silly fellow at times, and drove her nearly distracted, but she'd believed he loved her, believed he would put her happiness before any financial gain. He'd betrayed her. Though he did not understand her motives and thought Mr Skewes a nice fellow, Charlie knew she despised him. He knew she feared marrying a man she could not trust, and yet he'd tried to force her hand, to use her love for her nieces and nephews to coerce her to the altar.

Don't you want the girls to have dowries? Don't you want poor Harry to go to university?

As if it were her doing they couldn't! Then he'd dropped the final bombshell. He had debts, debts that he could not pay. All their savings had gone. He'd sold everything that wasn't nailed down or entailed, and it still wasn't enough, yet he'd still spent more buying stupid presents for Christmas… she wanted to weep. She *had* wept. For once she'd cried for herself, for a life wasted on trying to keep this family together when her brother was determined to undo all her good work.

Still she'd told him—spelled it out in words even he could understand—that she would not marry Mr Skewes under any circumstances, and that she had lost faith in him. It was impossible to trust Charlie now. She needed a plan, a way out. Livvy gave a despairing sob. Her only way out of her brother's house was to marry, and if he could no longer afford to keep her….

Well, there was more than one man in the world, not that she'd ever met more than a handful of them. Society was thin on the ground here, and she'd been too busy with Charlie's brood to meet the few there were very often. There were plenty of gentlemen farmers about who would snap her up but that would not help the children. She needed a wealthy man, wealthy enough to see Harry and George through school and university and give the girls their come out. A man like that would not be found in Bude or anywhere near here.

Great Aunt Agatha!

The idea hit her like a lightning strike. Her aunt was a daunting, mysterious figure, and one she only knew from the occasional letter that came their way and usually left Charlie in towering rage. Not that he ever let her read them. He said Aunt Agatha was a wicked creature, and Livvy must have nothing to do with her. It was one of the few things Charlie and their grandfather had ever agreed upon. Apparently, she had a *reputation.* She was also a very wealthy widow, and always gave a lavish New Year's Ball at her home in Bath.

Bath was not so very far away. Perhaps if Livvy could get there, her aunt might take pity on her, might lend her a gown and introduce her to some eligible men. Might give her a chance... might wave her magic wand and give her glass slippers and turn a pumpkin into a carriage. Livvy swallowed down a wave of misery. Yet it was her only chance, a straw to cling to against the torrent that seemed to be swirling around her, threatening to sweep her off her feet and tow her under.

"Miss Penrose?"

Oh, how bloody perfect. Livvy cursed the man to Hades. She must look a fright, soaked to the bone, her eyes burning from weeping too hard, and no doubt her nose was as red as a beacon from spending too long standing on the beach while the wind buffeted her back and forth. So, naturally, her nemesis had come to speak to her.

"Good heavens," Kingston said, his eyes widening as he took in the picture she made. She could only imagine how unattractive she must look. "You're soaked to the skin. Come inside at once."

Livvy balked, having had quite enough of men telling her what to do for one day.

"I am more than capable of looking after myself, I th-thank you, my l-lord," she retorted through chattering teeth, and then ruined it with a disgusting sneeze.

"There, you've caught a chill, you idiotic creature. What the devil were you thinking, wandering about in such weather with your skirts wet through? Don't you have the sense you were born with?"

He took her arm, no doubt some chivalrous instinct raising its head that had not quite been drowned in brandy, but Livvy felt a burst of alarm. Why, she could not have said, except that it felt as if another man were taking charge of her life, and she simply snapped.

"No!" she yelled, pulling herself free. "No, I won't go with you! I'll look after myself, I always look after myself, no… no one else… n-no one else…."

To her horror, the words stuck in her throat and her eyes burned hotter still. Though she'd believed she had no tears left to cry she broke down, sobbing in the middle of the garden with the Earl of Kingston staring at her in utter horror. Good lord, she'd be sent to a madhouse if he had anything to do with it. No doubt it would amuse him greatly. Yet she could not stop. The heavens opened once more and the rain hammered down, but Livvy could not move. Some dam inside her had burst, and all the misery and sadness she'd forced down for so many years exploded out in a disgusting show of emotion that would send any sane man running for the hills.

Except Kingston did not run.

Livvy gasped as he swept her up, strong arms holding her as though she weighed nothing at all, which she knew was not the case. She was too miserable to protest, too worn down to fight. For all she knew, he was going to take her to some dark place and murder her. She couldn't find the will to care. Instead, she rested her head on his shoulder and closed her eyes.

Somewhat to her surprise, he did nothing reprehensible, but carried her to the stables, out of the rain. The horses whickered a greeting, and the scent of hay and leather soothed her jagged edges a little. Kingston set her down on a bench and then sat beside her. He said nothing, only handed her a large white handkerchief.

Livvy took it from him and wiped her face, blew her nose, and took a shuddering breath, trying to find some semblance of calm.

"We'll go back inside once you feel able to face it. I know you don't wish me to interfere, but you'll catch your death if you don't change out of those wet things."

She nodded meekly, hardly able to dispute it whilst her limbs trembled so hard.

"Is he such an appalling prospect?"

Livvy blinked and turned her head to regard him in outrage. Curiosity glinted in his dark eyes, but he showed no sign of impatience or condemnation. The earl shrugged.

"Hard to keep a secret when the servants chatter. Walsh heard about it. So… is he? Appalling I mean."

"Y-Yes," she managed, wrapping her arms about herself.

He nodded and got to his feet, took off his coat and settled it about her shoulders. The warmth from his body still lingering in the fabric only made her shiver harder, but it was lovely.

"Th-Thank you."

"Don't mention it. We shall call it quits. You've seen me at my worst and now I've seen you. We're both human. Who would have thought it?"

Livvy snorted. "A passionate crying fit hardly equates to a lifetime of drink and debauchery, my lord."

He returned a grave nod. "True. You need a deal more practise. Perhaps you should try hitting me, or throwing things about?"

A sideways glance in his direction showed her a placid expression, but there was laughter in his eyes.

"Are you offering to present yourself as a target? I would be more than willing to try that, believe me."

He grinned at her then. "There you are. You feel better now you can be unkind to me, don't you?"

"Hmph. I do. How strange."

Kingston shook his head and stretched his long legs out before him. "Not strange at all. Like most young ladies, you've likely spent much of your life fighting back your feelings and smothering all the things you wish to say when things go awry, but you hold me in contempt, so you need not watch that sharp tongue of yours. You can vilify me to your heart's content and never feel a moment's guilt for having done so. Liberating, I should imagine."

Livvy pursed her lips. "That's not entirely accurate. Yes, I do enjoy scolding you. It is most satisfying, but the truth is I have always been a deal too free with my opinions. Though that's only because my brother is—"

She clamped her mouth shut against her words. Charlie might have betrayed her trust, but Kingston was a stranger. She'd not discuss her brother's shortcomings with him.

"Your brother is a good-hearted fool until he gets himself into deep water, and then he can be a selfish prick."

Livvy gasped and opened her mouth to remonstrate before thinking better of it.

"Yes," she said. "Precisely that."

"I know how you feel."

"I sincerely doubt it," Livvy replied, somewhat scathing at the idea they should have the least thing in common.

"My father cut me off because I won't marry to please him."

Livvy gaped at Kingston as he turned to face her.

"There see, I *have* shocked you."

"And is *she* appalling?" she asked.

Kingston shook his head. "No, but I should be if I married her. She's sixteen."

"Good God!"

"Oh, you think that's the worst of it," he said, bitterness lacing each word. "I assure you it is not. Her parents agreed to the match three years ago. Three years I have denied him, and made him so furious he set out to ruin me. I tried to make my own way, you see. Nearly succeeded, too, until my father—he's the Marquess of Eynsham—and the Duke of Olney got their heads together. The duke is the girl's father, of course. A splendid match, is it not?"

Livvy could hardly speak from considering a match between this big, dissolute fellow and a child of sixteen,... *thirteen* when the match was proposed. Good God, and she'd thought her brother a monster for treating her so, and she was a grown woman. She considered her oldest niece, Susan, thirteen years old and still playing with dolls and reading fairy stories, and her stomach lurched. Yet Kingston had denied them, despite losing what must have been a lavish lifestyle, when he could have married the chit and gone about his way... he'd stood firm.

Livvy took a breath. She respected his actions, and he ought to know that. "You did right, my lord. Though it sticks in my throat to admit it, I... I admire you for doing the right thing."

Kingston snorted and narrowed his eyes at her. "My, that *must* have stung."

"A bit," she admitted.

"There, there, Miss Penrose. Never fear, I shall say something shocking any moment now and the feeling will wear off."

Despite everything, she laughed. "I never doubted it."

They sat in silence for a while, which was surprisingly comfortable... or would have been if she wasn't freezing. Yet she was not ready to go indoors.

"What will you do?"

He shrugged. "Damned if I know. I made my way gambling until now, which I do well enough to get by, but... but it seems I have a bit of a... a problem."

"You cannot let yourself drink again, because next time you won't stop until you're dead in a ditch."

He sighed. "You don't mince your words, do you? I suppose I should say I find it refreshing, but it's rather like being scoured with a scrubbing brush."

"Invigorating," Livvy said, nodding, though she knew he meant nothing of the sort.

"Painful," he amended.

Livvy dared another glance at him and noted the troubled look in his eyes. "You *can* do it, you know. I recognise a stubborn individual when I see one, and yes, before you fling it in my face, it takes one to know one. I *am* stubborn, and so are you. You have the fortitude to resist your demons, my lord. Perhaps all you need is something else to focus your attention on."

He nodded, surprising her with the crooked smile that touched his mouth. Goodness, but he had a lovely mouth. Livvy tore her gaze away, horrified at having noticed such a thing. He might not be the monster she had believed him to be, but he was still a man with the morals of an alley cat. She ought not be alone with him, let alone notice his lovely, lush, sensuous mouth.

Oh, damnation.

"Yes, I have thought the same, the trouble being I cannot turn my attention to earning an honest living, for one because I am a nobleman, and it is not the done thing—"

"Which you don't give two hoots about," Livvy put in.

He gave her the benefit of another lopsided grin which was far too endearing. "I do not." His smile faded and he reached out, tugging a straw free from a nearby bale and twisting it between his long fingers. "But whatever I do, my father will ruin it. I've tried several times now and it isn't only me who suffers when he destroys whatever I try to build. I don't have the heart to try again, to make something work only to watch him reduce it all to rubble and dust. I certainly can't drag anyone else into it and now… now I haven't a farthing to my name."

"What if your father didn't know?"

Kingston shook his head. "He has an uncanny knack for finding things out. So, if earning my keep is not an option, that leaves me with gambling and dallying with the ladies… and we have gone full circle, I believe."

Livvy rolled her eyes at him. "I did not take you for a man who lacked imagination, my lord. Not with the vivid and horrible visions your mind created for you when you were out of your senses. Surely you can think of more to find in life than that?"

Suddenly she was the focus of his intense, dark gaze and her skin, which had been chilled and clammy, warmed until her cheeks burned. "Perhaps someone needs to teach me what else there is, for I can think of nothing."

"Perhaps," Livvy said, irritated to find her voice had gone all thready and breathless. Sensing danger, she got to her feet. "Thank you for your kindness, Lord Kingston. I am quite calm now, so I had best return to the house."

He stood too, reminding her just how big he was, how broad and powerful, even after having sunk so low. Livvy remembered how he had lifted her as if she weighed nothing at all, and her heart— irrational organ that it was—skipped to double time.

"I am at your service, Miss Penrose. If you feel yourself falling into a fit of the dismals, do feel free to come and remind me what a disgusting excuse for a man I am. I feel certain listing all my shortcomings will make you feel much more the thing."

He said it with such sincerity, with such a straight face that Livvy could not hold back a peal of laughter.

"You are quite the most baffling creature I have ever come across," she said.

Kingston bowed. "The feeling is entirely mutual."

Livvy shook her head in bewilderment and turned to walk back to the house. It wasn't until she closed the kitchen door behind her she realised she was still smiling. Somehow, Lord Kingston had pulled her out of the depths of misery and made her laugh. He'd lightened her heart when it had been at its most heavy and despondent.

Goodness, but what a strange and dangerous fellow he was.

Chapter Six

9th December 1818.

The bizarre nature of dreams, blackberry jam, and indelicate propositions.

Livvy spent an uncomfortable night tossing and turning, beset by strange dreams. It began with the horror of life as Mrs Skewes and a trapped panicky sensation that had her waking in the early hours, gasping for air. After giving herself a stern lecture not to be such an addle-brained twit, she had gone back to sleep only to fall into a nightmare of a different sort. This time she was Lord Kingston's wife, and was sharing his house with any number of misshapen goblins and terrifying demons. The walls of the house were lined with shelves, and the shelves were lined with endless bottles of brandy. Every time Livvy emptied one down the drain, Kingston would simply laugh and snatch another off the shelf and pour it down his throat. By the time she awoke again, far too early to get up, she was quite out of sorts and bleary-eyed. She wasn't entirely certain which dream had disturbed her the most, but having dreamed of Lord Kingston at all seemed so dreadfully inappropriate she could only wonder how she would look him in the eye at breakfast. After washing and dressing, Livvy decided she wouldn't be hungry this morning and solved her dilemma.

As the rest of the household was still abed, she enjoyed the peace of the early morning. She carried her candle down the stairs to the kitchens and stirred the fire back to life. Gelly would be here soon but, for now, she was free to sit in the warmth and allow her thoughts to wander. Somehow, she needed to think of a way to free herself from her brother's plans, and his influence. The only solution was to put herself into someone else's keeping, for she had no particular skills or contacts that would provide her a job as a governess. Her aunt might have pity and take her in, but Charlie would still be her legal guardian, and that was never again going to be a comfortable thought. Eventually, Charlie would land himself in debtor's prison. It seemed inevitable now, and then what would happen to the children? If Livvy was comfortably settled, she could take them in and provide for them. If she married a wealthy man, she could send Harry to university and give the girls the season they needed. She might not be selfless enough to accept Mr Skewes' tender mercies, but she was nothing if not practical. So she must marry.

But how to marry a man who would not be controlling, or cruel, or curb her freedom? She had long given up on the notion of marrying for love. Having a husband who would treat her kindly, who would respect her wishes and support her endeavours was a lovely one, but far less likely to come to pass than either of the peculiar visions she'd had last night, goblins and all. She must waste no time on fairytales. This was the real world, and she had a problem with which she must get to grips. The only man she could hope to marry her would be one who needed her rather than wanted her. Perhaps someone older, or infirm, or unsightly, or with some personal habit that might be off-putting. So long as he was not a reprehensible character, surely they could learn to rub along well enough. She might even be content if he was kind and good-natured. After all, she did not expect Prince Charming. She was no diamond of the first water herself. How to get such a man's attention and get him to the altar fast enough, though, that was the question. The one thing she knew about the marriage mart was that the competition was stiff. A man with a heartbeat and a fortune was in high demand, no matter his personal qualities. She on the other hand was too long in the tooth, had no dowry and was only passably pretty.

If she got herself to her aunt's in time for the party, she might have only days before Charlie came to fetch her back again. He would, too. She knew he was annoyed with her but, more than that, he did not like or trust their aunt. As selfish and idiotic as he was, Charlie did care for Livvy—in his own way—and would see it as his duty to rescue her from their aunt's pernicious influence. So, she must find the right man, and make him so desperate to marry her that he would carry her off to Gretna Green, or invest in a special licence. It seemed an unlikely scenario, whichever way you looked at it. Yet, on the few occasions she had read the scandal sheets, she had discovered that many of the most successful high-flyers were not great beauties. So what was it they did? How was it they gained a man's attention and made him so wild with desire that he'd pay huge sums just to be in their company? Not that she had pretensions to compete with them, or to become a Cyprian, but even a little of their skills—whatever they might be—could only help her get the desired outcome of a home of her own.

But who on earth could she ask about such a thing…?

She let out a little laugh and put her head in her hands. "Oh, Livvy, you absolute dolt."

Suddenly, she decided she fancied a spot of breakfast after all.

❧ ❧ ❧

"Yes, George, you really *must* wear clothes," Livvy said, struggling to fit the wriggling child into

91

his small clothes and skeleton suit before he ran off naked as usual. George protested and wailed but was no match for his aunt.

"He's a little savage," his eldest sister, Susan, remarked as she changed Birdie's clout and pilcher with expert hands.

Livvy fastened the last button on the skeleton suit with a triumphant laugh and kissed George's chubby cheek. "There! Now don't take it off."

George pouted, but wrapped his arms about Livvy's neck and hugged her to show she was forgiven.

"Oh, Livvy! Livvy, just look what that horrid girl has done to my hair!"

Livvy looked up as Rebecca burst into the nursery and just about rearranged her face into something solemn, smothering the laugh that threatened to erupt before she got herself into trouble. Rebecca's head had a Medusa-like complication of plaits and loops that had all slid to one side, and rendered her quite comical.

"I didn't do it on purpose," Lydia protested, hot on her heels. "It was supposed to look like that."

She waved a cutting from *Le Journal des Dames et des Modes,* which Ceci had brought back from London.

Livvy gave the illustration a dubious glance. "I think perhaps Parisian fashions might be a little *de trop* for breakfast at Boscawen, Lydia dear, even if the earl deigns to grace us with his presence. Do you think you can untangle that and put it in one nice, neat plait? You have ten minutes."

"Oh, you do it, Livvy," Rebecca wailed. "She'll make me cry again."

"Oh, don't be such a silly goose," Lydia muttered, taking her sister by the hand, and towing her out of the room again, with Rebecca protesting as Lydia remonstrated.

Livvy sighed as their bedroom door slammed down the hall and their bickering abruptly silenced.

"What the devil's going on?" Harry demanded, peering around the door. "It sounded like Lydia was murdering Becca down there."

"Well, it will be one less for breakfast, then," Livvy remarked, handing George over to his big brother. "You two take the little ones down. I'd best see if Gelly needs any help."

"Yes, Livvy," Harry said, as he hefted George into his arms and carried him off, with Susan carrying Birdie behind him.

Livvy hurried towards the servant's staircase and paused as she saw a flicker of movement out of the corner of her eye.

"Jane!" she called.

There was no reply.

"*Jane,*" she said again, a warning note lingering this time. The distinct sound of trotters on parquet gave the poor girl away.

Livvy bit her lip and took a breath.

"Jane Penrose, if you don't come out this minute…."

Jane slunk from around the corner with a piglet trotting at her heels.

Livvy folded her arms.

"Oh, but, Livvy, it's raining again and he was all wet and muddy," Jane protested, hoisting the piglet into her arms as the creature squealed and struggled.

"It's a pig, Jane. Pigs are at their happiest up to their necks in mud."

Jane scowled and shook her head. "Barnaby isn't. He's a clean boy."

Livvy put one hand on her hip and pointed in the general direction of the piggery. "Back to the sty with him. At *once.* And then wash your hands and get to the breakfast parlour or there will be nothing left for you."

"Yes, Livvy," Jane replied with a heavy sigh.

Livvy nodded and was about to turn away when a thought occurred to her. "Wait a moment. You said, he *was* all wet and muddy."

"Yes," Jane nodded. "I washed him in the scullery."

Oh, lovely. That would put Gelly in a marvellous temper. Livvy groaned and hurried down to the kitchen.

By the time she sat down to breakfast, Livvy really had worked up an appetite and helped herself to a thick slice of brown bread, spreading it with butter and jam. Kingston had not made an appearance, and she wondered if perhaps he wouldn't come. It was not the habit of the fashionable set to rise before noon, after all. Likely his habit was to sleep all day after a night of… of whatever it was the Earl of Kingston did. She pondered whether he had a mistress or not, or perhaps several mistresses, but then he hadn't any money, had he? They were supposed to be devilishly expensive.

"No, George," she said absently, grabbing hold of the child's hand before he could stick his fingers in the butter. She cut off a piece of her bread and jam and handed it to him instead.

"Fank," he said cheerfully and stuffed it in his mouth.

Livvy smiled. "What a good boy, George."

The breakfast table was absent of their parents, as usual. Ceci's habit was to take a cup of chocolate in her room and drift down after eleven. After that, she would drape herself upon a chaise lounge and take a nap after the exertions of readying herself for the day…or whatever was left of it. Charlie would have already eaten and escaped to his study before they arrived. So, the noise and chaos of the children was Livvy's and, as noisy and chaotic as it was, she didn't mind a bit. To her way of thinking, this was what family should be, and she only regretted that Ceci and Charlie did not seem to appreciate it more. Naturally, there were plenty of mornings when she didn't appreciate it much either, but mostly there was joy to be found in George's sticky face and in the way Susan carefully spooned porridge into little Birdie, and the children all talked at once and squabbled over the last of the strawberry jam.

Livvy looked up and saw the Earl of Kingston standing in the doorway. The expression on his face was that of a man steeling himself to walk onto a battlefield.

"You mustn't show fear, my lord. They can sense weakness," she counselled him.

"Like dogs?" he suggested, still looking dubious.

"Gog," George said. "Oof, oof."

"Quite," Kingston replied.

He gave his waistcoat a tug and walked into the room.

"Good morning. Do you always eat with the nursery?" he asked her as he pulled out the chair at her side.

Livvy rolled her eyes at him. "Only at breakfast and it won't kill you, I promise. They're only children, they don't bite. Well, George might if he's being very naughty, but generally speaking...."

She saw Kingston give George a frowning glance as she handed the boy another piece of her bread and jam.

"Oof, oof," George said.

"Hmm." The earl reached for a bread roll.

"Do you know the Prince Regent?"

"Have you been to Vauxhall Gardens?"

"Do pigs really like mud?"

"Is Lord Byron terribly handsome?"

Kingston paused as a barrage of questions hit him from all sides and Livvy held her breath, wondering if they were all about to get a terrible set down.

He frowned for a moment.

"Yes. Yes. Certainly, and no, he's overrated," he said, and put the roll down on his plate.

Livvy watched the children gather themselves for the next onslaught and got in first. "Children, Lord Kingston wishes to break his fast, not answer a lot of impertinent questions. Now, Harry, as you've already finished, do take Birdie up to Ceci. I'm sure she'd like to see her mama. Girls, if you've eaten your fill, take George to the nursery, and then begin the lesson I wrote on the board. I shall be up in a little while to see how you're doing."

"Yes, Livvy," they chorused, and for a moment there was the industrious chink of cutlery and teacups as everyone finished their tea and cleared their plates, followed by the scraping of chairs.

A short while thereafter, peace reigned.

"Thank you," the earl said with a sigh of relief.

Livvy suspected he was still feeling somewhat delicate and headachy, but it wouldn't do to pander to him.

"I didn't do it for you. We don't have an inexhaustible supply of jam, you know," Livvy replied.

"I beg your pardon. I shall content myself with the butter." Kingston said gravely.

Livvy's lips twitched. "I only meant that the children would eat it all if I let them linger too long."

"Ah. In that case, might I trouble you for the blackberry? It's my favourite."

"Certainly." Livvy passed it to him and took a moment study his face. "You're looking somewhat better than you did, at least."

He snorted. "Why, Miss Penrose, my heart is all a-flutter at your extravagant praise."

Livvy gave a huff of impatience and reached for her teacup. "I am not inclined to flirt with you, my lord. I merely observe that you appear a few steps farther from your impending demise than you did two days ago."

"Are you inclined to flirt with anyone?"

Livvy cursed herself for having walked into that one.

"Yes," she replied brightly. "Mr Moon."

His dark brows drew together. "Who the devil is… oh, wait. I remember. The crow. And where is the elegant Mr Moon this morning?"

"Oh, he comes and goes as he pleases. I shall likely meet him in the gardens later."

"Lucky Mr Moon," he murmured.

Livvy opened her mouth, quite prepared for the singular pleasure of giving the Earl of Kingston a set down, when she realised this was her opportunity and changed tack.

"I wish there were a Mr Moon to meet me in the gardens, but we are sadly lacking in beaus here at Boscawen. In fact, my lord, that's something I wish you to help me with."

Kingston's eyes widened and his knife clattered down upon his plate. He stared at her in astonishment.

Livvy frowned and thought again about what she'd just said.

"Oh!" she exclaimed, heat blooming in her cheeks. "Oh. Oh, I… I did not mean…."

"No," he replied with a wry smile. "I rather suspected you didn't. A pity. I am at your disposal, naturally."

Livvy fell silent and considered his words. Her heart picked up. Well, there was a thought. If seducing a man was anything like, say, baking, then reading a recipe was all well and good, but there was nothing like practical experience. Surely, a man as depraved as Kingston would have plenty to teach her, and no qualms whatsoever about doing so. The idea made her breathless. Livvy had squashed any hope of marrying years ago, but the longing to feel a man's arms about her, his lips upon hers, that had never gone away. It rose in her now, hot, and wicked. She slid him a sideways glance. He really was quite devilishly handsome, even with the dark circles under his eyes and the rather worn look about him. In fact, she wondered if it didn't add a little something to his appeal as he looked very much as if he'd been up to no good. Why was that an attractive quality? She wondered. There must be something very wrong with the feminine brain to find a man with the morals of an alley cat more appealing than a well-behaved one. Yet often being well-behaved was so dashed dull, so perhaps there was a kind of sense in it. Either way, a man like that could teach her a thing or two and have no qualms about doing it. All in a good cause, and *only* because she needed the experience to… to help her achieve her goal, obviously.

"Do I have jam on my chin?"

"Beg pardon?"

"You are staring at me, Miss Penrose, and whilst I am quite happy for you to admire the view, singular as it is, you are making me nervous."

"Forgive me, I was just considering what you'd said and wondering if I ought to take you up on it. It really might serve me well," Livvy replied, frowning into her teacup and trying to decide if it was a stroke of brilliance or if she'd run quite mad.

It was remarkably hard to tell in this house.

The earl frowned at her, obviously baffled.

"I asked if I had jam on my chin," he said, before taking a bite of bread and jam.

"What? No, no. How on earth does that serve me in any way? Do keep up. No, the bit before that. You said you were at my disposal, if I decided I would like to… to tryst with you."

Kingston choked. His eyes watered and he went quite red in the face, so Livvy sprang to her feet and pounded him on the back.

"Oh dear, that blackberry is quite tart. I ought to have warned you. We were rather low on sugar, so I scrimped a little. Likely why it didn't set as firm as it ought to have, either. I assure you it's not my best effort."

"Damn the bloody jam!" Kingston exclaimed once he could speak again. "And stop hitting me. I didn't even provoke you this time."

"Yes, you did," Livvy retorted, straightening, and returning to her seat. "You walked into the room. I don't know why, but that seems all the provocation required to want to throw things at you or do you bodily harm. Strange, isn't it?"

"Not in the least. My valet remarks on it often enough, but stop changing the subject. Did you say you were deciding whether to… to…?"

"Tryst with you," Livvy finished for him, realising she was babbling but quite unable to stop herself. "Yes. I was, though why you are getting so flustered about it I don't know. Isn't this the sort of thing you get up to all the time? I would think you'd be more sanguine by now."

Kingston opened and closed his mouth, opened it again and took a breath—looking for all the world as if he were about to tear her off a strip—and then closed it again.

"Do stop doing that, you look like a carp and they always make me shudder. All those little mouths opening and closing. Ugh." Livvy shook her head and wondered why the earl looked quite so outraged, but then she supposed his light skirts rarely compared him to a carp. It wasn't likely to make a man foolish with passion, was it? "There, you see, I'm certain your high-flyers don't speak about fish. This is why I need your help."

"My help?" he repeated, still staring at her like she'd grown a second head.

"Yes," Livvy said, pouring him out a cup of tea with hands that trembled suspiciously. She peered into the cup. "I'm afraid it's a little strong. Do you like it like that?"

"Like what?"

"Your tea, do you like it strong?" She frowned at him, wondering if he looked feverish. There was a definite flush to his cheeks. "Are you feeling quite well? You seem awfully out of sorts this morning."

"I have a headache," he said tersely.

"Ah, yes, I suspected you did. Bound to make you waspish."

"I am *not* waspish!"

Livvy gave him a doubtful look. He certainly sounded as if he'd taken a pet.

"As you like. Do drink your tea, though. I'm sure it will help. Also, I believe your vast experience will be invaluable to me, so I shall take you up on your kind offer. Now, when should we begin, do you think? I could probably spare half an hour before lunch if that suits?"

There followed a taut silence during which her heart thudded in her ears.

Livvy went to speak, but he raised a finger and pointed at her.

"No. Do not…. Not another word. My head is spinning and either I am going quite mad, or you are suggesting I meet you in the gardens before lunch, so I may… So we might…."

"Tr—"

"I said to be silent!"

Livvy closed her mouth again, folded her hands primly in her lap, and waited.

He let out a breath.

"Please, I beg you, do not use that word again," he said, looking as though he meant it. "I am not convinced you have the slightest idea what it means, or what you are suggesting, but I do know ladies of your…*type*…do not go around propositioning men like me."

"May I speak now?" Livvy asked politely.

Kingston waved a hand at her with an expression of resignation.

"I understand a tr—*that* word—to describe an illicit, romantic interlude between lovers, and what the devil do you mean, *ladies of my type?* Do you mean old maids?" she demanded with a surge of indignation. She supposed, strictly speaking, that was just what she was, but really one did not like to have it flung in one's face.

"No-oo," he replied, drawing the word out in such a way that suggested his patience was fraying. "I mean that gently bred young ladies do not go about propositioning men at the breakfast table."

"Oh," Livvy replied tartly, folding her arms. "Should I have waited for dinner? Is that how it's done? I just assumed my brother might interfere in the matter."

"Don't be facetious, and you know perfectly well that if there is any propositioning to be done, it's my job as the resident libertine to do it!"

He looked so indignant that Livvy had to work at keeping a straight face, but she was reasonably steady when she nodded her understanding and replied, "I do beg your forgiveness, my lord. You may proceed."

"Proceed?"

"Yes," she said impatiently. "If you are going to proposition me, you'd best get on with it. The children will wonder where I've got to."

To her immense frustration, he got to his feet, tossed his napkin to the table, and strode away.

"Where are you going?" she demanded.

He turned in the doorway and looked back at her. "To bed, Miss Penrose. I believe I have suffered a relapse. However, when I come down again, I feel certain I will discover this has all been a vastly disturbing dream. The result, I don't doubt, of my wasted life of dissipation. I admit I have never regretted indulging in drink more in my life. I bid you a good day."

With that, he bowed politely and left the room.

Chapter Seven

9th December 1818.

The sea, a seduction, a troubled conscience and a kiss.

Walsh gave his master a dubious glance. "You're pulling my leg."

King reclined against the pillows on his bed, massaging his temples with delicate fingertips. "I assure you I am not. Bold as brass she was, asking if I could spare half an hour before lunch. Half an hour! I ask you."

"Are you more upset that she beat you to it, or that she underestimates your stamina?" Walsh asked mildly.

King returned an arctic glare. "Neither. I have no designs on Miss Penrose. The poor woman is addled. She must be, to think I'd take liberties with my friend's sister under his own roof. Good God, what does she think I am?"

"Begging your pardon, my lord, but she thinks you're a libertine, and by definition—"

"Yes, yes, I thank you, Walsh," King retorted, realising Miss Penrose was correct, he really did sound waspish now, damn her eyes. "I have no requirement for you to spell out all the ways in which she believes me to be the devil incarnate, but that begs the question, what in blazes is she up to? Does she think to trap me in marriage?"

Walsh uttered a choked sound, very much like a smothered laugh.

"What the hell does that mean?"

His valet made a heroic effort to rearrange his face, but King knew the blighter well enough to realise he was enjoying a bit of sport at his employer's expense.

"Nothing, sir," Walsh replied, sounding like he might strain something.

"Yes, yes, vastly amusing," King groused. "But as far removed from eligible as I may be, I *am* an earl, and a woman in her position can't be too choosy. An earl in the hand is worth Mr Skewes in the bush, I don't doubt. My father will die one day, after all, and then I'll be a wealthy marquess."

"Your father is as hale and hearty as a man half his age, beg pardon for mentioning it."

King snorted. "Damn me if that ain't the truth, but I'll wager she doesn't know that."

Walsh shrugged. "Well, didn't you at least ask her why she wanted to meet you?"

"No!" King said, rolling his eyes. "I assumed that bit was obvious enough."

"Did it look obvious?"

"What?"

Walsh let out a long-suffering sigh. "I mean, did she look like a woman eager to be ravished in a dark corner?"

King frowned, casting his mind back. "No. She looked like a woman who would try to fit it into her busy day if she really must. Damn it, Walsh, whatever is she about?"

"Did it not occur to you to ask her?" Walsh asked with an air of mild exasperation King was all too familiar with.

"Well, I…."

"What *did* you say to her?"

"I…." King cleared his throat. "I told her I wasn't feeling well and was going for a lie down, and… and that I hoped it had all been a disagreeable dream."

"Very sophisticated, sir."

"Oh, shut up."

"Yes, sir."

King glowered at the ceiling. "With a bit of luck, whatever foolishness she had in that peculiar brain of hers will have worked its way free by now. I don't expect she'll mention it again."

"I don't expect so," Walsh replied with his most soothing tone.

King grunted and closed his eyes. He wanted a drink. No, the truth. It was important to be honest with himself at least. He wanted a bottle, possibly three, and he knew if he had them, he wouldn't stop until he passed out. *I'm not drinking. I am not drinking. I. Am. Not. Drinking.* It had become a mantra these past days, and it seemed necessary to repeat the words almost every minute, just in case. He would not let Walsh down when the man had shown such faith in him, he would not let himself down. His father might think him a worthless disappointment but that was no reason for proving the man right. He had lost control of himself, of his life, but it was *his* life, and he *would* take control of it again. King would not be governed by his father and certainly not by alcohol. *I want to live. I am not drinking.* This would pass and he would feel better. The drink did not control him, he would not allow it. He'd have a nap like he'd said he would, and with a bit of luck Miss Penrose would have reclaimed her sanity by the time he woke up.

Livvy gritted her teeth as Ceci let out another heavy sigh. Her sister-in-law put aside the latest copy of *Ackerman's Repository* and her study of the fashion plates and stared out of the window with a wistful expression. She was plump and pale, and lovely as a faded rose. Ceci had been a beauty once, but a combination of indolence, indulgence, and eight pregnancies would have worn upon even the brightest diamond. Still, she made a pretty picture, reclining on the daybed and looking as though she was waiting for someone to peel her a grape.

"Perhaps you ought to go back to bed," Livvy suggested, struggling to keep her tone that of a concerned sister.

"Oh, no, no. One must endure, mustn't one?"

Livvy dug her teeth into her bottom lip. She would not rise to the bait. She would not.

"Only it made me so sad to see little Birdie this morning wearing poor Rebecca's hand-me-downs. I mean, Becca is seven now, and—"

"Nine."

"Hmmm?"

"Rebecca is nine, and Birdie is wearing Jane's old clothes. *She's* seven," Livvy added helpfully.

"Yes, I know." Ceci gave a sad shake of her head. "To think we have been reduced to this. My darling Charlie hardly sleeps, you know. If only there was something to be done. It plays on his mind so, I fear for his health."

"A pity he spent all that money on Christmas presents, then," Livvy retorted and then cursed herself. *Don't do it. Do not.*

"Oh, but the poor, *poor* children. Imagine how they would feel not having presents for St Nicholas? Oh, dear me."

Yes, Livvy thought, but did they have to be quite such expensive presents? She suspected the children would rather have a roof over their heads and food in their bellies and not have to face their father being sent to Bodmin Gaol for his inability to repay his debts. Livvy drew in a deep breath and counted to ten, concentrating on the stocking she was darning.

"Here," she said, pushing the mending basket over towards Ceci with her foot. "Do some darning. It will occupy your mind and make you feel better."

"Oh, no. I haven't your skill for thrift and mending, Livvy, dear. You know that."

Another sigh.

One hundred and one, one hundred and two, one hundred and….

Ceci picked up her magazine again. "Oh. I should have liked to take dear Susan shopping for her gowns in a few years, but I don't suppose she'll have a season at all now."

"No," Livvy replied through gritted teeth, stuffing the mending back into the basket and rising to her feet. "I don't suppose she will."

Somehow, she held her tongue all the way out of the door.

She stood in the hallway for a moment, just breathing, and fighting the temptation to visit Ceci's wardrobe and pull out all the expensive gowns that had been bought for her over the years. The desire to fling them in her face and say, *there, that's why the girls can't have a season you selfish, ignorant creature,* was almost overwhelming. Knowing what kind of scene would follow was the only thing which made her swallow the words down. She had tried before now, tried to make them see, but it only ended up with Ceci crying and her brother shouting, the children frightened and upset and Livvy ever more aware of just how precarious her position in the household was. If she upset Ceci too badly or too often, Charlie would side with her, not Livvy. It would be her forced to leave, and then what?

Yet, this would not do. Sooner or later she would cause exactly such a scene and her brother *would* give her an ultimatum: marry Mr Skewes or get out. Once upon a time she would never have believed him capable of such a thing, but now he was determined she listen to reason. After all, he thought marrying Mr Skewes was reasonable. Mr Skewes was young and handsome and wealthy. Why would any young lady not wish to marry him? Indeed, if Livvy ever tried to justify what it was about him she found so reprehensible, she could never quite manage a satisfactory explanation herself. It was pure instinct, in the manner of a dog that shied away from a man likely to kick it. Charlie, who was used to Livvy being the practical one simply refused to listen to explanations about her *feelings*. He thought she was being an irrational female for no good reason. It was only a matter of time before he forced the issue and she would have to decide, give in, or runaway with nowhere to go to.

New Year was just three weeks away. Supposing she could even get to Bath in time for the party, she needed to prepare. She had toyed with the idea of writing to her aunt and asking for help, but decided against it. It was much harder to deny someone standing on your doorstep than it was to refuse them by letter. She must make it a *fait accompli*. Also, she must do something with her best gowns, such as they were, to make them presentable for a lavish house party. One might hope her aunt would lend her something, but it was always better to be prepared for the worst and pleasantly surprised by the best. Still, these were all practical problems, and Livvy saw no reason she could not deal with them herself. The problem of how to *be*, how to act around a man she wished to make her an offer with indecent haste was another entirely. She had never been in society, never flirted, or made scintillating conversation with a man, *with anyone*. No, she needed Kingston, and she needed him now.

Livvy glanced behind her to ensure no one was watching before she climbed the stairs and walked down the corridor that led to Lord Kingston's rooms. She wondered why she bothered being discreet. Birdie and George were both napping, and the older children were occupied downstairs. Charlie was ensconced in his study, pretending to work but more likely reading some sporting magazine, and Ceci wouldn't bestir herself unless the house was on fire. It would never occur to either of them that having such a man as the earl in the house might present a danger to Livvy. Though, to be fair, if there was any danger it was Livvy dragging him into it, not the other way about. Whoever would have thought it so difficult to get a man widely proclaimed a rake and a libertine to take liberties? Which only went to show how badly Livvy needed the help. If she couldn't get a man like Kingston to make love to her, she was hardly going to incite enough passion in a decent fellow to propose marriage.

With a final glance up and down the corridor, Livvy rapped smartly on the door. It was opened a moment later by Mr Walsh. Ah. Foolish of her not to have expected that. Deciding it better to brazen it out—Walsh must be privy to much of his master's goings on—she put up her chin and looked him in the eye.

To his credit, she saw only a momentary glimmer of shock in his eyes before he rallied.

"Might I speak to Lord Kingston, Mr Walsh?"

"I'm afraid his lordship is not here at present, Miss Penrose. I believe he has taken a walk to the beach to… blow the cobwebs away."

"Oh, has he still the headache?"

The valet nodded, but something in his expression led Livvy to believe it wasn't the headache that bothered him.

"Is he still suffering many ill effects from his drinking?"

Walsh seemed to debate a moment on how to reply before taking a step closer and lowering his voice. "He's trying hard to shake off his demons, Miss, but it's been a difficult year for him, and—"

"You worry for him," Livvy said.

Walsh nodded, and Livvy found herself pleased to discover a sensible man like Walsh worried for his employer. From what she had seen, the valet was hard-working, conscientious, and polite to everybody. If a man like that stayed, and even worried over his master, there had to be a reason for it. Kingston must have some finer qualities. Well, she knew he had. He'd not taken the easy route and married the poor child his father had selected for him. That spoke of a man with a conscience. She had always suspected the scandal sheets exaggerated but… to what extent? Was he not the wicked seducer he was purported to be?

"He's not the devil you might think him, Miss," Walsh said, echoing her thoughts. "Oh, that's not to say he don't deserve his reputation, for that would be a lie, but… but I reckon he'd reform, given a reason to do so."

Livvy frowned, an uncomfortable sensation of alarm crawling up her spine. There was a hopeful note to those words that made her believe…. "Mr Walsh, I do hope you are not labouring under the misapprehension that *I* wish reform him?"

Walsh shrugged, looking uncomfortable. "No, Miss. Truth be told, I ain't, but a fellow can hope, all the same. A fine strong-minded woman like you *could* handle King, I reckon, and there aren't many I've met I can say that about, though there's plenty willing to give it a go."

"But I have no desire to handle him," Livvy retorted. A flush rose over her skin as her words produced a rather vivid illustration in her mind of her hands literally upon the earl's person. Her breath snagged in her throat.

"No, of course not, Miss. I beg you to forgive me for speaking out of turn. I forgot myself."

Despite the apparent sincerity of his words, a knowing look gleamed in the valet's eyes for a moment before he bowed his head with every appearance of contrition. Livvy wasn't the least bit convinced.

"Yes, Mr Walsh, I believe you did. I beg you will not indulge in such foolishness again."

Whilst employing the *obey or suffer the consequences* voice she had perfected on the children was a little unfair, Livvy was thoroughly rattled and rather thought he deserved it. Seducing King was one thing. *Marrying* the man? Oh, dear heaven, no. She stalked back down the corridor and went in search of her pelisse. She might not want to marry the earl—good Lord, what an idea—but she still needed his invaluable assistance. She must at the very least learn to flirt a little to get the attention of someone she did wish to marry. Well, perhaps *wish* to marry was putting a rosy tint to it, *bear* to marry might be closer to reality. She may as well lower her expectations now, though how much lower they could reasonably get without sending her into a hysterical fit, she wasn't sure. Besides which if she was committed to marrying some old, broken down or unattractive fellow as seemed her only option, this might be her only chance to kiss a man who… who made her feel *something*. Whatever else Lord Kingston was, he was handsome and young and virile and despite her better judgement he made her heart thud harder. It would be nice to have an inkling of what passion felt like before she had to turn her back on it for good.

The path down to the beach was winding and circuitous. A buffeting wind tugged at her skirts and pushed her faster downhill on the steeper parts, as sand and loose pebbles skittered beneath her boots. The beach here continued in the same fashion, sand with swathes of pebbles and large areas of sharp rock. The children loved it here in the summer, searching the rockpools for darting shrimps and tiny crabs that scuttled away at the last moment, and exclaiming when they caught them. This was not a day for such innocent pleasures, however. The sea plunged and crashed with white-topped waves. Thankfully it was far enough out, though the sting of cold spray still drifted on the chill wind, making her skin tight and her lips taste salty.

Livvy hesitated as she saw the earl on the shore, staring out to sea. His shoulders were hunched against the cold and he looked as though he'd been there for some time. There was something stark and lonely about his posture, an air of desperation that tugged at her heart. Nonsense, she scolded herself. It would be foolish of her to consider him a romantic hero. There was nothing the least bit romantic about a man who would drink himself to death. He was troubled, no doubt. After nearly killing himself with liquor, one could hope he would take the time to reflect upon his life and the choices he'd made. That being the case, it was unfair of her to burden him with her own concerns at such a time. She ought not disturb him.

With her decision made, Livvy sighed and was about to turn back when he looked around and saw her. His dark hair whipped about his face and for a moment his expression appeared so bleak her breath caught. Then he smiled, and she wondered if she'd imagined it, the change in him was so sudden and forceful. He strode across the beach and bowed once he was close enough to greet her.

"Miss Penrose, a happy coincidence."

"Nothing of the sort, I'm afraid, my lord," Livvy replied, deciding she may as well tell him now.

Perhaps, if he had been feeling out of sorts, it would help him to have something else to think about. It was how she kept herself from becoming blue-devilled after all, by filling her days from morning till night...not that she had much choice in the matter.

"Oh?"

Livvy nodded. "I realise I was less than explicit about what it was I wanted from you when we spoke at breakfast."

"I beg to differ," he replied at once, frowning at her.

"No, no. I'm sorry, but you did not understand me. I have no interest in a romantic involvement with you. None at all, so you need not suppose me madly in love with you or plotting to trap you into marrying me. I understand your finances to be in dire straits, and so that won't help me in the least. In short, my lord, we do not suit."

He gave her a doubtful glance, which she found a little aggravating.

"I'm afraid not every woman wishes to fling themselves at your feet, as disturbing as this information may be to you."

He narrowed his eyes a little, which drew her notice to his eyelashes and gave her a stab of envy. How unfair that a man should have lashes as thick and long as that.

"What, then?" he demanded.

"I told you, I need your help."

"Help which involves meeting me in private to…." he hesitated and Livvy tutted with impatience.

"Tryst. Yes. I'm sorry, I know the word offends your tender sensibilities, but really one must call a spade a spade."

His expression darkened. "Oh, I know how to do that, Miss Penrose, I assure you, but then it would be you who was offended. What the devil are you playing at?"

Livvy took a breath, undaunted by his tone. "You know my brother wishes me to marry Mr Skewes. I do not. However, Boscawen is my brother; and I am at his mercy. He is going to ruin us, sooner or later. I have no doubt of that. I *must* marry, and I must do it soon. If Charlie gets any deeper into debt, I fear for what may happen to us all. If I marry a man of means who is willing to be generous, I can at least take care of the children."

"What the hell has that to do with me? As you so succinctly pointed out, I haven't a feather to fly with."

"If you would only listen and stop interrupting, I shall tell you, my lord," Livvy replied with a tut of impatience.

The earl gave a snort. "I'm all ears, but for heaven's sake call me King, everyone else does, and this conversation is so damned inappropriate already I don't see what harm it can do."

"Very well, *King.* My aunt holds a lavish New Year's Eve house party every year. The event runs for several days, and it is my intention to go there to find a man who will marry me. I will set my sights on someone less likely to be besieged with marriage-minded young women. An older man, perhaps, or one most ladies would find disagreeable for some aesthetic reason, or someone in trade. I'm really not the least bit picky, providing he is kind, and willing and able to help my nieces and nephews. I understand my aunt invites all sorts to her parties, so I hope there will be a few options. I won't have long, however, for if my brother realises where I am, he will come after me."

The earl said nothing, indeed he barely blinked, so Livvy ploughed on. "I must make some suitable man so besotted with me, in a short amount of time, that he will propose. I flatter myself that I am not such a dreadful prospect, even if I have no dowry. Please do not think me entirely foolish. I do realise it is a ridiculous plan and likely doomed to failure. I am desperate, though, and this is my only chance. I must take it. I must at least *try*."

King stared at her. He looked appalled. She waited, giving him time to gather himself and give her an answer.

"Well?" she demanded.

"Well, what? I still don't have the faintest notion what you want from me."

"Oh," Livvy replied, realising she hadn't exactly spelled it out. "Forgive me, I thought it obvious."

"I haven't the least idea why!"

Livvy huffed at his indignant tone. "Well, look at me," she said, holding her arms out as the wind made her skirts billow about her. "I'm hardly suited to seduction, am I? I need help, King. I need *your* help. Teach me how to be, how to talk and flirt, how to make a man want me. I don't need him to love me, only to want me enough to offer for me. I know there must be a knack to it, and you must have seen it in action countless times. Not every successful courtesan is a great beauty, are they? So teach me, teach me how to make a man wild with passion, for I haven't the least idea how to begin. I've never even been kissed. Not once! I must remedy this if I'm to have a chance."

For a moment he just gaped at her.

"Well? Say *something*," she pleaded.

"You're stark staring mad."

"Why?"

He gave a bark of laughter and strode away from her, shaking his head, before apparently thinking better of it and stalking back again. "You can't possibly think that I… that I would…."

He didn't seem to be able to put it into words and walked off again.

Livvy waited. He couldn't get off the beach in that direction, so he'd have to come back again. He did.

"Miss Penrose," he said, his tone suggesting she had tried his patience to its limits. "I am a guest in your brother's house. He was kind enough to take me in, and we both know he quite likely saved my sorry carcass. If you think me so utterly morally bankrupt as to seduce his sister whilst under his roof in such circumstances, then I... I...."

He threw up his hands, apparently lost for words.

"But you aren't seducing me," Livvy cried. "That's the whole point. You are helping me, *teaching* me. To seduce someone you need to persuade them to do something they wish for but know is wrong. I don't wish for this, I *need* it. I must have it! I need *you.* Please!"

Somehow, during her impassioned little speech, she had moved closer and clutched at his lapels. Now he put his hands to her wrists and tugged her hands free, taking a step backwards.

"No."

Livvy stared at him. Something about her words had made his eyes grow dark, and instinct told her that was a good sign. She would not give up. Knowing she was putting herself quite beyond the Pale, she gathered her courage, grasped his lapels once more, and kissed him.

For a moment he was perfectly still, no doubt stunned stupid by her outrageous behaviour. She quite understood the reaction. She was stunned herself, and not the least bit surprised when he once more broke away, putting distance between them.

"Hell and damnation," he cursed, staring at her. He was breathing hard, more colour in his cheeks than she'd seen since she'd met him, though that was likely the cold wind on the beach producing the effect. "You are out of your damned mind if you think I would… with *you*."

His tone was scathing, and for the first time it occurred to Livvy that she'd made one crucial mistake. She had assumed that a man of King's reputation would have no qualms about putting his hands on any woman. Yet she had observed herself that he was a handsome fellow. Women would desire him, without a doubt, so there would be no reason for him to waste his time dallying with a female who not only had no experience but could not pretend to be considered more than passably pretty. No doubt the women he associated with were Cyprians, beautiful creatures well-versed in all the ways of pleasing a man. Why on earth would King risk his friendship with her brother to dally with some dull, provincial old maid? He was right, she had been out of her mind.

The realisation brought shame and embarrassment, and a surge of colour rose to her cheeks.

"Of course," she said in a rush. Mortified and wishing now to be out of his company with all haste, the words tumbled out in a jerky, staccato fashion. "You're correct, naturally, it was quite… I never considered that you… that you wouldn't want…."

Her voice quavered and, to her horror, her eyes burned with tears. Worse than that, now she saw regret in his eyes. *Sympathy.* Oh, no. Not that. She could not bear it if he pitied her. What on earth had she been thinking? As if he could help her… as if kissing him would make the least bit of difference.

"It's of no matter. Forgive me, my lord. I… I must beg you to forget that… that I…."

She couldn't say another word. She was going to weep and so she must get away. Now. At once.

Livvy turned on her heel and hurried away. Humiliation filled her chest, making it hard to breathe, and she could hardly see for the tears blurring her vision. She stumbled on a rock, her foot twisting beneath her, and cursed, righting herself again, but suddenly a strong hand gripped her arm.

"Wait! Livvy, wait, damn you."

Livvy shook her head.

"Oh, please let me go," she said in despair. "I shan't bother you again, only please—"

"No, damn it, you started this. It's your own bloody fault."

"What…?"

Whatever it was she'd been about to say, the words died in her throat as she was pulled into his arms. He pressed his mouth to hers, stealing her breath, making her head spin as sensation overwhelmed her. His strong arms banded about her, holding her tight against his body. It gave her the oddest sense of security, which was ridiculous when she'd likely never been in such danger in her life. She didn't care. It was marvellous. His lips were soft and warm, and then his tongue traced along her bottom lip and everything feminine in her quivered with longing. Oh, yes, he *was* good at this. Livvy opened her mouth a little, sensing that was what he wanted from her, and his tongue swept in and… *good heavens*.

She was lost, beguiled by the heat and the slick slide of his tongue as it caressed hers, and then, quite abruptly, it was over. He lifted his head, his expression inscrutable, and Livvy dared to meet his eyes.

"You are, without a doubt, the most troublesome female I've ever had the misfortune to encounter," he said, sounding deeply aggrieved.

Livvy nodded. "I don't doubt it."

He made a harrumphing sound but no move to release his hold on her, which was a good thing. Livvy wasn't entirely certain her knees were up to the job at present.

"You do realise that, in all my years of wickedness, this is likely the most reprehensible thing I've ever done? And that's your fault, Miss Penrose, make no mistake. I tried to do the right thing, but… but then you went and *cried,* you infernal creature. I ask you… what is a man to do when you use such underhand tactics?"

"I didn't mean to," she said, with more of her usual asperity. "I tried very hard not to. Only I suddenly saw how ridiculous I was being and… and one doesn't like to consider oneself entirely undesirable, no matter all proof to the contrary. It was rather a blow to my pride."

"What proof?" he demanded in outrage. "What possible proof can you have for such a statement when you're stuck out here in the back of beyond, with hardly a soul for miles around, let alone a red-blooded male with enough sense to see what's right in front of him?"

"Oh, King," Livvy said, feeling a little dazed. "I do believe that was a compliment."

King frowned and let her go. Livvy staggered without his arms to hold her up, and was dismayed to realise she regretted the loss of his touch. A shiver ran over her. It was suddenly much colder without the warmth of his body against hers.

"Nonsense," he said briskly. "I was merely pointing out how idiotic you were. Nothing complimentary about it in the least."

As he seemed a little touchy about it, Livvy just gave a meek nod of agreement. There was no sense in upsetting him when he seemed to have resigned himself to helping her, *kissing her*. And that *had* been a compliment, and the way he'd kissed implied he wasn't just saying it. She was not undesirable after all. Oh, no doubt she didn't compare to his usual companions, but as they were all the way back in London and she was here… well, she may as well take it for what it was.

"So, you'll help me, then?" Her heart gave an erratic and hopeful thud in her chest.

King sighed and gave her a narrow-eyed glance. "Frankly, I'm not the least bit convinced you need the help."

"Oh, but I do," she said at once. "I could never have been so dreadful as to kiss anyone else, but you don't matter."

"I beg your pardon?"

Sensing she'd offended him again, Livvy hurried to explain. "I only mean that… that you don't like me, and I don't like you, and so… it doesn't signify if you think I've done something outrageous, because you already think me a dreadful creature."

"Hmph." He folded his arms and glowered at the sea.

"If you were a man I wished to ask to marry me, I could never be so direct. He'd think me a strumpet or... or a fortune hunter. I suppose he'd be right," she mused before shaking her head. She'd not think of that. "The point is, I must recognise that he *wants* to kiss me, at least. Then I say... no, not before we're married, and there we have it."

"Do we?" King muttered, sounding unconvinced.

Livvy nodded, hoping to encourage him. "I assume I must flirt with him, and perhaps even imply I might invite such liberties, but frankly it always seems like dissembling and I'm no good at that."

"You astonish me."

She tutted at his dry remark.

"I am being honest with you, so you understand the difficulty."

King pinched the bridge of his nose and drew in a deep breath. She wondered if he was counting to ten like she did when her patience was being tested.

"Very well," he said. "I shall help you, but we'd best get back before you're drenched for the second time in as many days. Those clouds look ominous. If you can slip away, you may come to my room this evening, and we shall discuss it further."

"Oh, thank—"

"Don't. I haven't finished. You will be discreet, damn you, and if we are discovered, you will tell your brother you knocked me over the head, drugged me, and forced yourself upon me. Are we clear on that point?"

"Perfectly clear," she said soothingly.

"Hmph."

He looked so disgruntled she thought she ought to make him feel better. "You are very kind to take the trouble, my lord."

"No, I am not," he retorted at once. "I've sunk beyond reproach, lower than a worm's belly, to consider… to think of… with *you*. With an innocent… Oh, damn me to hell. I'll see you later."

Livvy watched him go, admiring his long legs as he strode away from her. She knew he did not wish for her company in his present state of mind, and she did not wish to jeopardise their imminent rendezvous. So Livvy let him go and did not follow until he was out of sight, humming merrily to herself all the way home.

Chapter Eight

9th *December 1818.*

A whip or tar and feathers, rats, calves' feet, and pussy cats.

King strode back to the house, muttering to himself the entire way. He was out of his bloody mind. They'd be caught. They were bound to be. Even a brother as ridiculous and incompetent as Boscawen had to see what was right under his nose. He might be a selfish twit, but he no doubt loved his sister, misbegotten female that she was. Then there would be… what? A demand that he married her? Not if Boscawen had any sense. King had pockets to let. His father would be enraged if he married to disoblige him, and would likely disinherit King for good. There was nothing he could do about the title and the entailed property, but the family money could certainly be disposed of elsewhere. He could only imagine his father's glee in doing so. Perhaps pistols at dawn, then, but Charlie was a rotten shot and King was better than most, so that would be a stupid thing to do too. He wouldn't be able to tell anyone what he'd done, either, as that would ruin Livvy and then Charlie would never get her married off. No. There would be no repercussions for him other than Charlie's fury and disgust, and yet another stain on his soul, which he could ill afford. That was really quite enough. He ought to have told her no. He ought to turn around this instant and march back to her and tell her he'd changed her mind.

But he wasn't going to.

King groaned. He really was reprehensible. Not only because he would not tell her no, but because he didn't *want* to tell her no. There had been something quite marvellous about the prickly Miss Penrose becoming all pliant and willing in his arms. It had stirred his blood in a manner he had not experienced since… since….

Well… *Ever.*

This was another good reason men of his sort did not dally with well-bred young ladies. They were dangerous on too many levels.

King walked into the house, hung up his own coat as the loquacious Spargo never seemed to be about to do it for him, and went up the stairs. He ground to a halt on the landing as a piglet trotted past him. It was wearing a bonnet from which only its snout was visible.

The child Livvy had called George followed in its wake. The boy was bare-arsed except for a colourful scarf, which was draped about his shoulders, and he had two fingers stuck in his mouth. He withdrew them with a soft popping sound and gestured to the pig.

"Gog," he said.

"You can see it too, can you?" King asked, a little wary.

George nodded. "Gog. Oof, oof."

"Thank Christ for that," he muttered, before adding, for the sake of accuracy. "Actually, it's a pig. Er… oink, oink."

George frowned and shook his head. "Gog."

"As you like," King replied with a shrug, and watched the boy follow the piglet farther down the hall. "That's an interesting outfit you have there. Isn't it a bit draughty about your nether regions?"

"'Ot," George replied succinctly. "Too 'ot."

"Yes, I can quite understand the benefits." King nodded but felt compelled to point out: "But you can't just stroll about with your pego on display. It's not done. The ladies take offence."

"Pego?" George asked with an enquiring tone.

King pursed his lips, aware he might have spoken a little rashly.

"Best not say that word to your aunt."

George grinned. "Pego."

"Yes. I see. It runs in the family," he said with a sigh of resignation. "Well, run along then. The pig went that way."

"Gog," the child said, with a stubborn glint in his eyes. He snickered, and toddled off after the pig. "Pego!"

There was no escaping the fact that this was a bloody madhouse.

"I ought to be horsewhipped," King announced as he closed the bedroom door behind him.

Walsh looked up from the coat he was brushing without so much as a blink. "Very good, my lord. Would you like me to do it now?"

"Or perhaps tar and feathers? What do you think?"

Walsh's brow crinkled a little as he considered. "Tar and feathers is a terribly messy business, sir. Not to mention that it takes a good deal of preparation. If it's all the same to you, I prefer the whip."

"As you like. I shouldn't wish to put you to any trouble," King groused, flinging himself down in the chair by the fire. The wind gusted outside and a plume of smoke billowed down the chimney, filling the room.

"Needs sweeping," Walsh observed with a tut.

"The whole place needs pulling down and its occupants consigning to Bedlam."

"Might I observe you seem a trifle out of sorts, my lord? Am I correct in supposing that Miss Penrose caught up with you at the beach?"

King glowered at his valet in consternation. "You faithless cur! Do you mean to say you sent that she-devil after me?"

Walsh frowned and stood a little straighter. "I would not say I sent her, sir, merely that she was quite determined to speak with you and, seeing as you are staying under the same roof, it seemed inevitable that she would eventually. I assumed the beach would give you a greater chance of escape or evasion, should you wish to employ either tactic."

"What a load of cobblers!" King exclaimed, knowing his valet well enough to realise when he was pulling a fast one. "I ought to horsewhip you. I might have known I was being conspired against. I suppose you're in on it too, are you? *Et tu, Brute?*"

"I do not know to what you are referring," Walsh replied with all the offended dignity he could muster.

"All I wanted, Walsh, was a place to rusticate in peace. *Stay here*, you said, *just the place*, you said. Far from society, fresh sea air and no excitement. Bah!"

Walsh gave an affronted little sniff. "Would you like me to pack my bags, sir? I could have my letter of resignation to you within the hour."

"Ho! Oh no, my fine fellow, don't you try that, and don't pretend you don't keep that same letter to shove under my nose every time we're at outs. I'm not so green as I'm cabbage-looking. There's never a date on it, Walsh! *Ha!* So there. You thought I hadn't noticed, I bet."

"I like to be prepared, is all. I know where I'm not wanted, I'm sure." Walsh carefully hung up the coat he'd been brushing and made for the door, stony faced.

"Oh, pack it in, you old ham. We both know you're not going anywhere and I'm not angry at you, I'm angry with me. I've sunk beyond reproach this time, Walsh, and it's all her fault."

Walsh heaved a long-suffering sigh and turned around. "What happened?"

King explained the goings on he'd experienced on the beach with as much brevity as possible, though it would have been quicker had he left out several choice expletives which did not aid the story a whit, but which made him feel better.

"I see," Walsh replied.

"Do you?" King demanded bitterly. "For all I see is my sorry behind another few miles down the road to perdition."

Walsh snorted, a glimmer of amusement in his eyes.

"What the devil does that mean?"

King narrowed his eyes at his valet, who gave a nonchalant shrug. "Methinks the gentleman doth protest too much."

"I never said I didn't enjoy it," King retorted. "But you know as well as I do that a gentleman—even one as far removed from deserving the title as I am—does not dally with innocent, well-bred ladies. She is not a light skirt, nor a merry widow. Miss Penrose was brought up with the intention of marrying a man of her station and providing the necessary heir and spare, not having liaisons with her brother's blackguard of a friend and, what's more, under the poor fool's nose!"

"Horsewhipping is too good for you, sir," Walsh observed dispassionately.

"There, you see!" King threw up his hands before burying his head in them and groaning.

"If the idea offends you so deeply, why not just tell her no?"

King gave a bark of laughter that sounded just a tad too close to hysterical. "Have you tried saying no to Miss Penrose? I wish you would, Walsh, for I tell you now, she does not play fair."

"She cried?"

"Oh, she didn't just cry," King muttered, folding his arms. "She… she looked all… defeated and hurt and… and like a kitten I'd just tried to drown in a bucket, damn her."

Walsh gave a sympathetic nod. "I do see, sir, and I forgive you for your harsh words as you were clearly under duress. It is little wonder you took such a pet. It's enough to put any man on his high ropes, I'm sure. I shall go at once and make you a tisane and bring you some of Gelly's shortbread. You'll be right as ninepence in no time."

"Oh, no, I won't," King said darkly, staring into the fire in the hearth with the expression of one approaching the gallows. "She's coming here tonight, after supper. I'm doomed, Walsh. Doomed, I tell you."

❧ ❧ ❧

"Do stop behaving like such a ninny," Livvy scolded herself as she tiptoed along to King's room. No amount of scolding could stop her heart from thundering in her chest, though.

Livvy assured herself it was sneaking about after dark like a thief, and the possibility of getting caught, that made her pulse skitter about like a mad rabbit. It was assuredly not the idea of being in King's arms again, the thought of his lips against hers. *Oh, n-no, it's not that at all*. She swallowed a nervous giggle. Truly, it was ridiculous that a woman of her age should act in such a manner, giggling—good heavens. Yet for the first time in her life, she felt alive. That kiss had been better than anything she had ever dreamed of and she wanted to do it again. It didn't seem too much to ask before she gave up on such pleasures for good. It had been a pleasure too, the most sinful, thrilling moment of her entire life, and she wanted to experience it again. She knew full well she was doing something wicked and the knowledge was rather… invigorating.

Arriving at King's door, she raised her hand to knock, and then had to smother a squeak of alarm as it opened in front of her. She almost dropped the candlestick.

"Shhhh!" King hissed.

"I was shushed until you frightened the life out of me," she retorted in a furious whisper. "Why did you do that?"

"Change of plan," King said, closing the door behind him.

"Oh, no. You're not reneging on our agreement," Livvy said, shaking her head.

King tsked and took the candle from her. "No. Just changing location. We'll go to your room."

Livvy felt a flush of heat at the idea, though she did not understand why. His room, her room, it hardly mattered. "That won't help you if we're discovered. I thought I was supposed to have hit you over the head, drugged you, and taken advantage of your person."

He just shrugged and glanced over his shoulder at her. "Then you'll just have to lure me to your room first. To… rid you of a spider."

Livvy snorted. "No one would believe that. I get rid of the spiders in this house."

"A mouse, then."

"Do I look like the kind of creature to have a fit of hysterics over a mouse?"

King rolled his eyes at her. "You had a bad dream and screamed, and I came running."

"I'm not in my nightgown," she pointed out.

"Easily remedied."

Livvy opened her mouth in shock but saw the glint in his eyes. He was teasing her.

She huffed and pointed down the corridor. "Far end on the left."

She followed him back to her room and opened the door for him when he waited on the threshold.

"Why are we here, then?" she asked, turning to see him inspecting the room with interest.

Not that there was a great deal to see. A bed with a faded patchwork quilt, a few bits of furniture, good quality and well-tended. Inexpert sketches of the children and watercolours of the countryside tacked to the walls beside a sampler she'd done when she was far younger and less cynical, and not much else.

"If I am to help you with this… this…."

"Endeavour," she supplied for him.

"*Madness*," he corrected. "We may as well do it properly. As you have not been in society, I assume that your wardrobe for this party is somewhat challenging."

Livvy nodded. "That's putting it mildly."

"So, what you are planning to do? It isn't a costume ball, by any chance? You'd make a marvellous Cinderella."

Livvy opened her mouth, intending to tell him off for his rudeness when she glimpsed herself in the looking-glass on her dressing table. The reflection was hardly that of a well-dressed young lady. Her gown was faded and though like her furniture, once good quality and well cared for, it… well, she *would* make a marvellous Cinderella.

"No. It is not a masquerade and I shall need clothes for several days," she said, aware of a weary note lingering behind the words. Irritated with herself, she cleared her throat. "I have a couple of gowns I believe I may be able to make over and the others. The others…. Well, I may as well be frank…."

"Good Lord, do you mean you have been holding back until now?" King said with obvious alarm.

Livvy tutted and ignored him. "I shall borrow some of Ceci's clothes. Heaven knows she won't notice, and there's plenty to choose from."

"Ah, thievery. You never cease to impress me, Miss Penrose."

She continued and ignored that comment too. "I'm taller and a bit fuller in the bust, so I must lower the hems and let them out a little, but that's all. Since the last couple of pregnancies, we fill them out to a similar degree, so her more recent purchases might not even need that."

King's eyes were naturally drawn to her bosom after a comment like that, and he pursed his lips.

"Don't bother. I'm immune to lewd comments, I assure you."

"Really?" he asked with interest. "How do you know? Who has been making lewd comments about your person?"

Livvy returned an impatient glance. "No one, clearly, or I'd likely not be in this predicament. I just mean that I do not shock easily, so you may as well refrain from the effort. I suspect being wicked and lascivious at every moment of the day takes a deal of energy, so I am giving you leave to take a rest."

He looked so perplexed by the idea she felt compelled to elaborate.

"Well, isn't it tedious, always having to flirt and make women want to go to bed with you?"

His frown deepened.

"Because you need not try with me. I know you don't wish to bed me, and I most certainly have no wish for you to. This is merely a… a learning experience on my part. So you may relax and be at your ease with me. Treat me as you would one of your cronies."

There was a pause that felt significant, but Livvy could not put her finger on exactly why that was. After the significant pause had stretched almost to breaking point, and just before a fine prickle of sweat broke out on her forehead, he spoke.

"But you wish me to teach you how to seduce a man. That is not the kind of thing I would do with a pal, considering it must be a *practical* learning experience."

Livvy swallowed and willed her cheeks not to heat, glad for the dim candlelight. "Like on the beach?"

That had definitely sounded an octave higher and squeakier than she had intended or was in any way normal.

"Like on the beach," he replied, something simmering in his eyes that no amount of willing could stop bringing a flush of heat to her skin.

"W-Well, in those instances we shall be business-like, and… do what we must. There need be no lovemaking. As you say, it's merely practical experience."

Apart from a slight stutter, Livvy felt relieved her words had sounded cool and quite sensible, which was a relief and evidence of a new ability to dissemble she hadn't realised she possessed, for her insides trembled with longing at the idea that he might give her such an experience now. The look in his eyes suggested he was considering it.

"And outside of those *practical experiences,* I am to treat you as one of my cronies? A pal?" he repeated, frowning.

"Quite so," Livvy agreed, pleased that he had accepted the point.

"Very well," he said, perking up a little.

Livvy watched with consternation as he stripped off his coat, tugged his cravat undone, and threw both onto a chair. Then he strode to her bed and flopped down on it, lounging against the pillows with his hands behind his head, looking for all the world like some exotic pasha awaiting his harem.

"W-What…?" Livvy began.

"You said to treat you as one of my cronies. Pals are terribly informal, you see, we make ourselves at home with one another. You're right, you know, I do feel far more relaxed. Now then, show me these frocks you think can be made over. I confess I have grave doubts about their suitability."

Livvy stared at him for a long moment. Seeing him sprawled over her bed was giving her some very odd sensations in the pit of her belly. There was a peculiar coiling heat, a bit like writhing snakes only less unpleasant, and... and the strangest sense of *possessiveness*. As if by laying himself down upon her bed, in her room, he had somehow made himself... *hers*. What utter twaddle. One could no more own a man like that than keep a pet crocodile. Still, the sensation lingered.

He quirked one dark eyebrow. "See something you like?"

Livvy bristled instinctively. "Certainly not."

"Excellent. Show me the gowns."

Reminding herself that was what she was supposed to be doing, Livvy went to the chest at the end of her bed where the few decent items of clothing she owned were kept. Carefully, she drew out her best gown. It was a good five years out of date, with a deep, square neckline and in her favourite shade of blue. She remembered feeling quite pretty on the few occasions she'd worn it. Holding it up now for King's perusal felt a little like holding up an offering for a pagan god, and judging from the look in his eyes, being found wanting.

"The colour is well enough, I suppose," he said grudgingly. "Though it looks like something for some chit just out of the schoolroom, which won't do at all."

Livvy gave the dress a critical once over.

"Yes, I see what you mean," she said with a regretful sigh. "I'm too old for it."

There was a tsk of annoyance. "I never said that, grandmother dear. The dress is too childish for you. It does not suit the purpose. You will never snare a fellow who's looking for some silly simpering girl he can impress with gifts and bend to his will. No, you need to appeal to a man with a brain in his head looking for an intelligent companion. Preferably a companion who also gives the impression they'd be fun to bed."

Livvy stared at him, heart thudding with the prospect that she might have just heard another compliment. She desperately wanted to say something witty and amusing to underline her appeal to said *man with a brain in his head*. Sadly, after a few seconds of frantic thinking, the most she could come up with was, "Oh."

King nodded, as if she had said something halfway sensible. "Yes. If you combine those two ingredients successfully, you'll have a good chance of victory."

"Do you really think so?" Livvy asked, more than a little surprised. She had assumed he would do what he must—begrudgingly—all the time telling her she was being an idiot and doomed to failure.

He shrugged. "I don't see why not."

It was not exactly a ringing endorsement, but it was much more positive than she'd expected, so she could not help but smile at him.

"Thank you, King."

"Whatever for? I've just told you the dress is no good. Bodices are much narrower this season, though frankly I don't see how you'll get everything in. A bit like fitting a quart into a pint pot."

Once again, he gave her bosom a thorough perusal. As he was trying to be helpful—and she was giving him the benefit of the doubt on this— Livvy took her own advice and treated him as she would a friend, not a man. She ignored the weight of his gaze without comment.

"Er… King?"

He started at the sound of his name, and the slightly glazed look in his eyes was gone in a blink. "Ah. Yes. Next."

"Oh, well... this was my favourite one, once upon a time," she said, holding up a lemon yellow confection with a delicate frill of lace and a lot of ribbons.

"Good grief. In which century? Does it come with a stomacher and panniers?"

"How old do you think I am?" she demanded, wounded by his sarcasm.

"I think you're barely the right side of twenty. That ridiculous item, however, has enough fabric for a marquee. You're going to a ball, not hosting a garden party. I can't see anyone wearing it with no panniers to hoist all that fabric aloft, certainly not a little slip of a thing like you. You'd disappear."

Livvy opened and closed her mouth, torn between defending her favourite frock and... *little slip of a thing.* Dignity won out. "There are no circumstances under which you could describe me as a 'little slip of a thing.'"

"I beg to differ. There's nothing of you."

"There's plenty of me," she retorted.

King got to his feet, and strangely enough, she did feel rather smaller and slip-like as he did so. The room seemed to shrink a vast amount too, notably the space between her and the bed. Her idiotic heart thudded hopefully.

"May I illustrate?" he asked.

Illustrate? Her likeness to a slip, she supposed. What was a slip, anyway? Any further thoughts on the subject were suspended as he put his hands to her waist. She must have nodded her agreement. Yes, she had a vague recollection of moving her head in a jerky up and down motion. Now his large hands were at her waist, the heat of them burning through the worn material of her gown, and there was that odd quivering sensation again.

"There," he said, a definite tinge of smug satisfaction to the pronouncement.

"Where?" she asked, and only stared up at him, all in a dither and wondering what they'd been talking about.

"Here." He squeezed her waist, making her suck in a breath. "Do you eat at all?"

She nodded.

"You barely touched your dinner."

She wrinkled her nose at the memory. "I don't like calves' feet, or cabbage."

"Then why was it for dinner?"

"It's cheap."

"What about this morning?"

"Bread and jam."

He shook his head, his expression fierce. "You gave most of it to George."

"I did?" she replied, wondering why on earth he'd noticed.

"You did, and if you keep on, you'll not be a slip but a wisp. Men do not wish to marry wisps, Miss Penrose. They're dashed difficult to get hold of."

"You seem to have… have a hold… of… of me."

He nodded, a gleam in his eyes that made her silly, giddy, hopeful heart crash about like an unfortunate fishing boat around Vinegar Cove.

"I do," he murmured, his voice all low, velvety, and wicked, and… and he let go and resumed his imitation of an exotic pasha, his expression so utterly benign she knew he'd done it on purpose. The rat. "Well, so far we have a gown fit for Susan and a tent awning. Is that it?"

Livvy swallowed down a distasteful mixture of disappointment and ire and returned to the chest.

"The moths got into my pink, it's beyond saving. There's this…."

She held up her final offering and King stilled, an anxious glint in his eyes.

"Does that… it *does* have a tail, doesn't it?"

Livvy nodded. "Yes. We did some playacting one Christmas. I think perhaps I was supposed to be a cat?"

"Oh, good. I thought I was having a relapse."

She snorted as he put a dramatic hand to his forehead and affected a swoon.

"A pity you weren't in the play," she observed. "I was dreadful, but I suspect you'd be a fine actor."

He chuckled, tilting his head to one side. "Did you have ears?"

"Yes, out of paper. In fact…." Livvy searched about the chest for a moment. "Ah, yes, here we are."

She had fashioned the ears onto a headband and they were a little bent, but otherwise none the worse for wear. For some reason that escaped her, she put them on.

King beamed at her. "Adorable. Did you black your nose, too, and add whiskers?"

"As it happens, yes," she replied, feeling ridiculous.

"Such a pretty kitty," he murmured, and there was that predatory gleam again.

He grinned, and Livvy could think of nothing besides pet crocodiles. He held out his hand to her.

"Come here, puss."

Livvy swallowed and shook her head.

"Ah, don't be shy now. I won't bite."

Crocodile. Crocodile. Croco….

Livvy looked down, wondering at what point she'd put her hand in his. She frowned at her fingers, perplexed, and then squeaked as he gave a tug and she tumbled onto the bed and into his lap.

"There, now. That's more comfortable, isn't it, kitten?"

"I am *not* a kitten," Livvy retorted. "And it's not the least bit comfortable."

She was definitely getting better at dissembling. Her bottom was nestled perfectly in his lap and he was big and warm, and she wanted nothing more than to rest her head on his shoulder and close her eyes.

"But didn't you want some practical experience? Don't you want to make a man desperate to marry you?"

"Y-Yes," she said doubtfully.

"Well, then. There are many men who like to think of their sweethearts as delicate creatures, kittens, or birds. It brings out our protective instincts."

Livvy stared at him. "You're not suggesting I wear ears and a tail to the ball, I hope?"

King snorted. "Well, it would certainly gain you attention, but perhaps not of the kind you are hoping for."

"I should say not." Livvy replied, trying to sound tart, but his hand rested on the small of her back and her spine was melting beneath his touch. Just to make things worse, he rubbed it up and down in a soothing motion, and it took every ounce of willpower not to purr.

"I think, all things considered, that we need to investigate your sister-in-law's wardrobe."

"We?"

He nodded. "Judging on what I've seen so far, I dread to think what crimes against sartorial elegance you would commit if I left you to your own devices. No. This must be a team effort."

Once again, he'd distracted her from the implied insult, this time by the use of the word *team*. He was suggesting *they* were a team. The two of them, in it together. Something warm and fuzzy wrapped about her, like a snuggly blanket. It took her a moment to realise King had put his arms about her. She had never been a part of a team. It had always been her, by herself. Oh, there were the children, who were always on her side, except for when she was trying her best to instil discipline and they were cross with her. But the few friends she'd grown up with had long since married and moved away, and anyone else her age in the area had their own family and children. She was always at odds with her brother and Ceci barely distinguished between her and Gelly most of the time. Of late, her sister-in-law vacillated between seeing her as an unpaid governess or a drain on the family coffers when she refused to do the sensible thing and marry Mr Skewes.

The last remaining bit of spine she had wilted under King's caressing hand, and she leaned into him with a sigh.

"There," he said, and this time he didn't sound the least bit smug, only content. "That's comfy, isn't it?"

"Mmmm, marvellous," she said. "You are even more comfortable than my bed."

"I am at your service." His voice had gone all deep and gravelly and she didn't doubt it was the tone he used for seduction, but it only made her smile. "Are you going to sleep?"

There was a hint of outrage in the demand.

"Hmmm? Oh, no. Just… just resting my eyes."

"Miss Penrose, you are in the arms of a notorious rake and libertine. Your virtue is in grave peril."

"Is it?" Livvy replied, smothering a yawn. "That's nice."

"Livvy! You ought to be flustered and breathless, drat you. I swear you are the most unnatural female."

"It's true. I am. I'm so sorry, King. It's not your fault, though, so don't feel bad. Only it's been a dreadfully long day and... and you have the most splendid shoulders and you're so warm and cosy. I can't think when I have ever felt so... so... snug."

Livvy sighed, wondering why it was she felt so at peace. The little voice of her conscience yelled at her, but it was so faint and annoying it was hardly worth the trouble of paying attention to it.

Chapter Nine

Almost the 10th December 1818.

Dogs, crows, pegos and cravats, plus a terrifying suspicion.

King glowered at the woman in his arms. Well! The nerve of the creature. Here he was primed for a little jaunt down the road to perdition with a pleasurable detour via the abyss and a look in at damnation, and the blasted creature used him as a pillow.

"Snug," he muttered wrathfully. "Your maiden aunt's shawl is snug. The King of Sin is not *snug*, damn you."

"Hmm?" Livvy murmured sleepily. Her hand came up to his neck and she wriggled closer, her warm breath fluttering against his skin.

"Nothing, love," he murmured, frowning down at her. There was a peculiar sensation in his chest. Most likely the calves' feet kicking at his innards. "Go to sleep."

She sighed, and the gust of damp warmth stirred the attention of his flesh, already awakened by the proximity of a lovely female arse in his lap.

"Stand down," he grumbled. "We'll go to perdition another night. The wooden hill to Bedfordshire is as far as we are getting, it seems."

Bedfordshire. He snorted inwardly. Bloody Bedlam, more like. What the devil was he playing at? Had he just arranged to rifle her sister-in-law's wardrobe with her? For it very much sounded like he had. He must have taken leave of his senses. Yet then his senses remembered the girl asleep in his lap, her head upon his shoulder, her rather sharp features serene in repose, sweet and trusting. Trusting in him. Good God. Livvy might think she was up to all the tricks, and beyond falling for his particular brand of wickedness, but she did not understand. She was too delicious, all spiky on the outside, but once you navigated past those thorns....

Oh, hell. He was in a world of trouble.

Though he could not for the life of him fathom why, he stayed until dawn. His neck ached and left leg went to sleep sometime after midnight, which was more than the rest of him managed, but... but he was too tired to move. Besides, he'd only wake Miss Prickly Penrose, and she'd probably shriek on finding him still there and wake the house, and then they'd all be in the basket. That was what he told himself. When he finally moved, she didn't wake, though. She barely stirred and he stood staring down at her and her crumpled cat ears for far too long before he made himself walk away.

He managed an hour in his own bed before he faced the daily effort of not ransacking the entire house for a bottle of anything remotely intoxicating and getting dressed instead. By the time he was presentable, his hands were shaking.

I am not drinking. I am not drinking. I. Am. Not. Drinking.

It occurred to him then that he hadn't thought about drinking the entire time he was with Livvy last night. It next occurred to him that was a terrifying thought and one he'd do well not to dwell on. Which naturally meant he spent the next half hour staring blindly out of the window and dwelling on it. He fought down the anxious fidgety sensation in his belly and told himself to grow up, though if he'd not managed that in the past five and thirty years, it seemed unlikely to happen at this late stage. His one consolation was the fact that she would have to face him over the breakfast table, knowing she'd fallen asleep in his arms. With him in her bed. Well, *on* her bed. Which was still making it sound a lot more salacious and exciting than it had been, but still… Perhaps it hadn't been salacious or exciting, but it had been rather… he hunted about for an appropriate description. Pleasant? No. Peaceful? *No*. Lovely? Well….

"There'll be nothing left if you don't go now. Them children are like a ravening horde if you put bread and jam in front of them."

King nodded, more than a little distracted, but allowed Walsh to chivvy him down the stairs. He brightened on approaching the breakfast parlour, remembering he was about to see Miss Penrose blush and stammer and….

"Oh, there you are, King. Look who's come to see us."

Livvy beamed at him and held her hand aloft. A sleek black crow turned one beady eye on him and tilted his head to one side in a move King found mildly disturbing. The massive beak opened, and the bird gave an ear-splitting and, to King's mind, disapproving, caw. Marvellous, judged and found wanting by a bird.

"Isn't he handsome?"

King regarded the crow, who in turn looked him over as if he was something dead that may or may not be worth picking at.

"Yes, he is," Livvy crooned. Apparently, that had been a rhetorical question. "Mr Moon is a handsome fellow."

She stroked her finger over the crow's head, and he preened, giving King a look he could only describe as smug.

"Gog," said George.

"No, George, it's a crow," Livvy corrected gently. "A bird called a crow. Say birdie, George."

"Gog."

King sighed and shook his head.

"He has an affinity for dogs and is somewhat fixated at present," Livvy said, sounding a touch defensive. "It's a bird, George. A pretty birdie. Good morning, pretty birdie."

"He's probably confused." King observed. "His sister is called Birdie, isn't she?"

"No, she's called Henrietta, but yes, her pet name is Birdie. Perhaps you have a point."

Livvy gestured to Mr Moon. "George, *this* is a crow. Can you say crow, sweetheart? *Ke re oh*."

"Gog."

"Why do you have a pet crow?" King asked, not irritated in the least that Livvy was not blushing and stammering, and was more interested in a blasted bird and an obstinate child than him.

He was not jealous of a bird. Nor a small boy. No. Under no circumstances.

"I found him in the wood after a storm about three years ago. He was tiny and cold, and there were no parents about. So I fed him and kept him warm until he was ready to leave, but he never did.

162

He stays close to the house and often comes back to visit. Here, you take him."

Livvy held out her hand, gesturing for King to do the same. Reluctantly, King did as she suggested, and the bloody bird cawed and pecked at his fingers.

"Ouch!" King yelled, which sent Mr Moon off in a flurry of wings.

He swooped about the breakfast table, to the delighted shrieks of the children, before settling on the back of Livvy's chair.

"Oh, you frightened him," she said with reproach.

"He attacked me!" King held out his finger, which had a savage red mark on it, though the skin had not been broken.

"Don't be such a baby, it's barely a scratch."

"It's a sight more than a scratch. That thing is vicious. You should keep it away from the children."

Livvy gestured to where George was feeding the bird pieces of bread and jam. Mr Moon was taking the tasty morsels with a delicate, fastidious beak, and looked as if butter wouldn't melt, or whatever the crow equivalent was…worms wouldn't dissolve?

"Yes, he's a danger to society," she said dryly.

King glared at her and pulled out a chair, sitting down in it whilst keeping the monstrous bird in his line of sight.

"Is that an Obaldeston, my lord?" the oldest of the children asked him, regarding King's cravat with a covetous eye.

King dared tear his gaze from the attack bird for a moment to look at… Henry? Harvey? No… *Harry.* That was it.

"Certainly not. Far too fussy. It's a barrel knot."

"Father says you're the most stylish man in the *ton* and that everyone in town copies you."

Though the why of it escaped him, King felt a stab of discomfort at being described thus before Miss Penrose. It wasn't as if she didn't know he was a fribble and a fearful waste of space, after all. It was just, if one was committed to going to the devil, King didn't see why one ought not do the thing in style. Except, now he'd changed his mind about destroying his life through dissipation and vice, he felt rather a fool for having got so close to doing so.

Harry gave a wistful sigh. "I've almost mastered the *Trone d'amour.*"

King gave the boy's mangled neckcloth a doubtful glance, but kept his mouth shut. "I shouldn't bother. It'll make you look a right pillock.

All you need is the barrel knot, the ballroom and, perhaps for a change of scene, the oriental."

King saw the slump of Harry's shoulders and had a vivid and unwelcome recollection of being fourteen, in awe of everyone who seemed to be far better at being a man than he was, and living in utter terror of his father. Some sense of fellow feeling prompted him.

"If you come to my room before dinner tonight, I'll show you. If you like."

The boy's eyes grew wide with astonishment. "Oh, would you, sir? I... Oh, goodness, that... that would be *marvellous*."

King nodded, experiencing a strange little glow of pleasure at the boy's enthusiasm and gratitude.

Harry pushed to his feet, breakfast forgotten. "I'll see how many cravats I can muster. They... well, they aren't starched or... or terribly...."

King waved him off. "It's of no matter. I'll give you a couple of mine to practise with. Walsh always brings more than I could possibly need."

"Gosh," the boy said, his ears growing pink with pleasure. "I say... Thank you, my lord."

"Call me King," King said, smiling at the lad. "Everyone does."

Harry seemed to grow about a foot in height, his shoulders going back. "I should be honoured to, my lor… *King.*"

He walked out of the breakfast parlour with his head held high, only spoiling the effect once out of sight with an audible yip of excitement that echoed down the hallway.

"Thank you."

King turned to see Livvy regarding him with a rather unsettling misty expression.

He shrugged, concentrating on buttering the roll he'd taken, and wished his hands were steadier this morning.

"No, really, King. Poor Harry, he's… he's such a lovely young man, but painfully aware of… oh, of everything. Of the way his cuffs are fraying and he's growing out of his clothes, and… and his father doesn't seem to notice."

There was a bitter note to her words and a great deal of obvious frustration.

King hesitated, not knowing what to say. It was apparent the family were in financial difficulties, but one did *not* discuss such things, certainly not over breakfast.

And yet….

"Are things very bad?"

Livvy shrugged and lowered her voice so the children did not hear her words. "The house is entailed, at least but… Oh, well, you can see for yourself the place is falling down around us. My brother made some… *unwise* investments, but… but he has debts too, and…."

To his horror, her voice quavered, and she closed her mouth, blinking rapidly.

"Liv… Miss Penrose," he began, horrified to think she might cry at the breakfast table.

"Oh, dear," she said, forcing a laugh. "How horrid of me to subject you to such a scene before you've even broken your fast. No wonder you think me such a trial."

I don't think you're a trial. I think you're….

Thankfully, he stopped himself before he said the words out loud, or even in his head, but the effort left him shakier than ever and all on edge. What was happening to him? God, he needed a bloody drink.

No.

No.

I am not drinking.

"Gog."

"N-No, dear," Livvy said, sniffling a little and smiling at George. "That's Lord Kingston."

"Gog."

"King," King said to the child, his voice firm. "I am many things, young man, but I draw the line at being described as a dog."

"Ooof, ooof."

"*King.*"

George got a sly look in his eyes and said, carefully and deliberately: "Pego."

"George!" Livvy exclaimed. "Wherever…."

She turned an accusing eye upon King.

"It was an accident," he said defensively.

"What manner of accident results in you teaching the child that word?" she demanded.

King cleared his throat.

"He was walking about in the buff! I merely pointed out that ladies took exception to…." He waved his hand in an expressive manner. "*That* being on display."

"Oh, King," Livvy said, and put her head in her hands.

Her shoulders shook and King felt a wave of shame at being the fellow who had finally broken the indomitable Miss Penrose.

"Oh, Liv… Miss Penrose, please…. Don't… Don't…. I'm terribly sorry. Truly. I swear I'll try to teach him something else…."

Livvy raised her head, tears running down her face, and went off in a peal of laughter.

"Oh, you ridiculous creature," she said, gasping for breath. "I'm not crying. It's the funniest thing I've heard in… oh… oh…."

She clutched at her sides while the children stared at her, wide-eyed.

"Pego?" George enquired with interest.

Livvy went off in whoops again as the girls snickered and whispered behind their hands.

King sighed and got to his feet.

"Ladies," he said to the girls gravely. "Would you excuse us? Your aunt is a little… overwrought. I think perhaps she needs some air."

Somehow, he got Livvy to her feet and steered her, still spluttering and wheezing, out of the room, wrapped a shawl about her shoulders, and guided her outside. It was a beautiful winter's morning, with a sky the colour of the Madonna's cloak, and air so sweet and crisp it hurt his lungs.

Livvy sucked in a shaky breath and turned back to him, her eyes alight with merriment.

King had the oddest sensation of being kicked hard in the chest.

"Oh, King, thank you."

"Whatever for?" he asked crossly, finding he was suddenly breathless and out of sorts.

"For making me laugh when I felt like crying. Again."

He shrugged, frowning at his feet and avoiding her eyes, which he had just noticed were an even more intense shade of blue than the sky. She fell quiet and King kept staring at his feet until he couldn't stand not to look back at her. He'd known she was studying him. He could feel the weight of her appraisal, but still the act of meeting her gaze unbalanced him, as if he was on a ship that had pitched to one side.

"Are you well, King?"

The pitching sensation increased on hearing the soft concern in the question, the sincerity. So many people might ask, yet so few really wanted to hear the answer. In fact, besides Walsh, he couldn't think of a single one who truly cared, and wasn't that the most depressing realisation for a man of his years?

"Of course, fit as a flea," he remarked, trying to sound insouciant and at ease and managing neither.

The way she looked at him, her intense scrutiny, made him want to squirm like a child about to be birched, and he felt hot and uncomfortable.

"Does it pain you? Not drinking, I mean. I think it does. You're fighting it, aren't you? Terribly hard."

To his horror, she took his hand and squeezed.

"I'm proud of you, you know. I can't pretend to understand what it is you are feeling, but... but I'm sure it would be easier to just give in, and you haven't, and... well done, King. Oh, goodness, that sounded horribly patronising, didn't it? I didn't mean for it to, I promise, only—"

He kissed her.

Really, she'd left him no other option. He felt as if her words had cut his chest open and exposed his innards, rotten and festering as they no doubt were, and yet... yet she looked at him as if he might actually be worth something. It was too much. She made him feel too much, which was to say anything at all. It had been so long since he had allowed himself to feel anything, and then Miss Prickly bloody Penrose had waltzed into his life and scolded him and bossed him about, and... made him feel... *things.* It was damned inconvenient. Whatever those things were, he had not the least desire to examine them any closer, and so the only thing to do was to shut her up because she was making his throat tight and his eyes burn, and so he'd kissed her. Except now he'd only made matters worse because she melted into his arms without a murmur of protest and with a good deal of enthusiasm. Oh, and she was sweet, so much damned sweeter because he knew how strong she was and how no one else—barring perhaps the children—ever got to see beyond the prickles and strength, because she had to keep going, she had to hold them all together. She was doing it, too, with nothing more than string and sealing wax, and the sheer force of her will.

Desire was a searing ache in his chest and, damn, that was a strange thing because desire did not usually feel this way. Lust, he understood, but this was an uncertain blend of want and need and pain, and he did not know why or what to do with it.

He let her go, a little more abruptly than he had meant to, and she staggered, clutching at his arms. Her eyes were still bright, her cheeks flushed, and her lips reddened and swollen by the force of his kisses. He wanted to do it again. Hellfire, he wanted to haul her upstairs to his room and not let her leave until he'd made her understand just what manner of man he really was. Oddly, he wanted to protect her, too; he wanted for her to never know what kind of man he was, because he did not want to lose the look that was in her eyes now, as foolish as it was. Foolish of them both.

"Oh, my," she gasped, staring up at him. "Th-That was a practical lesson, I take it?"

He gave a jerky nod and tugged at his waistcoat. "Quite."

"Y-Yes, I thought that must be it."

"We'd best go in before someone sees us."

She nodded again, still staring at him. There was an unfocused, glassy look to her eyes now he could not help but feel a little smug about. Well, a fellow had his pride, dash it all! He couldn't be the only one who was feeling half seas over when he was more sober than he'd been in his life.

"When shall we go a-rifling?" she asked, a mischievous twitch to her lips that made him want to kiss her all over again.

"Rifling?"

"Yes. You promised to come and rifle Ceci's gowns with me, remember?"

"Ah, yes, rifling it is. Well, I don't know. When will she be the farthest from her wardrobe?"

"I believe she is going with Charlie to pay a call on Mr and Mrs Treloar over at Widemouth Bay. They ought to be gone at least a couple of hours. You've put Harry in such a good mood I'm sure he'll mind the children if I ask nicely."

"Very well. As soon as they're gone, then."

"Yes," she said, nodding, but making no move to return to the house.

"Well… we should…." He gestured awkwardly at the side door he'd ushered her out of.

"Oh, yes. We should."

King supposed he ought to be pleased by the reluctance with which she turned and went back into the house, but all he could hear were alarm bells ringing so loud his head was pounding, or was that his heart? Perhaps he was coming down with something. His hands were clammy and still not as steady as he'd like. God, he wanted a drink. Except he couldn't have a drink. *I am not drinking,* he reminded himself, but now it was not just because he didn't want to send himself to an early grave with nothing to show for his miserable existence, but… but because Livvy was *proud* of him. Damn her eyes! What business had she being proud of him? The next thing he knew she'd say she cared for him or… or that she….

He sucked in a sharp breath and clutched at his chest, wondering if perhaps he was about to turn up his toes after all.

"King? *King*! Are you sure you're quite well? You've gone the ghastliest shade of white, like a milk pudding."

King blinked and gave Livvy his haughtiest look of disdain, the one he reserved for presumptuous upstarts. "Quite well, I thank you. If you would excuse me, Miss Penrose, I… I must…"

His mind blanked. He didn't have the least idea of what was so pressing he must do it at once, and besides, she knew damn well he was an idle wastrel. He panicked, knowing only that he had to get away from her before he figured out what the hell it was that terrified him. He had a feeling knowing the answer would only make the situation increasingly dire.

So… he ran away.

Chapter Ten

10th December 1818.

One highly strung earl, a devious valet, and a gateway to fairyland.

Livvy watched King go with a frown. There was something about him that made her think of the children when they were hiding something. They knew they'd not be able to keep her from finding out eventually...so they ran away. He certainly had the look of a man running away. It had been the same when he'd kissed her, the sense that he was deflecting her attention. Not that she was complaining. It had been the most marvellous kiss. It lingered even now, the taste of him upon her lips, the warmth of his body against hers. *Oh.* She was all light and fluffy and floaty, like a billowy cloud. Before meeting King, she had never understood how any woman could be foolish enough to get themselves into difficulties with a man who was quite obviously trouble. Indeed, King was *so* obviously trouble he might as well have the word stencilled across his forehead in capital letters. She suspected it would in no way diminish his charm and women would continue to throw themselves at his feet. *Not,* she told herself firmly, *that she had done anything of the sort.*

After all, he had kissed her. Rather abruptly, it was true. Livvy frowned, considering that. What had she been saying that had set him off? Something about admiring his efforts to remain sober, if she remembered rightly, though remembering was more difficult than she liked to acknowledge, but really… that kiss. It was a wonder she was still standing, let alone had any grip remaining on her faculties.

She made her way back to the breakfast parlour, considering the Earl of Kingston as she went. It occurred to her that he was rather highly strung. He was clearly the kind of fellow who lived on his nerves and did not understand how to deal with emotional situations, so ran away before they bothered him too deeply, a man who needed reassurance at regular intervals, though he'd rather die than admit it, let alone ask for it. From the little she knew of his father, the Marquess of Eynsham— and that only what Charlie had told her—she very much doubted he'd ever had anything resembling reassurance or comfort of any kind. Livvy pondered this as she returned to the children, relieved to find that nothing had been broken or upset in her absence.

She sent them off to complete their various jobs, and Susan took Birdie off to change her clout, leaving Livvy with George.

"I think we'd best send King some breakfast up, George. The poor man didn't eat a thing between Harry's cravats and your performance."

George chuckled and reached out to tug on her skirts. "Libby Lib Lib."

"Hmmm, you may well Libby me, you little monster. You knew that was a naughty word, didn't you?"

George gave her a beaming smile of such innocent joy she could not help but bend and kiss his nose.

"Libby, Libby. Want gog."

"We don't have a dog, George, my sweet."

George huffed and tugged on her skirts again.

"No gog?"

"No dog," she said, making up a tray to send up to King with his favourite blackberry jam on.

"Libby. Ing?"

Livvy turned to look at him. "What, darling?"

"Ing?"

She blinked. "Do… do you mean King?"

"Es. Where is Ing?"

For some inexplicable reason, Livvy felt a tightening in her throat.

"Silly goose," she muttered to herself. "I think King has gone for a lie down. He's not feeling quite himself, but you'll see him later. Why don't we go and see Gelly?"

George put his arms up in the air, a demand to be lifted into her arms. "Gelly, cake!"

Livvy laughed and picked George up, heedless of his jammy hands on her frock. He could hardly make it worse at this stage. "You've just had breakfast."

George clutched her about the neck and gave her a sticky, blackberry flavoured kiss. "Cake!"

"Oh, very well. Let's go and see what we can find."

❧ ❧ ❧

Unsurprisingly, Ceci made herself and Charlie late by dithering over what to wear, but finally her husband ushered her out of the house. Birdie and George were taking a nap, Harry was reading and listening out in case they woke, and the girls were cutting pictures out of the latest fashion prints to stick on their walls. Free at last, Livvy went to find King, and bumped into Walsh on his way to the kitchen.

"Is Lord Kingston feeling better now?" she asked, wondering if his valet might give her some insight into why he'd run away in such a tizzy.

"I can't rightly say, Miss," Walsh said with a heavy sigh. "Keeps his thoughts to himself, he does. A deep one, as they say."

Well, that was hardly helpful. "Did he eat any of the breakfast I sent up?"

"No, Miss," the valet said mournfully. "I am afraid he didn't eat a bite of it. I worry for the poor devil. I do what I can, but I'm only a valet, when the fellow needs a wife. Lonely, he is, I reckon, not that he'd ever say so. He needs a bit of care and looking after, like any man, or I fear he'll take a turn for the worse."

"Mr Walsh," Livvy said sternly. "I have told you in no uncertain terms that I have no designs on Lord Kingston, so—"

"Oh, no, Miss!" Walsh broke in, his expression one of mortification she didn't entirely believe. "I didn't mean *you.* No, indeed. You made yourself quite plain and I wouldn't think to *ever* try to change your mind. Good heavens, what would you think of me? No, it's only that he's my master and a good fellow at heart. It plain tears me up to see him in such a way and if he goes and… and…."

Walsh's voice wobbled dramatically. He took a deep shuddering breath and cleared his throat.

"I just don't know what would become of me if he surrenders this time, and… and turns back to the bottle. For there won't be no one to save him next go around."

Livvy stared at the valet in horror. "Good heavens, is… is it so bad?"

Walsh shrugged. "Oh, he puts a brave face on it, Miss, and he's trying hard. Truth is, I never saw him try as hard as he's doing now and… and that is surely down to you and your kindness. He doesn't want to let you down see, Miss Penrose. You saved his life."

"Nonsense," Livvy said briskly, thoroughly unsettled by this entire conversation and not least the disturbing gleam in the valet's eyes, which was… she did not know what. "Boscawen saved him. I wanted to turn him out on his ear as you must surely know."

"Ah, but you didn't, Miss, and 'twas you not your brother what sat and nursed him and chased the devils away."

Livvy opened and closed her mouth to protest, but decided this conversation had gone on quite long enough. "Where is the earl now?"

"Sleeping, Miss," Walsh replied, with the regretful air of a man who expected King to shuffle off this mortal coil at any moment.

"Thank you, Mr Walsh," Livvy said, quite out of patience with the fellow, and set off to see for herself.

Livvy knocked quietly enough not to disturb King if he really was sleeping, but not so quietly that he'd not hear if he wasn't. When there was no reply, she cracked the door open and peered in. The room was dim, the curtains closed against the sunshine outside, and Livvy looked to the bed. Sure enough, King was sprawled across the mattress. He had rid himself of coat, waistcoat, and cravat, and he looked flushed and tousled, as if he'd had unpleasant dreams. Suddenly Walsh's words came back to her with more force and she remembered King earlier that morning, white as a sheet, and… and had his hands been trembling?

Oh, King.

Too overcome by anxiety to bother herself with her outrageous offence against both propriety and his own privacy, she hurried to the bed.

"King?" she whispered. There was no reply, and Livvy sat down on the mattress, taking one of his hands in hers and reaching up to push a dark lock of hair from his forehead. "King, are you well?"

When there was no response, she put her hand to his cheek, relieved to discover he was not feverish, but finding her concern undiminished. She laid her palm over his heart next and breathed a sigh of relief to find it beating strong and sure.

"Livvy? What the devil are you doing?"

Livvy gave a yelp of alarm. "Oh, my! You startled me. I thought you were asleep."

"I was asleep," he said, blinking at her in confusion. "Which does not answer the question. Why are you in my bedroom and putting your hands on me?"

"Oh… Ummm. Well, there is a reasonable explanation for that," she said, feeling suddenly breathless and annoyed with herself, not to mention furious with Mr Walsh. What *had* she been thinking?

"I'm all ears," he said, a tone to his voice which made shivers skitter down her spine.

"Well, I… er, I ran into Mr Walsh and enquired after you, because… Oh, because Ceci and Charlie have gone out now, only… only your wretched valet told me how you were lonely and dying of melancholy and drink, and…. Oh, I don't remember exactly what he said, but he put me such a pelter I was certain you were about to breathe your last, and…."

"And so you came to see for yourself?"

"Yes," Livvy said, relieved he'd understood. "I'm beginning to believe he… he…."

"Played you like a fiddle?" King suggested.

"Quite." Livvy scowled at him, wondering why on earth she'd allowed herself to be taken in. "What was he thinking?"

"I gave up trying to figure out what Walsh is thinking over a decade ago. I'm not about to try again now. Though I *believe* he acts with the best of intentions, the results can be… mixed."

"Yes, but you do realise the dreadful man is trying to get me to set my cap at you?"

King stilled and his voice when he next spoke was cool and remote, and not at all what she'd become used to. "Whatever gave you that ludicrous idea?"

"Well, he's all but put it in writing," she said caustically, not liking his tone.

"Well, do not fret unduly, Miss Penrose. We both know that I am of no earthly use to you beyond my limited ability in teaching you how to seduce another man of greater worth."

Livvy stiffened at the mockery behind his words. "There is no need to be unpleasant."

"Ah, but it was you who insisted we call a spade a spade, was it not?"

"I think I'd best go now. You are clearly in no mood for company."

"Oh, but you're quite wrong."

Livvy gasped as he pulled her down on to the bed with him and rolled them both so he was staring down at her.

"I find I'm quite in the mood," he said, his eyes glittering dangerously.

"You are supposed to be helping me find something to wear in Ceci's wardrobe," Livvy pointed out, wondering how on earth she sounded so calm when she was trembling all over.

She wanted to believe it was maidenly distress at being manhandled in such a cavalier fashion. Being the kind of person who thought it was the height of stupidity to lie to oneself, she was obliged to admit it was nothing of the sort. No, the thing that had her quivering and flustered was the feel of his large frame pressing hers into the mattress. She ought to be furious with him, she ought to demand he get off and let her go, but all she felt was a dizzying rush of exhilaration and a desire to ask for more.

"But I don't want to find you something new to wear. I'm only interested in getting you out of what you are wearing at present. You are in my bed, Livvy, you came to my room and put your hands on me. Some men might call that encouragement."

185

"What do you call it?" she asked, and there was no doubting the breathless quality of her voice this time.

"Recklessness. Idiocy. An utter lack of regard for the consequences of your actions?"

Livvy blinked, a little startled by the anger in his voice.

"Is this how you usually go about seducing women?" she asked. "Aren't you supposed to make me forget about all those things, not bring them to my attention?"

"For Christ's sake, Livvy. Do you want me to ruin you?"

Livvy stared up at him, her heart thudding too fast in her chest.

"Holy God!" he exclaimed, throwing himself away from her and scrambling to his feet. "You're not supposed to think about it!"

Livvy sat up on her elbows, staring at him in consternation. "Why did you ask me the question if you didn't wish me to think about it?"

"It oughtn't need thinking about, you wicked girl! The correct answer is an immediate *no,* followed by insults about the nature of my character and a good hard slap."

"You're awfully skittish for a libertine," Livvy replied, provoked now. "Are you quite sure you are the Earl of Kingston and not some imposter?"

"Quite sure," he replied acidly. "And if you really want to marry a man with more than ten shillings to his name, I suggest you leave. Now."

"No."

King threw up his hands and muttered a curse.

"There's no point in being all dramatic. I've had quite enough of that nonsense for one day," Livvy scolded. "You promised to help me find something to wear for this blasted ball and I am holding you to it."

"Oh, fine. Why the devil not? You've all but given me leave to ruin you, I don't see why I ought not rob your sister-in-law while I'm about it."

"I did not give you leave to ruin me," Livvy said, getting to her feet and putting her hands on her hips. Good Lord, but he was working himself up into a passion over nothing. "I was merely considering the possibility, and you are not robbing my sister-in-law. I am borrowing a few gowns which will be returned to her once I'm done with them. Really, King. I expect such tantrums and dramatics from George, but I believe you ought to have grown out of them."

"Do you?" he replied, folding his arms and glaring at her. "I don't have the faintest idea why.

Surely you know I'm a spoiled and indulged aristo with nothing between his ears but fluff and an urge to despoil every maiden within arm's reach."

"*I* was in arm's reach," Livvy pointed out. "And there was very little despoiling going on that I noticed."

"You needn't sound so blasted disappointed about it!" he yelled.

Livvy blinked at him, quite at a loss.

"King," she said gently, using the voice she employed for overtired toddlers. "You are becoming overwrought. I thought this morning that you were out of sorts, and now I'm certain of it. Why don't you come and have a lie down and I'll go and fetch a cold cloth for your head?"

"I don't want a lie down!" he growled.

"There's no need to get testy."

"I will get testy if I dashed well want to," he said through gritted teeth. "And I warn you now, if I get anywhere near that bed and you are still in the room, you'll see just how quickly I can despoil you, and you'll eat your words."

Livvy struggled with the temptation to see if he really meant it, but good sense won out. She took a breath, opting to soothe the beast instead. "I'm sure that's quite true, but you know you're just saying that because you're cross with me."

"Yes, I am!"

"I know, King. I do understand that I try your patience and I am sorry for it."

"No, you're not," he grumbled, stalking back and forth. "You're not the least bit sorry, you come in here all blue eyes and… and… lips and… *things* and… and *bother* me, and I'm the one who's in the wrong."

"I never said you were in the wrong," Livvy said, trying not to put too much store by his noticing her blue eyes and her lips and *things*. He had, after all, worked himself up to quite a pitch and was not the least bit rational. "And you are quite correct I did come and bother you when you were having a nice nap and that was a dreadful thing to do. I apologise. It was very bad of me."

"Yes, it was."

"Yes, I just said as much."

"Hmph." He folded his arms, scowling at her.

"Am I forgiven?" she asked gently.

He glowered a bit more.

"I am sorry. I quite understand if you prefer to continue your nap."

"I'm not three years old," he grumbled.

Livvy bit her lip, deciding it was not politic to point out the obvious. "I know. Forgive me. In that case, I should be most grateful if you'd help me choose what is best from Ceci's wardrobe."

King groused a bit more but turned to the door and opened it, glancing outside before gesturing for Livvy to go before him.

"Lead on, Macduff," he said with a somewhat sarcastic tone she chose to ignore.

"It's 'Lay on, Macduff,'" actually," she corrected him, even though she was poking the angry bear with a stick. "Macbeth is inviting Macduff to attack him, not to politely go through the door ahead of him."

"Don't tempt me," he gritted out, closing the door behind them.

Livvy led him to Ceci and Charlie's room, feeling all the while as if she was being stalked by a large, angry cat. She could not help but feel his mood did not spring from irritation at being rudely awoken, and he was clearly annoyed with her for not defending her maidenhead with more vigour. It occurred to her that, for a man of his reputation, King had a highly developed sense of honour. It was pointless to pretend that she wasn't tempted to… if not let him have his way with her, then let him have *some* of his way with her. Possibly rather more of his way than was required for the job she had asked him to help her with. It was his own dratted fault, though. If he would go around being sweet to the children and making her laugh when she wanted to cry, it was the least he could expect. Really, she was only human.

"Here we are," she said, pushing open the door to the master chambers.

She stilled as she went in. The last time she had been in here, she'd been so cross she'd sworn to never set foot in it again. Now she remembered exactly why that was, though in truth it was even worse than the last time.

"Good God!"

Livvy sighed. "Yes. I know."

"It's like a gateway to fairyland."

"It is," Livvy agreed, battering down the swell of resentment that rose on seeing all the lavish accoutrements that filled the room. The bed was swathed in rich fabrics, silk and velvet and satin in various shades of peach, and the room decorated with extravagant damask wall hangings. There were gilt mirrors and paintings. and a lovely tapestry fire screen. The pretty dressing table was crammed with bottles of perfume and expensive creams, and the floor layered with thick rugs. Everywhere there were clothes and shoes, carelessly abandoned, and the heavy curtains framing the windows puddled in an excess of frivolity upon the floor.

"You mean to say Lady Boscawen lives like… like this, while Harry hasn't a decent cravat to his name, and everyone's living on bloody cabbage, and you… and they treat you… like… like a damned skivvy?"

"Oh, it's… it's not that bad," Livvy said at once, some sense of loyalty stirring to life and making her defend Ceci and her brother, though it really was much as he described it. "I mean, Ceci doesn't mean to be extravagant, she's just—"

"Witless, thoughtless, and selfish?" King finished for her.

"Well… yes," Livvy said, folding her arms about herself. "But Charlie loves her to distraction, and he can't bear to say no to her. She could have married a duke, you see, but she chose him instead, and so…."

"And so he'll drag you all in penury before admitting he can't afford her."

Livvy shrugged.

King cursed a bit more before taking a deep breath. "We'd best see the gowns, then."

Livvy led him through to the dressing room and even she paused, wide-eyed, on the threshold. There was no point in saying anything further, though. She knew Ceci was an extravagant ninny and no amount of explaining their desperate situation seemed to change that.

Apparently, King understood the point too and held his tongue, though his expression was stony. "How many days is this party likely to go on for?"

"Three, at least, perhaps five, though I'd best not take anything too new, or she'll notice. So this corner here seems to be the most recent. I recognise that yellow as one she wore home a few weeks back."

King nodded, moved towards the far end of the dressing room, and set to work.

By the time they'd finished, Livvy had a collection of evening and ball gowns that weren't too badly out of style, morning attire, half dresses, a carriage dress and a riding habit, plus all the attendant gloves, hats and shoes. Luckily, Ceci's feet were the same size and most of the gowns only needed a little alteration. King had remained silent as they worked, either giving a nod or a tut of disapproval as they sifted through the selection on offer.

She did not think he was angry with her any longer, but she was uncertain of his mood and did not like to tempt him back into another display of ill humour. He made no protest when she asked if he might help her bring the travelling trunk down from the attics, and they installed it in one of the rooms that had been closed off, where no one would come across it. Livvy carefully folded each gown and packed it away, meaning to work on one at a time in her room of an evening. She closed the lid of the trunk and got to her feet, brushing dust from her gown as she straightened.

"Thank you, King. I know I've been a terrible nuisance, but I am grateful, I assure you."

"You're welcome," he said, though his eyes remained troubled.

She did not know how to ask him what was wrong, and he simply turned and walked away.

Chapter Eleven

12ᵗʰ December 1818.

Handsome farmers, secret assignations, and an episode of violent dusting.

Ross Moyle was a dreadfully handsome man. He was all wavy black hair, suntanned skin, and powerful shoulders. Livvy smiled to herself as she watched him work. There were worse ways of spending a morning than shovelling manure when one had such a pretty companion to look at. She pushed the hair from her eyes before setting to once more.

"There's no need for you to shovel muck with me, Livvy," Ross protested, the same as he had protested every time they'd done this for years now.

"Yes, there is," she said briskly. "We shall share the profits and that's only fair if we share the labour."

"Ah, but it's not right for a lady to be shovelling sh… this stuff... and 'twas your idea, and you what learned how it needed doin.' I would never have thought of it."

Livvy snorted. "And that may have been for the best. For all we know, it is a colossal waste of time and effort."

"Nah, reckon it's gonna work just as you said it would."

Livvy felt the fluttering of hope in her chest as she always did, but did not dare let it run away with her. Maybe… *maybe* by the summertime they would know. "Did you get hold of more oak bark? I'm certain ours needs replacing."

"Aye. It's a blasted nuisance not being able to fetch it from the tanner's in Bude, but I'll take the cart over to Holsworthy this afternoon."

"I'm sorry, Ross. I know it's time you can ill afford, but I daren't let anyone figure out what we're doing. If Boscawen were to hear of it…."

"Don't fret yourself to death, Liv," Ross said with an easy smile. "I weren't complaining to make ye feel bad. A fella likes to grumble about the state of affairs when he's workin,' 'tis all."

Livvy laughed. "And I don't blame you in the least."

They worked on in silence for a bit longer, the sun warm on their backs.

"There," Ross said with obvious satisfaction. "Give us a hand to lift the lids back in place and that should keep 'em warm and cosy. I'll replace the bark in the morning. If this sunshine keeps up and the frosts stay away, we'll have an easier time of it, an' that's for sure."

"I brought some of our oldest sheets and blankets to cover them over at night, like you said, though I'm sorry to give you another job to do."

"'Tis no bother, Liv. I'm happy to do it."

Livvy helped put everything back as it ought to be and watched Ross stash the tools away, out of sight.

"How's Sarah?" she asked as he walked with her back towards the garden.

"Fine and dandy and fat as a pig," he said, grinning at her, his blue eyes shining.

Livvy laughed. "I shall tell her you said that, you wicked man."

"Ah, she knows I love her, fat or thin. 'Sides, what kind of cheel would she be growing if she was all skin and bone?"

"How does Kensa feel about having a brother or sister?"

Ross chuckled and Livvy noticed the way his cheeks dimpled, and the flash of strong white teeth.

"Not best pleased, you ask me. Teasy she is, always clinging to her ma's skirts, but she'll get over it. Still the apple of my eye, anyway."

"I never doubted it. Well, you'd best get back or they'll wonder where you've got to."

"Aye, well. I'll tuck 'em in their blankets tonight and be here tomorrow, don't you fret. Best part of my day, it is. Look forward to it, you know. I feel like… like we're kind of growing a dream. Does that sound daft?"

Livvy shook her head.

"No. Not daft at all. I feel just the same way." Impulsively, she leaned in and kissed his cheek. "Thank you for… for being here for me, for trusting me with this foolishness."

He laughed at that. "Ah, I loved you when we was tiddlers, Liv. You know that, and I'd never let ye down."

"I know, Ross. I'll see you tomorrow."

"I'll be there."

King stalked the garden. It was a glorious morning, the sun warm despite the chill breeze blowing in, and yet he was still out of sorts. He'd kept away from Livvy since they'd gone to her sister-in-law's room, though he wasn't entirely certain why. Last night had been bad, the worst since he'd stopped seeing goblins and devils. He'd barely slept, anxious for no real reason other than that he needed a drink. Walsh had got up and made him tea, and sat up talking nonsense, which had irritated the hell out of him, even though he was grateful. They both knew Walsh was making sure he didn't go off searching for a drink. Livvy might be certain there was none in the house, but a thirsty man had a way of sniffing out liquor if he were desperate.

I am not drinking. I am not drinking. I. Am. Not. Drinking.

He drew in a deep breath, the cold air filling his lungs, cleansing him from the inside out. Eventually, this desperate need would dissipate, it would fade, he assured himself. He was not a feeble-minded creature. He would fight this. He was the Earl of Kingston, by God, and a bloody bottle would not rule him. Besides, he couldn't let Livvy down....

He stilled, closing his eyes as the thought settled in his chest.

I'm proud of you.

She'd said that, meant it too. He knew she'd meant it. The desire to seek her out, to pull her into his arms and kiss her and... and just the need to see her, to *talk* to her, was almost overwhelming, as bad as the need for a drink. It was worse, really, for he knew he'd stop thinking about finding a bottle the moment he was with her. God, but he wanted her company, and what manner of madness was that? Yes, he wanted her in his bed, badly, but he wanted to tease her, and hear her scold him and tease him in return. Impossible. She needed to marry money, someone who could support her and the children before that imbecile Boscawen and his feckless wife landed them all in the gutter.

What a bloody ridiculous situation. He ought to be one of the most eligible men of the *ton*, but when his father had cut him off and set out to ruin him as punishment for not marrying that poor silly child, he'd done a thorough job of it. Yes, if the man turned up his toes, King would be in clover, but as Walsh had pointed out, his father was as healthy as a horse and everyone bloody well knew it. He'd been only eighteen when he'd done his duty, got married and sired King, so he was hardly in his dotage. There had been three other children, two stillborn, both boys, and a sister who'd died before she reached her first year. Sadly for the old man, King's mother might now be infertile but was otherwise in good health or he'd have no doubt married again and kept trying. So King was the only heir and didn't that make his dear papa furious? The old bastard would likely live to be a hundred just to spite him.

Why was he considering that anyway? He didn't need prospects for marriage, he just needed enough money to live on. Even if he'd had the finances to do so, he wouldn't wish to marry. *Would he?* No, of course not. Why on earth would he do such a rash thing? He had a sudden vision of Livvy at his home, of showing her around the grounds and telling her stories about his childhood, and waking up with her beside him, and…. Good God, what the devil was wrong with him?

King paused, feeling hot and panicky.

"Pack it in, old man," he muttered under his breath. "No one is marrying anyone. She wouldn't have you even if you offered."

The truth of that was undeniable and yet still hit him in the chest with enough force to make his breath catch. He shook his head. *No. No, no, no.*

She didn't want him, and he didn't want her. Well, all right, he *wanted* her, but just for the usual reason a man wanted to dally with a pretty girl, not because he needed her, not because he….

Voices drifted towards him on the breeze from the other side of the hedge he'd been walking beside, and he let out a breath, grateful for the reprieve and the distraction from his own increasingly frantic thoughts. The voices grew closer, a man speaking now, his words indistinct.

"Best part of my day, it is. I feel like… like… a dream. Does that sound daft?"

King snorted, realising he must be about to intercept a courting couple and went to turn back, except then he recognised the woman's voice.

"No. Not daft at all. I feel just the same way."

Livvy.

His heart crashed about in his chest like the waves had done on the beach, the first time he'd kissed her. No… she had kissed him. She had kissed him, and so… and so what the devil was she up to now? He moved to a gap in the bushes and saw Livvy, one hand holding onto her bonnet, the wind tugging at her honey-coloured curls as she smiled up into the face of a bloody Adonis. Who the devil was this bastard? And… the strangest sensation filled his chest as he saw her lean in and kiss the man's cheek. It… *hurt*. He tried to breathe around the pain of it, but his lungs did not seem to want to cooperate.

He should not be here. He should not be here watching her like… like some blasted….

The Adonis gave a soft chuckle, staring at Livvy with affection. "Ah, I loved you when we was tiddlers, Liv. You know that, and I'd never let ye down."

"I know, Ross. I'll see you tomorrow."

Ross? So she was on first-name terms with him, was she?

Well, she must be to go about kissing the fellow and meeting him in secret, you imbecile.

"I'll be there."

King meant to leave. He really did. *None of his business,* he told himself. So what if she had told him she needed help and then… and then went and used that help to seduce the local… whatever he was. None of his affair. She was a free woman. Yet no matter what his intentions, or what furious words circled in his mind, his feet were planted and he stayed right where he was.

"Oh, King!" Livvy said as she turned the corner into the garden.

Her cheeks were flushed, her blue eyes bright and full of life and….

"Who is he?"

Oh, marvellous. He had not meant to say that. Now he sounded like a jealous prick.

"W-Who is who?" she asked, all wide-eyed innocence, though he could see she was nervous as hell and clearly did not want to answer the question, the little jade.

"The young Adonis you were just kissing."

The colour in her cheeks went from a pretty pink flush to a full scarlet burn, and did not make him feel any better.

"Oh," she said, standing a little taller. "That is our neighbour, Mr Moyles. I… I happened to bump into him on my walk. P-Purely by accident. He… He's like a brother to me. We used to play together as children, and it's been an age since I saw him last. It wasn't a kiss. N-Not… not a *kiss*."

"Really?" he said, folding his arms and wondering why the fact she was lying to him hurt quite so badly. They'd made each other no promises. Indeed, she'd told him from the start she had no interest in him. He had no interest in her either. None at all. He had no business giving her the third degree… and yet…. "That's why you've arranged to bump into him again at the same time tomorrow, is it?"

There was no mistaking the anger in his voice now, but Livvy just put her chin up, holding his gaze.

"It is not what you think, King, but either way, it is none of your affair."

"No. Quite right, but you might at least have been honest with me. Why not say you'd wanted to capture the heart of some local chap, rather than all this nonsense about your aunt's ball? Though how you think that fellow can save you and your family when he's clearly not got two pennies to rub together…."

"Oh, King!" she said, glaring at him in fury. "Do stop, you've not the faintest idea what you're talking about."

With blue eyes flashing, she turned on her heel, and King knew he ought to let her go, but his heart was racing, panic building in his chest at the idea she might… she might… that he might not….

"Then damned well explain it to me, Livvy," he said, grabbing hold of her arm and tugging her back around. "Explain to me how you can kiss me one day and go to him the next?"

He was overwrought, he knew he was, and he knew full well he sounded like the wronged hero in a bad melodrama, but he was quite unable to stop himself.

"King!" Livvy said, staring up at him, her eyes wide with surprise. "Why on earth do you care?"

"I don't bloody well know," he said desperately. "But either way, you'll get caught, Livvy. You'll be ruined and… and is he worth it? Will he marry you?"

Her expression softened. "Oh, you're worried for me."

"I'm bloody well not," he fumed. "I'm…."

He couldn't think of what the hell he was, so he didn't bother trying to explain it. Instead he pulled her into his arms and kissed her hard and, after a moment of resistance, she was all willingness in his arms, pliant and soft and… and had she been this way with Ross Moyles?

No. Don't think of it. Make her forget him.

Make her think of you.

Livvy pushed him away, and King let her go at once, though he did not want to. The realisation of just how much he did not want to was not a pleasant one.

"Good heavens, King, are… are you jealous?" Livvy asked, looking for all the world as if she'd said, *good heavens, King, are you the King of the Chimpanzees?* There was no possible way she could look more astonished, which was just as well as his ego could not take any more for one day.

"Don't be ridiculous," he said, just a little too quickly and with too much force. "We have already established that we don't like each other, so jealousy is out of the question. I just don't like to be misled or… damn it, Livvy, you *lied* to me!"

She stiffened at his accusation. "I did no such thing. I told you, my aunt has a New Year's Ball, I'm going to get myself a husband. What the devil did you think I was about taking all those gowns, if not for that?"

"I haven't the faintest idea. Perhaps you are planning to run away with your lover… *Ross*."

There was a flash of something in her eyes that suggested he might have pushed her over the line between anger and into incandescent fury. Well, good. Ever since he'd met the dratted woman, he'd been at the mercy of his… his *feelings*… ugh! But if he must experience all this… this unwelcome emotional *stuff*, then she dashed well had better be doing the same.

"My Lord Kingston," she said, her voice dangerously quiet. "Ross Moyles is married with a little daughter, and his wife is pregnant."

"Am I supposed to congratulate you on choosing the worst possible candidate for your illicit trysts?" he demanded.

"Oh, now you can say the word, can you?" she said, folding her arms. "Before it made you all hot and bothered."

"*Before,* I thought you were a nice young lady who was getting in over her head! Apparently, I was wrong," he retorted, the words out before he could think better of them.

She jolted as if he'd slapped her, and he was immediately aware of the fact he was a miserable brute. The possibility that he was likely not thinking clearly because he was out of his mind with resentment over her meeting another man was also a sudden consideration.

"Livvy," he said, his voice unsteady, holding out his hand to her.

She shook her head, her eyes too bright, and took a step away from him.

"Livvy, please, I… I didn't mean…."

He watched as she picked up her skirts and ran, and he could do nothing but let her go.

❧ ❧ ❧

After throwing herself down on her bed and enjoying a good cry, Livvy got up and splashed her face with cold water. Then she stomped about her room and did some aggressive tidying up while she cursed the Earl of Kingston, and thought of various ways in which he could best be punished for his outrageous behaviour. This ranged from him contracting various illnesses that would shrink his pego to the size of pea and/or covering it in large purple spots, to her being swept off her feet by the Duke of… of somewhere or other, just at the moment King realised he couldn't live without her. Both were equally satisfying, but she'd decided the duke was her favourite outcome. The vision of King on his knees and begging for her not to break his heart was too delicious not to give it her full consideration. After she had dreamily imagined various locations for his heartfelt declaration—from her front doorstep to Almack's ballroom—she was leaning towards Almack's—she felt a good deal better. Then, because she was a fair-minded sort of person, she considered that perhaps what King had seen or overhead *might* have appeared to be rather... damning. After all, she had been alone with Ross, and perhaps it had seemed rather intimate. Yes, obviously King *ought* to have given her the benefit of the doubt, but he was a man, and her—admittedly limited—experience of the male sex, was that they were inclined to be rash and emotional and not make a great deal of sense if their pride had been the least bit dented. Also, it was true that Ross Moyle's was devastatingly handsome and... and King had been jealous.

Livvy sat down on her bed with a thud, a little winded as she considered this. On pondering it further, her heart ceased its excited thudding as she realised it was only a case of possessiveness and there was nothing the least bit romantic about it. He had also been concerned for her welfare, as any friend might be, and no matter what he said, they did have a peculiar friendship of sorts, and naturally he would not like her kissing Ross so soon after she'd been kissing him. Not that she *had* been kissing Ross. If King had seen the kiss, he must have also seen that it was a chaste peck on the cheek, and nothing like the kisses they had shared. *Nothing* like. Not at all. Not even close. Like chalk and cheese. Really, a million miles away from anything she had experienced with....

Yes. Well. That was enough of that.

She let out a sigh of frustration. One thing was for certain, she could not stomp about in her room all morning. There was far too much to do. So, she took a deep breath, and headed down to the kitchen, resolved to put the Earl of Kingston out of her mind until such time as she could think sensibly about him. So possibly sometime in the next century. She'd put it in her diary.

Chapter Twelve

13th December 1818.

Things unsaid, a lot of silent longing, and stiff upper lips.

King gave himself a critical inspection in the looking-glass. Well, he looked a little less like he'd been dug up by body snatchers the week previous, but that was about the best he could say for himself. He thought perhaps he wasn't so pallid as before, and the dark circles beneath his eyes were a tad less pronounced. He'd put back on a bit of weight too, but his clothes were still loose and… and he kept remembering the ruddy good looks of Ross Moyles.

"Don't be an utter pillock," he muttered under his breath.

A knock at the door sounded and Walsh went to open it, smiling as he saw Harry's eager young face. "Ah, good morning, Mr Penrose, sir. I've some freshly starched cravats all ready and waiting for you."

Harry beamed at Walsh and came in. "Thank you, Walsh. Are you sure I'm not bothering you, my lord… I mean, King?"

"No, no," King said, smiling at the lad. "We didn't quite get the hang of it last time, did we? Practise makes perfect and all that."

King spent the next forty minutes going over the intricacies of tying the perfect cravat until Harry could do it himself with very tolerable results.

"Not bad. Not bad at all," King said, giving the boy's latest effort a slight tweak until it was just as it ought to be. "Keep practising, Harry. You'll make all the fellows wild with envy when you go back to school in the New Year."

The boy's face fell, and he coloured a little. "Oh, well, I… I'm not sure I'll be… that is, Father said I might stay at home this year, and—there's a tutor, you see—and… anyway, I'd best not take up any more of your time. Thank you again for helping me. It was jolly decent of you."

King watched him go, a heavy, impotent sensation sitting like lead in the pit of his stomach.

Walsh shook his head as he closed the door behind Harry. "Poor blighter. They ain't got the money to send him back."

"Yes, thank you, Walsh, I had figured that out myself," King snapped, and then let out a breath. "Forgive me. I…."

He did not know what to say, for he did not understand what he was doing or feeling.

"S'alright," Walsh replied gruffly. "It's frustrating. Feel it meself, truth be told. It's a nice place. Gelly's a good sort and even Spargo is all right, though he don't speak more'n two words at a time. The children are sweet natured and kind, and your Livvy...."

"She's not *my* Livvy," King said at once, stalking to the window.

He stood staring out with his hands behind his back as something twisted in his chest, and he accepted the truth of it.

"Aye, well. They don't deserve the hand they've been dealt, is all I was going to say. 'Tis a pity no one can help them. Still, perhaps Miss Penrose will find herself a husband with plump pockets who will take them on."

King snorted. "She'll find herself a husband, I don't doubt. Any man would have to be deaf, dumb, and blind not to see what they might have with her, but they'll not take the children. What newlywed wants to be lumbered with another man's get? Especially when the bloody fool is still alive and just too irresponsible to look after them as he ought. Though I don't doubt anyone wanting to court her will say the right things and make her believe they'll help."

"Reckon." Walsh nodded, his expression grim. "But that'll break her heart."

King rubbed the heel of his hand over his chest, irritable now. "Well, it's not as if there's anything I can do about it."

"No, my lord. I know it."

King made his way down to breakfast, uncertain if he was relieved or disappointed to discover Livvy wasn't there yet. He sat down with the children, somewhat disconcerted to realise he did not mind breakfasting with the nursery. Not so long ago, the idea would have horrified him.

The eldest girl was spooning porridge into the baby. King wondered if that was how she'd gotten her nickname, for she very much resembled a baby bird as she opened her mouth wide, waiting for the next spoonful to be delivered to her.

"Ing?"

King turned his attention towards George, a little startled to be addressed. At least, he thought that had been his name.

"Oh, he said your name," Harry chortled, confirming this. "Clever boy, George."

George beamed and held out his hand to King. "Ing?"

King hesitated, uncertain, but took the child's hand, wondering at how soft and warm it was as the tiny fingers closed over his much larger ones.

"Ing? Lib Lib?"

"Oh, I don't know where your aunty is," King said, though he realised he knew exactly where she was. She was with Ross Moyles. Perhaps she'd gone early this morning to warn him they must be more careful. The knowledge settled somewhere in his throat as if he'd swallowed a stone.

George let out a disconsolate huff, his lower lip pouting. King felt very much like mimicking the expression. He wondered what the children would do when their beloved aunty went off and got married and they were left to their parents' tender mercies.

"Here, George, have some bread and jam," King said briskly, taking a slice and spreading it with butter and a good amount of blackberry jam. He cut it into small pieces as he'd seen Livvy do and handed one to George.

"Ta," George said, taking it from him and beaming.

"You're welcome." King said.

He looked around at the children, at the older girls who were squabbling good-naturedly over the rules of some game they'd invented, and Jane, who was grumbling about whose turn it was to collect the eggs as it was drizzling with rain. The baby was fretting now she'd eaten all her porridge, and Harry was staring out of the window and picking at a thread on his cuff, his expression bleak.

"Damnation," King muttered under his breath. "If you'll excuse me."

He got to his feet and escaped the breakfast parlour. This wouldn't do. This simply would not do. He strode down the hall to Charlie's study, knocked twice and walked in, only to find the room empty.

"Gone to town," barked a low, rumbly voice that sounded like it had been dragged up from somewhere beneath the earth.

King spun around to discover Spargo standing in the hall behind him, as big as a boulder and about as easy to read.

"When?" King asked.

"This morning."

"When will he be back?"

A shrug was his only reply.

"Did he take his wife?"

Spargo shook his head.

King let out a sigh of frustration and wondered if perhaps that was sympathy in Spargo's eyes. The man must be well used to the vagaries of the household. It was likely why he'd given up on the art of conversation. There was no point in suggesting improvements or making plans when they were on a one-way trip to destruction. They both turned at the sound of trotters on parquet and watched as a piglet strolled along the hall towards the breakfast parlour. It had a string of pearls about its neck. Spargo didn't so much as blink. Well, at least there was something to pawn if things went to the devil, though he didn't think they'd get much for the pig.

"Oh, drat," muttered an impatient voice that King recognised from the other end of the hallway.

Spargo turned towards the sound, glanced back at King, and then strode off towards the kitchens, leaving King dithering, wondering whether he wanted to face Livvy after his outrageous behaviour the day before. Though he still hadn't decided, he couldn't seem to make himself walk away, so he was still standing by the open study door when she came down the hallway. Her hair was hanging in heavy damp curls about her face, and her skirts were sodden and dirty at the hem.

"Oh," she said on seeing him, her expression wary. "Good morning, my lord."

King gave an unhappy huff of irritation. "I see. It's that bad, is it? I suppose it must be if we're back to *my lord.* Though I suppose I can't honestly blame you."

He swallowed down the desire to demand to know where she'd been, if she'd been with Ross Moyles, and what manner of man would have her traipsing about in this weather to meet with him in secret.

"I am sorry, Livvy. I had no right—"

"No, wait," she said, stopping him in his tracks.

She moved towards him and took hold of his hands. King's heart did a peculiar little somersault in his chest as her cold fingers held his and squeezed.

"At least, no, you didn't have the right, but… but I can see how it must have looked so I wish to tell you something. I am *not* having an affair with Mr Moyles. There is nothing the least bit romantic between us, I swear to you, King."

Something in King's chest eased at her words and he nodded. "Very well."

"You believe me?"

"I do," he said, meaning it.

She wouldn't lie to him. Now that he'd had time to cool off and consider that, he felt the truth of it in his bones. Livvy wouldn't lie. Not ever.

"Thank you," she said, smiling at him.

The desire to ask her what she *was* doing was palpable. He held his tongue, yet there was something that needed saying.

"Livvy, whether there's anything between you won't matter if anyone sees you alone with him. You'll be ruined."

She nodded, but looked unconcerned. "I know, but we don't leave Boscawen's land, and you only saw us because you're a guest here. You may have realised by now, there is very little society to be had here. Especially at this time of the year."

"You don't mind it, though, do you? The quiet."

"Me?" she replied with a smile. "No. Not really. Oh, when I was young, I wished to go to town and wear pretty dresses and dance but... but I always imagined I would come back here, or somewhere very like it."

"My home is in Dorset," he blurted out, wondering why on earth he'd told her that. Whatever the reason, he didn't seem to be able to stop now he'd started and rambled on. "Wynford Castle. It's in a shocking state. I inherited it with the title but didn't pay it much mind until about five years ago. Too busy pickling my liver and creating the legend that is the King of Sin, I suppose. Except then I stopped. Drinking, that is. For a while, anyway. Obviously. I... I had some notion that.... Well, anyway, I was making improvements when my father… well, you know, the whole forced into marriage thing. I got the roof fixed, at least, but the rest is…. This place reminds me a little of home, actually."

Except that his home was empty, with big echoing rooms and no children running about. No piglets either, for that matter, or attack crows, and certainly no Livvy... and once his father had killed any hope for the future, he hadn't been able to bear going back there again.

"You love it there," Livvy said, something in her eyes he couldn't read.

King shrugged. "Once I thought that perhaps…"

He closed his mouth, uncertain what he might say if he continued. There was no point in making plans. He'd realised that a long time ago. It was foolish to think a man like him could have a home and a family of the kind that some men achieved...what dim-witted Charlie had right in front of him and was letting go to the devil, the stupid bastard. He didn't deserve what he had. Not that King did either, but at least he knew it, and knew better than to try. If a fellow was going to have a wife and children, he must be steady and dependable, and he'd better bloody well protect them with his last breath or… or what was the point, damn it?

"King?"

He looked up, only then realising he'd stopped halfway through a sentence and had been staring into space like an imbecile.

"Charlie's gone," he said, gesturing to the study.

"Oh." Livvy paled for a moment before pasting a smile to her face. "Oh, well. He'll have gone to see his man of business. Perhaps he'll come back with good news this time."

She laughed and the sound quavered, and King wanted nothing more than to put his arms about her and tell her it would be all right. Not because he wanted to kiss her, to touch her, but because he couldn't bear to see the worry in her eyes, and he longed to take it away. She rallied, though, as she always did, and smiled at him.

"I'd best go and see the children, they'll wonder where I've got to."

He nodded and watched her walk away, a sense of having come untethered nagging at him, though he didn't know why. King had always cherished his freedom, except for that brief little moment a few years ago that he'd forgotten all about but... but that had been an aberration, nothing more. It was better to be alone and free to do as he pleased. Growing up, he'd got himself out of his father's house as often as he could, staying at school for the holidays rather than going home, and he'd left for good the moment he was able. Having to explain himself to anyone, to be accountable to anyone, was abhorrent. At least having made his father too disgusted to look at him had given him freedom. Yes, freedom was everything. It was. Yet now that sense of freedom felt increasingly like loneliness, like a lack of purpose, as if he was adrift in unfriendly waters with no glimpse of safe harbour. He stared down the hallway in the direction Livvy had gone. Livvy and the children, and the bloody piglet, and… and they were nothing to do with him.

They were not his problem, and a damned good thing too, for there was sod all he could do to help them. King turned his back on them and walked off in the opposite direction.

After breakfast, Livvy took the children back upstairs and occupied them up with various endeavours. Harry had Latin exercises to complete and, though he hated it, he did not complain once. She wondered if Charlie had told him yet that he would not be returning to school and hated that Harry was probably putting a brave face on it so as not to worry her. Livvy had been helping Susan make over the blue gown King had said was too childish for her, and left the girl happily unpicking the stitching so it could be refitted to her more slender frame. Lydia and Rebecca were writing a story to read out later at bedtime, and Jane was busy doing some colourful illustrations. George was happily playing with his building bricks, and Birdie was in a sweet mood, so Livvy took her to Ceci to spend some time with her mama for a change. The baby gurgled and cooed for Ceci, which delighted her, and Livvy left them both to enjoy each other's company.

To be fair, Ceci never minded the children when they were in a good humour, and only found them fatiguing and sent them away once they'd stopped being easy company. It was the way of things, Livvy knew, and if they'd had a governess and a nursery maid... No, she decided, that would be worse. She and Charlie had experienced both sides of such women, from the sweet and docile but ineffectual, to the downright cruel. She'd never leave the children to people she did not know and trust. What if she wasn't here, though? What if she married a man who would support the children, but only at a distance? What if....

"Stop it," she muttered under her breath. Likely she would not marry at all, so it was a moot point. Eventually Charlie would realise they could no longer afford to live here. They would have to let Spargo and Gelly go and let out the house, though who on earth would want it in this sorry state she couldn't imagine. She closed her eyes and told herself not to be foolish. It was a beautiful property, even in such disrepair. No doubt some nobleman friend of Charlie's would enjoy coming here to rusticate and sea bathe and enjoy the glorious countryside, just like King had.

King.

She would not think of him. She would not think of him standing in the hall, of his imposing height and his broad shoulders and the soft concern in his dark eyes, and the way everything seemed as if it would be all right when she was with him—even though that was nonsense. Perhaps if things had been different, if his father hadn't cut him off, he might have come here, and she might have helped him, and he might have helped her….

"Stop it," Livvy said again, angry now as she blinked back tears.

She paused in the corridor, staring out of the window at the grey sky and the darker grey of the sea underlining the horizon. She could see white horses on the waves and hear the distant crash as they thundered to shore. Reality was as grey as the view beyond the window, and she'd be a fool not to face up to it. She'd heard what King hadn't said, that there had been a time when he'd hoped for a wife, for a family, but his father had made it impossible. Sooner or later, he would be forced to marry the girl the marquess had chosen for him, but he was waiting until such a time as he'd feel less of a monster to give in. No doubt when the girl was in her twenties, he'd have to let his father win. There must be an heir to the title, after all, and he couldn't live on fresh air any more than they could. She felt certain his decision had made him despair, had driven him to drink, but with just a little help he'd pulled back before it was too late. He was a strong man, stronger than he knew himself if she had the right of it, honourable too despite his reputation, despite his own estimation of his character. King would survive; he might even be happy one day. She hoped so. She hoped so very much.

Livvy stared at the sea for a while longer, allowing it to calm her jagged mind, to smooth over the sharp edges of jealousy and resentment and quiet the erratic thoughts that made her bad tempered and restless. As she stood there, she heard music and believed at first she had imagined it. Turning towards the stairs she followed the sound, realising it was coming from the back parlour where their ancient piano was. Not that she'd ever heard it produce a sound like this before. The children practised on it and Livvy herself could manage a few lively songs for people to dance to, but Ceci was the only one who could play with any skill, when she could be roused to do so. This, though... this was something else.

Though she knew she ought not, knew her emotions were too near the surface to be anywhere near him, Livvy hurried towards the sound. For there was only one person in the house who could be playing such music, such a beautiful, sorrowful melody that made her want to cry and laugh all at the same time, and she had to see him. She wanted to see him so badly she knew it was a terrible, dangerous idea, but she was going to do it anyway.

It was in her nature to be honest with herself, after all, and honestly, nothing could have kept her away.

Chapter Thirteen

13th December 1818.

Music and melody and the means of undoing an unhappy earl.

King had found the piano by chance, some happy stroke of luck that he was not about to question, though why it hadn't been pawned already he didn't know. Once Walsh had told him of the family's situation, King had noticed the spaces. There were picture-frame-shaped gaps on the walls, the paint or wall hanging exposed beneath a far brighter shade than elsewhere as the family's paintings had been sold off. In every room there was a space, sometimes several, where perhaps there had been a chair or a pretty piece of furniture. The more he looked about the place, the more he saw, and yes, he was an appalling guest, the nosy kind, poking his beak in where it wasn't wanted. There were too many rooms stripped bare, though, the layers being peeled away one by one. Lady Boscawen's bedroom was the only one that remained untouched. He could see it happening to

Livvy, too, could see the strain of hoping when experience had taught her not to be so foolish. Yet she kept on, kept hoping for better, striving for better, and not for herself but for those children whom she loved like her own, and whom she deserved more than their blessed mother did.

Something like rage swelled in his chest and he tamped it down. Not his fight. Even if it were, there was nothing he could do, nothing he could offer.

He sat down at the piano and smoothed his fingers over the keys, feeling a little of the tension in his shoulders ease as he did so. To his relief, and somewhat to his surprise, the piano was well tuned and cared for, and he ran through a few well-loved pieces before settling on something more personal and closer to his heart. Foolish of him, but he *was* a fool. He'd always been a fool, a dreamer, an idealist, until his father had finally taught him the lesson King had resisted learning, once and for all. Either he was the man the marquess wished him to be, or he was nothing. Anything King tried for that was his own, his father destroyed. Yet, he couldn't destroy this. He could take back the piano, which had been a gift to him as a very young man, but not the music he'd written himself. That was his own, except it didn't feel like it was his any longer. When he'd written it, he'd been foolish enough to hope, to hold on to a wistful longing, to believe there might be something more in his future, something rare and bright and hard to find, but he'd had that glimmer in the darkness. He'd clung to the fragile hope that he might find it for as long as he could. It had been lost to him too long ago now, drowned it in brandy as he let himself sink into the darker side of life, and yet here it was again, mocking him now, taunting him. Not that it mattered. He might as well never have seen it, seen *her,* for all the good it would do him.

He lost himself in the music, closing his eyes and letting it sweep him up and carry him away. When he played nothing could reach him, nothing could touch him. Prinny himself could have come and sat down beside him, and he wouldn't have batted an eyelid. Yet he knew when she opened the door, though she didn't make a sound. He knew it was her, though the door was at his back. He felt her presence like the sun warming his face on a frosty day, like the room had lit up with the glow of her. Oh, for pity's sake, how nauseating. He was turning into a bloody maudlin poet. Someone shoot him, for the love of God, and put him out of his misery.

"I've never heard anything so beautiful," she said, standing at his shoulder.

"You don't get out much," he replied dryly.

She gave an impatient tut but ignored the comment. "Who is it by? I don't recognise it at all."

King shrugged. "Don't remember."

Livvy moved around the piano and sat down on the stool beside him, forcing him to shove up a bit to give her room. He huffed but did not stop playing, did not look at her, could not look at her. She sat close, too close, the warmth of her body like sitting too near to open flame. A flush of heat and want burned up the back of his neck and he tried to concentrate on the music. He could feel her looking at him, as if she had peered inside his brain and seen the tangled mess churning inside his head.

"You wrote it."

He said nothing, and she gave a triumphant laugh.

"I knew it. You have hidden depths, don't you, King? There you are, drinking and carousing and making all the world believe you the epitome of depravity, when all along…"

He halted abruptly and reached for her. His hands sank into the warm silk of her hair and he kissed her, hard and desperate and out of control. She made a little squeak of surprise and then, like always, she softened in his arms, utterly pliant, perfectly biddable, wrapping her arms about his neck and pressing closer. The fierce, prickly Miss Penrose was entirely his the moment he touched her and, oh God, didn't that knowledge make him wild? Was it just him? Would she be this way for any man who touched her? *No.* No, she would not. She liked him, she… they… there was *something* between them, though he hadn't the faintest idea what.

Liar.

"Oh, King," she murmured, her voice so soft and sweet and loving, her hands in his hair as he kissed a path down her neck.

He pulled back, staring at her in alarm. Her blue eyes were hazy, gazing up at him like… like…. His heart crashed against his ribs like a trapped bird colliding against a closed window over and over, desperate for escape.

"Don't," he said, shaking his head. "Don't look at me like that." Because he wasn't what she needed, not even close. He'd ruined his own life, he'd not do it to Livvy too. He could never deserve the look he'd seen in her eyes.

"L-Like what?" she said, and yet he saw her face shutter up and become guarded at once, and something inside of him howled with misery. Her chin went up. "I'm merely following your lead. You're supposed to be teaching me how to seduce myself a husband, aren't you? I've had very little in the way of help and advice so far."

"You seem to be doing well enough," he said darkly, avoiding her gaze, knowing she was lying the same as he was. "And stop painting me in the colours of a good man. Just because I can play the blasted piano does not mean I have hidden depths. It is merely another means to get me what I want, another means of baiting the hook. The ladies love it, you see, as you have so clearly demonstrated."

He gave a bitter laugh at the outrage in her eyes.

"I see," she said, colouring a little.

"Yes, Livvy, now you see. My reputation sums me up to a nicety, I assure you, and you put yourself in harm's way every time you are alone with me. What little shred of honour I possess is the only thing keeping me from taking what you are apparently all too willing to give. If this were not my friend's home, to whom I owe a great debt, I would take it without a second thought."

There was a taut silence during which King prayed for her to slap him or curse him, or run away and slam the door, anything but sit there in silence. Every second that ticked by was a second closer to him breaking, begging her forgiveness, and kissing her again, and then… and then where would they be?

"Nonetheless, you promised to help me," she said, stubborn to the last. "So, playing the piano acts like catnip upon the ladies, does it? I wonder, does it work for gentlemen too? For I confess I have no great skill."

Thank God, King thought wildly, for he needed a reason not to want her, a reason to force himself to move away and put space between them. Perhaps if she murdered a piece of music, something delicate and beautiful, he'd be so offended by the assault he'd be able to think straight again, for it hadn't escaped his notice that she had not contradicted his statement. She was willing, and he could take her innocence if he chose to. A prickle of sweat broke out over his flesh.

"Show me," he said gruffly, gesturing to the keys.

He watched, intrigued, as she gathered herself and settled her fingers on the keys, and then broke into a stirring rendition of *No One Shall Govern Me.*

King's mouth fell open in surprise as Livvy's voice—by no means refined—but clear and strong, rang out through the room.

When young and thoughtless, Laura said

No one shall win my heart;

But little dreamt the simple maid,

Of love's delusive art.

At ball or play she'd flirt away and ever giddy be,

But always said, I ne'er shall wed, no one shall govern me. No, no, no. No, no, no. No one shall govern me.

But time on airy pinions flew

And Laura's charms decay'd;

Too soon, alas! The damsel grew.

A pettish, pert old maid.

At ball or play no longer gay, Poor Laura, now you'll see;

Nor does she cry, for reasons why, No one shall govern me.

No, no, no. No, no, no. No one shall govern me.

A lesson learn, ye ladies fair,

From Laura's wretched fate;

Lest you, like her, should in despair

Repent, Alas! Too late.

She finished with a flourish and a crash of keys that made King's ears ring and he sat staring at her, stunned into silence. There was a twinkle in her eyes and a slight twitch to her lips that told him she knew exactly what she'd been about. He wanted so badly to laugh and then to kiss her until neither of them could remember their names that he felt quite winded. But that way lay madness.

"Well," he said, once he could find words to form a stiff enough reply. "That should scare off any right thinking male within a ten mile radius."

"Oh?" Livvy said, all innocence and wide eyes. "Do you think so? I thought it rather appropriate, what with the description of *a pettish, pert old maid.* Fits me to a nicety, does it not?"

King gritted his teeth, aware of what she was doing.

"No," he said evenly. "But they'll all think it does with a performance like that, as you well know."

"Forgive me, King." And now she was all repentance, sighing with regret. "You see, I am a hopeless case. So... no piano. I cannot bait a hook to catch my husband, at least not with music. What next, then? Teach me all the tricks so I may play him like a fiddle. That is the expression, I think? I've never acted the fortune hunter before, so you'll forgive me for not knowing all the cant just yet, but fear not, I'm a quick study."

Something in King's gut twisted. He stared down at the keys of the piano, struggling to keep his breathing even. "You're not a fortune hunter, Livvy, and you're not... not like *me.* This isn't for your own pleasure, or even your own security. You've a nobler cause, I know that. Don't think that I don't."

There was another silence, this one fragile, with too much exposed between them.

The next time she spoke her voice was quiet, soft, but with more than a hint of teasing. "My goodness, King. Was that *another* compliment?"

He was grateful for the levity of the comment and laughed as he was supposed to. "Possibly. I must be feverish again."

"The only likely explanation," she agreed.

"I'd better have a lie down."

"Let me come."

King gasped and even Livvy looked shocked, but she held his gaze, not turning away.

"Why not?" she asked him, as if there weren't a million answers he could give. "I'm not a pretty young thing whose beauty and innocence is going to make a man want me. You said yourself I need to take another tack. So… why not this one? Teach me, King. I know you can. Teach me how to make a man wild with passion."

King's mind blanked and in his panic, he evaded in the only way he knew how by retreating into sarcasm. "At this hour of the morning? No man with an ounce of sense would have even broken his fast by now. You'll only make him wild with the need for another hour of sleep and possibly a hair of the dog that bit him."

Livvy glowered at him. "Be serious. I need help."

"You need to be spanked and told to behave like a good girl!" King retorted, leaping to his feet, and putting distance between them.

"Don't patronise me," she snapped back, her blue eyes flashing.

"Don't ask me to set you on the road to ruin, then."

"Why not?" she demanded tartly as she folded her arms. "You seem to be enjoying the scenic route to the same destination."

Desire burned beneath his skin, his muscles taut with wanting, his entire being aware of her, aware of what she was offering him. *Take it,* his mind and body demanded in complete accord. *She's offering herself up like the fatted calf. Take it all.* His heart, however, was having none of it. *No, this isn't what she wants, it isn't what you want. You're both lonely and afraid and desperate. This is desperate. This is wrong.* Oh, God, but he wanted her.

"*I* won't be ruined by taking that road," he growled, determined to keep from giving in to temptation, for once in his sorry life.

Livvy snorted. "No, you'll be dead."

His temper unravelled, fuelled by desire and frustration, and his words were cruel and hard and unthinking. "That's unlikely, as some harpy has hidden anything remotely alcoholic, and there's nothing resembling a comely wench for miles. That doesn't mean I'm desperate enough to seduce my friend's plain spinster sister."

Oh, God. The look in her eyes... and yet, perhaps that was the only way to make her stop, to make her believe….

"Oh," her voice quavered, and his heart ached. It was the beach all over again and he could not allow her to believe herself undesirable.

"Damnation, Livvy, I didn't mean that. You know I didn't. Why won't you let me be?"

"Because I'm desperate," she whispered. "We all are. We're going to lose our home, everything, unless I marry well, and I don't think anyone is going to want me. Not ever. Not at this stupid ball and not for the rest of my life, but… but I feel like maybe… maybe you do, and… and I want to know how it feels to be wanted, King. Just for a moment."

King sank his fingers into his hair, pulling on it in frustration. "Livvy, you little fool. If you show even a glimpse of the woman I have come to know these past weeks at that wretched ball, you'll have men falling at your feet. Some of them may even be good, decent men who will want you, want to marry you, and then you'll regret…."

"No." She shook her head, gazing at him. "No, I shan't regret it. Not ever. No matter what happens."

King closed his eyes, unable to look at her, to see the sincerity in her eyes, the hope, and all the things he could not give her.

"And what will you do on your wedding night when your husband realises you're not a virgin? Will you pretend it's your first time?"

"N-No, of course not. I should never be so deceitful."

"When, then, Livvy? After he's married you and it's too late? Or before? Don't you see? It will make him doubt you, doubt the kind of woman you are. It might ruin your chances."

He could see his words had struck home, and he did not know whether to breathe a sigh of relief or weep. No, strike that, weeping was certainly his favourite plan, along with howling with rage and frustration and drinking himself into an early grave. Damn it, no. No. He was not going to drink.

I am not drinking.

King hauled in an uneven breath, waiting only for Livvy to tell him she'd come to her senses before he made his escape. Then he'd go for a walk, or perhaps a swim. Yes, a swim in the sea should just be icy enough to cool his ardour. Perhaps then he'd be able to think straight again; perhaps he'd drown and end this misery now before it got worse. For it *would* get worse. He would have to leave sooner or later, and one day he'd read an announcement in the paper with details of her marriage to some lucky bastard who would not deserve her any more than King did.

"Well, you have a point."

King nodded, letting her words wash over him, so that he didn't really register the next ones until they shot straight to his groin like a lightning strike.

"But surely there is pleasure to be had without… you know, taking my… my maidenhead? We could do that, couldn't we? *Please*?"

Oh, damn him to hell.

She'd said, *please.*

Please.

Holy God and all his angels.

He was doomed.

Chapter Fourteen

13th December 1818.

Plans for seduction, George makes a conquest, and an unexpected visitor.

Livvy watched as the Earl of Kingston ran away. Again.

Were all libertines so highly strung? Honestly, it was infuriating that he kept stopping just when things were getting interesting. Only, she'd felt the desperation in his kiss, seen the heat in his eyes. For a moment she had doubted it when he'd spoken to her so cruelly, but he'd not been able to follow it through. He'd capitulated almost immediately, the moment he'd seen the hurt in her eyes, and that's when Livvy had known for certain. The Earl of Kingston was a good man, an honourable man, and he liked her, maybe he even cared for her, just a little, but more than that… he wanted her.

The knowledge was powerful. It simmered beneath her skin, making her too aware of all the empty spaces inside her. She felt like the damned house, decaying from neglect and lack of care and increasingly empty as everything of value was stripped from her. If she chose this, it would be for herself. She would marry any man who met her *increasingly* low standards—providing he wasn't cruel and didn't make her flesh creep—if it meant security for the children. If, as she suspected, no one would have her as she had no dowry and was getting too long in the tooth to ensure the production of enough babies to provide a boy, then she would stay with the children and do whatever it took to keep everyone together and safe and well. In all of that there was nothing for herself, besides providing for and being with her nieces and nephews whom she quite obviously doted on. But there was no hope for love or romance or her own happiness, so… why not? Why should she not have this and… and yes, damn it, use the experience to make a man of her choosing, choose her.

She knew it could not be King. She knew that. Her heart wanted to shrivel and die whenever she made herself face the truth, but she did know that. He had no money, and even if by some miracle he chose her, his father would never forgive him. She could never ask that of him. No, King could not help her and the children, even if he wanted to, and… and she did not think he wanted to. Oh, he was far kinder and gentler than he wished anyone to know and she knew their situation pained him, but wishing he could help and wanting to take on another man's family, children that weren't even hers…. No. No man in their right mind would want that. A fact which made the whole business of her aunt's party utterly pointless, but….

Livvy sighed and put her head in her hands. A smile tugged at her lips as she remembered the panic in King's expression when she'd asked him to take her to bed. His beautiful eyes had widened with alarm and grown as dark as a night sky, and she knew he would say yes. Which was, of course, why he'd run away. He'd hope she'd not have the nerve to go through with it and simply avoid her until she came to her senses. Except that Livvy felt like she had only come to her senses in these past few days. She had never really known what it was she wanted, let alone who, and… and now she did. Even if it was beyond her grasp, even if *he* was beyond her grasp and she wanted to sob for the impossibility of it, there was happiness too. It was a wistful, hopeless kind of happiness perhaps, but the dream was hers at least. It was more than she'd ever had before. So, if King was waiting for her to behave like a young lady ought to and act with good sense and decorum, well… he was going to be sorely disappointed.

"So, this is where you're hiding, is it?"

King looked up with a scowl to see Walsh standing with legs akimbo, arms crossed and a look of unrepressed merriment in his eyes which was, frankly, irritating.

"I am not hiding," King retorted, now both lying *and* hiding. Oh, bloody hell.

Walsh gave George, who was sitting on the floor beside King, a pointed look.

"Do you believe him, lad?"

"Ing?" George said, giving King a reassuring pat. "Pego."

Walsh snorted. "Aye, reckon so."

King glowered at his upstart valet and tried to remember why he kept him on and then remembered the poor bastard had been on half wages for months and kept his mouth shut. Perhaps George had a point. He gathered up the scattered bricks and began setting one on top of the other for perhaps the twentieth time that day, but George never seemed to tire of knocking them over again. He would shriek with laughter and clap his hands together with delight, and King wondered if he'd ever been that easy to please. Had he ever been so perfectly happy without being off his head drunk or wreathed in clouds of opium smoke? If he had, he certainly couldn't remember it.

He looked up at a decisive *tap, tap* at the window, to see Mr Moon's beady eye regarding him through the glass. King repressed a shudder.

"Don't you dare," he said to Walsh as the fellow moved towards the window. "The bloody thing is evil. It nearly took my finger off."

"Ing," George said soothingly, stroking his hand. "Gog, bite... oof, oof."

He pointed at the crow.

"Yes, he did bite," King said indignantly. "But he isn't a dog, George. It's a bird... er... a crow. Remember. Ke Re Ow."

"Gog?" George asked.

"No. Not a dog."

George gave a disconsolate sigh. So King turned the child's attention to the tower of bricks he'd just finished. "Look what I built, George, isn't it—"

George knocked the tower over, and the blocks crashed to the floor, scattering across the rug and clattering over the parquet beyond.

"--grand?," King finished, shaking his head and pretending to look sorrowful, which only delighted George all the more, naturally.

The little boy cackled with laughter, rocking back and forth and grabbing at his toes, almost toppling over backwards.

"Yes, yes, laugh at my misfortune why don't you? The universe seems to enjoy the same sense of humour as you do, my lad," he grumbled, reaching for the bricks again.

Walsh scuttled about the room too, gathering the bricks up and setting them down in front of King. Rather to King's surprise, Walsh deigned to sit on the floor too, and the two of them rebuilt the tower while George looked on with anticipation shining in his eyes.

"So, how did you come to be babysitting?" Walsh asked.

King frowned. "I'm not entirely certain. The eldest girl, Susan, is it? She was carrying him about, but then that blasted piglet ran past, apparently wearing the sash of her new dress. Well, I shouldn't like to be whoever was responsible for putting it on the creature, I can tell you. Set off like a little dervish, she did. So the next thing I know, George here is thrust at me, and she goes off in hot pursuit."

Walsh gave a bark of laughter and then narrowed his eyes at King. "So, why didn't you give him to one of the others or take him to the kitchen? Gelly would have taken the lad off your hands."

"I don't know," King said with a huff. "I couldn't be bothered. Besides, George has provided the most sensible conversation I've had since I got here."

"Ing? Where is Libby?" George asked, his expression grave, a little frown on his sweetly rounded face.

"Yes, King, where's Livvy?" Walsh asked, a knowing glint in his eyes.

King glowered at him. "Far from me, if she's got an ounce of sense."

"Where we find Libby, Lib, Lib?" George said, pointing at the door.

"I don't know, George," King replied, touching the child's cheek and wondering at how soft it was. "Shall I take you to Gelly? She might know."

"Gelly in the kitchen. Gelly got cake!" George said, grinning broadly and scrambling to his feet.

"That's a yes, then," King said, chuckling. He put out his hand to George, but George lifted both arms towards him.

"Up," he said, a determined glint in his eyes.

King hesitated. "Oh, very well, but no tugging on my cravat, do you hear?"

"No vat," George said solemnly, shaking his head.

King laughed and lifted the little boy up.

"Close enough, old man," he said, a little startled when the child curled his arms about his neck, crushing his cravat, naturally. King stilled, an odd sensation kicking about behind his ribs.

"That suits you, my lord. If you don't mind me observing it," Walsh said, smiling.

"What?" King looked back at his valet, too distracted to have heard his comment.

"You'd make a good father, I reckon. Pity you dislike the idea so much."

"Yes, well, I *do,*" King replied at once, almost angry now, frowning at Walsh.

"Ing?" George said, anxiety in his voice.

King let out a breath. "Sorry, George. Come along. Let's go and find Gelly and have some cake."

❧ ❧ ❧

"Need to be quick, Miss. Those clouds…." Spargo nodded at the darkening sky overhead.

"I will," Livvy nodded, jumping down from the dog cart.

She didn't bother pointing out she didn't have enough money to take long. Spargo knew it. As it was, having to spend coin on fripperies made her stomach turn, but she needed some ribbon and thread to finish making over Ceci's old gowns, and so it was rather more imperative than perhaps it appeared.

The door to the haberdasher's opened with a tinkling of the overhead bell, and Livvy smiled at Mrs Cardy.

"Miss Penrose," the woman said, her rosy apple cheeks dimpling with pleasure at the sight of Livvy. "I swear, I thought you'd forgotten us it's been so long."

"As if I could do such a thing, Mrs Cardy, and it has been too long. I hope you can forgive me. What with the children and one thing and another... well, I don't know where the time goes."

Mrs Cardy laughed. "Oh, I know it, and that brood is surely a handful. His lordship is lucky to have such a sister, though no doubt he must get used to the lack of you soon enough."

Livvy stilled, frowning in confusion. "Oh, whyever would he need to do that?"

"Oh." Mrs Cardy's rosy cheeks turned a slightly darker shade. "Forgive me, Miss Penrose, if I spoke out of turn only... well, it's all anyone can speak of at present."

"What is?" Livvy demanded, her stomach twisting with an unpleasant sense of certainty that she would not like Mrs Cardy's next words at all.

"Why that... that you and Mr Skewes...."

It was sometimes exhausting to be proven right all the time.

Livvy's jaw was so tight it was an effort to speak at all, but she forced her voice to remain calm and pleasant. "And where, pray, did this piece of nonsense spring from?"

Mrs Cardy looked truly unhappy now and Livvy felt bad for making the woman so uncomfortable, but really, it was too much to be borne. If her brother had been spreading the news when he knew damn well….

"Well, it were Mr Skewes himself what said it, or I'd have never… well, he didn't say it outright but he… intimated that…." Poor Mrs Cardy was hot and flustered now and looked very much as if she wanted to run from the room.

"Mr Skewes implied that… that we were engaged?" Livvy said, breathless but determined to know exactly what had been said.

"Yes, Miss Penrose."

"I see." Livvy's stomach was a churning mass of fury. "Well, Mrs Cardy, you have my permission to refute that rumour in the strongest possible terms. Not only am I not engaged to Mr Skewes, having never been asked, but I have no intention of *ever* becoming engaged to Mr Skewes, not even if he was the last eligible man in the country. I do hope that clarifies things."

"Oh, yes, Miss," Mrs Cardy said with an earnest nod, wringing her apron between anxious fingers, her usually cheerful countenance at once too pale and flushed at the same time.

Livvy let out a breath. She did not wish to punish the poor woman for something that was not in the least her fault and reached out to take Mrs Cardy's hand. "Don't fret, Mrs Cardy. I know you would never gossip about me, but there are those, and…. Well, anyway. Do not disturb yourself, I am not the least bit cross with you. Indeed, it is a pleasure as always. Now, I have a few items I must get, but I cannot linger."

"Oh, yes," Mrs Cardy said, her relief palpable. "I can see the skies growing darker as we speak, so you just give me that list of yours and it will be done in a trice, and don't you worry. I'll make sure I set everyone straight, and with pleasure too."

By the time Livvy exited the shop, she was seething with fury, though she had taken pains to ensure Mrs Cardy was unaware of it. Spargo, however, was family.

"Oh!" she fumed as she climbed back into the cart. "You'll never believe what that wretched man has done."

Spargo turned his head, eyes narrowing under his grizzled eyebrows.

"Mr Skewes," Livvy said, correctly interpreting Spargo's expression as a request for further information. "Has given everyone the impression we are engaged to be married.

Spargo sucked air in between his teeth and shook his head.

"Bleddy tuss," he muttered.

"Quite," Livvy replied. "If I were a man, I'd… I'd draw his cork."

"Calm, now, Miss," Spargo said, his gravelly voice low and soothing. "Won't do no good. Set 'em straight, diddy?"

"Yes, I did. I told Mrs Cardy in no uncertain terms and gave her permission to tell anyone else labouring under the same delusion. I can only hope it gets back to Mr Skewes, and he takes the hint, once and for all."

Spargo made a disparaging sound that Livvy did not find reassuring but understood to be true herself. Mr Skewes had decided to have her and believed it only a matter of time before she came to her senses. Not that he'd ever asked her to marry him. She suspected he wouldn't go that far all the time he knew he'd be rejected, but he believed she would change her mind, and she knew why that was. Bloody Charlie had likely told the man he need only wait her out. He was betting on the fact that Livvy would do the decent thing to save the family. Well, she would, but not with Mr Skewes. There was not much she wouldn't do for them, but she drew the line at selling her soul to the devil. Why she was being so dramatic she did not know, only that the idea made her breathless and panicky as nothing else could.

They made it back to the house, just as the heavens opened and Livvy hurried to the kitchen, eager for the comforts of home and a good hot cup of tea.

By late afternoon, Livvy had just about calmed herself, though only if she kept busy and her thoughts away from Mr Skewes. Once she'd peeled potatoes and set them in water for that night's dinner to help Gelly out, she had spent some time watching the deluge beyond the window before stirring herself to be more productive. Though it had been some time since they could employ a full staff, it was wash day tomorrow and a couple of laundry maids came up from the village to do the weekly wash. Livvy went in search of Sarah, their one remaining full-time maid, to ensure she had stripped the beds and put clean sheets on. Sarah was loyal, and more importantly cheap, but she was also a feather-brain who would forget what day it was if Livvy didn't constantly remind her. Relieved to discover Sarah had excelled herself, Livvy praised the girl for her hard work and was on her way to the laundry to check the dirty linen had been correctly sorted when there was a sharp knock at the front door.

Good heavens. What fool would be out and about in this weather? Though as Livvy glanced out the window on the way to the door, she realised the rain had cleared up since last she looked. Still, it was a wet, murky kind of day and best spent indoors. Whoever it was must have been determined indeed. That made her stomach knot, and she almost called for Spargo to open the door instead before scolding herself for being a ninny. She immediately regretted her bravery on coming face-to-face with Mr Skewes.

All the outraged fury she had felt in the haberdashers, when Mrs Cardy had told her she was the subject of local gossip, coalesced into a cold, slimy lump in her belly. It was always like this with Mr Skewes. He always wrong-footed her, as though she'd done something she ought not and as if… as if she were somehow lacking, a disappointment. It was a sensation she resented but could not shake off.

"Mr Skewes," she said woodenly, remembering she wanted to give the man a piece of her mind, but he had taken her by surprise, and she was unprepared.

"Do you think I might come in?" he said politely, just a slight quirk of his eyebrow indicating that good manners suggested she ought to have invited him by now.

The urge to deny him made her heart skitter with anxiety, but Charlie would be furious if he discovered she'd shut the door in their neighbour's face, and it wasn't her house.

Silently, Livvy stood back and allowed Mr Skewes to enter.

"Well, Livvy," Mr Skewes said. "You have set the cat among the pigeons, but I suppose that was your intention."

Livvy gaped at him, indignant in the first place that he'd addressed her so informally despite her reminding him before now she had not given him leave to use her Christian name. In the second place... *she'd* set the cat among the pigeons?

She crossed her arms, mostly so he could not see her hands trembling. Why did this wretched man always make her feel so... so... weak and uncertain? This was why she hated him so, she realised. She never doubted herself, *never*. Oh, sometimes she took time to determine the best course of action, but she always acted decisively and owned up to her mistakes if she got it wrong. It was better to act than dither, in her view, but this man... this man made her question everything about herself, and she despised him for it.

"If you mean to say it was my intention to ensure everyone knew the truth, then yes, Mr Skewes. I imagine it was."

Mr Skewes' mouth tilted up at the corner and Livvy wished for the thousandth time he was not so handsome. He had taken his hat off now to reveal thick hair of a soft brown with lighter shades of gold where the sun had touched it. His jaw was strong and his nose straight, and he was tall and well made. Everyone thought well of him, everyone thought her a crotchety, foolish… *petty pert old maid.* The words to *No One Shall Govern Me* came back to her, and she remembered singing it to King. She had wondered what his reaction would be to it, and as ever he had surprised her.

You're not a fortune hunter, Livvy, and you're not… not like me. This isn't for your own pleasure, or even your own security. You've a nobler cause, I know that. Don't think that I don't.

A nobler cause. King knew what she was doing, and why, but he would not fault her for not grasping at Mr Skewes' offer. She was not a fortune hunter, but there had to be some measure of peace in her decision. She must at least feel safe, secure, must know the children were too, and there was nothing about this man that made her feel that way. He was the kind of man that crushed your spirit, smiling sweetly all the while.

"Ah, Livvy, I admire your courage. I always have. Everyone knows this place only keeps going because of you, but I'm afraid it is time you stopped fighting."

His voice was gentle, almost apologetic, and a shiver ran down Livvy's spine.

"For the last time, Mr Skewes, you will address me as Miss Penrose, and I don't have the faintest idea what you mean."

Somehow, the words were forceful enough, but she was aware of the tremor of fear beneath them. She suspected Skewes heard it too, for there was a satisfied glint in his pale blue eyes. Yes, he liked that. He liked the fact that she was afraid.

He gave her an assessing look, and then his tone became brisk and businesslike. "Your brother is in debt. He has invested in the most ridiculous schemes, as I'm sure you are aware, but perhaps you do not know that he has compounded the problem with yet another get rich quick scheme which has also failed. He told me he would be away for a few days, for he must do what he can to placate those he cannot pay. In short, Boscawen suggested I use this time to bring you to your senses. I can make it all go away, Livvy. I can pay his debts, the children can remain in their own home, Harry can go back to school, and the girls can have their season. All you need to do, is say yes."

Livvy felt as though the world had tilted, as though everything had shifted, and she could not keep her balance. She stumbled back, dizzy with shock, and felt a strong arm at her elbow, steadying her.

"Miss Penrose, are you quite well? You look rather peaked." King said, his dark eyes moving from her to Mr Skewes.

She did not know if he had heard their conversation, but something in his expression told her he had taken an instant dislike to Mr Skewes. Whatever his reasons for it, she felt a sudden surge of vindication. King felt it too. He wasn't the kind of man who could be taken in with polite words and smiles. He saw the truth in people, in himself. Even when it was ugly, King didn't look away. In that moment she could have kissed him, almost did, just for the satisfaction of seeing the look on that odious man's face.

"No, I'm afraid I don't feel terribly well," Livvy said, meeting those dark eyes and hoping he understood her gratitude. She was not a feeble creature, she never had been, but she had not been prepared for this. Next time, she would be ready.

"I do not believe I've had the pleasure, sir," Mr Skewes said, his voice cool with displeasure.

"*My lord*," King corrected, and Livvy watched with delight as he held Mr Skewes' gaze, a sardonic smile playing at his lips.

"My lord," Livvy said, suddenly relishing the moment. "Allow me to introduce our neighbour, Mr Skewes. Mr Skewes, The Earl of Kingston."

Livvy had never believed herself to be a vindictive creature, and she loathed it when people of higher station looked down upon those they considered beneath them, but she was honest enough to admit that watching Mr Skewes bow— albeit grudgingly—to King, was one of the most satisfying moments of her life. Skewes had a way of being so precisely polite and attentive to those beneath his station that it smacked of condescension, though sometimes Livvy thought she was the only person who saw it. He believed himself better than most everyone around here, though, and certainly better than Boscawen despite his title, because he thought her brother was a fool. Sadly, she could not gainsay him on that point.

King, however, was not a fool.

"If you will excuse me, Mr Skewes," Livvy said, urgently needing to be away from him now. "But I am feeling rather unwell."

"Livvy," Mr Skewes said, a warning tone to his voice that made Livvy's skin prickle and her heart pick up speed.

"*Miss Penrose* is indisposed, Mr Skewes," King said, taking a step closer to the man and for the first time Livvy truly appreciated his height and breadth. He could be intimidating when he put his mind to it, she realised, and yet he had never once made her feel anything but secure, even when he was angry with her. She had never once doubted her safety or feared his temper, despite his reputation. "Do go and rest now, Miss Penrose. I shall send Lady Boscawen to you directly after I have shown Mr Skewes out."

He gestured to the front door, leaving Skewes no other option but to leave.

Livvy saw the way Mr Skewes' jaw set, saw the furious glint in his eyes as he addressed her. "We shall speak again, when you are feeling more composed and able to listen to reason," Mr Skewes promised, sketched a half-hearted bow, and stalked away.

She couldn't speak for a long moment after the door had closed, just stood there, staring at it, wondering what she might have said or done if King had not been there to give her a moment's respite.

"Come along," he said, his voice gentle, and he took her arm and guided her to the parlour. He sat her down in a chair by the hearth before ringing the bell and then stooped to stir up the embers and get the fire blazing again.

Spargo appeared a moment later.

"Mr Skewes just called on Miss Penrose," King said with no preamble. "I do not believe she wishes for a repeat of the experience. In the future, you alone will answer the door and under no circumstances is the lady at home unless she expressly tells you otherwise."

"Zackly," Spargo said at once with a determined nod, before turning to Livvy. "Miss… I were in the kitchens…."

Livvy shook her head and returned a wan smile. "It was my own fault. I ought not have answered the door. After this morning I should have known what I was in for, and you cannot be in two places at once. Goodness knows you do too much for us as it is."

Spargo rubbed the back of his neck, looking miserable and awkward.

"Might we have some tea, and perhaps some of Gelly's excellent cake, if there is any?" King suggested.

Spargo nodded at once, looking relieved to have something he could do. "Right on, my lord."

Once he was gone, King turned back to Livvy, and she looked up at him. "What a feeble creature you must think me, though I do thank you for playing knight in shining armour. I confess I have never been more grateful to see anyone in all my life…."

Her voice quavered and, to her horror, a fat tear rolled down her cheek.

"Oh, Christ, Livvy, no. Oh, damnation, don't cry. Why don't you scold me for my appalling behaviour or… or list all my failings one by one? You know being horrid to me always makes you feel better. You can hit me if you want to," he offered, his voice so earnestly sincere that Livvy laughed and sobbed at the same time.

"Oh, K-King, you are the most r-ridiculous creature," she hiccoughed.

"There, see. You feel better already, don't you?" he said, a note of triumph in his voice.

"Yes," she said, staring at him through a haze of tears. "You always make me feel better. Since you got here, whenever the world is bleak and unfriendly and I feel all alone, I turn around and there you are and… and you make it all better, King. How? How do you do that?"

He swallowed, his eyes dark and sombre and anxious. "I don't know, Livvy, but I don't make it better. I only make you forget it for a bit. I would though… if I could, I would make it better, but…"

She reached out and pressed a finger to his lips, silencing him. "I know."

King took her hand, holding it for a long moment before he pressed a kiss to her palm that made her stomach do a peculiar flip flop, and then he let it go. Livvy longed for him to take it back, but he drew in an uneven breath and got to his feet. She watched as he straightened his waistcoat and looked down at her.

"Well, then, that was Mr Skewes. I'm afraid you had the right of it, Livvy, my girl. He's appalling."

Livvy nodded. "Yes, though you have no idea how you relieve my mind by saying that. Charlies and Ceci think I'm all about in my head to refuse the man. They see only a handsome fellow with pretty manners, a lovely home, and money enough to solve all of our problems."

King made a sound of disgust. "Ceci is oblivious to the world at large, and I'm afraid to say your brother is a selfish prick. I know that seems wicked of me to say so when he took it upon himself to save my sorry carcass when he could have looked away, and I know he means well, but really he just dragged me out of the gutter and threw me at your feet. It was you who did the hard bit, Livvy. It was you who saved me. More than you realise, I think."

There was something in his voice, something sincere and wistful, and Livvy felt emotion bubble up in her chest.

On impulse she sprang to her feet and ran to him, throwing her arms about his waist and holding on tight, her face buried against his chest. Oh, and he smelled so wonderful. Fresh linen and soap and a clean, male, musky scent that made her a little giddy. He froze, rigid beneath her embrace at first, and then his arms closed about her and he held her tight.

"Livvy," he said, his voice soft. "I can't…."

"Shut up," she told him, using her most severe scolding tone and clinging harder.

His chest moved in a slight huff of laughter and he stroked her hair.

"Don't speak," she said, barely a whisper now. "Don't tell me no. Just hold me. Please."

She felt rather than heard him nod, and he did as she asked, holding her silently until Spargo knocked to announce the arrival of the tea tray.

Chapter Fifteen

15th December 1818.

Wrapped about a small boy's finger.

After the stresses of the day, Livvy was too weary to implement her plan to seduce King. Her heart was heavy and her mind too troubled. That Charlie had been such a fool by repeating the same mistake was more than she could accept. She wanted to scream and cry with frustration, but it was too much to face yet, and depression brought a strange sense of lethargy. The future seemed an unfriendly and frightening expanse that stretched before her, and the thought of dealing with it had exhaustion settling heavily in her bones. She just wanted to curl up in her bed and pull the covers over her head and stay there, possibly forever. Except once she was there, she wished King were with her. Oh, but he gave the most marvellous hugs. It was like being wrapped up in a deliciously warm blanket and knowing you were quite perfectly safe, that nothing bad could ever happen to you again. Nonsense, of course, but it was how he made her feel and that was all that mattered. Still, she knew he would balk if she pursued him now. He would believe she was upset and not thinking straight and that she would regret her actions in the morning. Livvy knew better but judged it best to leave things a couple of days, so he could see she wasn't acting out of impulse. So, life went on as before.

King did not exactly avoid her, but he kept his distance, surprisingly spending more time with the children than she would have expected. He seemed to have taken a shine to George, and the feeling was obviously mutual as the little boy trailed after him and constantly asked for "Ing" whenever he was out of sight. Harry too was in awe of him, and if his clothes had allowed for it, would have become quite the peacock as he tried to emulate his hero. Even Susan was smitten and would go all pink and silly, and giggle whenever King spoke to her, for which Jane teased her mercilessly.

Preparations for the coming festivities continued, though to Livvy there was a Last Supper feel to the affair now. She was determined that the children would have a wonderful Christmas, a celebration that they could remember as a happy time and something to cheer them when they were forced to face leaving their home and… and what, Livvy did not know. She did not know yet how bad the debts were, if they could be managed by renting out the house and selling off anything with any value. She wondered how Ceci would take it when she realised her gowns and jewellery must be sold off. The cold, panicky sensation that would sometimes clutch at her heart and send her stomach roiling when Mr Skewes' offer repeated in her ears she tried hard to ignore. Would she accept him, if things were truly desperate? For once, she could not face the truth but shied away from it, clinging to the impossible hope that lingered with her attending her aunt's party. She did not allow herself to think about the likelihood her aunt might send her packing the moment she got there, or that she would simply look like a rustic old maid in a dress three seasons out of date and be a figure of ridicule, or that no man would give her a second glance. Instead she clung to her impossible dream of finding a kind man who would be generous enough to give the children the life they deserved. In her quiet, private moments she dreamed of other things too. She dreamed of what she really wanted for herself, a dream so extraordinary she might as well have King riding up on a unicorn and carrying her off to fairyland where they could live happily ever after in a castle in the clouds. Inevitably these dreams made her cry and she ended up feeling cross and out of sorts, scolding herself for being such an utter ninny. It didn't stop her from indulging in her ridiculous imaginings, though, and longing for a man who might be in the same house, but was so far out of her reach he might as well live on the moon.

"Fancy a game of cards?" Walsh asked, waving the pack at King.

King turned from his position at the bedroom window and scowled. "No."

"Chess?"

"No."

"Gelly made some shortbread this morning—"

"I'm not bloody well hungry," King snapped and then scrubbed his hand over his face. "I beg your pardon, Walsh."

"Don't trouble yourself," Walsh said with a shrug.

King groaned and went and sat on the bed. He put his head in his hands. He'd tried to occupy himself, to keep his mind quiet by entertaining the children. He was of little enough use to Livvy, but at least he might give her a bit of peace by keeping them busy. Strangely, it had been no hardship either. He wondered whether he'd always eschewed children before now because he'd met none like these, or if he'd just not given them a chance, for they were rather entertaining. He seemed to have a quite undeserved heroic status in their eyes, too, which was both flattering and daunting.

Harry's worship, he well understood. He was a boy on the cusp of manhood and King was obviously a man of the world, the kind of man an impressionable boy like that might choose to emulate. Even Susan's newly acquired infatuation was something he could comprehend. He was, after all, male, had all his limbs, hair and teeth, and that seemed all that was required for a susceptible girl to form an attachment. So he treated her with kid gloves and made very certain they were never alone together.

The younger children, though…. The girls had him playing piano for them to dance to, and demanded endless games of ludo and chess and cards, and had gifted him with dozens of pictures. Many of them were drawings of him, wildly out of proportion with a head like a sun and legs almost to his neck, and a beaming smile. In his favourite one, which Jane had done that morning, they were all in a line, hand in stick-like hand, with him and Livvy side-by-side in the middle of the picture. He had kept them all, placing them carefully under his folded shirts.

George though, George adored him and seemed to view him as a combination of moveable climbing frame and personal court jester. Even little Birdie had deigned to be held, and cooed and giggled at him, tweaking his nose with her tiny hand and messing up his cravat. King had never experienced the like of it. He told himself it was all a crushing bore, and he would be glad to get away, to get back to London, to his life and his friends and… and it was the most damnable lie.

There was something here, in this place, with the children and Livvy and Spargo and Gelly. It was a home, filled with people who loved and cared about each other, no matter that they bickered and argued and drove each other to distraction now and then. Ceci and Charlie were a part of it too, albeit on the periphery and on their own terms, dancing in and out of the scene like bit players in a theatrical. That Charlie had all this and had cocked it up… that he expected Livvy to marry that… that vile man to make his mistakes come right…. Fury was a living thing in his chest. It burned and ached and made him wild with frustration to the point where he had to be on his own and pace and fret or stare endlessly out of the window in impotent rage. It made him want to find a bottle and drink himself back into oblivion, for he was such a bloody sorry excuse for a man that he might as well. Any man worth his salt could rescue Livvy, surely? A real man could extricate her from this god awful tangle and make her and the children safe.

King leaned his forehead against the window. The glass was cold, though a feeble warmth emanated from the sun, which was high in the sky now. It was mid-afternoon and George was taking a nap, much against his will. Livvy had peeled the boy from him as George wept piteously and clung to his lapels and was only placated by the promise of seeing King again if he was a good boy and had a little sleep. It had left King with a lump in his throat which was so utterly bloody ridiculous that he'd had to escape to do a bit more pacing and muttering and be bad-tempered and unreasonable with his faithful valet.

"Hell and the devil, Walsh. What am I to do?"

"You could marry her."

"Yes," King said with a sigh, despairing that Walsh had come up with the only possible answer. "If I married that silly chit, I'd have access to my funds again and I could pay that idiot Charlie's debts and make it so Livvy and the children were safe. I'd set her up in a place of her own if I could, but... well, you know how that would look."

"No, you bleedin' twit!" Walsh exclaimed.

King's mouth fell open. He allowed Walsh a good deal of freedom of speech, but he'd never been spoken to with such a lack of respect and quite so much irritation.

Walsh coloured and cleared his throat. "Beg pardon, sir, but I meant... you could marry Miss Penrose."

King stilled, turning to stare at Walsh in outrage. "And then what? Invite her to escape this crumbling pile, to come to my own crumbling pile and live on sunshine and fresh air. How does that help? How does that keep the children safe?"

Walsh shrugged. "You'd think of something. Always have afore now."

"Walsh," King said with a derisive tone. "Your belief in me is admirable but entirely misplaced. I have barely muddled though, and become a raging alcoholic in the process. Somehow, I made a few quid here on there on cards and horses. As I will end up killing myself if I go back to that way of life, it is no longer an option. As history has proven time and again, anything legitimate will get my father's attention, and he will destroy it with a smile on his face."

His first enterprise had been a sporting gentleman's club, a place where a fellow could box or fence, or improve his skills in any number of sporting activities. He'd set it up with a friend and the response in the early months had been very encouraging, they'd even been talking of finding better premises, and then his father had discovered his involvement. He still didn't know how. Within days the new members stopped enquiring and the old ones were suddenly too busy to attend. Amazing the influence a marquess and a duke combined could bring to bear when they put their minds to it. It had ruined both him and his friend, a fact he could not forgive himself for. He'd been foolish to involve anyone else and a man he had liked and respected had suffered for it.

"Maybe, maybe not," Walsh said.

"You are not, surely, suggesting my father might have had a change of heart?" King demanded, so stunned by the absurdity of this idea he didn't know where to begin with it.

"No," Walsh said, the word spoken slow and drawn out. "But he's doing it to force your hand, to get you to marry the girl of his choosing. Once you're married, there nothing anyone can do about it, even Lord high and mighty bleedin' Eynsham."

King snorted, amused. "I feel certain I ought to reprimand you for speaking of the marquess so, but I'm damned if I will. However, you are talking rubbish. He'll be apoplectic with fury and only more determined to destroy me."

Walsh shook his head. "I've tried to tell you this afore, my lord, but as you was generally half seas over I'll forgive you for not paying me no mind, but your father has been taken to task before now for his treatment of you."

"The devil he has," King retorted, though felt a little less certain of this as Walsh rolled his eyes to the ceiling. The man appeared to be praying for patience.

"He *has*," Walsh said again, his tone firm now. "You might remember my old pal, Jack Taylor, him what's valet to the Duke of Sandon? Well, he told me how the duke told your pa his treatment of you was a disgrace and an embarrassment. He said even Prinny has remarked that forcing you to scrabble about for money when your father was as rich as Croesus made your pa look like a miserly curmudgeon at best, and at worst like the only way he could control his only son was by beggaring him. Well, you know Prinny's had experience of that kind of managing himself. And as everyone knows you're stubborn enough to live in the gutter before you give in…." Walsh shrugged. "Well, you got the Prince Regent in your corner, and the Duke of Sandon. You reckon they're the only ones who've remarked it, or that there isn't gossip about your father, that he isn't being ridiculed for his behaviour? Sure, there's some what might agree with him after the way you've kept company with the devil these past few years, but not all. Not by a long chalk."

King digested this information in silence, frowning. "My father hates being backed into a corner, Walsh. He'll come out fighting."

Walsh shrugged. "Maybe, maybe not, but we both know Livvy ain't gonna find a bloke to take them little 'uns on. At best, *if* she finds a decent bloke he might pay for Harry's schooling, but I wouldn't have no faith in more than that. Would you?"

King didn't answer. His instinct was in accord with everything Walsh had just said, and the knowledge made him prickly with anxiety. What would happen to little George and Birdie if Charlie landed himself in debtor's prison? Ceci would need looking after herself, never mind having the strength to keep the babies safe, and the girls. He swallowed, running a hand through his hair. Poor Harry would have to find work, but he'd been raised a gentleman. He had no practical skills and had not even finished his schooling. King let out an uneven breath. As soon as Charlie got home, he was going to have a frank talk with him and discover how bad things were. Perhaps he had no financial aid to give, but he wasn't a fool. Hell, compared to Charlie, he was a blasted genius. Perhaps he could find a way to keep the family here and pay Charlie's debts, something the man had missed. He doubted it, and there was every chance Charlie would tell him to go to the devil, but he'd have to risk it, for Livvy's sake.

As Charlie was still away and Ceci opted to dine in her room, Livvy brought the children down for dinner rather than them eating in the nursery. King was glad of it, glad of the distraction. Eating dinner alone with Livvy was far too appealing, too intimate, but there was no chance of intimacy among the chaos the children brought.

The first hurdle was explaining to Jane that the piglet would not be dining with them. She had named the creature Barnaby, despite Livvy having strictly forbidden naming it at all. Tonight it was wearing a colourful paper crown and King was certain he could see rouge on its whiskery black cheeks. After some persuasion, Jane reluctantly bade Barnaby a good evening and allowed Spargo to take him back outside, but only on condition he got his pick of the left over vegetable peelings. Next was the task of encouraging George to put his clothes back on. As ever, he was running about bare arsed, though he had at least kept his top half covered tonight, which proved he was an intelligent lad as it was chilly in the dining room.

"George!" Livvy exclaimed, hands on hips, as George ran away from her, giggling.

"Allow me," King said, smothering a grin as he took the child's abandoned clothes in one hand and snatched George up with his free arm as he careened past.

George squealed and kicked, laughing and wriggling like an eel to get free as King carried him out of the room and back into the parlour.

"Pack that in, you little devil," King said, lifting the boy to eye level.

"Ing!" George said, grinning at him unrepentantly.

"What have I told you about covering yourself up, young man?" King said gravely.

George snickered. "Naughty boy, George. Girls scream loud, Ing."

Emma V Leech

King felt his lips twitch and fought not to laugh.

"Yes, I quite understand the urge to shock them, believe me, but it's really not very gentlemanly." He sat down and released George, who took the opportunity to make a break for it. "Oh, no you don't."

King was too quick and caught him again, tickling the child until he was screaming,

"No, no, no, lemme go, lemme go!" George protested breathlessly, cackling with laughter at the same time.

"There, see? That's what you get, my lad. Now, then, I'm starving, and I want my dinner. Are you hungry?"

George nodded.

"Well, you're not having dinner until you put these on, but if you're a good boy and get dressed, you may sit next to me."

Somewhat to King's surprise, the boy subsided at once and submitted to being wrestled inexpertly into small clothes and trousers. Once all his buttons were buttoned, King looked him over, taking a moment to straighten the collar on the boy's skeleton suit.

"Very smart, George. Now then, shall we dine with the ladies?"

277

"Es," George replied, nodding. "George hungry. Ing wants dinner."

"Yes, I do," King confirmed, taking the boy's hand.

"Barn'by hungry," George said hopefully.

"He may well be, but pigs don't eat at the dining table."

"Barn'by gog. Oof, oof."

King shook his head. "You know very well Barnaby is a pig, not a dog."

George slanted him a mischievous look, but only murmured: "Oof, oof."

When Livvy saw them walk back into the dining room, hand in hand, with George dressed and smiling, the look she gave King made something shift in his chest. He looked quickly away from her and lifted George into his seat, sitting down beside him.

The meal was simple but excellent, Gelly having a knack for making plain fare exceptionally well. A thick vegetable soup and good bread was followed with a mutton pie with a divine golden pastry that melted in the mouth, boiled potatoes with butter, carrots and—naturally—cabbage. Strangely enough, King was getting a taste for it.

For some reason, his mind returned to meals when he was Harry's age. When he was old enough to be allowed to dine with his parents, on the rare occasions he was home from school, mealtimes had been anxious, stilted affairs. His mother often dined in her room rather than face the ordeal, for which he perhaps ought not to have blamed her, but he did, for it left him alone with his father. King would either scoff his food as fast as he could manage hoping to escape quicker and then getting reprimanded for his appalling manners, or barely be able to choke down a morsel as terror of his father's moods made his throat tight. The table would be covered with dozens of dishes and a ridiculous number of courses, many of which would go untouched as his father prided himself on his restraint. Indulgence in any form was an abominable offence to the Marquess of Eynsham.

King was not so blind to his own nature that he did not recognise what had driven his horrendous behaviour and subsequent fall into dissipation.

He looked about the table now, at the animated conversation and the laughter, and smiled as George offered him a piece of carrot.

"Thank you, I have some. You eat it."

George shrugged and stuffed it into his mouth, chewing happily.

Some fierce sense of urgency burned in King's chest, a swell of protectiveness that was quite out of character. King had never cared for anyone but himself before now. He'd allowed no one close, allowed no one to know him. He wasn't certain he'd even known himself before he'd arrived here, out of his mind with drink. He'd always held back, acting the charming devil, flirting and laughing but never really engaging with anyone, never really feeling anything fully. He hadn't wanted to. That had been the marvellous thing about drinking, it had numbed him and made everything wonderfully simple, until it hadn't.

Out of habit he reached for a glass of wine that wasn't there and took a breath, taking up his water glass instead and downing it. Somehow, he must protect this, this imperfectly perfect family with all its madness and peculiarities and the love they all clearly had for one another. He would not allow Charlie's heedless decisions to destroy their peace and happiness. There had to be a way. Whatever it was, whatever he must do, he would do it. For once in his sorry life he'd do something for someone else, for someone who deserved it, and yes it was for Livvy, but not just her. He looked about the table again, at the rosy cheeks and bright eyes of the children as they bickered and chattered and laughed. Beside him, George banged his spoon on his plate and grinned. King laughed and reached out a hand to the child, smoothing down an errant curl that stuck up in an irrepressible fashion. The boy's hair was impossibly soft, silky and warm.

"Eat up, George, a little bird told me there's jam roly poly for pudding if you clear your plate."

George perked up at once and King smiled as the boy picked up another carrot and shoved it in his mouth, chewing with a determined expression.

King chuckled and then met Livvy's eyes. He saw the warmth there, the gratitude and admiration, and something else, something too terrifying to contemplate, so he looked away and returned his attention to George.

Chapter Sixteen

15ᵗʰ December 1818.

A night brim full of surprises and regret.

There was no point in pretending otherwise. Livvy had fallen in love with the Earl of Kingston. She was also an idiot. Really, though, what chance had she, when the man was so patient with Harry's incessant questions about London life, and Susan's sighing over him, and the girls teasing him, and then… and then with George. *Oh stop it, you hen-witted creature,* she scolded herself, but to no avail. She'd peeked in on them earlier to see George climbing over King like a monkey scaling a tree. The poor man's cravat was crumpled beyond saving, his dark hair tousled, and his boots scuffed from crawling about on the floor. Yet he was smiling, watching George with a combination of wonder and fascination. Was it any surprise her heart had turned to mush, and her womb had quivered with longing? She was only human, and there was only so much a woman could take. Then tonight, at the dinner table… Livvy pressed a hand to her heart, which felt like it had swollen to twice its normal size in her chest. This could not be borne.

She had never realised how different a man could be from her first perception of him. Livvy had always believed herself a good judge of character and yet she had condemned King as a vile seducer and a drunkard at first sight. How horribly judgemental she'd been. How naïve not to have wondered what might have brought him to that point. For now she could see the truth of him, a man who desperately needed to be loved, who wanted a family, a home. She wondered if he knew it himself, if he had realised what he was doing with the children, taking just a little of the affection they so abundantly offered him as though he was stealing from them. Livvy had seen him run away from them too, when it got too much, when he was overwhelmed by their happiness in having his attention, and by his own reaction to it.

She wished she could give him everything he needed, but even if things were different, she knew this wasn't how it should be for him. He did not need another man's family. He needed his own. Hopefully, he would see that in time. For now, though, he was here, and they could share something that might sustain them both until life shone a kinder light upon them.

Tonight.

She would go to him tonight and pray she could persuade him to be less of a gentleman before she spontaneously combusted. It wasn't as if she had unrealistic expectations. Despite her foolish daydreams, she knew this was nothing more than a brief affair. After Christmas, King would leave, and she would escape to her aunt's party and likely their paths would never cross again. It was for the best. For now, though, just until after Christmas, he would be hers. She would spell it out so there was no question of anything else, so that she would not frighten him off and give the impression she was hoping for more. They both knew it was impossible, but she would underscore it to reassure him. It was just for now, just for Christmas, and then… and then it would be over, and they would go their separate ways and that would be an end to it. The idea made her lip tremble, and her eyes burn, but she swallowed down the foolish emotions that threatened to undo her. She was a practical woman, and it was better to have half a loaf than none. It was.

So her decision was made.

King stared up at the ceiling, his arms behind his head. He'd left the curtains open to admire the great expanse of sky, velvet black and jostling with stars. Moonlight filtered in, casting odd shadows which would have had him gibbering and screaming about goblins and demons not so very long ago. The thought brought a wash of shame that he had sunk so low, that he had almost fallen off the edge, the point of no return. Even now his hands trembled at the idea he might fail, that he might be offered a drink the moment he returned to London, and he'd not be able to say no. Well, it was bound to happen. All his cronies had been a hard drinking lot, well, except Charlie, but then they'd never been friends. Acquaintances perhaps, King being someone Charlie felt he owed a debt to.

King wasn't sure he *had* friends. He had people he'd go out carousing with, those who were the best, most amusing company, and those who were inoffensive enough not to make him want to throttle them when he was hungover. Friends though…

A friend would understand he could never allow himself to fall so far again, a friend would help him, support him. The only man he might have named friend had been ruined by King's father and no longer wished to know him. King could hardly blame him for it. He tried to think of anyone among his circle who would understand when he told them he would not drink anymore, that he could not, if he wanted to live. Try as he might, King could not think of a single person who wouldn't just laugh and make a joke of it. They'd put a drink in his hand and tell him not to be such a crashing bore. Though he had known it in the back of his mind, it was only now that he allowed himself to accept the truth of it. If he returned to his rooms in London, to his friends and their endless parties and gambling and drinking, he would be drawn back in. He could not go back. His life must change.

The idea was frightening. It was as frightening as the thought he might give in the first time someone offered him a drink, or if he was alone and free to help himself. He would have to go back to Wynford. The castle was enormous and would swallow him whole and even thinking about it gave him such a sense of loneliness and abandonment he did not know how he would bear it. His dog was there at least, Argos, a big, loyal fellow who did not deserve to be abandoned with such regularity as he was. He felt a pang of longing for the creature, wishing he could keep him in London but it was no place for such a big, energetic dog. It would be selfish of him.

Though he knew it was a dangerous game to play, for a moment he allowed himself to imagine doing what Walsh had suggested, the impossible notion that he might marry Livvy. He allowed himself to glimpse the image of Livvy at his home. Livvy and the children, filling the endless empty rooms, their chaos and laughter chasing away the silence that had always been a part of his life, unless he was drunk and raising hell. He closed his eyes and forced the image away, unnerved by the swell of emotion that rose in his chest, the force of longing. Closing his eyes did not help though, for now he remembered the feel of her in his arms, the sweetness of her lips and the warmth and softness of her body. His skin ached with wanting her, his body growing hard and hot, a flush that burned over his skin with such intensity he flung the covers back, unable to stand them against his naked flesh. He groaned and covered his face with his hands.

"Stop it, stop it, stop it," he murmured to himself, trying to regain control of his body before it spiralled out of control.

"King?"

He jolted, scrambling to sit up and snatch at the bedclothes at once as Livvy's soft voice pierced the silvered darkness of his room. King couldn't breathe, let alone demand what the bloody hell she was playing at, coming to his room alone in the middle of the night. Though now, judging from the fact she'd just undone the ribbon tie on her nightrail and allowed it to fall to the floor... her intentions needed no explanation whatsoever.

King's mind was a blank. He simply could not think. At all. His vision was filled with the sight of Livvy, all glorious curves and soft skin, her hair loose, tumbled curls about her shoulders. The moonlight shone upon her skin, a pearlescent glow, shimmering silver, her golden hair a shining mass of platinum now as the moon transformed her into a creature of myth, a succubus come to drive him to madness.

"King," she said again, a tremor audible in her voice.

She was nervous, as well she might be, a lamb trotting willingly into the lion's den.

"Livvy," he said, struggling to find breath enough to say that much, striving to find the will to command her to leave, now, at once, before any hold he had on his sanity snapped once and for all. He gave a soft bark of laughter, realising that moment had long since been lost. She was here of her own volition, willingly offering herself to him.

Still, he didn't move, giving her the chance to come to her senses, torn between desperation that she stay and wanting her to take that chance and run from him, to find the strength that he lacked to deny her, and to save herself. She did not run. Livvy came closer and his heart thudded so hard he felt giddy and light-headed. Was he still not recovered? Was this an echo of his night sweats and terrifying visions of strange creatures with horns and tails come to take him down into the darkness? For he had never felt this out of control. He'd bedded women enough to know objectively that Livvy was no great beauty. She was lovely, yes, but not exceptional, not the kind of woman for whom men fought duels and drove themselves to madness. Except his heart disagreed vehemently, crashing about behind his ribs like it fought to get free, like it might stutter to a halt and die if he didn't touch her. His heart recognised a goddess, a queen, a woman he might spend his entire life worshipping, trying to be worthy of, if he were only given the chance.

"Say something," she said, close enough to him now that he could reach out and touch her.

He wanted to so badly, but hardly dared, in case he'd dreamed the whole thing and would wake the moment he tried to put his hands on her.

"Can't," he said, his voice husky. "Forgotten how."

Livvy laughed, and the sound rioted through him. "Are you quite certain you're a libertine? I mean, aren't you supposed to be eloquent and full of seductive teasing?"

"Not with you, Livvy," he said helplessly. "It's all smoke and mirrors, love. Haven't you understood that yet? I can't pretend with you. You saw behind the mask from the first, you broke the illusion. So you just get me, I'm afraid. Sorry to disappoint you."

It was her that reached for him, of course. Brave, beautiful Livvy, undaunted, facing the world head on. Her fingers traced the line of his jaw and he shivered beneath her touch, shaken by the depth of his desire, at the force of his own need.

"If you think that disappoints me, you are sadly mistaken, King. I could never live a lie. I have only ever wanted honesty. That's why I like you so much."

"I should send you away," he said, even as he reached for her.

"Perhaps," she said, a crooked smile at her lips. "But you wouldn't be so cruel to me. I want you, King. I want you so much I feel like I might die if you don't touch me."

"Oh, God," he said, and pulled her down onto the bed.

Livvy fell with a stunned gasp, the touch of King's skin against her own so explicit, the feel of his body against hers so shocking her brain simply refused to function. She stared down at him, her hair falling about her face, her hands braced on his chest. *On his chest!* Against his naked skin with… with hair and nipples and…. Oh, she was going to pass out. *Olivia Penrose, don't you bloody dare,* she told herself, holding onto some semblance of calm by her fingertips—fingertips currently tangled in the thick wiry hair *on his chest*. She made a small sound, akin to a whimper.

"Livvy," King said, his eyes dark and utterly focused upon hers. "If you want to leave—"

"No!" she practically shrieked and then slapped a hand over her mouth as she realised she was supposed to keep quiet.

He grinned at her then, a wolfish, pleased grin that reminded her forcefully that no matter the man she had come to know, he had gained his reputation for a reason. She hauled in an uneven breath and sat back, taking a moment to look at him. For really, it was foolish to waste the opportunity. It wasn't the first time she'd seen his top half naked, but then he'd been so sick, reeking of drink and out of his senses. This was different. So different.

"May I...?" she began, uncertain how to ask if she could put her hands on him again but trembling with the need to do so.

King huffed out a laugh. "If you don't touch me in the next thirty seconds, I shall be on my knees begging before a minute has passed."

"Oh, well, we can't have that," Livvy said, relieved to discover she wasn't the only one experiencing such emotions.

Tentatively, she returned her hands to his chest, finding his skin not only warm but hot, surprisingly silky too, except where that dark hair curled. She ran her fingers through it, pleased when he shivered again. His reaction had surprised her when she had touched his face and seen the shiver of pleasure over his skin. *It's not just me,* she thought with a surge of triumph, *he feels it too.* The idea gave her courage, and she bent, pressing her lips to his. King groaned, and the sound had a visceral effect, turning her insides hot and achy and making her press harder against him. Livvy gasped as a jolt of sensation lanced through her and she realised she was straddling him, his arousal in precisely the place she needed it, with only the sheet keeping them apart.

"Oh, Christ, Livvy, you're going to kill me," King muttered, his hand sliding to the nape of her neck and pulling her down. His mouth was demanding, urgent now as his free hand slid down her back to her hips and tugged her closer.

"Oh!" Livvy gasped against his lips as that exquisite sensation came again as he rolled his own hips up, creating the kind of friction she thought really might end with her going up in flames. "Oh, my, King, that's… that's really quite…."

He chuckled and turned her onto her back, kissing a path down her neck, lingering along her collarbone, tracing patterns with his tongue that made her shiver and gasp. His hand slid up from her waist, slow and caressing until it reached her breast. The devil stopped just short, nuzzling her neck and kissing the soft, sensitive skin beneath her ear. Livvy bit her lip, wanting to tell him to bloody well get on with it before she went mad.

"Stop thinking," he scolded her, his voice low, a rumble through his chest that she felt as much as heard.

"I can't," she protested. "I want it, all of it, everything, and we have so little time and—"

He pressed his mouth to hers, stopping her words.

"Don't," he said, the word ragged, his breathing harsh. "Don't ask me for everything, and we have tonight."

"No. Longer than that," she said, allowing a steely note to underline the words. "Christmas. I know there's no more than that, King. I expect nothing from you, only this. I'll be yours until Christmas, and… and you'll be mine."

He was silent for a moment, and though she'd been grateful for the darkness up until now, she wished she could see his face better. She wanted to look into his eyes, to see what he was thinking, but there was nothing but the moonlight upon the hard planes of his face, a glitter like starlight in his eyes.

"And then?" he asked, his tone unreadable.

"And then, we go our separate ways. I go in search of a husband and… and you do whatever it is the Earl of Kingston does… until your bride is of an age where you feel comfortable marrying her, I suppose."

He reared back at that.

"What?"

She reached up and stroked his cheek. "King. You cannot go back to the life you were leading, and you were not meant to be alone. You need a wife, a family. If you treat her kindly, the girl will be desperately in love with you in a matter of days, I know I... I know you can do it. Make a family, you foolish man. It's what you want, or had you not realised that yet?"

There was a taut silence. Livvy's hand fell to his arm, braced upon the mattress, the muscles bunched and hard under her touch. The tension sang through him and she regretted her words, regretted making him face them, especially now of all times. What a fool she was. Desperate to distract him, she put her arms up, linking them behind his neck and kissing him, tugging him back down. After a moment's resistance, he followed with a muttered curse and a groan that made her pulse skitter. He settled between her legs and she wrapped her body around his, clinging to him, too aware of how perfectly they fit, of how nothing in her life would ever feel this way again, so utterly right.

"Livvy," he murmured. "Oh, God, Livvy...."

"Ing?"

Oh good Lord.

George.

King yelped and simultaneously threw the covers over Livvy's head and sat up to face the small, shadowy figure in the doorway.

"George!" King said, breathless and horrified. Bloody hell. "Y-You gave me a turn. What is it? Is something the matter?"

George sniffled, wiping his nose on his sleeve. "Livvy not there."

King's experienced a surge of such shame he wanted to fall to his knees and beg the child's forgiveness. Oh god. Poor George had been frightened and wanting Livvy and he… and they…. He felt sick.

"Oh, George, I…." King swallowed, gathering himself. "I… I expect she's… er… in the kitchen. Gone to get some milk, perhaps? Did you have a bad dream?"

"'Es." George nodded, his bottom lip quivering a little.

"Well, that's rotten luck," King said, utterly wretched now. "I'll take you back to bed and I expect Livvy will come and look in on you before she goes back to bed. You… er… just hold on while I put some clothes on."

"'Es. Ing, must wear clothes. Girls scream loud. No pego," George said solemnly.

A choked sound escaped King, somewhere between a laugh and a moan. He was an utter bastard, a selfish, wicked man who would have taken from Livvy when he had nothing of any worth to give her. Christ, what if George had come into his room just a little later? King went hot and cold, appalled. Once he was decently attired, King lifted George into his arms, hesitating in the doorway.

"Let's get you back to bed then, young man. I bet your aunt will have gone to get you a glass of milk, that's why you couldn't find her."

Hopefully, Livvy would take the hint. He could not face returning to his bed with her still in it.

"Come along, young man."

King carried George down the hall and up the stairs to the nursery and padded into the room. Little Birdie was snoring softly, arms and legs akimbo. Susan must have the benefit of a room of her own now, but Lydia and Rebecca were here, sleeping neatly, tucked under their blankets. Jane, however, had kicked the covers off, sleeping on her stomach with one leg and one arm hanging off the side of the bed. King experienced another wave of heat and humiliation as he considered what he'd been doing. God, he was despicable. That he could think to have a love affair with Livvy and then just walk away, that she would accept that….

"Here we are," he said, his voice sounding odd, too loud, in the darkness of the nursery. He felt too big among all the child-sized furniture, too wicked and tainted, to be anywhere near this… this remarkable, beautiful family. He lay George down in his bed and pulled up the covers, tucking the boy in tight and picking up a rather odd looking fabric dog from the floor. It was made from ticking, one of its legs was longer than the other, and the ears and tail were out of proportion, far too big for its body, but it was definitely a dog.

"Gog, oof, oof," George said softly, reaching for the toy.

"He's a very handsome fellow," King said, sitting down gingerly on the edge of the bed. "Did Livvy make him for you?"

George nodded.

"What's he called?"

"Bob," George said, holding the dog out again to King.

King inspected it critically. "Yes," he said, smiling at George. "He's definitely a Bob. A good strong name. Fierce enough to chase bad dreams away."

George nodded and drew Bob under the covers with him before tucking his thumb into his mouth.

"I have a dog," King said then, the words blurted out before he could think about it.

George sat up, his thumb leaving his mouth with a soft *pop*, wide-eyed with interest now. "Ing, you got gog?"

King nodded. It was too late to take it back now, though it had been a stupid thing to say. Now George would want to see it.

"Is big? Ing's gog big?"

"Yes. He's a Newfoundland. His fur is black and white and he's very brave, very loyal. His name is Argos, like Odysseus' dog."

"Arrrgos," George repeated, pronouncing the word perfectly.

King smiled. "Yes."

"Want see Argos," George said, reaching out and grasping King's hand. "Morrow, we go? See Argos?"

King swallowed, cursing himself. Emotion surged in his chest and he wasn't certain why. Perhaps thinking of poor Argos sitting on the steps that rose to the massive front door of the castle, waiting for him to come home again after being abandoned for so long. King had missed him horribly, but London was no place for a dog like that. Argos had boundless energy, he needed the fields and open spaces, and besides, the housekeeper and her husband, Mr and Mrs Dibben, doted on him. It wasn't as if he'd been neglected. He was better off there, away from King and his wicked lifestyle. Everyone was better off away from him. He ought to leave, ought to go away before he could do this family any more harm. God knew they had troubles enough already.

"Ing?"

King shook his head, his throat tight. "No, George. Not… Not tomorrow. My home is a long way away."

"'Nother day?"

King did not want to tell the boy falsehoods, but it was late, and he did not know what to say, could not think past his own misery and self-loathing.

"We'll see," he said, forcing a smile. "We'll see."

Chapter Seventeen

15th December 1818.

A rude awakening.

Once King had gone, Livvy dressed hurriedly and went to fetch a glass of milk. How stupid of her not to have checked on George first, though he hadn't woken in the night in an age, so it hadn't occurred to her. No doubt the whole incident would have horrified King. She could almost imagine his train of thought, something along the lines of debauching innocents and bringing immorality into the children's lives. It was bound to be something of the sort. She knew him well enough now to know he had a very low opinion of himself and that he would instinctively take the blame. Why was that? Weren't noblemen supposed to be arrogant and full of themselves with an unshakeable belief in their superiority? Yes, there were certainly glimpses of arrogance in King, but only when he was playing the rogue, like he was wearing the role of the Earl of Kingston in the way an actor would Hamlet or King Lear. Goodness, but he was an enigma, and she wanted so badly to unravel him and put him back together again in a way that meant he might realise just how wonderful he truly was. She paused in the doorway to the nursery as she heard King's voice speaking low. She peered around the door to see him sitting down on George's bed.

"He's a very handsome fellow. Did Livvy make him for you?" he asked, inspecting the ridiculous dog she'd sewn. It was a dreadful thing, barely dog-like at all, but poor George had wanted one so badly after having seen one in the village. "What's he called?" King asked George.

"Bob."

Livvy smothered a grin as King made a show of inspecting the strange creature.

"Yes," he said, smiling at George. "He's definitely a Bob. A good strong name. Fierce enough to chase bad dreams away."

Stop it, Livvy told her idiotic heart as it fluttered in her chest. Oh, who was she trying to fool? She was a lost cause.

"I have a dog."

King's words surprised her, and she bit her lip, knowing this information would have George demanding to meet the animal.

"Ing, you got gog?" George demanded, breathless with excitement. "Is big? Ing's gog big?"

"Yes. He's a Newfoundland. His fur is black and white and he's very brave, very loyal. His name is Argos, like Odysseus' dog."

"Arrrgos," George repeated, and Livvy felt a burst of pride in him for grasping it so quickly.

"Yes."

"Want see Argos," George said, reaching out and grasping King's hand. "Morrow, we go? See Argos?"

Oh, dear. Livvy watched King, watched the way his broad shoulders slumped, and he shook his head, the picture of misery.

"Ing?"

"No, George. Not… Not tomorrow. My home is a long way away."

Livvy's heart clenched. There was too much emotion behind the words, sorrow and longing and… *oh, King.*

"'Nother day?" George asked, such a plaintive question that Livvy wanted to cry, for him and for King. Oh, why was life so bloody cruel?

"We'll see," King said, a catch in his voice that made tears prick at Livvy's eyes. They both knew it would never happen. "We'll see."

Livvy cleared her throat and bustled into the room.

"Oh, George, you've fetched King. I was down in the kitchens getting you some warm milk. Here you are."

Livvy sat down on the other side of the bed as King got to his feet.

"I'll… er…." he said awkwardly, waving at the door.

"Oh, there's no need," Livvy said at once, hoping to make him stay.

King made a low sound of disgust. "Yes, there is. Night night, George. Goodnight, Miss Penrose. I shall see you both *in the morning*."

Livvy sighed as she watched King go, closing the door quietly behind her.

"Ing, got big gog, Libby," George said. "I like Ing."

"Yes," Livvy said, stroking George's hair as he sipped his milk. "I like King too."

❦ ❦ ❦

King did not sleep, tormented by the scent of Livvy on his sheets and the memory of her warm skin against his. He forced the images away, self-loathing for his actions giving him the strength to think of other things, for short periods anyway. Then the hopelessness of his life would stir the desire to get himself a bloody drink, and he'd grasp hold of anything that would distract him. Naturally, he ended up thinking of Livvy again as his heart ached in his chest and he went full circle, over and again. Sometime after dawn he fell into a fitful sleep and then woke with a jolt of alarm as a tremendous crash echoed through the house.

"Bloody hell!"

He scrambled out of bed, gritty eyed and stiff and slung on his clothes in a haphazard fashion that would give Walsh a nervous collapse when he saw. Surely, though, there had been some manner of disaster? The roof falling in, a wall coming down? Oh, God, the children!

King bolted for the door as he heard a female scream and ran pell mell down the corridor only to come up short as he discovered Ceci at the top of the stairs with her head in her hands, weeping.

"What is it?" he demanded, so terrified he could hardly get the words out. "Are you hurt? Is it the children? What…?"

Ceci pointed a trembling hand towards the bottom of the stairs and King turned his unwilling eyes in that direction, expecting to see a crumpled body. There she was, little Jane in a tumble of skirts and petticoats, laying in a heap.

"Oh, God. No!" King cried, taking the stairs two at a time but not getting to the poor child before Livvy.

King stared at her, helpless, wanting to save her from the pain, to shield her from….

"Jane Penrose, you little devil!" Livvy said, clearly extremely cross as she hauled Jane to her feet. "How many times have I told you that our best silver tray is *not* a toboggan!"

"Oh, they'll be the death of me," Ceci wailed from the top of the stairs. "My poor heart! I thought she was dead."

The child's mother put her head in her hands and wept. For once, King thought she had a point. His heart was still hammering in his ears and he felt sick.

"There, see?" Livvy said, pointing past King to Ceci. "You've made your poor mama cry, not to mention giving Lord Kingston a terrible fright. Oh, and, Jane… Oh… oh, Jane…."

Livvy paused as her gaze landed on the silver tray. King watched, truly horrified this time as Livvy pressed her fingers to her mouth, trying not to cry.

He saw what she saw. A family heirloom, no doubt, but something that had been beautiful, and valuable, and was now scratched and dented and… well, there was still the price of the silver to be had but… *Oh, Livvy.* His heart ached, not knowing who to comfort first. Jane did not understand perhaps the full extent of what she had done, but seeing her indomitable auntie struggling not to cry was clearly a shock. The girl's bottom lip trembled, not helped by Ceci still sobbing piteously at the top of the stairs.

King took a proper look at Livvy to see she was soaked through, the hem of her gown muddy. She'd been with Ross, then. Rain droplets clung to her hair and her cheeks and nose were red from the cold, redder still as she fought the tears that were forcing strange little hiccoughing noises from her. It was too much, though. The emotion got the better of her and she stood, sobbing and crying, clutching her arms about herself as her eyes and nose ran. She certainly wasn't an attractive sight when she cried, which was the oddest thing to realise, as King only wanted her more than ever. He wanted to hold her tight and comfort her and make everything all right, but he could not. Still, he could manage this mess. Weeping females were surely not too much for the King of Sin's legendary charm.

"What the devil is going on?" Harry said, appearing in the hallway with Susan in tow.

"Oh, good Lord," King murmured as the crying ratcheted up a notch.

Birdie, who was in Susan's arms, had looked up at her mother—now sunk to the floor at the top of the stairs and sobbing noisily—and promptly decided she needed to join in too. At this point the piglet trotted through the hallway with a pink bow around its neck. George followed, shedding clothes as he went.

"H'lo, Ing," he said, waving cheerfully as he kicked his breeches free and wandered off after the pig.

King took a deep breath.

"Harry, handkerchief," he commanded, nodding his thanks as Harry gave his over.

King was still only in his shirt and breeches and had nothing so useful to hand. He pressed it into Livvy's fingers, relieved when she used it to wipe her eyes and give her nose an enthusiastic blow.

"Right," he said, moving to pick up the silver tray.

He turned to Jane, who looked wretched too, fat tears rolling down her pink cheeks.

"Now, then, Miss Jane. I think you owe your aunt and your mother an apology for giving them a horrid fright, and a promise never to do such dreadful a thing again," he said gently, reaching for her hand and giving it an encouraging squeeze.

"I… I *am* s-sorry, L-Livvy," the girl stammered. "I won't do it again, Mama. N-Not ever. Promise."

Livvy said nothing, all her energy and concentration focused on not falling to pieces in front of everyone again.

"You're not hurt?" King said, crouching down to meet the girl's eyes.

"My knee hurts a b-bit," Jane stammered, sniffling now. "And I scraped my hand."

"Oh, dear. Well, be a brave girl, and Harry will take you and your sisters to the kitchen and Gelly will patch you up. Harry, give this tray to Spargo and see what can be done with it. And your mama needs the sal volatile and a nice strong cup of tea in her room, please."

"Yes, King, at once," Harry said, snapping to attention like King was Wellington commanding the troops. "Come along, Jane, you silly goose," he said, with all the tender sympathy of a male sibling as he took his little sister's arm and hauled her off to Gelly with Lydia and Rebecca trailing behind them.

"Susan, give Birdie to me and get George dressed again, then see that piglet back to where it belongs."

"Yes, King," Susan said, fluttering her eyelashes at him and sighing heavily. She gazed adoringly at him as he took Birdie from her. King cleared his throat.

"Ahem, er… yes, well, run along then before George is completely bare ar… around the house."

Susan giggled, blushed, and then ran after her brother.

King turned back to Livvy and took a moment to squeeze her hand. She had stopped crying now at least, though the blank expression on her face was somehow worse.

"Deep breaths. I'll be back in just a moment," he promised.

Livvy didn't so much as blink, just stared into some place in the far distance, her arms clutched about her middle.

King hurried up the stairs, carrying the wailing baby.

"There, there, now," he soothed the child, feeling like an idiot. Had *there, there now,* ever made anyone feel remotely better? Though, strangely, the child soothed a little, staring up at him with watery eyes, her eyelashes all spiky as she sniffled. King stroked the baby's head and kissed her silky cheek. "There's a good girl."

When he reached Lady Boscawen, he reached down a hand to help her up. "Come now, my lady. No one was hurt and Jane is sorry for giving you such a horrid scare, but poor Birdie is frightened by all the upset and needs her mama."

"Oh," Ceci said, wiping her cheeks. "My poor baby."

She cried much more prettily than Livvy it had to be said, but then Livvy only cried when she was feeling defeated, and very little defeated Olivia

Penrose. She didn't cry over trifles like he suspected Ceci did, and so she could not disguise the depths of her misery. Her tears were ugly because the emotion was so heartfelt, so raw that there was no hiding it.

King escorted Ceci back to her room with Birdie and promised that her ladyship's smelling salts, and a good hot cup of tea were coming soon and so she wasn't to upset herself further. This suggestion, given with King's most solicitous tone, seemed to go a long way to calming her and the lady settled in a chair with Birdie who was now all smiles for her pretty mama and the crisis appeared to have been averted. Here, at least.

King closed the door and hurried back to Livvy, uncertain whether he was relieved or alarmed to discover she hadn't moved a muscle.

"Come now, love," he said, taking her by the arm and guiding her back up the stairs. Though he had promised himself to stay away from her, she was in no fit state to be by herself and everyone else was occupied. King took her to her room and began undoing the ties on her clothes. That at least got her attention. Her cheeks flushed, and she lifted her gaze to his, her expression one of such naked longing that King's heart stuttered.

"Don't," he said, shaking his head. "Please, don't. I cannot, but you must get out of these wet things before you catch your death."

He moved behind her, undoing everything he could see and then retreating to the door.

"Get changed, Livvy," he said, keeping his voice firm and no nonsense because the slightest quaver was going to spell ruin for them both. "I'll be right outside. Let me know when you're decent."

He turned to leave before thinking better of it and adding.

"And I do mean decent. No... No tricks, love, I beg you. I... Not today, please."

She looked away from him, the light in her eyes dying, but she nodded listlessly. Oh God. King felt like a brute for walking away from her, but he reminded himself it was for her own sake. Poor Livvy was all about in her head, to be looking at him in such a way. *Him,* of all people. He was saving her from herself. He must remember that.

King leaned back against the wall outside Livvy's door, frowning down at his boots.

"Is Livvy all right?"

He looked up to see Harry regarding him anxiously. King straightened, aware that it was extremely inappropriate for him to be here. Not that Harry seemed to have registered that King ought to be nowhere near his maiden aunt's bedroom.

"A bit worn out, I think," King said with a smile. "I've only been here a few weeks and I feel like I might suffer a nervous collapse. Your poor aunt has been doing it for years."

Harry's expression grew serious, and he nodded. "Father has made a dreadful mess of things, hasn't he?"

King hesitated, unwilling to say anything less than complimentary about the boy's father, and worried that if he began, he might let his tongue run away with him.

The boy snorted and shook his head. "It's all right. I'm not a child. There have been times this past year I've felt more of a grown-up than Papa, to be honest. I mean, don't misunderstand me, he's a wonderful father, he truly is. I've always felt that. He's such fun, or at least… he used to be before the money troubles got so bad. We used to play games, and everyone was always laughing, well, except for Livvy the past year or so, but then she saw what was happening before we did."

King didn't know what to say. He had long thought Harry was an exceptional young man, kind-hearted and serious, but with a sense of humour too. He looked after his siblings, even when they drove him to distraction, and did his best to be the man of the house.

"Livvy should have been in charge of the estate," Harry went on. "She's always been far cleverer than Papa. He knows it too, only…."

He shrugged and went to stand by the window, staring out a day that was full of soft grey mists that hung low and clung to everything like spun sugar.

"Pride, Harry," King said with a sigh. "We're all guilty of it. Hard for your father to let his little sister take over the running of the estate."

"Yes, so he ruined us instead."

The bitterness of the words was so raw King's heart ached.

"Harry," he said, moving closer to the lad.

To his astonishment, Harry turned and flung his arms about him, sobbing, his thin frame racked with emotion.

King froze, uncertain what on earth to do. Small children and women were one thing, but.... He had a sudden, vivid memory of being about Harry's age and his beloved dog dying. She had been old and sick, and the end hardly unexpected, but he had been distraught all the same and had turned to his father for comfort.

"Emotion is for the lower orders," the marquess had said coldly. "Go to your room until you can behave in a manner that does not bring you disgrace."

It had helped, at least, for misery had become anger, and King had sworn to hate his father until the day he died.

With the memory clear in his mind, King hugged the boy tight.

"I'm so sorry, Harry."

Harry wept a moment longer before getting himself back under control. His cheeks were burning, and he could barely meet King's eye.

"I… I beg your pardon, my lord."

"Oh, stuff that," King said impatiently. "I told you, it's King, and we all feel like blubbing now and then. God knows I have of late."

"Y-You?" Harry looked at him with such frank astonishment that King could not help but laugh.

"Yes, me!" he exclaimed. "Did you think I was made of stone? Did you not hear me weeping and screaming in terror when I was out of my senses with drink? My God, Harry. We are none of us perfect. Not your father, not you, and most certainly not me. We are all flawed, doing our best, muddling through. Sometimes we will succeed and sometimes we will fail. It's how you face failure that makes you a man though, Harry. Taking responsibility for your own actions and dealing with the consequences is what makes us stronger, not weaker."

Harry nodded, standing a little taller. He was pale and his eyes were red, but he looked thoughtful. He took a deep breath before he spoke again, "I won't ever be able to go back to school, will I? Nor go to university?"

The words were flat, spoken with no inflection, no emotion, just a finality that was heartbreaking.

King felt impotent rage swell in his chest. "Yes, Harry, you will. If there is anything I can do about it, you will. I... I don't know how, and it might take me a little time, but...."

Surely he could get someone to pay for such a promising young man's education. He cast about in his mind, coming up with the names of two wealthy widows who had promised him a reward for... well, never mind what for, he didn't wish to remember that, but they might do this for him.

Harry was staring at him, wide-eyed. "B-But I couldn't ask—"

"You didn't ask, I offered," King retorted. "And if I wasn't in such a... a bind myself I'd pay for every last farthing gladly, but... well, my father is a good deal worse than yours, lad, so take comfort in that, at least."

"I don't know what to say." Harry was bright-eyed, looking very much as if he might weep again.

"Don't say anything, not to anyone," King said firmly. "I can't say for certain I can do it but... but I swear I'll do my very best for you, Harry. Word of honour."

King held out his hand and Harry took it, shaking it with such an expression of sincere earnestness that King's throat grew tight.

"King, I… I know I ought not ask such an… indelicate question...."

King snorted at that. "Ah, Harry. It's a bit late for that and we're both men of the world are we not. Out with it."

"Couldn't you marry Livvy? I think she likes you very much."

Damn him for not seeing that coming. It took him a moment to shift the stone that had somehow lodged in his throat. "I can't," he said, hardly able to meet the boy's eye. "I would if… but I can't. Besides, she deserves better than me."

The disappointment in the boy's eyes was almost enough to dissolve any remaining shreds of dignity that King had been clinging to, but he nodded his understanding. "I see. Well, that's… that's a pity."

"Yes," King replied, somehow forcing the words out. "A pity."

They stood in silence a little longer before King got himself under control again.

"Go and fetch Susan will you and help her with George and that blasted piglet. Send her up to Livvy as soon as you can. Your aunt needs some help and looking after."

With his troops all set upon their various tasks, King did what he did best when it all got too much, and ran away.

Chapter Eighteen

16th December 1818.

The earl's prickly surprise.

The next time, Livvy decided, she would be better organised and if King thought he was getting away from her, he would have a fight on his hands. It would be another matter if he didn't want her, but that clearly wasn't the issue. It was some nonsense about her virginity and his dreadful past and… oh, good heavens, what did it matter now? She was hardly just out of the schoolroom and being a virgin did not make her innocent. Honestly, she'd helped Ceci give birth, heard a deal of village gossip she probably ought not to have, and had seen the ram servicing the ewes… was she supposed to be deaf, dumb, and blind? Apparently so, but she refused to play the game. Well, with those she cared for, at least. Besides, people had affairs all the time if the scandal sheets were anything to go by, not that they saw many of them at Boscawen as Charlie wouldn't have them in the house. For a man with a burgeoning family, he was remarkably prudish about such things. Her grandfather's influence, she supposed. He had been a wonderful man, but he'd always leaned towards the fire and brimstone outlook on life and religion. Though he'd had a very strict moral code that Livvy had admired—up to a point—it hadn't exactly rubbed off on her. She was far more... *realistic.* Practical. After all, human beings were what they were and were bound to mess up more often than not, and wasn't the whole point about loving thy neighbour and not casting the first stone to do with forgiving and accepting people for what they were? Not that she was a sterling example of that either, as she'd judged King at first glance and found him wanting, but she had admitted her mistake.

Oh, Lord, what a day. She didn't know what had gotten into her, making such a scene over a stupid silver tray. Except it was an item she had used to calculate how much money they might have if they were forced to sell everything of value and... her chest felt tight again and she forced her mind away from the subject. *Not now, Livvy,* she told herself. She had promised herself the days until Christmas would be for her, and for the children. They would be merry and bright if it bloody killed her, and King was going to help. He was so wonderful with her nieces and nephews that would be no trouble at all. It was getting him to be wonderful to her which would be trickier, but she would get there. Oh, yes, she would.

"Thank you for your help, Susan," Livvy said, giving the girl a kiss on the cheek. She had come to help Livvy dress, giving King the chance to bolt again, of course. "And I'm sorry I made such a silly scene before."

Susan rolled her eyes. "Don't be daft. Gelly says it's a wonder we haven't all sent you screaming to Bedlam for a bit of peace."

Livvy gave a startled little laugh and pulled Susan into a hug. "Sometimes I forget what a grown-up young lady you are becoming."

Susan sighed and leaned her head against Livvy. "Not that it will do me any good to grow up. I shan't have a season, shall I, Livvy? Nor the others."

Livvy closed her eyes and held Susan tightly. "I… I don't think so, Susan. Not unless I marry a kind, rich man."

Susan looked up then, her eyes wide. "You won't marry Mr Skewes, will you? Promise, Livvy."

Obviously Livvy hadn't the slightest intention of marrying the man, but Susan's request was so surprising she could only stare.

The girl held her gaze, and gone was any trace of the giggling schoolgirl, replaced by a maturity Livvy had not seen before. "I could never sleep peacefully again, knowing you'd married him to save us. We don't want you to do it, Livvy."

"D-Don't you like Mr Skewes?" Livvy asked, for none of the children had ever mentioned him one way or the other as far as she knew. She didn't think they were even aware of the situation, but then in a family like this, secrets were hard to keep for long.

Susan wrinkled her nose.

"None of us do! He's so... *ugh*. He treats us all like charity cases and... and he keeps patting me on the head like... like a dog!" she said with a burst of indignation.

Livvy bit her lip, aware that a girl on the cusp of womanhood would not appreciate being treated like a child. Mr Skewes' particular brand of condescension was enough to make Livvy want to throw things, so why not Susan too.

"Oh, Susan, you have no idea how it gladdens my heart to know what a sensible girl you are. No, I shall not marry Mr Skewes, well... unless things are very desperate indeed. Even he would be better than the workhouse...I *think*," Livvy said, a touch doubtfully.

"Are things as bad as that?" Susan said, and Livvy cursed herself for her wayward tongue.

"Oh, no," she said at once, but Susan's shrewd gaze stopped her. She took a breath. "No, not so dreadful as that, but the truth is I don't know how bad. Your father has not told me, but… but I suspect we must leave this house in the New Year. It must be rented out. Hopefully, the income will be enough to keep us and pay off your father's debts, but…."

Susan swallowed hard but did not cry. "Will… Will I need to… to go to work?"

Livvy felt emotion bubbling up in her chest again, threatening to explode in another wretched scene. She forced it back down.

"No," she said, her voice firm. "I won't let that happen. We're not done yet, Susan."

Susan nodded and grasped Livvy's hand. "I know if anyone can find a way, you can." She hesitated then. "You could marry King."

Livvy smiled and fought back the tears that prickled behind her eyes. "I'm afraid King is no better off than we are, love."

"Oh. Well, I'd marry him anyway," Susan said dreamily. "He's wonderful."

Yes, Livvy thought. *He is.*

Having sent Susan off to check Jane had recovered from her fright, Livvy thought she'd best look in on Ceci. She was a tender-hearted creature, and little Jane must have frightened her half to death this morning. Livvy's heart was still jittering, and she considered herself nigh on unshakeable. She knocked on the door of Ceci's room and went in, finding Ceci standing and gazing out of the window. Birdie was asleep on the bed, barricaded in with pillows and bolsters so she couldn't roll off.

"Adorable," Livvy said with a sigh, watching the baby sleep.

Ceci turned and smiled, a wistful expression on her soft features. Livvy frowned, noting Ceci's eyes were still red.

"Ceci, is everything all right?"

Ceci's lip quivered. "I l-lost the baby, Livvy."

Livvy stared at her in shock.

"Oh, oh, my dear." She ran to her sister-in-law and hugged her tightly as Ceci clung to her and sobbed. "But when? Why didn't you say anything?"

Ceci shrugged, pulling away to wipe at her eyes. "Last night, and there didn't seem any reason to. There was nothing you could do. I wasn't very far along after all, and it's hardly the first time it's happened. There seemed no point in bothering anyone, only... only I wish Charlie had been here."

Livvy opened her mouth to say that Ceci ought to have come and fetched her, but then thought better of it. Goodness, what a night it might have been. Perhaps it was an omen, some strange force telling her that King was not to be hers, even for a short while.

"Livvy," Ceci said, taking her attention once more. "I feel so guilty."

"Why?" Livvy exclaimed in astonishment.

"B-Because I'm glad. It's not that I wouldn't mind more babies, but…. Oh, Livvy, we're poor, aren't we?"

Livvy sighed, looking into Ceci's frightened eyes. She wrestled a handkerchief out of her sleeve and handed it to her. "Yes, love, I rather think we are."

Ceci nodded and wiped her eyes. "Is it my fault? Charlie keeps telling me not to worry but… he keeps going away and he's s-so changed. He doesn't sleep."

For a moment all Livvy's old resentments rose in a wave as she looked about the opulent room, but that wasn't entirely Ceci's fault.

"I've been trying to tell you for some time, Ceci," she said, as gently as she could. "But Charlie loves you so much he wants you to be happy. He thinks you'll leave him if you don't have pretty things and gifts all the time."

"What?" Ceci looked genuinely aghast at the idea.

"Oh, come now," Livvy said, a touch impatient. "We all know you could have married the Duke of Hartington."

"That fat old man!" Ceci retorted in disgust. "You think that… that I'd rather marry that fat old man and be rich than starve with my darling Charlie?"

Livvy stared back at her, surprised and gratified by Ceci's vehemence. The truth was, she had wondered. She knew Ceci loved Charlie, but she was so lethargic about everything that Livvy had questioned how deep the emotion ran. Now she knew. She smiled at Ceci, a genuine, heartfelt smile of affection. "Oh, Ceci, if only you'd told Charlie that before now, but I am so glad to know it's true."

"Well, it is," she said, putting her chin up and showing a glimmer of steel that Livvy had never seen.

Livvy nodded and took Ceci's hands. "Tell Charlie that. Please, Ceci, for I think we may have to leave this place and rent it out. It will be a terrible come down for you, I'm afraid."

Ceci's lip quivered, but she nodded. "M-My clothes… jewellery…?"

Livvy said nothing, just held her gaze and Ceci nodded again.

"Be brave, Ceci. We shall find a way."

"And… and you really won't m-marry…?"

"No!" Livvy said, her voice brooking no argument. "You wouldn't marry a fat old duke and I won't marry Mr Skewes."

"Oh," Ceci replied, understanding dawning. She patted Livvy's hand. "No, dear. In that case, of course you must not marry him."

Livvy let out a breath of surprise and hugged Ceci tightly. "Thank you, and I'm so sorry about the baby, but you must not feel guilty. Of course it is heartbreaking, and if it had been born we would all have loved it with our whole hearts, but it would have been hard, Ceci. It's a weight off all our minds, truth be told, for another mouth to feed now…."

"Yes," Ceci said, her voice thready with emotion. "Yes, I know and… and those things you said about… about how to not have… a-another one."

Livvy drew back in surprise to see Ceci's cheeks burning scarlet.

"I shall speak to Charlie," Ceci said, clearly embarrassed but determined too.

For a moment, Livvy only stared in astonishment. Goodness, what a day this was turning out to be. "Well done, Ceci. I'm so proud of you."

"I can be practical too, Livvy," Ceci said with dignity, and Livvy could only smile.

❧ ❧ ❧

King looked up from the piano keys to find Walsh watching him.

"Calmed down now, have you?" Walsh enquired.

"No," King replied, glowering at the keys. "This is a bloody madhouse."

Walsh snorted. "Must be why you like it so much."

There was a tap, tap, tap, on the window and King jumped, turning to glare at the crow. It tilted its head, regarding King sideways through the glass, one obsidian eye glinting.

"That damned bird," he muttered wrathfully. "I swear it's an omen of doom."

"Or it just wants to come in," Walsh pointed out. He moved to the window.

"No! Walsh, don't you dare—"

But it was too late. The bird flew in with a flurry of black feathers and skidded to a halt on top of the piano. Its big black beak opened and emitted a discordant caw.

"Stay away from me, demon spawn," King said, glaring at it.

It glared back, unblinking.

"Caw!"

At that moment Livvy entered the room, smiling to discover her crow.

"Mr Moon," she said with obvious delight. The crow flew to her, landed on her finger, and allowed her to pet him for a moment before flying back to the top of the piano to bother King.

"Away, you starveling, you elf-skin, you dried neat's-tongue, bull's-pizzle, you stock-fish!" King cursed it.

"Oh, here we go," Walsh muttered, while Livvy looked on with interest.

"Caw!"

"Away, you three-inch fool!"

"King, really," Livvy protested.

"Caw!"

"I am sick when I do look on thee," King said, getting into his stride now.

Mr Moon cocked his head to one side and took a step closer to him. *"Caw!"*

"I scorn you, scurvy companion!"

"Caw!"

"Oh," Livvy said, realisation dawning. "That was Henry IV."

"Thou art a boil, a plague sore!"

"Oh, oh, King Lear!" Livvy said, putting up her hand. She was getting the hang of it now.

"Caw," said Mr Moon, unimpressed.

"Thou art unfit for any place but hell!"

Livvy hesitated and then yelled, *"Richard III!"*

King chuckled, amused despite himself. He looked back at the crow and shuddered. "Oh, Livvy, make it go away. It gives me the pip."

Livvy rolled her eyes at him, clearly thinking him quite ridiculous.

"Come here, my handsome fellow," she said to Mr Moon, obviously seeking to irritate King all the more.

Sadly, it worked, but it was a relief to see her back to her usual self after the morning's upset, so King let it go.

"I'm going for a walk," she said, turning back to King with Mr Moon perched on her shoulder like a parrot. "I should like to show you… *something."*

She made an odd jerking motion with her head in the direction of the garden, making it clear she had an ulterior motive.

Walsh cleared his throat and made himself scarce, clearly interpreting her words in the same way King had.

"Now, Livvy," he scolded, even as his body tightened with anticipation. "If I won't debauch you in the comfort of a bed, you can't think I'm so bloody mad as to do it in this filthy weather. We'd catch our deaths, and frankly—"

"No!" Livvy said, interrupting and tutting at him. "Honestly, is that all you can think of?"

"Me?" King retorted, stung. "Well, I like that!"

Livvy folded her arms, narrowing her eyes at him. "Do you want to see what I've been doing with Ross Moyles, or do you not?"

King's eyes widened.

"Oh," he said, surprised.

"Yes, *oh,"* Livvy repeated, adding a sarcastic tone. "I shall be in the garden in ten minutes. Don't keep me waiting."

"I shouldn't dream of it," King murmured, and watched her hurry away.

King slanted Livvy a look as they walked in silence through the wet garden. The rain had cleared, the sky a bright white, but everything was sodden, and moisture hung in the air. It clung to Livvy's hair, giving her a rather ethereal appearance. God, but she was lovely.

"Stop looking at me like that or I shall drag you into a bush and ravish you," she said tartly, though her beautiful lips twitched with amusement.

King snorted. "You would too."

Livvy nodded. "So, don't tempt me."

He sighed and wondered why life was such a damned bitch. Why now? Why had fate thrown her into his path now and lit her up like a beacon, screaming *love and salvation this way*, if he wasn't allowed to have her. It was too bloody cruel.

"It's this way," she said, taking his hand now they were out of sight of the house and pulling him across an open field.

"Will Mr Moyles be there?" King asked, curious what this was about.

Livvy shook her head.

"No, he has a farm to run." She glanced up at the sky overhead and sighed. "If only there were more sunshine. Still, it's mild enough, that's a blessing. A hard frost is the big concern."

"Is it?" King said, perplexed.

Livvy noted his bemused expression and laughed. "Yes, it is."

She dragged him behind a large, tumble-down barn. Brambles grew thickly here and snagged at their clothes. It looked as if no one had been here for years… until you moved farther around the back. There was a neat path cut through the overgrowth and a well-trodden track. They walked single file now with Livvy leading the way, still holding King's hand as though she were afraid he'd run away. More buildings appeared, decrepit, with holes in their roofs and ivy tangling through broken windows, or the toothy gaps where windows had been.

"Where are we going?" King asked, wondering what on earth she'd been up to.

"Not long now," she called over her shoulder.

They turned a corner and…

"Here!"

King looked about him.

"Well?" Livvy said.

He frowned. "Er…"

She tsked at him and tugged his hand. "Here," she said, pointing down at the remains of what looked to be a storeroom on the side of another small brick building. The walls had been knocked down, leaving perhaps three feet of wall backing onto the barn, which was still intact. Sitting on top of what remained were large windows, clearly salvaged from the other crumbling buildings, fitted to make a kind of cold frame. King moved closer, peering through the glass.

"Good heavens," he said, straightening to stare at Livvy. "Is… is that…?"

"Yes!" Livvy said, beaming at him, clearly proud of herself and enjoying his flummoxed expression. "Isn't it marvellous?"

"But… But how?" King demanded, wondering how they had managed it.

"Well, they're in a bed of manure and oak bark. Both create heat around the roots, you see. Then, in the little building behind, we've piled tons more manure, which also heats the air through those holes in the wall. So, the plants are nice and snug. They do take a lot of tending, but Ross comes every night to cover the frames with blankets and put straw bales around the walls in case of frost."

King gaped at her, so astonished by her resourcefulness he was lost for words.

"Pineapples," he said in wonder, shaking his head. "You're growing *pineapples*. Good heavens. I would never have guessed that was what you were up to. Not in a million years."

Livvy laughed, clapping her hands together and looking thoroughly smug. He wanted to kiss her.

"When?" he said once he had his wits about him again. "How?"

Livvy leaned back against the wall of the barn, looking fondly down at the pineapple plants.

"A few years ago, Charlie and Ceci came back from a grand party and they brought the top off a pineapple. Charlie asked if he could take it to show the children, and his friend agreed. Well, our old gardener, Mr Trethewey, retired years ago, but I often visit him and so I took the top to show him too. He was so excited," she said, grinning now. "He showed me how to peel off the outer spikes and put the top into water. After a few weeks, it had begun forming roots. Oh, King, it was so marvellous. Like magic!"

She laughed, and King moved closer to her, drawn like a magnet, like a man too long in the cold seeking the warmth of a cosy hearth.

"Then what?" he asked, hypnotised by the light in her eyes, the flush in her cheeks from the pleasure of sharing her story with him.

"Well, Mr Trethewey had a friend that worked in the Duke of Hartington's hothouses, and so he wrote to his friend and asked how one might go about growing a pineapple. We assumed he might not wish to tell us, gardeners often keep their secrets close you see, but the fellow had been Mr Trethewey's apprentice as a young man and remembered him fondly, so he sent clear instructions and said to contact him again if ever we needed to."

"And so you roped in your old friend Ross to help you?" King said, wondering at this astonishing woman who had seen an opportunity and grasped at it, made it happen.

Livvy nodded. "I didn't dare tell Charlie. He's so enthusiastic about schemes to get rich, I was worried he'd start spending on the strength of it or get his hopes up too high. We had our first fruit off the original plant the year before last, but the summer was poor, and it was small and green. We got a little for it, enough to keep going, but the plant produced lots of baby plants. Last year we had one, magnificent pineapple. We sold it for two guineas," she said, her pride apparent. "I believe we could have achieved a far greater price if we had the contacts, but as I couldn't tell Charlie or sell it myself, Ross had to, and…. Well, we were pleased enough. And look now."

King looked back at the plants, and at the three healthy looking pineapples.

"I know it's not a fortune, not in the grand scheme of things, but it's been such a blessing for Ross with another baby on the way, and these plants will produce yet more plants after they've fruited. Ross will build another frame next to this one to house them."

"Walsh," King said at once, a flicker of hope stirring in his chest.

"What?"

"Walsh is the fellow you need." King gave a huff of laughter. "Lord knows I don't understand it myself, but being my valet has a certain… *cachet*. Everyone knows him and he knows everyone. Indeed, his bosom pal is valet to the Duke of Sandon. You want contacts with the ear of the rich and powerful, Walsh is your man. He'll get you the best price. I swear the fellow could sell dirt, given strong enough motivation."

"Oh," Livvy said, staring at him in wonder. "Oh, thank you, King. Oh, that's… that's wonderful!"

King shook his head.

"The very least I can do for everything you've given me, Livvy. Though in truth, I am not lifting a finger. It is Walsh who will be of service to you. I am of neither use nor ornament, as ever," he said with a bitter laugh.

"Don't say that!" she said, her anger startling him. "Don't say it and don't ever think it. King… my goodness. Don't you have any idea of the kind of man you are?"

He stared at her for a moment, perplexed by her outburst, but his lips quirked in a wry grin. "Sadly, yes," he replied.

"No." She folded her arms, glaring at him. "No, you don't. You don't have the least clue, you great numbskull. Honestly, if only I could make you see—"

"You've made me see so much," King said, smiling. "You've made me realise what is important, and I can never thank you enough for that. My God, Livvy. You are the most astonishing creature. Truly remarkable. To think of everything you have achieved here. I am so proud of you."

She flushed with pleasure at the compliment. "Oh, well, it was hardly just me. Mr Trethewey had the idea to grow it, and then the information from his friend, and without Ross…"

King stepped closer, unable to stop himself, and pressed his finger to his lips.

"You made it happen, Livvy. You've kept this family together, been mother and father when you've had to be; you are the strongest person I have ever met and you make me feel ashamed for having buckled and given in when you kept going under far harder circumstances."

Livvy shook her head, tears in her eyes now.

"Oh, no. Not harder, for I had my family. I was surrounded by the people I loved and who loved me. They lifted me up when I was utterly blue devilled. You were all alone, King, and that is the hardest thing in the world, and I am so, *so* proud of you. Whatever happens after Christmas, don't be alone anymore. Find someone to care for, someone who cares for you. Please, my love…."

Her voice quavered and King could not bear it. He took her in his arms and held her tight.

"Don't be alone anymore," she whispered.

King buried his face in her hair and squeezed his eyes shut. The idea of not being alone if Livvy was not with him…

He could not bear the thought of anyone taking her place, for no one could. She had snuck into his heart despite his best efforts, and now she'd gotten a hold of him. It was only now he realised how weak he'd been in the past, for his loneliness and despair was nothing to pain of knowing he must give her up. Yet he would bear it, for her. He would not let her down, not let her faith in him be proven hollow. He would survive, he would watch from a distance, cheering her on as she married another and saved her family, and no doubt grew a bloody pineapple empire. God only knew she could do it. She could do it, and he would be glad for her, even as he died a little more for every day that she was not in his life.

Chapter Nineteen

16th December 1818.

And the scales fall...

Livvy padded through the darkened corridor, candle in hand until she got to King's door. Silently, she turned the knob and pushed it open, about to step through when she came face to face with Mr Walsh.

Livvy gave a little squeal as Walsh stepped hurriedly out into the corridor, closing the door behind him.

"I'm so sorry, Miss," he said, looking wretched. "I've tried talking sense to him, but he won't have it and… and I'm to sleep in his room until we leave."

Despite the darkness hiding the furious flush of colour that was scalding Livvy's face, she did not doubt Walsh was aware of her heightened colour. The heat being given off her cheeks must be akin to standing before a crackling fire. *Damn you, King!*

"I see," she said, mortified that the bloody man had employed a… a *bodyguard* to defend his honour. *Argh*.

"Please, Miss, you've got to understand, for all his wild ways, his lordship… he's…"

"Noble and generous and kind, and honourable to his bones," she finished with a heavy sigh.

Walsh's lips turned up in a smile. "Ah, you have got him figured out then."

Livvy nodded. "I suspected when you came after him. You are obviously a very accomplished valet, Mr Walsh, and no doubt in some demand. Why you would stick to a man of the kind his reputation suggested he was made no sense at all… unless there were something about him that inspired a deep sense of loyalty."

"That's, King, a regular conundrum he is. I don't mind telling you I've been at my wit's end these past few years. It's been so good to see him here, to see him heal. He's happy, or at least, he would be if it weren't all about to end."

"Oh, Walsh," Livvy snivelled. "Stop, for heaven's sake. I have become the most dreadful watering pot of late."

Walsh silently handed her a handkerchief. Livvy snatched it from him and buried her face in it until she was calm again.

"You love him," Walsh observed.

"Oh, of course I'm in love with him," she said irritably, flapping the handkerchief at him. "Do stop stating the obvious. Not that it does anyone the least bit of good for I c-can't have him, can I?"

Walsh sighed, scowling, and looking remarkably fierce. "There must be a way. Bleedin' hell! Beg pardon, excuse my French."

Livvy snorted. "Don't mind me. Believe me, I've uttered a few choice words on the subject."

The valet gave her an approving smile. "Reckon you did an' all, Miss. Oh, and I shall get to work on your little project tomorrow if I might borrow some writing materials. I've a good few people in mind who ought to come in handy."

"Thank you, Walsh. That… That is marvellous, and so kind, and I shall ensure you are compensated for your help too."

Walsh waved this off, shaking his head. "Tis a pleasure to help you, Miss. It is truly."

"Oh, don't be nice," Livvy begged, her throat thick. "You'll start me off again."

"Sorry, Miss."

They stood in awkward silence for a moment until Livvy sighed. "So, he will not come out and face me then?" she said, putting her chin up.

"Don't reckon so, Miss, but don't give up. Between us… surely we can think of something."

"If you have a way of turning pineapples into solid gold, I'm all ears," Livvy remarked bitterly, and then turned on her heel and stalked back down the corridor.

❧ ❧ ❧

"Is she gone?" King asked as Walsh returned to his room.

Walsh glowered at him but said nothing.

"Oh, I see," King said, folding his arms. "I'm the monster for keeping an innocent out of my bed. Good to know. Damned if I do, damned if I don't. Nothing new there, I suppose."

"Keep your hair on," Walsh said, tutting. "I know you're doing the right thing it's only… ah well. I wish you'd just marry the girl. You'll never meet another like her, and you know it. Don't let her get away, my lord."

"Tell me how," King growled, frustration and longing making him angry now. "For the love of god, give me something solid, something real, not dreams and fairy tales and *you'll figure something out*. Give me a plan, Walsh, something I can *do.*"

Walsh stared back at him, shoulders hunched.

"No, I didn't think so," King replied with a cynical twist to his lips. "Then keep your bloody mouth shut."

King gritted his teeth, his jaw so tight it hurt. He ought not have spoken to Walsh so, ought not have been so bloody rude, but he couldn't stand it. The days were rushing past. It would be Christmas soon, and then Livvy would leave. She'd go off to her aunt's party and be lost to him for good. He'd go back to Wynford Castle, where only poor Argos would be pleased to see him, to keep him company in the vast echoing expanse of the crumbling estate. He pressed the heels of his hands into his eyes and tried to breathe, but his lungs were tight. *I am not drinking,* he reminded himself. *I am not drinking. I. Am. Not. Drinking.* A hand rested on his shoulder for a moment, a silent show of understanding, before Walsh moved away again.

King looked out the window the next morning to see Charlie had returned. He must have got the driver to push on through the night to have arrived so early. Was that bad news or good news, or just a desperate need to be home? King would do such a thing if Livvy were waiting for him. He pushed the thought away and hurried downstairs. He needed to have a frank discussion with Charlie, and he may as well get it over with.

On reaching the entrance hall, he almost collided with Livvy, holding onto her arm to steady her.

"Good morning," he said, testing the waters to see what mood she was in after last night's foiling of her plans. He doubted she was thrilled with him.

"My lord," she said with a pleasant smile, confirming that she was planning his imminent demise.

"Livvy," he said, his tone low, but she stalked past him, nose in the air to greet her brother.

King hurried out of the door in her wake, pleased for her it was a bright sunny day. That at least ought to put her in better humour, as it was good for her pineapples.

"Charlie, I'm so glad you're home," she said with a smile. "Do hurry up to see Ceci, she's missed you dreadfully."

She embraced her brother warmly, which rather surprised King as he knew how angry she was with him. Personally, he wanted to break the fool's nose, not hug him, but then Charlie wasn't his brother. He'd never had a sibling, so must assume that was normal.

Charlie paled visibly at mention of his beloved.

"She's not ill, is she?" he asked in alarm.

Livvy shook her head but took both of Charlie's hand's lowering her voice. "No, no, she is quite well and apart from missing you, in good spirits, but… Oh, Charlie, I'm afraid she lost the baby. I'm so sorry."

"Oh," her brother's face fell, and King was glad not to have come storming out to confront him as his temper had wanted him to.

The man looked as if he'd just been punched in the gut.

"Oh, well. Not to be, then. I… I suppose… for the best," he said, but with such a sorrowful smile King knew he didn't mean it.

For all that Charlie was a blasted fool who couldn't keep a shilling in his pocket if there was something idiotic to spend it on, he loved his family, that much was obvious.

"Papa! Papa!"

A chorus of little voices echoed from inside the house, and a moment later Charlie disappeared under the onslaught of children. His sorrow vanished in the light of his warm greeting and he hugged each child, handing out lemon drops in return for a kiss. A burst of jealousy ripped through King, so intense it stole his breath. Not because the children wanted to greet their father and did not run to him, not that. Just that… that Charlie had *all this*. King had always known he'd wanted this too, a home, a family, but he hadn't quite realised how badly, how deep the wound had been when his father had tied his future up with some silly child he would feel more a father to than a husband. God, the idea sickened him.

"Ah, Boscawen. A word, if I may."

King stiffened as he turned towards the voice, the sound of footsteps having been drowned out by the children's excitement. He looked to Livvy, who shrank back, moving towards him. King wondered if she knew she'd done it and felt a burst of pride in knowing she felt she could rely on him, and utter fury that this creature could make Livvy shrink away. His bold, fierce Livvy who looked the world square in the eye was afraid of this man, and that made him furious.

He went to move forward, to tell Mr Skewes to get the hell away from her, but Livvy caught his sleeve. Her eyes held a warning light as he glanced back. *Not your place,* they said silently.

King clenched his fists, frustrated by the knowledge that she was correct.

"Mr Skewes," Charlie replied, smiling warmly, and holding out a hand to his neighbour. "Good to see you."

"I wish I might believe you, my lord," Mr Skewes said, an angry edge to his reply. "I'm afraid I have come to doubt my welcome in this house."

His cold blue eyes glared at Livvy and King moved in front of her, blocking his view, meeting that hard stare with one of his own.

Charlie glanced between Skewes and his sister, and then King.

"I'm afraid I don't follow, Mr Skewes," he said. "Come along into my study and we can talk in private. I'll have some tea brought. I'm parched, I don't mind telling you. Such a journey..."

"Oh, stop prattling on, you damned fool," Mr Skewes said. "Your sister has made me a laughingstock, telling the whole bloody world that she'd not marry me if I were the last eligible man in the country. Well, either she marries me before the year is out or you can all take up residence in debtor's prison for all I care. You can bloody rot there."

Charlie gaped, clearly never having seen this side of Mr Skewes before now, nor having suspected it was there. The fellow never could see when someone was playing him for a fool; he'd been a magnet for bullies at school.

The children gasped, huddling around their father at the man's words, which had clearly terrified them. Anger rose in King's chest and he stepped forward, but a furious Livvy pushed past him.

"You get away from here, you sorry excuse for a man. What the devil do you think you are playing at, speaking to Lord Boscawen with such disrespect and saying such vile things in front of the children? Can't you see you are frightening them?"

Mr Skewes sneered at her. "It's only the truth, Livvy, and it's about time they discovered what a witless creature their father has been. He's the one they should be afraid of, he's the one whose condemned them all to a life in the gutter… if they're lucky. You could save them that, you could save them all of it. But no. Miss hoity toity Penrose thinks she's too good for me because her brother is a viscount. Well, I tell you this, if you want me to save your blasted family from the mire, you'll come to me on bended knee and beg me, and you will come Livvy, crawling through the dirt like a dog. *You will come to heel."*

Livvy gasped, colour rushing to her cheeks as her anger rose. "You call yourself a gentleman? You do not know the meaning of the word, you, smug, pompous, *vile little man."*

Mr Skewes jolted as if she'd slapped him and raised his hand.

Livvy gasped, stumbling back.

King saw red.

He snatched at the hand before it could make contact, yanking Skewes around to face him.

"Don't you dare!" King growled.

Skewes glared at him in fury. "This is none of your business, you interfering bastard."

King didn't budge, standing between Skewes and Livvy. "It's not yours either, Livvy has made her choice."

Mr Skewes made a sound of impotent rage and threw a punch which King dodged and then planted his fist in the man's face with a such a burst of rage he heard the crunch as much as felt it. Skewes howled as he fell to the ground, clutching his nose. The desire to pick him up and do it again was a thrum in King's blood, his heart thudding with the desire to hurt the man who would raise his hand to a woman. He struggled to calm himself, to remember he was a gentleman, a better man than this wretched creature, not that it was much of an accomplishment.

"Get out before I throttle you," King said through his teeth, his fists clenched. "And don't you ever, *ever*, come back "

Skewes scrambled away from King, getting to his feet.

"You'll regret this when you are all out in the street," he yelled back at them, except with his hand clutching his broken nose it sounded rather more like—*Yoogretis wenarou ina steet*—and it rather lost some of its sting.

349

Charlie stared after the man as he stumbled away from them before turning to Livvy.

"Oh, Liv. Livvy, I… I swear I didn't know. I would never have suggested…"

Livvy let out a breath King suspected she'd been holding for some time and gave her brother a wan smile.

"Least said, soonest mended, I think, Charlie."

Her brother's expression was pained, but he nodded.

"I'd say I'd make it up to you, but…" He spread his hands in a rather hopeless gesture.

"Oh, Charlie," Livvy said, and ran into his arms.

King rounded up the children, who were still white-faced and round-eyed with shock.

"Come along, now," he said, urging them inside to give Livvy and her brother some privacy. "That's enough excitement for one day. Let's see if Gelly has some cake for us."

"Cake," George said, giving King an anxious glance.

King hated the fact that the children had seen him hit Mr Skewes and could only imagine what they thought of him now. Probably for the best but… but the idea that they might think badly of him or be afraid of him… his heart hurt.

He felt soft fingers touch his and looked down to see Jane inspecting his knuckles. "Come along," she said, shaking her head in a perfect imitation of her Aunt Livvy. "That needs seeing to."

"Ing?" George said, leaning away from Lydia, who was carrying him and holding his arms out.

King felt a lump in his throat as he took the boy and George curled his arms tight about his neck. "Bad man gone. You made bad man go away, Ing. I not like that man."

King drew in a sharp breath and held George's warm little body close. "I didn't like him either, George, and yes, he's gone. He won't be back."

George kissed his cheek. "Cake now, Ing."

King laughed, though there was an odd, quaver to the sound that disturbed him. Bloody twit, getting all emotional. What the devil was wrong with him?

Feeling the weight of eyes upon him, King turned to see Susan staring at him. She blushed and smiled and looked away.

"I say, King, that was a smashing facer you landed him," Harry said with breathless enthusiasm. "Did you ever fight with Gentleman Jackson? Is he as marvellous as they say? Would you show me?"

King let Harry's excited questions carry him along, hoping by the time he arrived in the kitchen, he'd be calm enough to answer the lad.

Livvy waited until later that day to speak with her brother. Now that he had stopped pushing her to marry Mr Skewes and was feeling wretched about having done so, she had an opportunity. It would be so much easier to go to her aunt's party if she had his blessing after all. It was a risk. Charlie could be remarkably stubborn, especially if propriety was in question, but they were clearly inching closer to desperation. He must see that they needed to grasp every opportunity they had.

She heard laughter from inside the study as she raised her hand to knock. Ceci was with him, and in much better spirits now her beloved was home. Livvy had underestimated her, she realised. Ceci was a frivolous creature it was true, but she would stand strong beside Charlie, no matter what.

"Come," her brother called, and Livvy went in. "Livvy, come and have some tea and scones. It's the last of strawberry jam too."

Ceci patted the seat beside her and Livvy went and sat down, helping herself to a cup of tea.

"I need to speak with you both," she said, once she was settled with her teacup in hand. "I... I have an idea. I planned to do this without your knowledge, but now you see what kind of man Mr Skewes is, I hope you might feel happier in trusting my judgement. I warn you though, I shall do this, with or without your blessing."

Charlie got to his feet, frowning down at her.

"Go on," he said, moving to stand beside the fire.

Livvy took a breath. "I intend to go to Aunt Agatha's New Year's house party in the hopes of finding a husband."

Charlie gaped at her, and even Ceci let out a little gasp.

"Out of the question," Charlie said at once. "Aunt Agatha is… good heaven's Livvy, she's scandalous. Do you have any idea how many lovers she's had?"

Livvy shrugged. "None whatsoever. You will never speak of her to me, but she can't be considered so scandalous as that for she's still the height of fashion, is she not? Even I know her parties are legendary."

Charlie stared at her. "Livvy, Agatha is a wealthy widow. Such women are allowed a deal more license than unmarried ones, but…."

"Respectable people go to her parties, don't they?" Livvy pressed.

"Y-Yes," Charlie said, for he was the kind of man who would tell the truth even if he didn't like it. "But she is… she will… she's a bad influence, Livvy."

"Oh, stuff," Livvy said, impatient now. "I'm four and twenty, Charlie, not a silly child of sixteen. I am beyond being influenced."

"Charlie," Ceci said tentatively. "Be reasonable. You know how sensible Livvy is. Far more than we are," she added with a smile.

Livvy looked at Ceci in surprise, not having expected her support.

"Thank you," she said.

Charlie still looked doubtful.

"Look, Charlie," Livvy said with a sigh. "The chances are it will come to nothing but, in the first place, we have very few opportunities left to us, and in the second, I have never met my aunt. I should like the chance to do so, and if she is as wealthy as all that, perhaps she might at least sponsor Harry through school. We do not have the luxury of pride any longer, or are you going to tell me that things are not as bad as I think?"

A flush of colour tinged her brother's cheeks and his shoulders sagged. Livvy watched as he sat down again.

"No, Livvy. I cannot tell you that. We shall have to leave here. I have a few options, fellows who might rent it from me. We won't be in the gutter as Mr Skewes so eloquently described our situation, but… but the truth is things are going to be very tight indeed. I have debts to pay and…" He put his head in his hands and took a deep breath. "Livvy, I am your brother, it is my job to protect you so… so if you must go to this wretched party… I shall escort you."

Livvy let out a breath of relief.

"Thank you," she said, wondering why she did not feel more relieved. "Like I said, it's unlikely to come to anything but… well, even if all I manage is to get Aunt Agatha to help Harry, it will have been more than worthwhile."

"Oh, Livvy. Don't be a silly goose. You'll be a great success, I'm sure you will," Ceci said, smiling at her. "Though I really think you ought to marry Lord Kingston, the poor man is in love with you, after all."

"King?" Charlie said in shock.

Livvy stared at Ceci, too stunned to speak for a moment. That Ceci had even noticed there was something between them was shocking enough, but that King might… that he could be….

"In l-love," she stammered. "W-With me?"

Ceci rolled her eyes to the ceiling. "Good heavens, I'm not that oblivious to what goes on in this house, Livvy. Oh, Charlie, you should see them together, it's adorable. He's head over ears, I swear it."

Charlie looked back at Livvy with interest.

"No," she said, shaking her head, though her throat was tight. "You know as well as I do Ceci is a hopeless romantic. I believe that… that Lord Kingston is *fond* of me, yes, but… but as for being in love… Besides, it's impossible. His father has already selected a bride and won't accept any other. King has no money and, if he married me, his father would cut him off for good. There would be no hope of reconciliation. I could not ask that of him, even… even if he did wish to and I might point out, Ceci, he has not given me reason to believe he… he loves me, or he would want to m-marry me."

"Livvy," Charlie said, anxiety in his blue eyes. "King is an awfully charming fellow and a dreadful one for the ladies. He… he hasn't…?"

"No!" Livvy said at once, flushing scarlet. "No, he has taken no liberties, so I beg you not to speak to him on the subject. He has been a perfect gentleman."

More's the pity, she added silently.

Charlie looked a little sceptical but nodded and Livvy let out a breath.

"Very well, Livvy, we shall leave after Christmas and I will escort you to Aunt Agatha's, though heaven alone knows what kind of reception we shall receive. I only met her once and… it did not go well."

Livvy sighed. One problem at a time.

Chapter Twenty

24th December 1818.

A Christmas like no other.

King had woken early. It was strange how his life had changed. Not so long ago, he would have slept the day away, for there was nothing worth getting up for. Sleeping off the previous night's excesses was what the daylight hours were for. Not so now. Now he woke earlier and earlier, eager for the day ahead, desperate to snatch every moment he could with Livvy before this enchanted period of his life was over and gone. Time was passing too quickly, the minutes falling away like trying to hold sand in his grasp.

Christmas Eve already.

King forced the ache in his chest down, the panicky sensation that rose when he considered how little time was left. It could be measured in hours now, the time until he would be forced to say goodbye, to watch Livvy leave and never see her again.

Don't. Don't think on it.

He took a deep breath and concentrated on tying his cravat, but his fingers were all thumbs today. By some unspoken agreement, they had all made the past days as full and happy as was possible. Charlie and Ceci had joined in and they had played games with the children, King had played piano for impromptu dances and they had gone for long walks when the sun shone. Mealtimes were animated and filled with laughter and conversation and… and how would he carry on when his nights were spent with only Argos and poor devoted Walsh for company.

Don't think on it.

"Here, let me do that," Walsh said, exasperated with his mangling of the cravat. "A right pig's ear you've made of it."

King huffed but allowed Walsh to take over. Foolish to realise he'd even miss seeing the wretched piglet trotting about, though he was happy enough never to see the blasted crow again. He'd bring it home and happily, however, if Livvy came too.

"So, they've agreed she can go to her aunt's party then," Walsh said.

King felt his valet's gaze upon him, studying him. "They have."

"Reckon she'll find herself a husband then."

"I suppose so," King replied, terse. He knew damn well what Walsh was up to.

"Think you can live with that?"

"Damn it, Walsh, that will do." King knocked Walsh's hand aside and reached for his coat, shrugging it on without help. "What the devil do you want me to say?"

"That you'll not be such a damn fool and let her go," Walsh said stubbornly.

"How can I not?" King said, opening his arms out in a look at me gesture. "This is all I can offer her. A bloody drunkard with nothing but a crumbling castle he can't afford to live in. I have no friends, my parents can't bear to look at me, I've wasted my bloody life…"

"You do have friends," Walsh retorted. "These people are your friends, and Miss Penrose isn't some fragile flower what needs protecting. She's a worker, and she's used to scrimping and saving. She wouldn't turn a hair."

"But she ought not have to scrimp and save, for the love of god!" King raged. "She deserves better, far better. Better than me, that's for good and certain."

"Perhaps," Walsh said, shaking his head. "But does she want better? You ever thought to ask her?"

King shook his head. "She's had her head turned by the first fellow to show her any notice, that's all. Once she's out in the world…"

Walsh made an angry sound and stalked to the door. "So, you're saying she don't know her own mind, right?"

"Women are easy," King said dully, trying to make himself believe that was all it was. "You know that. A handsome face and few pretty compliments… putty in my hands, Walsh. It's not like you haven't seen it a hundred times before."

"Not like this," Walsh growled, glaring at him. "Nothing like this and you know it."

King shrugged and Walsh left the room, slamming the door behind him.

For a long moment, King stood, staring out of the window. It was a beautifully sunny, frosty morning, and he hoped Mr Moyles had tucked the pineapples up nice and warm last night. Today they were going to cut greenery to decorate the house for Christmas. The children were excited and Livvy had been busy in the kitchens, helping Gelly prepare for the feast.

Don't be maudlin, he scolded himself. The children were going to have a wonderful Christmas. He'd promised Livvy he would help her ensure that and… and so he would. So he plastered a smile onto his face and tried to ignore the pain in his chest that was growing steadily with every minute that passed. He would survive. They would both survive. They would move on and go back to their lives and… and everything would be just fine. It would.

Oh, God.

Livvy crouched on the floor, doing the buttons up on George's coat before winding a thick scarf around his neck and pulling on his hat, next mittens. Once everything was properly covered, she stood straight again.

"There," she said.

"Good heavens, the poor child looks like a starfish."

Livvy turned, her heart doing its usual little dance in her chest at the sound of King's voice. "It's cold out."

"Yes, but he can't move. George, are you in there?" King demanded, crouching down to inspect the child.

There was a muffled sound and King tsked, moving the scarf so it no longer covered George's mouth.

"Ah, there he is," King said.

"'Ot," George said plaintively. "Too 'ot!"

"I'm not surprised, my lad. No wonder you're always undressing. Well come along, it's cooler outside, though hardly arctic as your aunt seems to believe."

King scooped George up as the other children gathered about them.

"Ah, everybody is ready," Charlie said, clapping his hands together.

"Here's your scarf, dear," Ceci said, handing it over to her husband. Birdie was in her arms, watching proceedings with interest. "Now don't forget to find me some mistletoe," she added with a mischievous glint in her eyes.

"Your wish is my command, dearest." Charlie kissed her and Ceci gazed adoringly at him.

"Are you sure you won't come, Ceci?" Livvy asked.

"Oh, no," Ceci said. "It's too cold for Birdie, and all that tramping about in the mud. No, I shall stay here with my little bird and have a lovely morning, I assure you."

Once everyone was ready, they set out. Spargo was waiting for them with a large barrow to collect their wares, and everyone else had baskets. The children set off at a run, giggling and shouting, their breath blowing clouds on the chill air. Charlie walked with Spargo and Harry, the three of them chatting amicably.

Livvy glanced sideways at King with little George in his arms. She wondered what would become of him when he left them. Fretting over this was something she was doing more and more, indeed it kept her awake at night. King needed company, needed looking after. He might be a big, strong looking fellow, and he was filling his clothes out properly now after plenty of rest and good healthy meals, but he wasn't nearly as unbreakable as his appearance might suggest. There was a gentle soul beneath that fierce exterior. Seeing him with George was enough to illustrate that fact with no doubt. He adored the boy, and she feared leaving the children would hurt him more than he realised. If ever a man needed a family, it was King.

They had fallen behind the others and no one was paying them any mind, so Livvy slipped her hand into his. His gloves were of the finest leather and she felt the heat of him as his fingers curled about hers. He glanced down at her.

"Christmas already," he said, smiling. "I don't know where the time went."

Livvy shook her head. "Me either. I… I wish…."

"Don't," he said, and she looked up sharply, aware of a desperate edge to his voice. He met her eyes, and she saw the apology there as he shook his head. He did not wish for them to speak of it, to acknowledge it. Well, perhaps that was for the best.

"Look, *Ke re ow,* " George sounded out, pointing as a large black bird swooped overhead.

"Crow!" Livvy said, smiling at him. "Quite right, well done, George, clever boy. It's Mr Moon."

King glowered. "Ugh."

"Be nice," Livvy warned him, smiling, even though she wanted to cry.

"S'alright, Ing," George said, patting his shoulder. "No be 'fraid. George keep Ing safe."

King gave a surprised little laugh and hugged George to him. "Thank you. Thank you, George," he said, and Livvy had to hurry away as tears pricked at her eyes and her throat grew tight.

By lunchtime, they had a huge barrow full of greenery, holy and ivy and evergreen, laurel and hawthorn, but still no mistletoe. The children were cold and hungry by now though, so everyone headed back towards the house. Livvy turned to see where King was, realising he was not giving up the hunt. Charlie had taken George and the other children were rushing home with the prospect of hot chocolate and food giving them a last burst of energy. No one was paying her any mind, and though she knew he would be cross with her, she would not let King leave with nothing said between them. She was desperate to feel his arms about her again, and the very least he owed her was a kiss after thwarting her plans so thoroughly.

She crept through the woodland as quietly as she could so he did not realise she was there until she was quite close to him.

He turned and saw her and let out a huff of laughter. "I should have known."

"You did know," she said, smiling at him. "You wanted me to come after you."

He lowered his eyes and looked away from her.

"Yes," he said simply. "Though I thought perhaps good sense might prevail."

"Don't be silly."

She moved closer to him and then stilled as something caught her eye. "Oh, King, look," she said, laughing now. "How perfect."

King looked up, to see a large ball of mistletoe in the branches of the tree he was standing beneath. He shook his head. "The universe is conspiring against me as usual," he said with a snort.

Livvy moved closer, relieved when he didn't step away. "Perhaps the universe knows a thing or two that we don't," she said softly and slid her arms about his waist.

King let out a breath. "I wish it would give me a bit of help in that case."

"I think this one is easy enough to interpret," Livvy said, reaching up with one hand and drawing his head down, seeking his mouth.

"Livvy," he protested, but it was a half-hearted effort at best.

He kissed her, pulling her into his arms, so tight she could hardly breathe, his kiss so fierce it was as though he needed it like he needed air. Livvy's heart raced in her chest, giddy with desire and happiness and longing and the desperation of knowing this was all she would have of him.

"King, oh, King, I can't bear it."

"Don't, Livvy, don't say it, I can't…"

Livvy heard the pain in his voice and her heart leapt even as she knew it changed nothing. He did care, perhaps he even loved her a little…

She kissed him again, pressing herself against his hard body and wanting… wanting so much, *everything.*

"Oh, God, don't, don't… I… Christ, love." King gasped as she wrestled his shirt free and slid her cold hands beneath. She laughed at his shock, revelling in the feel of his hot skin beneath her palms. "You little wretch."

"You never did teach me how to seduce a man, King. You never taught me what I needed to know."

King cupped her face between his large hands, staring down at her, his dark eyes warm and gentle. "Ah, love. You never needed it. Did you never realise? I've been yours since the beginning, Livvy. If I didn't love you so much, I would never be able to resist you, I would never be able to let you go, but I could never hurt you, beautiful Olivia. You deserve the world, and I cannot give it to you."

"Oh," Livvy stared up at him, hardly able to take in his words. He loved her. He loved her, but he was still going to let her go. She burst into tears and clung to him, and he held her tight.

"Come along, we'd best cut this mistletoe and get back before they send out a search party. I have no wish to answer a lot of awkward questions from your brother."

He kissed her forehead and let her go and Livvy almost stamped her foot with frustration, but she knew that was no way to get what she wanted, what she needed. For that… for that she would need a plan.

By the evening, the house was bedecked with greenery. They had adorned the mantelpieces with fir and berry studded holly, and there had been much muttering and cursing over the tying of red ribbons as the vicious leaves stabbed at tender fingers. Candles glowed, and Spargo and Charlie had hauled in a massive Yule log which was burning in the hearth. The house was quiet now, though. The children had gone to bed, chattering and merry, full of excitement for the great feast tomorrow. Everyone would be up early in the morning with plenty of jobs for everyone to do before they could get to the business of celebrating. Once upon a time this house had been filled with servants, and the idea that Livvy or any of them should dirty their hands with chores too ridiculous for words. Times had changed though, and in truth, Livvy did not mind it. Though her hands were not pretty and smooth as they had once been, she did not enjoy sitting idle. Tonight, however, she was not thinking about the jobs that needed doing, nor the day ahead, she was lying in wait.

"Mr Walsh."

Walsh leapt about a foot in the air as she stepped out of the parlour door to intercept him in the corridor.

"Saints preserve me," Walsh said, clutching at his heart. "Lord, but you gave me a turn."

"I do beg your pardon, Mr Walsh. I did not intend to startle you."

She stood silently for a moment while the man drew in a steadying breath. "Thought everyone had gone to bed long since," he said, turning towards her at last.

Livvy gave him an apologetic smile and shook her head. "I waited up. I… I need to speak with you about… Well, it's a little indelicate, but… but I have come to trust you, Mr Walsh, and I flatter myself that you like me enough to—"

"He's expecting me, Miss," Walsh said, giving her a sad smile. "If I don't come, he'll go looking. It won't work, not tonight…" He broke off and pursed his lips. "Tomorrow night though, I've said I'll pitch in and help Gelly and Spargo with the cleaning up. Reckon that could take… Oh, hours and hours. I'll not want to disturb him by the time I'm done, I reckon."

Livvy let out a breath. "Thank you."

Walsh nodded.

Heat burned up the back of her neck as Livvy considered just what it was she was doing, and that this man knew about it. "You must think me such a—"

Walsh reached out and squeezed her hand. "I think people do desperate things when they're in love, and I hope you might use the time to talk some bloody sense into him. He needs you, Miss. I told you that from the start. I never seen anyone handle him how he needs handling and… ah, bloody hell. If you want a bit of advice, you'll get him to ruin you, then he'd be duty bound to make you his wife. He'd never consider not marrying you then. Honour, you see, Miss."

Livvy laughed, the sound startled out of her. "Well, I thank you for your advice, Mr Walsh, but I'd never trap him in such a way. I cannot ask him to choose me over his father. Somehow, they must be reconciled, and his fortunes restored to him. Living in poverty with me hardly has anything to recommend it, now does it?"

"It has you, Miss," Walsh said firmly, and Livvy's heart warmed at the compliment.

"I wish that were enough," she whispered, a catch in her voice. "Thank you, though, for tomorrow night. I… I just need time… time to say goodbye."

Walsh nodded, and Livvy turned away and hurried up to bed.

25th December 1818.

"Do you think…?"

"Yes!" Walsh said, exasperated. It might not have been the first time King had mentioned this. "Yes, I think the presents are perfect and they'll love them."

King huffed, unconvinced. "They're hardly presents, mere trifles. I feel ridiculous giving such paltry offerings."

Walsh took a deep breath. King got the impression he was praying for patience. "My lord, those children adore you. They'd be happy with anything you gave them, but the gifts are personal and thoughtful, they'll be chuffed to bits, you mark my words."

Mollified, King nodded and gathered the little collection of wrapped gifts together. He had something for Livvy too, but that would have to wait until later.

King hurried downstairs and hid the presents in an out of the way corner before investigating what was going on. The hub of activity seemed naturally to be focused between the kitchen and the dining room.

"Look, King," Jane called, waving him into the dining room where the children were helping Spargo decorate the table. The best china and crystal and silverware had been polished and shined, and King tried not to think about the possibility of it all being sold off. He hoped things weren't so very dire. "Doesn't it look lovely?"

King nodded, smiling at her and picking up a hand drawn place marker. "Beautiful, Jane. Did you make these? They're fabulous."

Jane shook her head.

"Rebecca did them."

King looked at the girl. She was by far the quietest of the siblings and the most serious. She pushed her glasses up her nose, flushed with pleasure at his words. King inspected the place marker with each person's name carefully drawn in different coloured ink. She had illustrated the names too, with whatever she thought appropriate. King's was drawn with a large curly K and there were little golden crowns and musical notes all around it.

"You have a very fair hand with a pen, Rebecca. These are quite lovely. May I keep mine after dinner?"

"Oh. Oh, yes, of course," she said shyly. "I should like you to have it."

"Thank you. I shall treasure it."

Leaving the girl flustered and pink, King went to investigate the kitchens.

He paused on the threshold, enveloped by the delicious scents of Christmas, and enjoying the bustling scene before him. Livvy was in the thick of things as he had expected, her cheeks flushed, golden curls falling around her face.

"Good morning," he said, causing Livvy to jump and drop the spoon she was holding. It clattered into the saucepan she'd been peering into.

"Oh, King. Good morning to you."

"Is there anything I can do to help? You all look rather frantic," he said, noticing that even Ceci was here, though to be honest, she looked rather less frantic and was stirring a saucepan with a lazy hand and a dreamy expression.

Gelly glanced up at him in horror.

"An earl… in my kitchen? I think not, my lord," she tsked. "What would people say?"

"Oh, nonsense," Livvy said briskly. "No one will ever know. Why shouldn't he help if he wants to? There's all those Brussels sprouts to peel, for one thing."

Brussels sprouts? Damn. He'd had to open his mouth.

Livvy took his arm and guided him to the kitchen table. Then she fetched a large bowl of sprouts and gave him an empty saucepan and a small knife.

"Like this," she said, demonstrating how to peel off the outer leaves and cut the base of the sprout.

Well, that didn't look too challenging.

King set to work, enjoying the hum of conversation as Gelly and Livvy and Ceci chattered. The children came and went, fetching and carrying, and Spargo with a tray full of wine glasses. He shot Livvy an apologetic glance.

"Forgot," he said. "Sorry."

374

"Oh," King looked up, realising they'd be forgoing wine on his account. "No, don't… You ought not have to…"

"We don't have to," Livvy said firmly. It was her *obey or suffer the consequences* voice and he knew better than to argue with her. "We are choosing to. None of us are great drinkers so it is no vast sacrifice, I assure you. We will be far happier knowing you are comfortable than making you restless for the sake of a few sips of wine."

"I… Thank you." King held her gaze, not knowing quite what to say. He'd never felt so entirely at home, so very welcomed as he had in this rather unconventional household. For a moment he imagined his father's reaction if he'd ever come across him peeling sprouts in the kitchen. Good God, he'd have an apoplexy on the spot. Yet King was happy. True, he would not wish to do it every day, nor did he imagine Gelly would welcome him. As it was, she kept giving him sceptical glances and inspecting the sprouts to see if he was making a mess of it. But today was Christmas, and it seemed truly to be full of gladness in a way he had never experienced it before. The holiday had meant nothing to him other than a day of suffering through his parent's company and trying his best to be visibly grateful for a lavish gift that he never seemed to be grateful enough for. Not enough to please his father, at least.

Once preparations were well advanced and the increasingly over excited children were on the point of bursting, they ate a hurried breakfast and then it was declared to be time for presents. Everyone gathered in the parlour and Charlie began distributing gifts to the children.

"They were already bought," he whispered to his sister, an apologetic glimmer in his eyes.

Livvy only gave a slightly exasperated laugh and shook her head, kissing Charlie's cheek. "Merry Christmas, Charlie."

Everything was unwrapped and exclaimed over, and Charlie thoroughly scolded for having bought George a drum.

"Look, Ing," George said, proudly striding up and down with the drum on a string about his neck. He hit it with great enthusiasm until all the girls were holding their ears.

"Marvellous," King said, relieved he was no longer drinking. That would have been a hellish noise for a man with a hangover. It was quite trying enough sober. "I tell you what though, George. I have a little something for you too, but… you must put the drum down to unwrap it."

George pursed his lips, considering this, before casting the drum to one side. Everyone let out a breath of relief.

"Present, Ing?" George said, bouncing eagerly on his toes.

"Only a very little present," King warned him, anxious now in case he'd over egged the pudding and the child was disappointed. After all, it wasn't an exciting gift for a small boy.

King handed it over to him, watching nervously as George unwrapped it with surprising care.

"Oh!" George said, staring at it. "Argos?"

King nodded, pleased he'd made the connection. "Yes. I'm no great artist, but I think it's a fair likeness."

"Look! Look, Libby. Argos." He ran to his aunt, waving the little pencil drawing.

Livvy looked at it and King's heart ached at the look she sent him, so very happy and proud. "Why, how modest you are, my lord. It's beautiful. He looks a very fine fellow indeed, doesn't he, George?"

George nodded and sat staring at the picture for a moment before remembering his drum. "Take Argos for me, Lib Lib," he said, thrusting the picture at her and rushing off to commence bursting everyone's eardrums again.

"Oh, George, do take it into the hallway," Ceci wailed, clutching at her ears.

Thankfully he did, and the sound muted somewhat as he strode up and down the length of the house. Everyone laughed with relief.

"Right, er… Susan, Lydia and Rebecca, Jane and Birdie." King handed over small parcels containing a variety of colourful ribbons that Mrs Cardy in the haberdasher's had assured him would find favour with the girls. He was relieved to discover she was correct. Ceci exclaimed happily over Birdie's pink ribbon and insisted on making a bow on top of the baby's head with her little golden curls. She looked so adorably silly that everyone had to kiss her, which made Birdie giggle and coo. The largest parcel King gave to Harry, who exclaimed with delight to discover five of King's best cravats.

"Oh, King, I… but you won't have anything left to wear," Harry protested.

King laughed and shook his head. "Walsh always packs far too many, and I've plenty more at home. Do not trouble yourself on that count."

"Well, that… that's marvellous. Thank you so much." Harry had gone a bright pink and was staring down at the cravats with something akin to awe. King smiled, a little dazed to discover that Walsh had been correct. They had been more than pleased with his gifts.

As it was the tradition of the house that only the children got gifts on Christmas day, King was a little stunned to discover they all had something for him. There were drawings from the younger children, a carefully written letter from Harry thanking him earnestly for his cravat tying lessons, a colourful scribble from George which the boy presented alongside a big wet kiss, and a handkerchief from Susan with a large, slightly askew K embroidered in one corner. By the time they were done, King was thoroughly overwhelmed. He stammered his thanks, gathered up his gifts and made a hurried excuse, disappearing out of the door. He most certainly needed a moment to compose himself.

Chapter Twenty One

25th *December 1818.*

The most marvellous Brussels sprouts, and a change of heart.

Livvy watched King escape with a sigh. She wished she could make a home for him where he could get used to being treated with such love and affection without the need to run away when it all got too much.

"Is he all right?"

Livvy turned to her brother, who looked puzzled over King's hurried exit.

"Do you know much about his parents, Charlie?" she asked.

Her brother pulled a face. "Ugh, the Marquess of Eynsham and his lady. More than I need to, I assure you. Very high in the instep."

Livvy nodded, unsurprised. "Can you imagine being an only child with them at Christmas?"

Charlie's eyes grew wide. "The poor devil. I… I never considered."

Livvy nodded sadly as Charlie confirmed what she had guessed to be true. "He's not used to being so welcomed, not by a family of our peculiar variety anyway," she amended wryly. They both knew he'd been welcomed with open arms by a certain section of society, but that was not an appropriate topic of conversation.

"You told me once that King didn't have friends," she said, her voice low. "Is that true?"

"Yes, I believe it probably is," Charlie said, thoughtful now. "He was always a popular boy at school. Idolised actually, but… but I don't remember him ever having close friends. Nothing changed since either. He's always seen out carousing with the same old faces but I… No. I can't imagine him being friends with them exactly."

Livvy frowned, wondering what he would do next. Surely, he could not mean to return to those fair-weather friends. It would a terrible strain on him to return to that life and not begin drinking again.

"Will he be all right?" she asked, unable to still the fear in her heart for him. "When he leaves us, I mean."

Charlie gave her a searching look. "You are in love with him, Livvy."

Livvy shrugged, unable to deny it. "I… Oh, Charlie, I worry for him so."

Her brother sighed and took her hand. "I've let you down, Livvy. I know I have. If I hadn't made such a blasted mull of things, you might have married him and…"

"Don't," she said, shaking her head, understanding now why King had stopped her from saying what she wanted. It was too raw to speak of.

"Whatever happens, I shall stay in touch with him, Livvy. I shall make certain he is well, and he will always be welcome with us, no matter where we end up."

Livvy nodded, her throat tight, and clung to her brother's hand.

By the time dinner was ready, King had composed himself and Livvy had buried her heartbreak convincingly enough to make merry with the rest of the family.

Gelly had made them a splendid feast and there was a large roasted goose and a dozen other dishes from roasted potatoes to glazed carrots and peas and, to Charlie's delight, not a single dish of cabbage. Everyone exclaimed that the Brussels sprouts were the finest they had ever eaten and made King laugh with their increasingly ridiculous compliments. All except for George, who had taken one look at the sprout on his plate and handed it back to King.

"Ugh," he said, screwing up his little face.

Everyone dissolved.

The Christmas pudding was served with thick cream and whilst a little less indulgent than usual, having been fed with plum juice instead of brandy over the past weeks, was no less delicious.

Once dinner was done, parlour games ensued and Livvy wondered at how she was falling ever deeper in love with King as he happily made a fool of himself with the silly games everyone insisted he take part in.

Too soon the day was over, and the children were reluctantly put to bed, all except for George, who had fallen asleep in King's lap an hour earlier than usual, utterly exhausted.

Finally the house was silent, and Livvy met Walsh's eye as they passed in the corridor. "Got a deal of clearing up to do in the kitchens," he said awkwardly. "Then I told Spargo I'd play cards, as it's our day off tomorrow. Don't need to get up early see, so…"

Livvy moved closer and kissed Walsh's cheek. "Thank you," she said simply. "I shall be leaving early in the morning. It will take two or three days to get to Bath and my brother wishes to go to my aunt's before the party begins to ensure, well… that we are not thrown into the gutter in front of all her guests, I think. I believe they are rather at outs."

Walsh nodded his understanding.

Livvy turned away and then thought better of it. "Don't… don't wake him tomorrow, then. You should both enjoy a lie in. I shall say everything I wish to tonight and… I don't think I could bear to say goodbye to him. Not in front of everyone. You do understand?"

Walsh nodded, and she was surprised to see his eyes glitter with emotion. "I do, Miss, and… I wish things were different."

Livvy nodded. "So do I. Merry Christmas, Walsh. Take good care of him for me."

"I'll do my best, Miss Penrose. Merry Christmas to you too."

Livvy hurried away, returning to her room before she gave into the urge to weep. She would not cry tonight. No matter what, she would not have King's last memory of her to be one of a weeping female. Besides, that would hardly persuade him to give her the night of passion she was hoping to get from him. For she had made up her mind, and this time, she would not be thwarted.

King sat in his room, staring down at the gifts the children had given him. George's colourful scribble was crumpled up where the child had got a little over excited and almost ripped the paper. King smoothed it out carefully and allowed himself to imagine a child of his own, a child that Livvy had given him. His heart felt like it would burst free of his chest, it was so filled with longing at the image in his mind. He drew in a deep breath. How could he bear it? How could he let her go? Compared to losing Livvy, giving up drinking had been a mere trifle. Living without drink was a choice he could make and force himself to stick to. Living without Livvy… It seemed like choosing to live without air, without water or salt. She was necessary. She was everything.

The door handle snicked quietly as it opened. King got to his feet as it closed again, and he heard the key turn. He'd known she would come. Of course he'd known. No doubt she'd conspired with Walsh, who would have been only too happy to help her stake her claim on his heart. Not that there was anything left of him to tie down. He was entirely hers, had been from the beginning.

"Ah, Miss Penrose, I'm glad you've come."

"You are?" she said softly, her surprise apparent.

"Why yes, for I have not had the chance to give you your Christmas present."

Pleasure lit her eyes, and he wished he had something else to give her. He wanted to lavish her with gifts, not that she would ever wish for such extravagant things he knew. Livvy had taught him what was truly of value, and he knew his gift would please her more than jewels or pretty fripperies.

"Here," he said, reaching for the roll of paper he had tied with a red silk ribbon, one he'd bought especially for her.

She took it from his hand and sat down on the bed, carefully tugging the ribbon free.

King watched as she looked at the sheet music he had written himself, and at the title. *Dreams of Olivia.*

"This is the music you were playing," she said, looking up at him.

King nodded, moving to stand before her. "I wrote that piece a long time ago, Livvy," he said, his voice low. "I was far younger and less cynical then and it was filled with hope, with dreams for my future, for the possibility of a happier life. It was filled *with you*, love, though I didn't know it then. It was you I have always dreamed of. I'd come to believe nothing so lovely and perfect could exist in real life, only in foolish dreams. I was wrong. You're flesh and blood and as real as I am and… I love you, Livvy. I always shall."

She made a choked sound and got up, flinging her arms about his neck. "Oh, you wretched man. I promised myself I wouldn't cry all over you tonight and n-now l-look. You've turned me into a p-perfect watering pot."

King laughed, holding her tight as she sobbed against his shirt. "I wouldn't have you any other way. I am very fond of your red nose."

"Oh," she wailed. "Don't tell me my nose is red. I suppose my eyes match, do they? How very attractive. I imagine you can't wait to get your hands on me."

"Ah, Livvy," he said, cupping her face in his hands. "I've never seen anything so perfect as you in my life. You make my heart sing, and I can hear music again when it had been lost to me for such a long time."

"Oh, King, do stop saying such wonderful things to me. My poor heart can't take it. It's so terribly in love with you too, you see."

King's heart skipped at the words. He'd hoped, had wanted to believe it, but to hear it said out loud… "Is it, Livvy? Truly?"

She made an odd snorting sound and buried her face in his shirt again. "Oh, you know it is. You knew I was in lust with you from the beginning. Then you made it so very enjoyable to scold you, honestly, you lured me in, you dreadful man."

"Did I?" he asked, grinning now.

"You know very well no woman can help but fall in love with a man who cuddles babies and plays on the floor with small children. It was very bad of you, King, really it was."

"I know, love," he said apologetically. "But I'm not the least bit sorry I'm afraid."

Livvy sighed and stared up at him, her eyes shining in the candlelight. "Me either, my lovely rogue. I should not have missed these past weeks for the world. You've made me so very happy."

"I don't want it to end," he said, wondering how he could bear to let her walk away.

"Neither do I," she said, her eyes still bright with tears. "But what choice do we have? It was just for the holidays, just for Christmas. A beautiful gift."

King bent his head and pressed his lips to hers. He couldn't listen to those words, could not only keep her for Christmas and let her go. Her mouth was soft and warm and sweet, and desire was an ache beneath his skin. She pressed closer, her body warm beneath the thin cotton of her nightgown. King deepened the kiss, his hands sliding down her back to cup her lovely behind and pull her closer against him. Her breath hitched as she felt his arousal and King smiled against her mouth as she reached for his shirt, tugging it up so she could slide her hands beneath it.

"Take it off," she muttered, breathless.

King obeyed, only too happy to oblige her.

"The rest too," she demanded, her hot gaze making his blood heat, surging through his veins like it was on fire.

"You are dreadfully bossy," he said mildly, throwing his shirt down and reaching for the buttons on the fall of his trousers.

"I know, but I think you like it," Livvy said, never taking her eyes from him. The desire he saw there, the need, was enough to make him move faster still, and he kicked the rest of his clothes off to stand naked before her.

"I do," he said, his body growing harder still as she stared at him in wonder. "I like that you know what you want, Livvy, that you speak your mind."

Her gaze travelled up, lingering on the place where his arousal was blatantly obvious, up his stomach and chest to his face. "I know what I want," she agreed, moving closer to him. "I want you, King. All of you. Make me yours, even if it is only for tonight. I will manage whatever comes next. If I must sacrifice my heart to keep the children safe, I will do it, but let me have this. I feel like I might die if I never know how it feels to be with you."

"Livvy," he said, his heart breaking. He felt the same way, but he didn't think he could do it, didn't think he could sacrifice her, or allow her to give up their future. The children must be safe, but… but surely he could find another way. He would strip the castle bear if he must, sell every painting, every stick of furniture, his soul if it came to it, but he could not give her up. "Livvy," he said again, needing to tell her, but she pressed her mouth to his.

"No. Stop talking," she commanded. "Kiss me."

King laughed, unable to deny her anything, and there was time enough to talk, to convince her to take a chance on him. It would take some persuading, he didn't doubt. She loved him, but to put the children's future in his hands, a man with his reputation. Livvy would worry for them and rightfully so, worry he might start drinking again and let them down. For once, King was not afraid. He had something to fight for now, something to believe in, and he would not mess it up.

The ribbon tying her nightgown up slid free with ease, and King watched with his heart thudding as the material tumbled to the floor. He went to touch her and hesitated.

"Is George…" he began anxiously.

Livvy laughed. "There's nothing on earth that will wake him tonight, but I did lock your door just in case."

Still he hesitated, remembering the children sleeping on the floor above.

"There is no shame in loving me, King," she whispered, moving into his embrace.

King smiled, unable to refuse her anything and contenting himself with the knowledge that he would make it right. He would do whatever it took to persuade her, but Livvy would be his wife. She would be his. He would make certain of it.

He lifted her into his arms, making her gasp as he swung her legs up and carried her to the bed. Her hands slid over his shoulders, down his arms and she sighed happily.

"So strong."

King chuckled and lay her down and concentrated on making his wife to be lose her mind.

❧ ❧ ❧

Livvy was dazed and gasping, clutching at the bed. Good heavens. The man was utterly wicked, depraved, the king of sin indeed. It was marvellous. When she had seen him naked, she had simply *wanted,* with such force she had trembled with it. Not that it had been the first time she'd seen him naked, but it was the first time she had been able to properly study him. He was magnificent. His shoulders were broad, his arms thick and strong enough to lift her with ease, and his chest... *Oh.* His skin was hot like the summer sun burning upon stone, that dark hair that rasped so deliciously against her breasts curling about her fingers, and then there were the superb proportions of his… well, his everything. He was perfection.

His hands and mouth seemed to be everywhere, and she had simply closed her eyes and allowed him to do as he would with her. It had been a revelation. He had already sent her body into a burst of rapture, forcing her to turn her head into the pillow to smother her cries, but now he was kissing a path down her body, his tongue painting decadent patterns over her belly and moving lower and… and she believed she knew where he was going. Her mind became a blank, anything resembling a coherent thought lost to her as King sought out her most intimate flesh and…

"Hush, love," he murmured, the amusement in his voice audible. "You'll wake the house."

"What did you expect? How am I supposed to…" she retorted, but the words trailed off as he went back to work and she arched beneath him. There was nothing but sensation, the warmth of his mouth and the slick slide of his tongue, and oh good heavens she would lose her mind. Now his fingers had joined his bid to turn her brain to jelly, and Livvy gasped as his clever hands caressed her in a new and intriguing way. The excited gathering sensation that his touch commanded was rippling through her once more, beckoning her on and…

Suddenly he stopped and Livvy blinked into the dim light, disappointed.

"King?" she said, sitting up and almost head butting him in the process as he moved towards her. "Oh!"

"Easy there, love," he chuckled, gently pushing her back down onto the mattress. "I can't wait any longer. I need…"

What he needed was evident as he settled between her thighs and Livvy's eyes widened as she stared up at him. She had thought she would have to persuade him into making love to her, to cajole and wheedle and beg. Apparently not. What had changed his mind she did not know and did not care to ask in case he changed it back again.

"Will it hurt?" she asked him, a little nervous now despite everything.

"Perhaps a little," he said, his voice soothing. "I'll try not to cause you any discomfort, love. Relax if you can."

Livvy smothered a laugh at the idea of relaxing when his straining member was hot and hard and sliding against the place where her body was throbbing insistently. She might well burst into flame at any moment, relaxing she wasn't so certain of.

She closed her eyes and sighed as King's mouth pressed to her throat, butterfly soft kisses moving over her skin. One large hand cupped her breast, and he ducked his head to take it into his mouth, suckling until she cried out in surprise.

"Like that, do you?" he asked, sounding dreadfully smug.

"I like all of it," she admitted. "I like you."

King did it again, humming with pleasure as he did so until Livvy thought she might pass out. "I'm pleased to hear it," he murmured as he drew back, flicking at her nipple with his tongue and then looking up at her, a mischievous glint in his eyes. "Are you relaxed yet? Please say yes."

Livvy laughed, as was obviously his intention. "Yes, yes, yes, yes."

Her laughter stopped abruptly as he grasped her leg, bending her knee and pressing his erection against the seam of her core. Her sensitive flesh responded at once to the press and slide as he sought entry and she jolted. King soothed her, kissing her deeply, caressing her body, easing his way inside with a gentle push and retreat that had her panting with a combination of pleasure and pain that her mind did not seem able to make sense of.

"Oh, God, Livvy, so… so perfect… just a little… a little more…"

"More?" she squeaked, a tad outraged as he stole her breath, and then he was fully inside her. He stilled, allowing her body to accept him. Livvy tried to steady her breathing, clutching at his big shoulders, concentrating on her palms gliding over his damp skin, moving down his body to grasp his buttocks and relish the feel of him so close, and then he moved.

"Oh!" she cried, her eyes flying open as he retreated and thrust home again, gently at first and then with increasing speed and force and he moaned, the guttural pleasure in the sound detonating something primal inside her that had her body squeezing around him. From the fierce sound he made King liked it when she did that, so she repeated it and he gasped.

"Don't..." he said, his voice ragged. "Won't last if you... Oh, Christ, Livvy."

He kissed her and Livvy wrapped herself around him, delighting in this newfound pleasure, heart soaring as she held him close to her, to the place where he should always be. Thoughts of tomorrow, of how she would carry on without him, were all swept away as he loved her, with the startling combination of passion and tenderness that he gave her as he made her his. She would always be his. The realisation brought her back to herself for a moment, a shining beacon of clarity through the haze of desire. There was no way she could marry another man when she would always belong to King. Perhaps he felt the way her heart leapt at the realisation for he pulled back, staring down at her in wonder.

"I love you," he said. "I love you. I need… always, Livvy, always…"

His body shuddered and jerked, and the coarse exclamation he uttered sent a thrill of pleasure singing through her. The delicious sensations he had brought forth earlier were back again, stronger and more insistent, sparks firing inside her, along her spine and gathering low and all at once her body was pulsing, squeezing, grasping at him as she held on tight and called his name as the world fell away.

King was floating… somewhere. His mind was bobbing along on a fluffy cloud of dazed happiness, warm and sleepy. His body was heavy, sated, utterly spent. He had never felt so… so complete, so perfectly content, so entirely himself, as he did in this moment, and it was all because of Livvy. Oh, Christ…

"Livvy?" he pushed himself off her, belatedly realising he was crushing her into the mattress.

"Hmmmm," she said, a pleased murmur that reassured him she was floating too.

She barely stirred as he withdrew and settled himself by her side, pulling her back into his arms. He spooned around her, nuzzling her neck, and she sighed.

"Are you well, love? I didn't hurt you?"

A barely there shake of her head and another contented mumble was all the answer he got. King smiled, not above feeling a little smug. Not bad for her first time then, and now they would have plenty of time to practise. Practise did make perfect, after all. His hand slid to her belly, and he experienced a jolt of shock as he realised there might be child taking root there even now. *Now, now, King, don't get ahead of yourself.* There was a deal to organise before they began their own brood. He would not be as heedless as Charlie had been, though granted he could understand the temptation well enough now. Perhaps he ought to have taken precautions this time too, but… but it had been the first time and he had wanted it to be perfect and… and it had been. He must hope that he had got away with it this once and be more careful until they were properly settled. Asking her to marry him would be a good start, he realised.

"Livvy," he said, leaning over to look at her face. Her hair had fallen over her eyes and he smoothed it back again. "Livvy, darling. We need to talk."

"Hmmmm," she said, not opening her eyes.

"It's important."

He stared down at her, but there was not even a flicker of her eyelids.

"Livvy. I want you to marry me… I can't go on without you, love. I won't. I'll find a way to make things right. I will, I swear but… but say you'll have me, love. Please?"

King waited, his heart beating in his throat, until a soft snore made him realise he was not about to get an answer.

"Olivia Penrose, you are the most frustrating creature on god's earth," he said with a huff. "Of all the times to fall asleep."

King listened to her breathing, slow and steady, remembering then that she'd been up since dawn and had hardly stopped all day. What a marvellous day it had been too, so full of joy and laughter, so full of Livvy. Well, let her sleep then. The morning would come soon enough, and then he would do whatever it took to make her his wife.

Chapter Twenty Two

26th December 1818.

No goodbyes, no fond farewells, but a startling revelation.

Livvy stared down at King. He was sprawled on his belly, dark hair a tousled mess, one arm flung across the mattress in the place she'd been laying just moments ago. She let out a ragged breath, drinking him in, engraving the sight of him on her mind. Last night was something she would never forget. That he had made love to her was still a surprise, a shock really, for she had thought he would not do so if… but it was of no matter. He loved her. They'd just got so carried away that… that he'd not stopped at the crucial moment. Oh dear. Something else not to think of. No doubt it was nothing to trouble herself about. Ceci was often pregnant, it was true, but it had taken them some months to conceive Harry. It would be dreadfully bad luck to fall pregnant the first time so she would not dwell on it.

She really must go. All her things were packed already, had been since before Christmas, so there were only a few bits and pieces to arrange, but she must wash and dress. Livvy sighed, wanting desperately to reach out and stroke his hair but not daring to disturb him. If he woke and came down to see her off, she could not keep her composure. She doubted she would leave at all. She would weep and cling to him and he would be honour bound to ask her to marry him, for everyone would guess and… No.

Her plans to marry another man might be ruined, but there was still her Aunt Agatha. If only she could get the woman on side. Just because Charlie thought badly of her was no reason Livvy would not like and respect her. Just the reverse, in fact. She had been dying to meet her forthright aunt ever since she'd first heard talk of her. If only she could persuade her to sponsor Harry, maybe even give Susan a come out… Oh, surely it was not too much to ask if she was as wealthy as Charlie seemed to think. He might be too proud to ask, but she was not, and Charlie would just have to bear it. If he hadn't got them into this fix it wouldn't be necessary, so his pride would have to be swallowed.

With one last, longing look at the man who had stolen her heart, Livvy padded silently to the door and left.

King awoke slowly. He was drowsy and content, and the bed was warm. As his senses returned to him, he remembered the night before, making love to Livvy, and the little devil falling asleep when he was trying to propose to her. A smile curved over his mouth and he reached for her, finding only an empty space. Blinking in the dim light of the bedroom, he sat up and looked about, realising that the house was awake. Of course, Livvy would have left before anyone saw her. Not to worry, he would corner her after breakfast. They could take a walk down to the beach. That would be a romantic place to propose again, in the place where he'd first kissed her. He could hear George and the distant *bang, bang* of his new drum. Good God, what had Charlie been thinking? He chuckled and got to his feet, about to ring the bell for Walsh when he remembered it was Boxing Day and all the servants had a day off. Ah well, he'd have to see to himself then. A shame. He'd have liked to have seen Walsh's face when he told him he was going to marry Livvy. The devil would be dreadfully smug, but King didn't care a jot. He was too happy.

It took him a deal longer than usual to wash, shave and dress, not least because he couldn't find half of the things he needed, and the water was freezing bloody cold. It woke him up, at least. By the time he was decent, he made his way down the stairs to the breakfast parlour to discover the table had not been laid. Frowning, he moved towards the kitchens to discover Susan holding court. The children were all sat around the big table eating their breakfast while she made up a tray.

"Right, I'm going to take this up to Mama. Harry, do keep an eye on George. He's not to have the jam pot again. He ate two whole mouthfuls before I got it off him. I don't want him to be sick."

She turned and jumped a little as she saw him. "Oh, g-good morning."

"Good morning," he said, smiling at everyone. They were looking at him a little strangely and his hand went to his cravat. Perhaps he'd made a mess of it. "Are we breakfasting in here today? That's cosy."

"Well, it seemed easier than laying everything up for just us. Mama is too tired to come down this morning," Harry said, a little stiffly.

"Oh, yes, of course. Is Li... is your aunt up yet, Harry?"

Harry's eyes widened. "Why... why yes. I thought... Oh... that's why you didn't come down to see her off. I did think it rather out of character for you to be so..." He broke off.

King's heart did an odd little jump in his chest and thudded harder. "See her off," he repeated, frowning. "Off where?"

"She's gone to Bath," Susan said, watching him carefully. "You knew she was going today."

"Well yes, but…" But it had never occurred to him that she would leave without saying goodbye, that she would leave him sleeping and… and go off to her bloody aunt's party to find herself a husband. "When?" he asked. His stomach had tied itself in a knot and he felt sick.

"Two hours ago, at least," Harry said, sympathy in his eyes now.

"I must go after her," he said, panic setting in. Oh God, she didn't know he wanted to marry her. She thought he'd taken his pleasure with her and… and… Heaven's above surely the wretched woman knew him well enough to realise he would never have done so if he hadn't meant to make it right. "I need a carriage, a horse… anything."

He must have sounded desperate as Harry leapt to his feet and took his arm.

"King, come and sit down and have some breakfast and…"

"I don't want any bloody breakfast," he said, with such force Harry jumped and George stared at him wide eyed.

"Ing?" he said.

King gathered himself. "I… I beg your pardon, Harry but… but I wish to marry Livvy and… and she's gone off to your aunt's to find herself a husband and…"

Harry let out a little whoop and Susan ran to him, clutching at his arm and tugging at him until he bent for a kiss. "Oh, I say, King, that's… that's marvellous news," Harry exclaimed.

"No, it isn't," King said in frustration. "Not if she's gone. I must go after her, she doesn't know…"

The back door crashed open and Walsh staggered through. His normally immaculate valet was dishevelled, unshaven, and looked very much like he'd slept in a bush.

"Morning," he rasped, swaying a little. "Any chance of some coffee."

"Never mind coffee," King said, striding over to Walsh and grabbing his arms. "This is an emergency. Livvy has gone and *before I got the chance to ask her to marry me.*" He gave the man a hard, meaningful glare until the significance of what he'd said sunk into Walsh's sodden brain. From the stench of him, he'd had a skinful. A good job King hadn't known wherever the stash was all this time, but he and Spargo had clearly made a night of it. Spargo was now lumbering up the garden towards them, weaving back and forth across the path as he went.

"Before you asked…" Walsh repeated, hazily trying to focus on King. His eyes widened abruptly. *"Oh."*

"Yes. Oh," King growled. "I must go after her at once."

"How, though, that's the question," Harry said thoughtfully. "Papa took the carriage. We've no other horses. You'll have to take the dog cart and pony into Bude and see if you can hire a carriage but seeing as it's Boxing day…" he trailed off with a shrug.

King wanted very much to scream but forced the urge back down.

"Right, well. I'll deal with that when I get there. Harry, brew some strong coffee and pour as much of it into Walsh as you can manage. I'll go and pack."

"Oh, no, sir," Walsh said, taking a stumbling step forward and then clutching at a chair back. He'd gone an alarming shade of green.

"Oh, yes. If you want to stop me, you must sober up. Come on, Walsh, old man. I need you."

Walsh gave a sharp nod and then clutched at his head. "Yes. Yes, sir. I'll… work on that."

King ran back to his room and dragged out his travelling chest. Everything got thrown in with more speed than efficiency, and he knew Walsh would give him hell for days, but he couldn't care less. He must get to Livvy. That she had snuck away from him… No, not thinking of that. She had her reasons, no doubt. Bloody ridiculous ones, but there would have been reasons, and she could damned well explain them to him in detail once they were married. Once his worldly goods had been crammed into the chest and the lid forced shut, King went and gave Walsh's belongings the same treatment. He cringed to think what retribution his valet would have in store for this outrageous turn of events, but at least the fellow could boast about having had the Earl of Kingston pack his belonging for him. No doubt he would too, the devil.

With a bit of help from Harry, who came when King yelled for help, they carried the trunks down to the front step where Harry, bless the lad, had readied the pony and cart for them.

"Thank you, Harry. You're a fine man, you know that I hope. I shan't forget your help."

Harry blushed and stood a little taller. "A pleasure to help, King, truly. You've… you've been marvellous with all of us and we should be honoured to call you uncle, sir."

"Oh," King paused, staring at Harry as the rest of the children came out to see him off. He would be their uncle. "Well, it… it will be I who is honoured, Harry. I promise you that, but I must catch up with your aunt first."

King looked up as Ceci came out with Walsh on her arm. "Oh, the poor man really isn't fit to travel, my lord," she said, giving Walsh's arm a gentle pat.

"No help for it," King said mercilessly. "Walsh, I shall owe you until the end of time, but please, please help me get to Livvy."

"Just try to stop me," Walsh replied gamely, though it looked like a gentle breeze could stop him he was swaying so, his complexion the colour of cold porridge. "Trouble is, my lord… we… we got no blunt."

King paused, horrified to realise Walsh had a point. He hunted about for his coin purse and looked at the pitiful amount remaining to him after buying the presents for the children and giving what he could to Gelly for their keep.

"You?" King asked hopefully.

Walsh shook his head. "Thruppence ha'penny."

King snatched his hat off his head and flung it to the ground, his fists clenched. He strode away into the garden, fighting for calm. *Think, think, man.* There must be a way. Whichever way he turned it, he needed money, and he had no way of getting it. Perhaps if he could find a card game somewhere but… Oh, Christ the longer they delayed the farther away Livvy got. He didn't know what to do and several minutes of frantic pacing did not produce an answer.

King turned back to the house to see everyone had gone back inside. Sick to his stomach with fear and frustration, he followed suit and stalked back to the kitchen. As he walked in, Jane ran up to him clutching a small pewter cup which… which was stuffed full of money.

"W-What…?" he began, staring at them.

"We've collected together all our pocket money, sir," Harry explained, smiling at him. "And Spargo and Gelly put some in too. It's not much but… is it enough?"

King felt his throat tighten as he looked about their hopeful faces. He glanced at Walsh and saw that he felt it too, the enormity of what this family would give to help him.

"Harry…" King said, his voice thick. "Harry… All of you, this… this is too much. I can't…"

"Course you can," Gelly said, banging her fist on the kitchen table so hard Walsh and Spargo looked like they might vomit. "You go and marry that girl. Lord knows she deserves a bit of luck and happiness. You will make her happy, won't you, my lord?" she demanded, a slightly daunting glint in her eyes.

King nodded.

"Please, King," Harry said, squeezing his arm. "Livvy needs you. We all need you. Don't give up now. Take the money and put it to good use. I can't think of anything better I should want to spend it on."

"Ah, Harry, lad," King said, choked now. He pulled Harry into a fierce hug for a moment before straightening again and turning to Walsh. "Come on, Walsh. Chin up. I've found a wonderful woman daft enough to fall in love with me. We mustn't let her get away."

"Ing! Ing get Libby?" George demanded.

"Yes, George. I'm going to get Livvy." King turned to his valet who was struggling to his feet. "Aren't we, Walsh?"

"Right you are, sir," Walsh said, before turning green, heaving, and running for the back door.

King sighed. They'd go and get Livvy in a few minutes then.

"Oh," Susan said, staring at King with stars in her eyes. "Isn't it romantic?"

King smiled at her. He certainly hoped so. He hoped this would be a story they would tell their children and grandchildren, but for now he felt very much like doing as Walsh was doing and throwing his guts up, he was so bloody terrified. They were only hours behind her, he reasoned. She could hardly meet a man and get married before he tracked her down. Her aunt's party didn't even start until... when did it start? Come to think of it, where did her aunt even live. He knew it was Bath but...

"What is your aunt's address, Susan?" he asked her.

"Oh, I have it somewhere," the girl said, hurrying to a big dresser, packed with china and odds and ends and tugging open a drawer. "Livvy keeps them all in a little book. Yes, here it is."

King waited while she flicked through the pages. "Ah yes, Aunt Agatha. Dudley House, Somerset Place..."

"Wait..." King's heart, already bruised from the events of the morning, leapt to his throat and lodged fast. "Did... did you say, Dudley House? Do you mean to say... is she..."

"Oh, Lord," Walsh said faintly, having just come back into the kitchen and heard what Susan had said too.

"Is your aunt...?" King began.

"Mrs Dudley," Harry said before Susan could reply, flushing a little. "Yes. She's been widowed for years of course, but... well, she's rather a scandal, I'm afraid."

"Walsh." King moved to his valet and clutched at his shoulders. His heart was thudding in his ears now. "Where was my father spending Christmas?"

Walsh swallowed.

King didn't hesitate. He stuffed the money into his pocket, snatched up his hat, grabbed Walsh and towed him out of the kitchen.

"We must catch up with her," he hissed to Walsh, who just nodded miserably.

"King… King, what is it?" Harry called, hurrying behind them as King propelled Walsh out the front door. "What has this to do with your father?"

King hesitated, but Harry wasn't a fool, he was a young man, already aware of why his Aunt Agatha had the reputation she had most certainly earned.

"Harry," King said, helping Walsh collapse into the seat of the dog cart and turning back to him. "Mrs Agatha Dudley is my father's mistress."

Chapter Twenty Three

28th December 1818.

Retribution for some, forgiveness for others.

Livvy looked up at the magnificent house in front of her. Good heavens. Aunt Agatha lived in grand style. It was everything that was modern and elegant and certainly one of the finest houses on Somerset Place, though to be fair, some were not yet finished.

Charlie hesitated, glowering unhappily at the front door. He'd been very kind to her for the past two days, kind enough not to ask her why she was so quiet and morose. The answer was obvious enough not to need an explanation.

"It's for Harry," she reminded him. "Harry and Susan and all of them, Charlie. If you must eat humble pie, what better cause could you possibly have?"

Livvy watched as Charlie set his jaw, smacked his hat onto his head, and held out his arm to her. "Very well. I've made this wretched mess. I suppose this is my comeuppance, so I'd best get it over with. I only hope you're not disappointed, Livvy. My abiding memory of her is a woman who does not mince words. We'll likely find ourselves ejected after she's rung a peal over us, well me anyway. That's if we get in at all."

"We won't know until we try," Livvy said, squeezing his arm.

"Right you are." Charlie took a deep breath and strode to the front door.

A smart, liveried footman opened the door, resplendent in dark blue and canary yellow trimmed uniform.

Charlie handed his card over. "Lord Boscawen to see my aunt, Mrs Dudley," he said, looking every inch the nobleman and not a bit like he was quaking in his boots. Livvy admitted herself impressed.

They were seen into a drawing room so grand Livvy could not help but stare. Everything was of the finest quality and the most impeccable taste. The walls were a delicate shade of pale pink, the ceiling and glorious plasterwork all white with the fancier bits picked out in gold leaf. The curtains were gold too, the fabric thick and luxurious, shimmering in the sunlight through the huge windows. Every piece of furniture was elegance itself and placed with a deftness of touch that made this a grand room indeed, yet still a homely one. Livvy could well imagine curling up in the comfortable looking chair before one of the windows and reading a book or simply watching the world go by. Not that she dared now, instead staring nervously at the huge ormolu clock on the mantel that seemed to tick with such enthusiasm it rang in her ears.

"She won't see us," Charlie said, pacing now. They'd been waiting for at least ten minutes. "She'll just make me sweat and then decide she's not at home."

"Will *she* indeed?" came an imperious voice from behind them.

They both span around and Livvy gasped. She wasn't entirely certain what she had been expecting of her mother's sister, but it was not the glorious creature standing in the doorway. Good heavens, she was stunning. A woman in her early fifties, her hair was still lustrous and a dark honey colour, her eyes were a piercing blue, and the outrageously stylish gown she wore made no bones about the quality of the figure beneath the fabric.

"Aunt Agatha?" Livvy said, gaping at her. "Good heavens, you're... you're exquisite."

Her aunt sniffed and looked at Livvy with interest. "You're not that silly creature he brought last time," she said, frowning and stepping closer. Her expression changed, her eyes growing wide. "Oh. Oh, my, you must be Olivia." She pressed her fingers to her mouth.

414

Emma V Leech

"Yes, aunt," Livvy said, dipping a curtsey. "I am very pleased to make your acquaintance at last."

"You are the image of your mother," Agatha said, her eyes suddenly very bright, then her expression hardened. "And why, pray, has it taken so many years for me to make your acquaintance? Hmmmm?"

Livvy opened her mouth and closed it again.

"You know very well our grandfather did not think you a respectable woman, Aunt," Charlie said. "You also know he would not allow Livvy to have contact with you. I have enforced his wishes since he died. It is none of my sister's doing."

Aunt Agatha made a derisive sound and took Livvy's arm. "Come and sit with me, child."

Livvy sent her brother an anxious glance but allowed the woman to sit her down on an elegant gold love seat. Agatha inspected her critically.

"You're not as beautiful as my sister was, but you have a certain something. Those eyes... yes, those eyes are very fine. Have you a beau?"

Livvy flushed scarlet and her aunt chuckled.

"Ah, you do. Is he going to marry you?"

Livvy stammered and stumbled, unable to provide a coherent answer.

"She cannot marry the man she loves, Aunt Agatha," Charlie said, his voice full of certainty now. "He is a fine man, a nobleman, but he has no money and… and as you once predicted I have made a damned mess of everything. I've no doubt you will enjoy your triumph over me, but I cannot give Livvy the dowry she needs, that she deserves. I had hoped to ask you to help my children, Harry needs schooling, university and the girls need to be presented at court and come out… but… but the truth is Livvy needs your help every bit as much as they do. I've been a damned fool and I… I need your help. *Please,* Aunt. I ask not a farthing for myself, I swear, but for them…."

Livvy gaped at her brother, touched that he should humiliate himself so to help her.

"Oh, Charlie," she said, getting up and running to embrace him.

"There, there, Liv," Charlie said with a sad smile. "It's all true. You've kept my family together, kept us all in one piece. I know it. I didn't see it for a long while, but… but I do now. I should have listened to you. I wish I had. King loves you, though. Ceci was right, it's plain enough whenever the two of you are in the same room. He's head over ears in love with you and he needs you, Livvy."

Livvy put her hand to her mouth and stifled a sob.

"Yes, yes, very touching," Agatha said briskly, patting the seat beside her again. "Now, come and explain yourself to me, girl. Did you say… *King*? You are surely not speaking of the man we know as the King of Sin?"

Livvy nodded, wiping her eyes and sniffling. "Yes, aunt. The Earl of Kingston."

"In love with *you*?" Aunt Agatha said again, clearly astonished.

Livvy put her chin up, a little irritated by that. "Yes, aunt. *Me*."

"Well, well," Agatha said, her blue eyes sparkling. "I think you had best start at the beginning."

29ᵗʰ *December 1818.*

King stood on the doorstep of Dudley House and did his best to smooth his hair down. The last three days had been an unmitigated nightmare. The terrible travelling conditions, poor accommodation, and King's appalling packing skills meant he looked nothing close to the elegant model of a fashionable gentleman he usually resembled. Instead, he looked as if he'd not slept in days, and had spent a deal of that time in a hedge, which wasn't too terribly far from the truth.

Walsh made a flapping motion to him from the pavement.

"Bloody hell," King muttered, sucking in a deep breath. It must be well over a year since he last saw his father, and this was not the way he'd wished to repeat the experience. He'd not *intended* to see him ever again. If he discovered King meant to marry Livvy…. Oh, good God. He rapped smartly on the door. There was no getting away from it. He needed to see Livvy, and Livvy was here. So….

A po-faced butler opened the door, his nose wrinkling a little at the sight of King.

"Lord Kingston," King said, handing his card over.

The butler's eyes grew wide.

"I've had the very devil of a time getting here," King said tersely.

As soon as the butler realised he had an earl standing before him and that he was the son of the man his mistress was entertaining at present, the fellow almost bent double. Nothing was too much trouble, and King was shown into a very elegant drawing room to await Mrs Dudley.

He stared out of the window, heart thudding, wondering if Livvy was here even now. If he might see her at any moment… then a crash sounded. King hurried to the door and stepped out into the huge entrance hall, looking up as movement caught his eye.

Livvy was hurrying down the stairs.

"I thought I heard...."

She paused halfway down, staring at him.

"King?" she said faintly.

"Darling," he said, rushing to her, taking the stairs two at a time, heedless of who might see. He swept her up into his arms. "Oh, Livvy, how could you do it? How could you leave without saying goodbye?"

"Oh, King," she sobbed, clutching at his lapels. "I couldn't bear to say goodbye to you at all, and certainly not in front of everyone. I should have wept all over you and everyone would have known and... and it would have been so embarrassing for you."

"You silly goose," he muttered fondly, shaking his head. "If you hadn't fallen asleep with quite such alacrity, you wouldn't have left me at all."

She blinked up at him, blushing a little, and he grinned.

"And I made you such a romantic proposal too. Imagine my chagrin when I discovered you snoring through it."

Livvy's mouth dropped open. "Y-You p-proposed?" she stammered.

"I did, and my only response was a snore. It was most provoking, love."

"Oh! I do not snore," she said indignantly.

"I beg to differ."

She narrowed her eyes at him and then her face went all soft and her eyes sparkled. "You did ask me? Truly?"

"If you doubt me. I shall just have to ask you again, won't I?" King got to one knee, which was dashed awkward as they were halfway up a staircase, but he took her hand and gazed up at the woman he loved with all his heart. "Olivia Penrose, my dearest Livvy, would you do me the honour of becoming my wife? And I'd better warn you, love, I'm not taking no for an answer."

"Oh," Livvy said, blinking rapidly. "Yes! Yes, of course, King. But how can we? Where shall we live, and what about the children? *Oh,* what about your father? King, he'll never speak to you again. I cannot make you choose between…."

King was about to retort that there simply wasn't a choice to make, when the shouting that had continued faintly from somewhere else in the house got a deal louder. A door crashed open and Mrs Dudley stalked out, head held high.

"Agatha. Agatha, darling, *please*… don't be like that," came a man's pleading voice from behind her. "I can only apologise for my youthful mistakes so many times."

King stared, mouth open, as his father rushed out of the room in her wake. At least… King thought it was his father, but the Marquess of Eynsham was always immaculate and never so much as raised his voice. This fellow was frantic and dishevelled, his cravat all askew, and he looked like a man who'd been mown down by a woman in a fury.

"Don't you *Agatha darling* me," Mrs Dudley said, rounding on him. "You damned snob. You turned your back on me thirty-five years ago because I wasn't good enough to marry, and now… and now you think to make your son do the same thing to my niece. Well, I'll see your name dragged through every scandal sheet in the country before I let that happen, Arthur, and don't think I wouldn't."

"Agatha, I *couldn't* marry you," Lord Eynsham said, pleading for understanding. "You know this. My father would not allow me—"

Agatha's eyes flashed as she turned on him. "King isn't asking for your permission, Arthur. You've had that poor boy all but beggared, and he's still not dancing to your tune. He'll marry the woman he loves, even if you never speak to him again, even if he never sees a penny of your money until you're cold in your grave. *That's* a man in love, my dear."

"But I was just a boy," the marquess said, reaching for Agatha and taking her in his arms. "I did not know what I was doing, what I was throwing away. If I had only known, love, I should never have done it. I swear, I would have married you, my father be damned."

"So you say," Agatha said, clearly unimpressed by this heartfelt declaration.

"It's true. I have loved you since we were children. You and you alone, Agatha. My wife and I have never cared for each other; it was an alliance, not a marriage. You must believe me."

Agatha turned to look at him, her lovely face cool.

"Prove it," she said. "Give your son his blessing to marry my niece. Prove to me you have learned your lesson and truly regret casting me aside. Do this… or I shall *never* see you again."

King heard Livvy gasp beside him, felt her hold on him tighten, but in truth he was too dazed to comprehend… what the bloody hell was going on? To see his father so out of control, so clearly out of his mind for Mrs Dudley, who was apparently the woman he'd loved all his life… it was astonishing. The Marquess of Eynsham had never experienced anything remotely resembling an emotion in his entire life as far as King was concerned, so this was a revelation.

King was utterly speechless.

"Darling, you don't know what you ask of me. It's not a question of snobbery, but the girl is Olney's daughter. It would be the match of the century—"

King watched as his father's mouth snapped shut, as well it might at the look Mrs Dudley sent him.

"Goodbye, Arthur." She walked away from him, head held high.

"*Wait*! Wait, Agatha… oh, damnation. Very well. Anything, love, anything you want only… don't leave me. Please, my darling. I've only just got you back after all these years. I can't lose you again. I can't live without you any longer."

Agatha turned back to him, her expression thoughtful. "You mean it, Arthur? Upon your honour? Your son can marry my niece with your blessing? You'll return his fortune to him?"

King's father swallowed hard. Oh, that was a bitter pill indeed, King thought wryly.

"Upon my honour, Aggie. May God strike me dead if I tell a lie."

"Thank you, darling," Agatha said, moving to kiss the marquess' cheek.

Then the wicked creature looked up the stairs, to where she'd obviously been well aware they had an audience.

"Did you hear that, King? Livvy? Arthur says you have his blessing. Isn't that wonderful?"

King watched as his father's gaze lifted to his and the man's colour rose dramatically through several shades until it settled on something that could only be described as puce. It clashed rather wonderfully with his waistcoat. God might not have struck him down, but King suspected it was a close-run thing. He looked on the verge of an apoplexy.

"Oh, Aunt!" Livvy flew down the stairs to embrace the woman, who held her in her arms like a long-lost daughter.

"There, there now, Olivia, dear," she said with perfect calm. "I told you to trust me, did I not?"

King walked slowly down the stairs, assuming with every step that his father would take it back, deny his permission, and swear he'd see him in the gutter before he allowed him to marry for love, of all things. It never happened.

He moved to Livvy and took her hand in his, facing the Marquess of Eynsham, his father, and looking him in the eye.

"My lord, may I present my fiancée, Miss Olivia Penrose?"

King waited, holding his breath in case his father was rude, gave her the cut direct, or made any number of cruel comments for which he was so famous.

"Miss Penrose," his father said at length. "You have your aunt's spirit, I suspect. I can see it in your eyes. In which case… my son has made a very wise choice. A wiser one than I ever made."

With that, he gave King a curt nod and walked away.

Chapter Twenty Four

12th *January 1819.*

Sparkling snow, sparkling eyes and the happiest of days.

They were married two weeks later in the ancient church of St Andrew's in Bude. Everything was a sparkling white after snowfall the night before, and King's breath clouded on the frosty air as they emerged from the church.

Livvy shivered beside him and he pulled her close.

"Well, Countess, we'd best get you warmed up," he said with a wicked glint in his eyes.

Livvy returned a warning glance. "We have a wedding breakfast, remember. Gelly will have your guts for garters if you don't do it justice."

"Ah, well. I'll do my best on the carriage ride home, then. Can't have the Countess of Kingston arriving with a red nose, can we?"

Livvy gasped and covered her nose with her hand. "Oh, it isn't, is it?"

King laughed and pulled her hand away, giving her nose a kiss. "It's perfect, love. You are perfect as always."

"'Ing! 'Ing!"

"Come on then, George," King said, holding his arms out to the little boy.

He'd been thoroughly over-excited throughout the service, and nothing anyone did could stop him tearing up and down the aisle giggling like a lunatic, much to the disapproval of the vicar. King lifted him up and kissed his cheek, then blew a raspberry against his neck, which only made George shriek and laugh all the more.

"Stop getting him all excited," Walsh said, shaking his head. "We won't be able to manage him if you keep this up."

"Ah, he's just enjoying himself," King protested.

Walsh gave a dignified sniff. "I was speaking to Master George."

Livvy spluttered with laughter and King snorted. "Oh-ho, very droll."

"Well done, King," Charlie said, coming up to shake his new brother-in-law's hand. "Welcome to the family, and thank you again...."

King shook his head. "No more thanks, Charlie. You just let Mr Moyles grow that pineapple business, don't make any investments without talking to us first, and listen to Livvy the next time she gives you good advice. That's all the thanks I need."

Charlie nodded ruefully. "My word on it. And you're quite sure about having all the children come and stay?"

"If you don't send them, I shall come and fetch them myself," King said, his voice firm.

"See Argos, 'Ing? At the castle?" George demanded.

King nodded. "Yes, George. At Easter. You will come and stay with me and Livvy and Argos."

George gave a little whoop of delight and then wriggled his way free, running off after his big brother. "'Arry, 'Arry, we go to 'Ing's castle!"

King laughed and turned back to Charlie. "I'd have them sooner, but the place needs a deal of work before we have visitors. Besides, if you don't take Ceci to Paris at Easter like you promised, you'll be in the doghouse."

Charlie laughed. "Indeed I shall. Well, I shall say it again, anyway. Thank you, King. You've saved me once again, it seems. I shan't forget it."

"Ah, Charlie, let's call it quits this time, eh?" He tugged Livvy closer, smiling at her. "I was saved too, after all."

To Livvy's delight, her glamorous Aunt Agatha had deigned to come to the wedding. It was quite clear now where Livvy had inherited her forthright nature from, and the women had formed a strong bond almost at once. King was pleased for her, and even more so that Livvy felt she had regained a connection to the mother she had lost in hearing Agatha's stories about them growing up together. Agatha and Charlie were not exactly reconciled, but they were thawing towards each other. Agatha had to admit that there was some truth in her not being entirely respectable, and she was perhaps not the perfect role model for her great-nieces. Charlie, in turn, had to confess that Agatha was not the wicked harlot his grandfather had made her out to be, and that she had many fine qualities which his children would do well to emulate. There was an understanding there, and King felt certain that they would find a way forward.

King had not invited his parents. There would be no warm reconciliation there. King did not expect or even want one. He pitied his mother for their loveless marriage and his father for having made the wrong choice all those years ago. He even understood that he might not have withstood the pressure himself if he'd been a boy of eighteen instead of a man of five and thirty. As it was, there had been no other choice for him. He could not have let Livvy go, and he knew he would have found a way to care for her, and for the children, even if things had not turned out so perfectly. Though he had fallen a very long way down, he had faith in himself now, in his ability to stand strong, to resist temptation and choose what was right over what was easy. He could do it because he had chosen Livvy. She had changed him, she had changed everything, and he had never been so grateful for anything in his life.

King looked around as Walsh laid a hand on his arm. "If I might say so, my lord, well done. I'm… well, I'm right proud of you, and so happy, too. I knew from the start she was the one for you."

"Yes, you did, didn't you?" King said with a smile. He reached for Walsh's hand, grasping it in both of his. "What you did for me, keeping me alive when I barely cared what happened…."

"Ah, no," Walsh protested, shaking his head.

"No, Walsh. It needs saying. You are loyal and true, and far more to me than just a valet. I hope you know that. You've been a friend, the only one I've ever been able to count on. I just want you know you have a friend in me, too."

Walsh choked, and fumbled for a handkerchief, wiping his eyes, and giving his nose a forceful blow.

"Well, thank you, sir. You're like a son to me, truth be told," he said and then cleared his throat and gave King a look of utter guilelessness. "Does this mean I'll get a raise, then?"

King snorted, amused. "Devil. Never mind a raise, I owe you at least six months back pay. But of course, Walsh. Goes without saying."

Walsh chuckled, looking a bit guilty. "I was only ragging you."

"I know." King nodded. "But I wasn't. You deserve every penny."

The moment the carriage door closed on them, King pulled Livvy into his lap.

"Right, Countess, you have twenty-five minutes to have your wicked way with me," he said, grinning at her.

"I've had it," Livvy said tartly. "More times than I can count, you dreadful man. I never realised quite how apt your nickname was."

"Yes, you did," he said, his voice low as he made quick work of the buttons on her elegant new pelisse and slid his fingers beneath, up her side to cup her breast. "You knew the first time you set eyes on me."

Livvy sighed as his thumb brushed back and forth over her nipple. "Oh, very well. You win."

King chuckled and kissed a path down her neck.

"This is a beautiful gown, by the way," he said. "I am looking forward to taking it off you later."

"It was dreadfully expensive," Livvy said, and he could still hear the anxiety in her voice.

King sighed and looked up at her. "Good. Stop worrying about money. Now my inheritance has been restored to me, I am quite disgustingly wealthy. I'm afraid you'll just have to get used to it."

"Yes, King," she said meekly. "I shall try."

"I should think so. Now… where was I?"

"I think you were about to tug my dress down and kiss me until I scream," Livvy said, utterly deadpan.

King's entire body stood to attention.

"God, I love you," he said. "Come here."

Livvy chuckled and did as he instructed, climbing over and straddling him.

"Oh," she said, as his aching cock pressed against her in just the right place. Her blue eyes darkened, glittering with mischief. "King… can you… *you know*… in a carriage?"

"Of course *I* can," he said, aware he sounded far too pleased with himself. "But we must hurry."

"I don't think that will be a problem," Livvy gasped as he tugged up her skirts and she fumbled at his buttons.

"Quick, quick," he muttered, as they snatched desperately at each other. "Yes, yes… Oh, oh, Livvy."

His head fell back against the squabs as she sank down onto him, and he was engulfed in heat and pleasure and Livvy.

"Heaven, love," he whispered against her neck. "You are heaven. I can't believe you are really mine."

"All yours," she whispered. "All yours for always, King, and not *just* for Christmas."

Epilogue

24th December 1820.

The Christmas season once again, and family, in all its messy perfection.

"Someone's here!" Susan cried, climbing down from her position at the window seat and rushing from the room with Lydia and Rebecca in pursuit.

"Oh, is it your mother and father?" Livvy called, springing up from her seat by the fire and following her out.

"It's Harry!" Jane shrieked, somehow having got to the door before any of them.

Bascombe, their dreadfully efficient butler, gave the girl an amused glance as she passed him on the way out.

Livvy turned to see King coming down the stairs, carrying their baby daughter, Bea. Lady Beatrice Agatha St John had been born five months ago and was the apple of her father's eye.

"I thought you were giving her to Nanny to put her down for a nap," Livvy said, hiding a smile and knowing exactly what had happened.

"I was," King admitted. "But she sleeps much better when I'm holding her."

Livvy sighed as he walked up to her and she kissed his cheek.

"Like her mother," she said softly.

King tore his eyes away from his daughter long enough to grin at her.

"Give her to me," Livvy instructed firmly. "Harry has just arrived, and you know he'll be bursting to see you."

Reluctantly, King handed the baby over, kissed Bea's head, then Livvy's, and hurried out to greet Harry.

Livvy waited inside in the warmth until everyone rushed in with a burst of noise and laughter. Her heart soared as she saw Harry. He'd grown at least another inch since last she'd seen him, and he was broader across the shoulders. His cravat was tied with absolute precision, and he looked the image of a fashionable young man, home for the holidays. She held back, not wanting to embarrass him by hugging and kissing him as if he were still a little boy, but Harry took one look and ran to her, hugging her carefully around the baby and gazing down at Bea.

"She's got so big, and yet she's still tiny," he said, lifting his gaze back to Livvy. "It's so good to see you, Livvy, and little Bea."

"Oh, it's good to see you too, Harry. We have missed you dreadfully."

Harry laughed, blushing a little, and kissed her cheek. "Are Mama and Papa here yet?"

"Not yet," Livvy began as the sound of carriage wheels reached her. "I spoke too soon...."

Harry grinned and ran back outside again.

"Here, give me my little princess," King said, stealing the baby back.

Naturally, the child had woken now and cooed at her father, kicking her little legs gleefully.

"King!" Livvy protested, though in truth it made her heart melt to see how her husband doted on their baby. Not that it meant any of the other children got any less attention. George was his constant shadow whenever he was at Wynford, which begged the question....

"Where's George?"

King looked around. "He... He was here a moment ago."

"Oh," Livvy said, wondering where to start looking. The castle was vast, and—

King held up a hand. "Argos! Here, boy!"

A moment later, there was the scratching of claws on the flagstones and Argos came trotting into the grand entrance hall, wearing one of Livvy's best bonnets, and with George following on behind. Mr Moon swooped across the space, diving low over King and making him duck with a huff of annoyance.

"Blasted bird!"

"I can't undo the bow," George said crossly, pointing at Argos. "Silly Jane dressed him up again. He's not a girl dog, King. Can't you tell her?"

"Well, I'm sure Argos doesn't mind," King said, eyeing the dog doubtfully.

Livvy laughed as Argos gave a long-suffering sigh and lay down on the floor.

"Oh, dear. Poor darling. Come here and let me free you."

After Livvy had disentangled Argos, and the entire family were installed at the dinner table, King looked about him with a deep sense of satisfaction. The castle was the kind of project that would last him his lifetime, and probably his children's too, but that was just fine. He was proud of everything he and Livvy had achieved to date, and especially of his daughter, who had taken a little longer to arrive than they'd expected, but he was making up for lost time. King wondered when Livvy was going to tell him she was expecting again. He would look dreadfully surprised, naturally. A smile curved over his mouth.

"What are you looking so smug about?" Aunt Agatha demanded of him. "You look like the cat that got the cream."

King shook his head.

"Just happy, Aunt," he said, lifting her hand to his mouth and kissing her fingers. "I am so very pleased to have you here with us for Christmas."

"Oh, piffle," Agatha said, laughing. "You're still pleased as punch over your lovely daughter, I know. Not that I blame you. I think she has my eyes. She will be a great beauty."

"She has her mother's eyes," King said firmly. "And yes, she certainly will be."

Agatha snorted and tapped her knife on the side of her glass until she had everyone's attention. "A toast, I think. To my beautiful new great-niece and namesake, Beatrice Agatha."

Everyone raised their wine glasses, except King, who reached for a glass of water without a flicker of regret.

"To Beatrice Agatha," he said, wishing his daughter everything that was good in life.

He looked down the table at Charlie, and Ceci, who had little Birdie sitting on her lap; at Susan,

Lydia, Rebecca, and Jane, who were all laughing and chattering; at his special little man, George, and his big brother, Harry, who was helping him cut up his meat. He knew that Walsh, Gelly, and Spargo were all enjoying a good get-together down in the kitchens, and looking forward to Boxing Day. King felt a rush of warmth and happiness, of pride in this family, *his* family. He looked to the end of the table to his wife, to Livvy, and she met his eyes, smiling at him and blowing him a kiss.

King raised his glass to her.

"To you, my dearest love," he said, too quietly for her to hear the words, but he knew she understood all the same.

Also, just in time for the Holidays….

Winter's Wild Melody
A Rogues & Gentlemen Christmas Novella

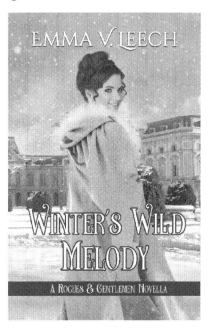

Caught in the storm on his way home after a week of overindulgence, Viscount Debdon takes shelter in an abandoned farmhouse, only to realise…

He is not alone.

When his ghostly companion is revealed to be not only an earthly body but a heavenly one too, the temptation to remain lost in the woods is hard to resist.

Out Christmas Day, December 25, 2020

Pre-order your copy here: <u>Winter's Wild Melody</u>

Want more Emma?

If you enjoyed this book, please support this indie author and take a moment to leave a few words in a review. *Thank you!*

To be kept informed of special offers and free deals (which I do regularly) follow me on *https://www.bookbub.com/authors/emma-v-leech*

To find out more and to get news and sneak peeks of the first chapter of upcoming works, go to my website and sign up for the newsletter.

http://www.emmavleech.com/

Come and join the fans in my Facebook group for news, info and exciting discussion...

Emmas Book Club

Or Follow me here......

https://www.instagram.com/leech.emma/?hl=en

http://viewauthor.at/EmmaVLeechAmazon

Emma's Twitter page

About Me!

I started this incredible journey way back in 2010 with The Key to Erebus but didn't summon the courage to hit publish until October 2012. For anyone who's done it, you'll know publishing your first title is a terribly scary thing! I still get butterflies on the morning a new title releases but the terror has subsided at least. Now I just live in dread of the day my daughters are old enough to read them.

The horror! (On both sides I suspect.)

2017 marked the year that I made my first foray into Historical Romance and the world of the Regency Romance, and my word what a year! I was delighted by the response to this series and can't wait to add more titles. Paranormal Romance readers need not despair however as there is much more to come there too. Writing has become an addiction and as soon as one book is over I'm hugely excited to start the next so you can expect plenty more in the future.

As many of my works reflect I am greatly influenced by the beautiful French countryside in which I live. I've been here in the South West for the past twenty years though I was born and raised in England. My three gorgeous girls are all bilingual and the youngest who is only six, is showing signs of following in my footsteps after producing *The Lonely Princess* all by herself.

I'm told book two is coming soon ...

She's keeping me on my toes, so I'd better get cracking!

KEEP READING TO DISCOVER MY OTHER BOOKS!

Other Works by Emma V. Leech

(For those of you who have read The French Fae Legend series, please remember that chronologically The Heart of Arima precedes The Dark Prince)

Rogues & Gentlemen

The Rogue

The Earl's Temptation

Scandal's Daughter

The Devil May Care

Nearly Ruining Mr. Russell

One Wicked Winter

To Tame a Savage Heart

Persuading Patience

The Last Man in London

Girls Who Dare

Daring Daughters

The Regency Romance Mysteries

Dying for a Duke

A Dog in a Doublet

The Rum and the Fox

The French Vampire Legend

The Key to Erebus

The Heart of Arima

The Fires of Tartarus

The Boxset (The Key to Erebus, The Heart of Arima)

The Son of Darkness

The French Fae Legend

The Dark Prince

The Dark Heart

The Dark Deceit

The Darkest Night

Short Stories: A Dark Collection.

Stand Alone

The Book Lover (a paranormal novella)

This Girl is Not for Christmas (Regency Romance)

Audio Books!

Don't have time to read but still need your romance fix? The wait is over…

By popular demand, get your favourite Emma V Leech Regency Romance books on audio at Audible as performed by the incomparable Philip Battley and Gerard Marzilli. Several titles available and more added each month!

Click the links to choose your favourite and start listening now.

Rogues & Gentlemen

The Rogue ***

The Earl's Tempation

Scandal's Daughter

451

The Key to Erebus (coming soon)

** *Available on Chirp*

*** *Available on Chirp and Audible/Amazon*

Also check out Emma's regency romance series, Rogues & Gentlemen. Available now!

The Rogue

Rogues & Gentlemen Book 1

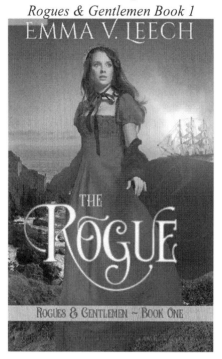

1815

Along the wild and untamed coast of Cornwall, smuggling is not only a way of life, but a means of survival.

Henrietta Morton knows well to look the other way when the free trading 'gentlemen' are at work.

Yet when a notorious pirate, known as The Rogue, bursts in on her in the village shop, she takes things one step further.

Bewitched by a pair of wicked blue eyes, in a moment of insanity she hides the handsome fugitive from the local Militia. Her reward is a kiss that she just cannot forget. But in his haste to escape with his life, her pirate drops a letter, inadvertently giving Henri incriminating information about the man she just helped free.

When her father gives her hand in marriage to a wealthy and villainous nobleman in return for the payment of his debts, Henri becomes desperate.

Blackmailing a pirate may be her only hope for freedom.

Read for free on Kindle Unlimited

The Rogue

Girls Who Dare– The exciting new series from Emma V Leech, the multi-award-winning, Amazon Top 10 romance writer behind the Rogues & Gentlemen series.

Inside every wallflower is the beating heart of a lioness, a passionate individual willing to risk all for their dream, if only they can find the courage to begin. When these overlooked girls make a pact to change their lives, anything can happen.

Eleven girls – Eleven dares in a hat. Twelve stories of passion. Who will dare to risk it all?

To Dare a Duke

Girls Who Dare Book 1

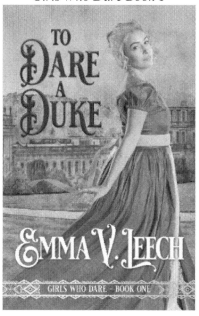

Dreams of true love and happy ever afters

Dreams of love are all well and good, but all Prunella Chuffington-Smythe wants is to publish her novel. Marriage at the price of her independence is something she will not consider. Having tasted success writing under a false name in The Lady's Weekly Review, her alter ego is attaining notoriety and fame and Prue rather likes it.

A Duty that must be endured

Robert Adolphus, The Duke of Bedwin, is in no hurry to marry, he's done it once and repeating that disaster is the last thing he desires. Yet, an heir is a necessary evil for a duke and one he cannot shirk. A dark reputation precedes him though, his first wife may have died young, but the scandals the beautiful, vivacious and spiteful creature supplied the ton have not. A wife must be found. A wife who is neither beautiful or vivacious but sweet and dull, and certain to stay out of trouble.

Dared to do something drastic

The sudden interest of a certain dastardly duke is as bewildering as it is unwelcome. She'll not throw her ambitions aside to marry a scoundrel just as her plans for self-sufficiency and freedom are coming to fruition. Surely showing the man she's not actually the meek little wallflower he is looking for should be enough to put paid to his intentions? When Prue is dared by her friends to do something drastic, it seems the perfect opportunity to kill two birds.

However, Prue cannot help being intrigued by the rogue who has inspired so many of her romances.

Ordinarily, he plays the part of handsome rake, set on destroying her plucky heroine. But is he really the villain of the piece this time, or could he be the hero?

Finding out will be dangerous, but it just might inspire her greatest story yet.

To Dare a Duke

From the author of the bestselling Girls Who Dare Series – An exciting new series featuring the children of the Girls Who Dare...

The stories of the **Peculiar Ladies Book Club** and their hatful of dares has become legend among their children. When the hat is rediscovered, dusty and forlorn, the remaining dares spark a series of events that will echo through all the families... and their

Daring Daughters

Dare to be Wicked
Daring Daughters Book One

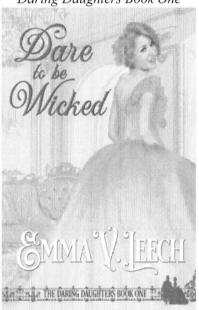

Two daring daughters ...

Lady Elizabeth and Lady Charlotte are the daughters of the Duke and Duchess of Bedwin. Raised by an unconventional mother and an indulgent, if overprotective father, they both strain against the rigid morality of the era.

The fashionable image of a meek, weak young lady, prone to swooning at the least provocation, is one that makes them seethe with frustration.

Their handsome childhood friend ...

Cassius Cadogen, Viscount Oakley, is the only child of the Earl and Countess St Clair. Beloved and indulged, he is popular, gloriously handsome, and a talented artist.

Returning from two years of study in France, his friendship with both sisters becomes strained as jealousy raises its head. A situation not helped by the two mysterious Frenchmen who have accompanied him home.

And simmering sibling rivalry ...

Passion, art, and secrets prove to be a combustible combination, and someone will undoubtedly get burned.

Pre Order your copy here: Dare to be Wicked

Interested in a Regency Romance with a twist?

Dying for a Duke

The Regency Romance Mysteries Book 1

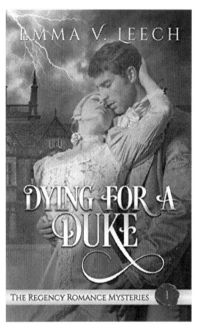

Straight-laced, imperious and morally rigid,
Benedict Rutland - the darkly handsome Earl of
Rothay - gained his title too young. Responsible for
a large family of younger siblings that his frivolous
parents have brought to bankruptcy, his youth was
spent clawing back the family fortunes.

Now a man in his prime and financially secure he is betrothed to a strict, sensible and cool-headed woman who will never upset the balance of his life or disturb his emotions ...

But then Miss Skeffington-Fox arrives.

Brought up solely by her rake of a step-father, Benedict is scandalised by everything about the dashing Miss.

But as family members in line for the dukedom begin to die at an alarming rate, all fingers point at Benedict, and Miss Skeffington-Fox may be the only one who can save him.

FREE to read on Amazon Kindle Unlimited..
Dying for a Duke

Lose yourself in Emma's paranormal world
with The French Vampire Legend series…..

The Key to Erebus
The French Vampire Legend Book 1

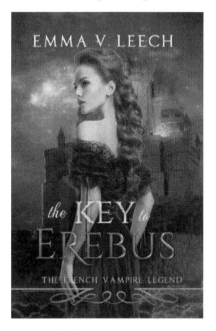

The truth can kill you.

Taken away as a small child, from a life where
vampires, the Fae, and other mythical creatures are
real and treacherous, the beautiful young witch,
Jéhenne Corbeaux is totally unprepared when she
returns to rural France to live with her eccentric
Grandmother.

Thrown headlong into a world she knows nothing about she seeks to learn the truth about herself, uncovering secrets more shocking than anything she could ever have imagined and finding that she is by no means powerless to protect the ones she loves.

Despite her Gran's dire warnings, she is inexorably drawn to the dark and terrifying figure of Corvus, an ancient vampire and master of the vast Albinus family.

Jéhenne is about to find her answers and discover that, not only is Corvus far more dangerous than she could ever imagine, but that he holds much more than the key to her heart ...

FREE to read on Kindle Unlimited The Key to Erebus

Check out Emma's exciting fantasy series with hailed by Kirkus Reviews as "An enchanting fantasy with a likable heroine, romantic intrigue, and clever narrative flourishes."

The Dark Prince

The French Fae Legend Book 1

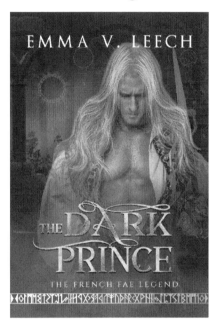

Two Fae Princes
One Human Woman
And a world ready to tear them all apart

Laen Braed is Prince of the Dark fae, with a temper and reputation to match his black eyes, and a heart that despises the human race. When he is sent back through the forbidden gates between realms to retrieve an ancient fae artefact, he returns home with far more than he bargained for.

Corin Albrecht, the most powerful Elven Prince ever born. His golden eyes are rumoured to be a gift from the gods, and destiny is calling him. With a love for the human world that runs deep, his friendship with Laen is being torn apart by his prejudices.

Océane DeBeauvoir is an artist and bookbinder who has always relied on her lively imagination to get her through an unhappy and uneventful life. A jewelled dagger put on display at a nearby museum hits the headlines with speculation of another race, the Fae. But the discovery also inspires Océane to create an extraordinary piece of art that cannot be confined to the pages of a book.

With two powerful men vying for her attention and their friendship stretched to the breaking point, the only question that remains...who is truly The Dark Prince.

The man of your dreams is coming...or is it your nightmares he visits? Find out in Book One of The French Fae Legend.

Available now to read for FREE on Kindle Unlimited.

The Dark Prince

Acknowledgements

Thanks, of course, to my wonderful editor Kezia Cole.

To Victoria Cooper for all your hard work, amazing artwork and above all your unending patience!!! Thank you so much. You are amazing!

To my BFF, PA, personal cheerleader and bringer of chocolate, Varsi Appel, for moral support, confidence boosting and for reading my work more times than I have. I love you loads!

A huge thank you to all of Emma's Book Club members! You guys are the best!

I'm always so happy to hear from you so do email or message me :)

emmavleech@orange.fr

To my husband Pat and my family ... For always being proud of me.

Printed in Great Britain
by Amazon

54017277R00279